Lucien's Hart

Anthony Blodgett

BLODGETT VENTURES LLC

Published in the United States by Blodgett Ventures LLC

First edition, June 2025

Cover design, formatting, and layout by Anthony Blodgett

Interior formatting and typography by Anthony Blodgett

For permissions or rights inquiries:

blodgettventures@gmail.com

Before You Begin

This is not a safe book.

Inside, you'll find blood on silk sheets.

Love tangled with violence.

Loyalty so brutal it borders on madness.

Sex that doesn't apologize.

Language that cuts.

And choices that leave stains you won't wash off.

This isn't a love story.

It's obsession. It's betrayal.

It's consequence dragged through fire.

This wasn't written just to entertain, but to leave a mark.

If you came for polite, close the book.

But if you came to bleed. To burn.

To fall in love with the dark.

Welcome to the world of Lucien's Hart.

One more thing.

This is not the whole truth.

Not yet.

What you're about to read is the opening fracture, not the final reckoning.

Some answers are delayed on purpose.

Some truths don't survive first contact.

This story was built to unfold.

To break, then return changed.

If you reach the end and feel unfinished, that isn't a mistake.

It's the design.

Don't say I didn't warn you.

Anthony Blodgett

Author's Note

I didn't write this book in comfort.

I wrote it in a season where sleep was short and certainty was thinner.

This story was born from pressure, from questions that refused to quiet down,

from a need to turn chaos into something that meant more than pain.

I wasn't trying to write a genre.

I was trying to understand obsession, power, love, and what it costs to become someone new.

Every page carries intensity because it came from a place that demanded honesty.

Not perfection.

Not polish.

Just truth.

This book is fiction.

But the questions inside it were real.

Thank you for stepping into the fire with me.

Welcome to Part One of the Lucien's Hart Saga.

The beginning of everything that follows.

Anthony Blodgett

Prologue

Rain fell like shattered vows, pouring from a heaven that had long since turned its face from the world.

Cities stood broken across continents.

Towers clawed at bruised clouds, black spires crowned in lightning.

Every flash revealed what had become of us.

Roads split open.

Bridges sagged beneath ash.

Windows stared over the ruins like the hollow eyes of giants long dead.

People would later say the end came out of nowhere.

They were wrong.

The end had been approaching for a very long time.

Not the end of humanity.

The end of the world that ruled it.

For generations, people would argue about where the fracture began. Some blamed nations. Others blamed greed, power, the slow corruption of institutions that believed themselves immortal.

They were wrong too.

Because the truth was smaller than any empire and far more dangerous.

It did not begin with war.

It did not begin with revolution.

It began with two lives colliding in the dark.

A spark thrown across the void.

A man who chose her over the world.

A love so immediate it felt older than memory, violent in its certainty, sharp enough to cut through fate itself.

No one understood it then.

Not governments.

Not prophets.

Not the men who believed they shaped history from behind quiet doors.

The first fracture was not political.

It was personal.

It began the moment one man refused to let them take her from him.

He could not have known the woman he fought to protect would one day stand beside him and help him tear the world apart.

That refusal woke something inside him no one was prepared for.

Something ancient.

Something relentless.

The storms came after.

The uprisings.

The Pulse that split reality at the seams.

The collapse of the old order until even the oceans seemed to recoil.

When the children born after the fire ask how everything changed, we tell them the same story.

But the story did not begin with the fire.

It began here.

The moment he chose her.

From that moment forward,

the world was never the same again.

Contents

1. THE CITY DONT SLEEP, IT WATCHES   1

2. FOR THE PURPOSE OF BEING REMEMBERED   5

3. THE NIGHT THAT CHOSE HER   9

4. MONSTER IN THE SHADOWS   15

5. WHAT HE LEFT BEHIND   25

6. THE THRESHOLD   29

7. THE SUMMONS   35

8. SURRENDER TO THE NIGHT   47

9. INTO THE FLAMES   53

10. MARKED BACK   63

11. NO SAFE EXIT   71

12. NO SAFE PLACE   81

13. THE HOUSE ABOVE THE RIVER   87

14. ROOMS THAT REMEMBER   93

15. LOVER IN THE WALLS   101

16. SECRETS BENEATH THE STONES   109

17. THE FOOLISH PRINCE   115

18. THE FUSE BETWEEN US   127

19. NO REST BETWEEN US   131

20. THE CALM BEFORE IT ALL WENT DARK   137

21. AND THEN CAME THE DARK   145

22. LUGGAGE AND LOOSE ENDS   165

23. FIRST IMPRESSIONS LAST FOREVER   181

24. MIAMI BURNS BLACK   191

25. DAWN SHARPENS THE BLADE   203

26. CHECKMATE MOVES ONLY   207

27. THE ART OF CONTROL   223

28. LEAVE NOTHING HIDDEN   235

29. WHEN GOD BLINKED   247

30. MIDNIGHT MASS   253

31. ON THE RECORD, OFF THE LEASH   261

32. CUT LOOSE, WAR BOUND   267

33. OASIS ON THE EDGE   277

34. HOUSE MONEY, HOLY SIN   289

35. ENEMIES IN THE GARDEN   303

36. PULL THE THREAD   317

37. SEVER THE HEAD, BURN THE CROWN   325

38. VICTORY WAKES THE WOLVES   333

39. BEHOLD A BLACK HORSE   343

40. AND HELL FOLLOWED WITH HIM   349

41. THE ENEMY ALREADY INSIDE   361

42. TONIGHT WE FIGHT IN HEAVEN   367

43. THE JUDAS CLAUSE   379

44. THE STRIKE BEFORE THE STORM   391

45. RADIOACTIVE   403

46. BLOOD FOR BLOOD   415

47. THE SIGNAL THAT LIED   425

48. THE GRAVE THAT WOKE   439

49. THE FUTURE   455

50. HAPPY EVER AFTER?   467

CHAPTER ONE

THE CITY DONT SLEEP, IT WATCHES

Dawn cut the city open and left it bleeding light.

Some cities woke. Manhattan resurrected, every morning paid for in blood and rent.

Steam shouldered through ventilation grates. Engines growled, idle and waiting. The skyline held still like a patient under glass, deciding what would be taken and what might be spared.

Lena Hart walked the part of morning most people skipped, the hour when the city was not waking so much as counting survivors. She kept to old concrete that looked like it had survived more than it would ever tell. The air smelled of worn-out brakes and last night's rain. Somewhere a bodega gate rolled up and screamed metal.

She moved like someone the city had already forgotten.

For her, forgetting had been a skill long before it became a preference.

Exits mapped themselves without effort. Subway mouths. Service alleys. Doors she could jam with her heel if she had to. Here, you learned to walk by reflection, not faith, catching yourself in storefronts, bus mirrors, the black tint of limousine windows. That was how you stayed unhurt here, by noticing what didn't belong.

A box truck idled at a red light, lights off, diesel breathing steady. The driver watched the crosswalk instead of the signal, waiting for something that was not the light.

A cook leaned in a doorway, apron stained, cigarette trembling in the wind.

A woman stood on the corner, practicing a smile she did not mean.

None of them saw Lena. Better that way.

She knew this route, the timing of lights, the mirrors that told more truth than faces. But the tempo was wrong, as if someone else was scoring the morning behind her back.

Two blocks later, the city threw color like a dare.

A mural swallowed the wall of a tenement that survived three landlords and a fire. It was no saint, no slogan. Just illegal, aggressive, impossible to ignore.

A woman rose across the brick, not falling but ascending, body stretched toward a sky that was not there. Her hair streamed upward like gravity had changed its mind. Below her, broken spires tilted and buckled, skyscrapers bending as if bowing or breaking under her lift.

Somewhere in the painted ruin, a man's shadow stood beneath the rising woman. Not clear enough to name. Not close enough to touch. But the whole city seemed to bend around the shape of him.

Black police tape curled behind her in the shape of wings, twisted until warning became a halo. Gold leaf streaked through her limbs, veins of light running across her body like someone had repaired her with fire instead of metal. The brick glowed behind her, heat clinging to the mortar, more brand than painting.

Words arced around the ascending figure in sharp, deliberate script:
YOU WERE NOT BORN FOR QUIET GRAVES
YOU WERE BORN FOR FIRE
FOR RUIN
FOR THE DAY THE WORLD CRACKS

Paint bled down the wall as if it had not dried. Razor blades lacquered into the strokes glinted in the morning light. The whole thing carried the kind of truth that did not ask permission.

Lena slowed when the mural caught her.

La Maison Élite, where she worked, opened at eight sharp. She had eleven minutes. Still she didn't move.

Cold moved up her spine and settled at the base of her skull.

She raised her phone out of habit, like she needed proof it existed, framing the mural in the lens.

Her reflection hit first in the glass. Hair clean. Eyes tired.

A tidy version of a woman living smaller than she was meant to live.

Most days, her life came down to numbers that never stopped moving. Rent. Transit. Coffee bought like medicine. Commission tallies that rose and fell on the moods of women who wore sunglasses indoors and men who touched silk with the same hand they used to dismiss her. She sold luxury for a living, folded it into black ribbon, smiled like she belonged near it, then

2

rode home with sore feet and someone else's perfume in her hair.

She had told herself for two years that the job was temporary. Long enough to get steady. Long enough to breathe. Long enough to become the kind of woman who did not check her balance before buying lunch. But New York was full of temporary things that hardened into a life while you were busy enduring them. You woke up one morning and realized survival had not led anywhere. It had only taught you how to do it again.

She had gotten too good at mistaking that for adulthood.

Her breath caught because the mural wasn't only beautiful. It was true.

And truth always landed hardest when it found you disguised as art.

Truth never felt like revelation. It felt like the floor giving way under a life you had just learned to carry.

An old ache stirred beneath her ribs, one she had trained herself to ignore. She liked to think she had stopped looking backward years ago. The mural knew better.

The mural felt like a line drawn for her.

The next block stank of bleach and copper.

Police tape sagged between light poles, fluttering like tired flags. A white sheet clung to the body beneath it.

Roof jumper. That was the story.

In this city, lies came ready-made. The wrong deaths got buried inside the right ones.

She stepped off the curb. Gutter water ran red, then cleared. The city did not stop for blood. It only rerouted traffic.

She scanned an alley as she passed. A kid stood in a doorway, still as a photograph, eyes too dark to catch the light.

The waking hours were no gentler than the night. In this city, it was smart to assume you were being watched. This morning, something kept time with her steps.

She kept moving.

Baristas yawned behind fogged glass.

Traders clutched triple shots like communion.

A florist whistled while arranging roses the color of fresh wounds. His wife hosed down the sidewalk. Water ran green with stems, red with crushed petals. Buckets of lilies waited by the door.

The sight hit something sharp and unwelcome beneath her ribs.

The city snapped into focus, but not for her.

Then she saw it.

A shadow out of sync.

A figure with a jacket too clean. A gait too neutral.

Someone who had practiced not existing.

At the crosswalk, she caught it in the edge of her vision. The shadow stopped when she did.

She crossed anyway. The game was simple. You pretended you didn't see it until you did.

Something tugged behind her, not fear, but a door cracking open.

Broadway swelled, early suits and late stragglers blending into a single pulse.

The shadow did not follow. That was worse.

Distance could be measured.

Disappearance was its own kind of violence.

Her pulse overruled reason. Something had shifted. The city had changed weight, like a bridge taking on a truck.

Two blocks out, she could see it already. La Maison Élite rising like a courthouse for people who could hire better gods. Black glass. Gilded serif letters. Marble floors cold as a sentence. Perfume that never had to ask the price.

It wasn't sanctuary.

It was containment.

Inside, the mirrors would be clean enough to accuse. The music low. The air expensive enough to make people stand straighter.

By eight-fifteen she'd be fastening clasps for women who never remembered her name, translating hunger into compliments, reading bank accounts off posture, watches, wedding stones.

At La Maison Élite, she was trusted to touch things she could not afford to replace. In this city, proximity was sold as access.

She had gotten good at making rich people feel inevitable. That was the skill.

Never envy them out loud. Never flinch at the price tag.

And never let them see that after ten hours under gold light and polished glass, she still went home to a life where nothing matched, nothing stayed fixed, where every beautiful thing she handled all day stopped belonging to the world the second the lock turned behind her.

Whatever color the city offered drained out of the morning as she turned the corner.

Somewhere behind her, the day closed a door she didn't hear.

Lena straightened her shoulders and walked into it like the trial was already over.

Chapter Two

FOR THE PURPOSE OF BEING REMEMBERED

Two blocks away, the streets still bared their teeth, sirens drilling through gridlock, vendors shouting over steel trays, jackhammers rattling like bones in a tin can.

On the block La Maison Élite occupied, it became another species entirely. By the time she reached it, the street had cooled to a courtroom hush.

Her reflection stared back from the glass, lipstick precise, eyes carrying a weight the glass only sharpened. The face she wore when the world expected grace.

Grace was easier to sell than contempt.

She palmed the handle. The door gave with a soft chime, the kind that sounded expensive for the sake of it.

The boutique had the moral temperature of a bank vault. Silk hung in armed rows. Every mannequin a disciple of perfection. Every hem a small confession. The place smelled like money trying to remember its manners. Somewhere, a hidden compressor sighed.

"Lena."

Her name sliced from behind her, sharp enough to take skin. Mr. Donovan: tailored cruelty, cufflinks like guillotines. He didn't approach so much as materialize.

"Main display. New arrivals." His gaze moved down and up, measuring, pricing.

"And try not to look so tired."

Men like Donovan always mistook exhaustion for failure.

The insult landed where he wanted it. She gave him the smallest smile and no apology. He was already gone, absorbed by the back office like a stain pulled into dark carpet.

Work swallowed minutes. She dressed a mannequin in satin the color of bruised peaches, fingers steady while her mind replayed gold paint and razor glitter. The lilies from outside seemed to have followed her; she caught their funeral sweetness on a customer's scarf and breathed shallowly.

Her phone buzzed once in her coat pocket. Christina.

Enigma tonight. Jessica's birthday

Christina and Jessica were the only friends she had made since moving here, bright, chaotic women who made surviving feel easier.

Lena typed back, automatic.

I'll make it

She set the phone face down and slid a final pin through silk. The mannequin didn't flinch. Figures never did. That was why people loved them.

The door chimed.

The light changed when he entered, as if the building adjusted its exposure to flatter him.

He didn't walk in. He arrived.

She didn't look up; she had learned not to reward bells. But the room noticed. Conversations thinned. Two clients remembered posture.

At the register, Donovan's smile shifted into something careful.

Men with money were treated well in places like this.

Men with power were treated carefully.

Donovan was being careful.

He crossed the floor first, head lowered in a respect she had never seen him extend to anyone who paid retail.

Only when Donovan angled away did Lena turn fully toward the man who had entered.

He wore a charcoal suit that seemed to absorb light, collar open, no tie, as if control required nothing extra. His watch kept its own counsel. He moved as though the space had been measured to his dimensions and everything else was clutter.

He didn't bother with Donovan. His attention swept the boutique like a scanner: glass, exits, sightlines. Then Lena. When his gaze settled, it held her still, as if he had found what he came for.

He came toward her. Unhurried. Certain. The kind of walk that made people step aside without understanding why. His eyes dipped once to the name on her jacket.

"Lena."

He didn't ask it. He claimed it. The word found a place between her ribs and stayed there.

She kept her hands on the fabric. "Good morning."

"I need something." His voice was low and controlled. "A dress."

"For whom?"

"For the purpose of being remembered."

Her breath slipped. "Color?"

"A question you already know the answer to."

Gold.

Of course.

Gold was worship and warning, the color cities used to paint saints before burning them.

She selected pieces with the same instinct that had taught her where to stand when things were about to collapse.

He watched her method, not her taste. How she moved. How her shoulders settled. What she reached for when instinct outpaced thought.

Men like him didn't study surfaces unless they meant to get past them.

For a second, something unguarded crossed his face. He looked like a man recognizing a wound he knew intimately.

He hid it fast, but not before she caught it.

Up close, he smelled faintly of smoke without fire, night without sleep.

At the far rack he paused, fingers tracing a silk column as if testing a blade. "Tell me." His voice softened. "Do you sell dreams here, or alibis?"

His gaze searched past makeup and practiced calm, as if checking her face against something he almost remembered.

"Depends who's paying." She met his eyes because most people didn't.

Something in him paused, as if she had reached a part of him the world rarely touched.

A corner of his mouth acknowledged it. "Show me what works."

She did. Three options, no chatter. He didn't ask the price. Donovan hovered, pretending not to hover.

When he chose, he did it the way men choose coordinates.

At the counter, paper slid. A card tapped.

The name flashed across the terminal before Donovan could hide his reverence.

LUCIEN COLE

Respect curdled in Donovan's eyes into something obedient.

Lucien's attention flicked once to the mirrored column beside the register. The mirror gave him the room twice. He seemed to like that.

On his way out he stopped close enough to tilt the temperature of the air.

"I'll see you again."

It sounded less like a prediction than a forecast.

He turned, and the boutique loosened around his absence. The room softened, but no one mistook it for safety.

People resumed being rich. Donovan resumed being cruel. Lena rang up three scarves and a lie about how good they looked, the kind boutiques charged extra for, before catching herself glancing at the door, half expecting him to still be there.

The air had not warmed back yet.

Chapter Three

THE NIGHT THAT CHOSE HER

By late afternoon, the city's chaos pressed at the windows, sirens ricocheting off glass, horns braiding with the grind of gears.

The mural's words kept circling her thoughts, refusing to go.

The bell chimed. The sound died. She kept moving.

When she finally made it home, the apartment felt staged, everything neat, nothing true.

She stood in front of the mirror and began to build someone who could pass through Enigma's door without being turned away.

Foundation for armor. Liner for edge. Shadow to sharpen what softness had no place tonight.

The black dress wasn't fabric anymore; it was permission.

She pinned her hair not for softness but for structure.

A touch of gold at her throat, less jewelry than signal.

She looked herself in the eye long enough to feel the lie settle into a shape she could carry.

Enigma wasn't for the rich; it was for the reckless, the beautiful, the untouchable. The city's rumor mill talked about it the way soldiers talk about ghost units: it existed only if it wanted you.

They didn't come for champagne. They came to be baptized in light and noise, to let the city erase their outlines for a few hours. And if they were lucky, they walked out instead of being absorbed.

Her phone lit. Christina, efficient as ever: **We'll be there in fifteen**

Lena killed the screen, took her keys, and stepped into the hall.

She touched the black dress at her hip and adjusted it once, a habit she trusted.

She checked the lock twice, turned the knob once, and stepped into the stairwell without looking back.

The cab ride to Enigma blurred into wet asphalt and neon scars. Night had hardened over the city, reds and violets smeared across the glass.

Lena's pulse stayed high, a drumbeat in her wrists. She wasn't nervous, exactly. It felt less like nerves and more like inevitability.

When the cab slowed, she saw it.

Enigma didn't sit on the block. It dominated it.

Smoked glass panes reflected the street back at itself, broken by veins of molten red light running like arteries up its columns.

Across the entrance, the name blazed in letters three stories tall, burnished chrome and crimson light: ENIGMA, the font jagged and beautiful, like a weapon etched into the building's skin.

Rumor had it Enigma was built over the bones of an old cathedral condemned years ago.

Some nights, people swore they still heard the choir through the bass.

Door staff stood in black coats, earpieces glinting like scalpel steel.

The crowd surged against the velvet rope like a tide pulled by an unseen moon.

Christina and Jessica waited by the curb, framed in the spill of light and the restless hum of the line. Their laughter cut through the night like a spark.

"There she is," Christina called, sly grin tugging at her mouth. "We thought you were gonna ghost us."

Lena exhaled a laugh, heels clicking as she approached, eyes flicking to Jessica. "I wouldn't miss your birthday, Jess."

Jessica smiled, but her eyes kept flicking toward the door as if she were looking at an altar.

They joined the line, letting the crowd press them forward until the velvet rope was in reach. The guard, a slab of muscle, scanned the queue with eyes that measured without interest.

"Names?"

Christina, always the bold one, shook her head.

"We're not on the guest list, sir."

The guard didn't blink. "Max capacity. Guest list only."

Jessica let out a breath, disappointment flickering across her face.

"Great. So much for that."

Christina rolled her eyes. "We should've tried Atlas."

Lena glanced once at the glowing doors of Enigma, then back to her friends.

"Come on," she said. "There's always somewhere else."

She was reaching for Jessica's hand when a low, unmistakable growl of a sports car split the night.

A machine built to outrun consequences slid to the curb.

Conversations thinned. Heads turned.

Then he stepped out.

Lucien Cole.

Sharp as ever in a tailored suit that turned the club's lights into something darker, he moved with the kind of quiet command that changed a room before he even crossed its threshold.

On his arm was a woman draped in the dress Lena had helped him choose earlier that day.

His gaze swept the crowd until it landed on her.

Lena's breath caught.

She expected distance from him, the untouchable kind.

Instead he looked at her like the recognition went both ways.

Something tightened low in her stomach, sharp and unfamiliar.

She hadn't expected to see him again. Least of all like this.

Before she could stop herself, she lifted a hand.

It wasn't a wave.

It was a signal flare she couldn't stop herself from sending.

Lucien's steps slowed. Then, without a word, he shifted course and came toward her. The crowd parted like fabric being cut.

"Didn't take you for someone into this scene," he said, voice low, laced with amusement that didn't reach his eyes.

Before Lena could answer, Christina grinned. "Oh, she's not."

Jessica smirked. "It's my birthday. We dragged her out."

Lena shook her head, soft laugh breaking under the noise. "Not that it matters, we can't get in. Guest list only."

Lucien didn't glance at the guard. "These three are allowed in."

He said it the way men like him said everything that mattered, as if refusal had already been removed from the air.

The shift in energy was immediate.

The guard straightened.

"Of course, Mr. Cole."

The velvet rope dropped.

Jessica and Christina exchanged wide-eyed looks and slipped past the barrier.

Inside, the world changed.

Heat from the lights mixed with perfume so expensive it smelled like an idea of sin.

Bass rolled through the walls like subway tremors, invisible but structural.

Black marble. Chrome edges.

Balconies rimmed in ultraviolet glow stared down like jury boxes.

Grids in the floor leaked color upward, washing faces in cyan, then magenta, then slow pulses of blood-red.

This wasn't a club.

It was the city's heart suspended in glass, still beating.

Beautiful predators and reckless saints pressed toward the center, moths trying to touch flame without burning.

Chaos wore designer heels. Deals were sealed with a handshake and undone with a glance.

No posted rules. No cameras you could see.

Only the promise that whatever you touched in here would cost you exactly as much as it bought you.

Near the lobby's center, beneath a wall of backlit onyx, Lucien leaned in to whisper something to the woman on his arm.

She nodded once, elegant, and headed for the grand staircase without looking back.

"I'll be right up," he whispered before turning to Lena.

"My apologies for the front door situation," he said. "The guards are instructed not to let just anyone in."

Lena let out a soft breath of a laugh.

"You must hold serious power to overrule them like that."

Lucien's mouth curved, controlled, nothing like a smile.

"Well. I do own the place."

He said it lightly, like ownership was too ordinary to announce.

The heat of it lingered after the words were gone.

Behind Lena, Jessica and Christina stared at him as if he'd descended from another world.

His gaze flicked toward them, then returned to Lena.

"Head up to VIP. Ask for James. There's a table waiting. Drinks are on me."

He paused. "Maybe I'll see you around."

Just as he turned to leave, he looked at Jessica. "Happy birthday."

Then he disappeared into the crowd, walking toward the stairs like the ground was built for him.

At the landing, he looked back.

Men like that didn't look back by accident.

Their eyes met, and something in his stare carried weight, not curiosity but certainty. For a second, the world seemed to step back.

Christina nudged her, snapping the moment. "The night just crowned us."

Lena steadied herself, heart knocking once against her ribs, with the quiet, impossible sense that he had seen the real her and hadn't looked away.

She followed, pulse steadying, already cataloging what this night had cost her.

The night had already changed the rules. She just didn't know which ones yet.

CHAPTER FOUR

MONSTER IN THE SHADOWS

Hours unraveled in a blur of bass, cocktails, and velvet laughter. Lena, Christina, and Jessica moved like they belonged, riding the current of a night Lucien had quietly handed them. Enigma throbbed beneath their heels, music pulsing through marble and muscle.

Lena had lost count of the drinks. She didn't care. Tonight she felt unchained, loosened from the gravity of her own life.

As they danced, bodies folding and breaking around them, a prickle climbed the back of her neck. It felt slow. Intentional. The kind that didn't come from cold, but from being watched.

Her gaze lifted to the balcony above.

A man stood there, completely motionless in the chaos, half-sculpted by the crimson light. His stare locked onto her with an intensity that didn't blink. His smile twitched crookedly, wrong in a way liquor couldn't explain. Something hungry lived behind his eyes, not desire, something sharper, meaner.

Lena's stomach tightened, instinct flaring before thought could catch up.

When she looked back again, he was no longer on the balcony.

That should have felt like relief. It didn't.

A voice pushed through the music behind her, slurred and thick with liquor.

The wrongness from the balcony had found her.

"Wanna dance?"

He pushed closer.

Lena shook her head, stepping back. "No thanks, I'm good."

He didn't move. He leaned in, his body reeking of sweat.

"Come on, baby. One dance won't kill you."

His hand shot out, fingers locking around her arm. Lena froze, heart stalling, then yanked herself free.

"Get lost, asshole," she snapped, shoving his hand away.

His grin turned mean.

"Alright, alright. Didn't take you for a bitch."

Shock prickled through her, but before she could respond, he slipped backward, dissolving into the moving crowd.

Christina looped an arm around her waist, concern sharpening her gaze. "What happened?"

"Nothing," Lena lied, forcing a smile. "Some guys just don't know when to quit."

They let it go. The night pressed on, more drinks, more dancing, more laughter, but the ease she'd felt earlier had soured. Every few minutes, Lena glanced over her shoulder, convinced she caught glimpses of his face, his leering eyes slicing through the crush of dancers.

But each time she looked again, he was gone.

Maybe she'd imagined him.

That was how danger first learned your shape, by teaching you to doubt whether it had ever really been there.

Eventually, Lena excused herself, needing air, needing one moment where no one touched her.

She pushed through the dense crowd, the music swallowing her whole, lights strobing like warnings.

But something shifted. The air thickened. The rhythm that had carried her minutes ago now dragged across her nerves like grit.

What had been vibrant now felt distorted, off-kilter. Eyes lingered too long. Faces blurred, then snapped into masks. Strangers knocked into her without turning, shoulders clipping her arms, hands brushing her hips as if she weren't there at all.

The music was still playing, but the joy was gone.

And then she felt it.

A chill crept beneath her skin, without reason.

Like something had followed her out of the light.

The club still throbbed with dark, animal energy, a heavy heartbeat that echoed through Lena's bones. But the corridor leading to the private restrooms felt disconnected, forgotten, a vein severed from the heart of the party.

The bass dropped to a distant, haunting thrum. No voices carried this far. No laughter. Only her footsteps, too loud, too alone.

Golden sconces flickered along velvet-black walls, barely touching the shadows. The air felt colder here.

Lena's heels clicked louder with every step, nerves tightening beneath her skin. Something urged her to turn back. She ignored it, fingers brushing the bathroom door.

The place felt detached, like she had stepped out of the club and into something waiting.

She reached for the handle.

A shift in the air stopped her. No sound. No movement. Just pressure, space tightening around her.

A hand clamped around her wrist.

Cold and brutal.

Her breath locked in her throat. She spun, vision jerking, heartbeat slamming high in her ribs.

It was him.

The same man. The one she'd told to get lost. The one who had watched her from the balcony like she was prey.

His eyes were glazed, pupils blown wide into pits of black that didn't register her fear. Liquor soured the air between them as he dragged her in, mouth brushing her ear.

"You didn't look so fucking tough back there."

Her stomach caved. Something inside her went still.

Before she could scream, he yanked her sideways.

Her heels scraped the concrete as he dragged her.

Her shoulder cracked against the wall, her vision blurring at the edges.

The world narrowed to his grip and the dark.

She clawed at him, nails raking his neck, face, and chest. He didn't flinch.

The pain meant nothing to him.

He shoved her through a half-open door marked MAINTENANCE. It swung shut behind them.

The hallway beyond was a tomb.

A single naked bulb flickered overhead, throwing broken shadows across unfinished walls, rusted pipes, forgotten ladders, and hanging plastic tarps.

This wasn't part of the club guests were supposed to see.

This was a place screams couldn't escape.

The realization hit too late. He slammed her into the concrete again, breath ripping from her lungs.

His mouth crashed against her neck, wet and desperate, leaving bruises that burned. Teeth scraped her skin, then bit down. Pain tore through her.

"No!" she gasped, twisting against his hold.

He laughed, a low, drunken rumble.

"You walked around all night like a fucking tease. Pretending you didn't know exactly what you were doing."

His hands grabbed at her waist, lifting her off her feet and pinning her against the wall.

"You think you're special?"

"Stop!" she cried as panic burst through her chest.

But her voice died against the walls, the music outside too loud to notice.

He pressed harder, hips grinding into her.

She struggled, hitting, clawing.

He barely noticed, strength thick with alcohol and rage.

He hiked up her dress, fingers bruising her thighs. A sob tore from her as air hit skin that shouldn't have been exposed.

"Get the fuck off me!" Her voice cracked.

He laughed, thick with drink and certainty.

His hand shot up, fisting the gold chain at her throat.

The links snapped, sharp and final.

He stuffed it into his pocket like loose change.

"Please," she gasped, reaching for it, voice breaking. "That was my mother's."

Her throat closed around the word. She hadn't said it aloud in years.

The words felt older than the room.

He ignored her, fingers hooking into her panties, pulling them down roughly, inch by agonizing inch. Air rushed in, cold and unforgiving.

"Shh," he hissed into her ear. "Pretend you don't want it."

"No!" she gasped again, the word breaking apart.

He shoved harder, parting her thighs with a knee, the weight of him crushing against her.

She squeezed her eyes shut, desperate to escape. But reality dragged her back.

His belt buckle rattled.

His zipper opened.

And then a voice sliced through the dark.

"Let her go, motherfucker."

The man barely had time to turn before two figures came out of the shadows and hit him like a verdict. One tore him off her. The other drove him into the wall hard enough to shake dust from the pipes above. The sound that came out of him was ugly and short, more air than voice.

Lena's legs gave the second his weight left her. Her heels slipped on the concrete. Cold slammed up through her feet. Her attacker's eyes went wide, not with remorse, with disbelief, like men like him never imagined the night might turn and bite back.

"Wait," he choked.

A fist buried itself in his stomach and folded the word in half. Another followed, cleaner, harder, the kind of blow that didn't come from anger. It came from practice.

Then Lucien stepped into the hallway.

He didn't rush in. He appeared through the dark like the hallway had been waiting to give him shape. The weak bulb overhead caught the angles of his face and left the rest to shadow. His eyes found her first.

Not the man.

Her.

Something cold and enormous moved through the air.

"You alright?" he asked.

His voice was low enough to calm a room.

It did nothing to hide the violence under it.

She nodded because speaking felt too far away. "I'm, yeah. I think so. Thank you."

For the first time since that man's hands had closed on her, the world stopped pitching under her feet. It was as if her fear saw Lucien and stepped back.

He came to her in slow, measured strides, every movement controlled so completely it felt worse than rage.

"You're safe with me," he said.

Not softly. With certainty.

The words should have meant nothing from a man she barely knew. Instead they struck something buried deep, somewhere old enough to remember what it cost to believe in safety at all. She hated that her body trusted him before her mind had the chance to object.

He turned then, just slightly.

His men still had the attacker pinned to the wall, his face half crushed into concrete, his breathing wrecked and wet. They looked to Lucien and waited.

Lucien's gaze dropped to Lena's throat.

Bare skin.

The chain gone.

Something in his face emptied out.

No flare of anger. No spectacle. Just a stillness so complete it made the whole hallway feel smaller.

He looked back at the man.

"Which hand."

The man blinked at him, drunk and dazed and too stupid to understand the mercy of being asked.

"What?"

Lucien took one step closer.

"The hand you used to touch her."

Silence fell so hard it felt physical.

The man started to shake his head. Maybe to deny it. Maybe to beg. It didn't matter. Lucien was already finished with him.

He looked at his men.

"Break it."

He turned back to Lena before the scream came, as if what happened next was too inevitable to watch.

When he looked back at Lena, his expression had softened, but not the danger in it. "Come on." He offered his arm. "Let's get you back."

Her fingers found his forearm, clutching tight as though he was the only thing anchoring her to reality. Beneath the expensive suit and the warmth of his skin, she felt steel.

As he guided her back into the club, the pulsing bass and flashing lights blurred around them. People parted instinctively, like a river around a rock, sensing something dangerous moving among them.

When they reached the VIP section, Lucien turned and summoned another figure from the shadows, broad-shouldered, sharp-eyed, clearly a man accustomed to violence.

"Michael," Lucien said, the name more threat than introduction. "Take Lena and her friends wherever they want to go. Anyone so much as looks at them wrong."

Michael's expression hardened. "Understood."

Lena swallowed hard, heart racing. "Thank you, Mr. Cole."

Lucien's eyes darkened, holding hers with unsettling intensity. "Don't thank me," he murmured. "You're under my roof."

She didn't know which part of that frightened her.

And with a last glance, Lucien vanished back into the crush of the club.

Things moved quickly after that. Security flowed where Lucien pointed, and by the time Michael guided them outside, police lights were already washing the curb, but Lena barely noticed.

Enigma's fame came with a price. The city kept patrol cars nearby after midnight, just in case the wrong kind of trouble spilled onto the sidewalk.

Across the pavement, the man from the hallway stood with his head down, wrists cuffed in front, one arm hanging at a wrong angle, already swelling.

Before officers pushed him into the car, he lifted his eyes and locked them on Lena.

His stare didn't scream or curse. It lingered, slow, unsettling, strangely calm.

It wasn't the look of a man who had lost.

It was the look of a man who was remembering.

Lena didn't flinch.

But something deep within her did.

Because the true threat, the real power, was already gone, swallowed by the dark and the roar of his own domain.

The ride home stretched in uneasy silence. The city blurred past in streaks of red, gold, and sickly white, each light smearing across the glass like something trying to keep up with them. Inside the SUV, the air felt sealed, expensive, and wrong, too quiet after the violence, too controlled to trust.

Michael drove without wasted motion, one hand on the wheel, eyes shifting between the road and the mirror. He had the kind of stillness that didn't read as calm until you looked twice. Then it read as discipline, the kind men earned the hard way.

By the time she finished telling them what happened in the hallway, the car had gone quiet again.

Christina broke first, voice frayed thin. "Jesus, Lena. What the fuck just happened?"

Jessica sat forward, arms wrapped tight around herself. "That wasn't protection. That was vengeance."

Michael didn't turn around. "Sometimes they're the same thing."

The words sat there like a blade left on the table.

Lena kept her cheek against the cold window. Beneath the fading adrenaline, something deeper kept moving through her, like her body had not finished understanding what almost happened.

Her fingers rose to her throat.

Bare.

Still gone.

The absence burned hotter than the bruise beneath it.

Her mother's chain.

The last piece of her past, sitting in a stranger's pocket like loose change.

Somewhere between the hallway, the lights, and the police, she had forgotten to make sure she got it back.

For a second her lungs forgot their job.

Michael's eyes lifted to the mirror. He saw it. Of course he did.

"There's water in the door," he said. "Clean cloth in the console."

The line should have been small. It wasn't. It was the first thing anyone had said to her all night that didn't demand panic.

Christina reached for the bottle and handed it over. Lena took it, but didn't drink.

Jessica stared ahead. "Is he always that calm after?"

No one needed to ask who.

Michael took the next turn smooth as thought. "No."

That single word changed the air more than a speech would have.

Jessica looked at him then. "Could've fooled me."

A faint shadow crossed his face, not amusement, not quite.

"Men like the one Lena ran into tonight count on the room forgiving them," he said. "Tonight it didn't."

Lena watched the city slide by in reflections, neon breaking over Michael's profile, then gone.

"You've been with him a long time," she said.

He met her eyes in the mirror for a second. "Long enough."

It wasn't an answer. It was a boundary.

Jessica shook her head. "I still don't understand what kind of man does something like that and then just walks away."

Michael was quiet for a moment. When he spoke, his voice was level, almost thoughtful.

"The kind who's already handled what comes after."

No one had anything to say to that.

Lena's grip tightened around the water bottle. "My chain," she said, surprised by how small her own voice sounded. "He took my chain."

Michael's jaw shifted once. The only visible sign that the detail had found somewhere to land.

"If it was on him, it's in evidence now," he said. "Things have a way of turning up eventually."

Christina turned toward Lena, eyes glossy now, anger and fear fighting for space. "You should come stay with one of us tonight."

"I'm fine," Lena said automatically.

Nobody in the car believed her.

Michael slowed for a red light. Blood-colored glow washed through the interior, painting everyone in the same uneasy shade.

His eyes lifted to the rearview mirror again.

"You fought him," he said.

Lena looked up.

"Most people freeze."

Lena swallowed, eyes drifting back to the window. "He asked which hand," she said quietly.

Michael's gaze stayed on the light.

"He gave him a chance to pick which one he kept."

Jessica shook her head. "That's not mercy."

"No," Michael said. "It's a lesson."

Silence settled over the car.

After a moment, Lena spoke again. "He looked at me like this wasn't over."

Michael didn't turn around.

"It is."

The light changed.

Michael pulled through the intersection.

No one in the car doubted him.

A few blocks later, the SUV eased to the curb outside Lena's building.

For the first time, Michael turned slightly in his seat, enough for her to see him fully.

"Get inside," he said. "Lock the door. If anything feels wrong. Call the number."

Lena frowned. "What number?"

Michael held out a card between two fingers. Black. One number. No name.

She took it.

Christina reached across the seat and caught Lena's wrist. "Call us in the morning, okay?"

Jessica's eyes held on her, fierce and frightened. "Text us when you're inside."

Lena nodded and stepped out into the night.

The air was cold and alert, the kind that made the city feel awake in all the wrong ways. New York looked hungriest at this hour, when the masks came off and the real teeth stayed out.

She shut the door and glanced back once.

Michael was watching to make sure she got inside.

Not staring. Not lingering.

Just watching like a man finishing a job.

Then the locks clicked, the SUV pulled away, and its taillights disappeared into the dark.

Lena stood in the doorway a second longer than she meant to, black card in one hand, the bruise on her throat alive under her skin.

Then she climbed the stairs, one heartbeat at a time.

Chapter Five

WHAT HE LEFT BEHIND

Lena closed the door and leaned back, spine hitting the wood like it might hold her together. Her heart was still catching up, fluttering beneath her ribs. Her body hadn't decided yet whether it had escaped or been released.

Everything had moved too fast.

Drinks.

Music.

Danger.

Lucien.

She barely knew the man, two brief encounters and a disaster, yet her thoughts kept orbiting him like he was the only solid thing left.

Stability, she realized, didn't have to be gentle to feel real.

One moment replayed above all the rest, the instant he appeared, silent and lethal, flanked by men who didn't ask questions, only obeyed.

The adrenaline that had carried her home began to ebb, shifting into something slower.

A hum. A heat. The memory of the way he'd looked at her, not like another girl in a crowded club, but like something chosen.

She drifted toward the bathroom, toes brushing cool hardwood. The switch clicked, too loud in the quiet.

Her reflection stared back, flushed and disheveled. A faint bruise marked her neck where that creep had pressed too close.

Her hand rose to her collarbone. Bare skin.

The chain, her mother's, was still gone. Another thing she hadn't been able to protect.

She'd let the night move too fast, too bright, too dangerous to stop and demand it back. The realization stung worse than the bruise.

She pressed her fingers to the empty place, anger flaring through her chest.

The thought burned, then cooled into something heavier.

She should have been thinking about the man in cuffs.

Instead, she kept hearing Lucien's voice.

It felt wrong to want the man who stepped into the nightmare more than she feared the one who caused it. But wrong or not, the wanting stayed.

His voice echoed inside her: *Are you alright?*

The way the room had seemed to fall away when he turned toward her.

She picked up her toothbrush, trying to shake the memory. It followed her anyway.

By the time she shut off the light, her heartbeat was rising again, not from fear, but from the slow, curling ache he'd left behind.

She crossed the room and slipped beneath the covers, pulling the sheets over bare skin.

Sleep didn't come.

Lucien Cole lingered with her. In her thoughts. In the air around her. In the space between the knot in her chest and the heat pooling low in her belly.

She needed proof that the night had edges.

She unlocked her phone and typed his name.

Lucien Cole

Public posts. Tagged images.

What struck her first was the restraint. Almost nothing. Only a few photographs, each one placed.

One outside a gallery opening, suit black, expression unreadable, the caption nothing more than a date. Behind him, two men in suits watched the room instead of the art.

Another at a charity event she remembered seeing on the news, Lucien standing just behind the mayor, close enough to speak but never smiling.

A third from some rooftop reception, city burning behind him in gold hour light, his eyes on the distance like he was measuring the city.

Then the one that made her breath lock.

A tagged photo, not his. Grainy, caught across a table on someone's yacht. He wasn't posing. He wasn't aware.

Shirt open, sleeves rolled, a half-smile curving like he'd just finished saying something dangerous.

Not relaxed. Not casual.

A man in control even while doing nothing at all.

Even blurred by motion, he radiated authority.

It wasn't beauty that held her there. It was control.

In every frame, he looked carved from something colder than the men around him. Like danger shaped into a man.

She leaned back, tugging the covers higher, not for warmth, but to contain the heat pulsing between her thighs. The glow of her phone lit her face, his outline burned into her thoughts.

Her body hadn't learned the difference between terror and desire; it only knew who had walked into the dark and pulled her back out.

He didn't smile. He didn't pose. He existed, threaded with something dark enough to ruin her.

Her nails trailed down her stomach, slow, raising goosebumps like tiny confessions. The sheets twisted around her thighs. Restless heat pooled low, insistent, pulling her hand beneath the waistband before reason could intervene.

She was already slick, already aching, her body answering a want she hadn't dared name.

A soft sound escaped her, half whimper, half surrender, as her fingers found the rhythm her mind had already set. Lucien's voice rose inside her, low and controlled, intimate as a blade against skin: *Don't stop.*

Her hips lifted off the mattress, chasing the filth she imagined him saying. She imagined his hand there instead, larger, heavier, merciless.

She wanted him past permission, because permission had already been given somewhere deeper than words. Taking. Pinning her wrists above her head with one grip while the other closed around her throat, just tight enough to remind her who she had chosen to surrender to.

He would put his mouth where the bruise already lived, claim the hurt and turn it sacred.

Say it, he'd put in her ear, right against her pulse. *Who do you belong to?*

The question alone sent a tremor through her. Her fingers moved faster, harder, the pressure tightening, winding, like something pulling tight inside her, ready to snap. She pictured him not bothering with gentleness, pulling fabric aside, entering her in one deep, unrelenting claim. She would open for him, scream for him, break for him because some part of her had always been waiting to be broken this way.

Take it, the voice in her head commanded.

And she did.

The release came like surrender to a god she had invited into the dark. Her back arched off the mattress, a cry breaking out of her before she could stop it, her hand flying to her mouth too late. Every muscle locked, then shook as it tore through her, so hard it almost hurt, his name sitting right there in her throat where she refused to let it out.

She lay still for a long moment, chest heaving, sheets damp with sweat. The city hummed beyond the window, indifferent. Her thighs trembled; her skin felt branded from the inside out.

She drew her hand free and curled it against her stomach, shaken by how real it felt, how much of herself she had given to a man who had never touched her.

Not for pleasure.

For witness.

As if somewhere across the dark miles of the city, Lucien Cole could feel what she had surrendered without ever needing to see it.

She cleaned herself in silence, wiped away the evidence, and dimmed the lamp with a hand that still shook.

The clock blinked.

3:01 A.M.

Lucien Cole hadn't touched her.

Hadn't said more than a handful of words.

But something had already changed.

Chapter Six

THE THRESHOLD

The alarm cut through the quiet.

Lena rolled out of the dark and into the morning.

Morning here wasn't mercy. It was judgment.

She already felt sentenced.

Yesterday still clung to her skin. Sleep had rinsed nothing away. The cut of his voice, the gravity around him, the feeling she'd stepped into a story that already knew its ending.

The worst part was how right that ending felt. Too soon. Too strong. Too certain.

Somehow, she was already written into it.

Routine was armor. She built it piece by piece. Coffee like penance. Black on black. Hair pulled clean. She moved quickly enough to outpace thought.

Outside, Manhattan glittered the way knives glitter, pretty until you touched them. Sunlight ricocheted off windshields in hard white slashes. Sirens stirred somewhere beneath the traffic.

By the time she reached La Maison Élite, the street had settled back into ritual. The glass doors waited. The silence inside waited with them.

The boutique performed discretion; Lena performed control. Hangers whispered. Satin slid. The air smelled of perfume and money, both meant to disappear. She moved with the economy of a dancer and the silence of a witness.

And still, he kept sliding through her mind like static in a wire, something that refused to fade.

The phone rang, sharp as a scalpel.

Stacey, who worked the front counter, caught it, voice sugar on steel, then turned, smile lacquered and lethal. "It's for you."

"For me?"

Stacey said nothing.

Lena lifted the receiver. "This is Lena."

A pause, long enough to make the room feel smaller.

"Lena."

Her name in his voice landed slow, heat spreading under her skin.

"Lucien," she answered, her tone steady even though nothing inside her was.

"My sister is already on her way. Victoria. She needs help picking something out for her birthday."

"Understood."

"I know."

For a second neither of them spoke. She could hear his breathing, slow and close, like he was standing just behind her instead of somewhere across the city.

"Last night, you moved through the dark and didn't flinch. Most people do."

It wasn't praise. It was recognition. A matching spark he hadn't expected.

Recognition was more dangerous than kindness ever was.

She felt it in her spine.

"Thanks to your intervention."

"I don't send amateurs. And I don't save anyone unless I want them breathing tomorrow."

She should have been chilled by that. Instead something inside her aligned with it, like her pulse recognized the cadence.

"She'll be there soon. Give her what she wants. But you..."

A pause, just for her.

"You'll learn quickly what I expect."

Hunger answered before judgment could.

"Lucien..."

He let the word hang between them, gentle but absolute.

"Good."

And the line died.

But her body didn't.

Lena set the receiver down like it might bite.

The door chimed.

A woman entered smelling of old money and impatience. Diamonds like verdicts. "Is anyone working the floor," the woman asked without looking, "or is elegance self-serve now?"

"That would be me," Lena said.

A measured glance up and down. "In that?"

"We make the client the mirror," Lena answered, steady. "The clothes do the talking."

"We'll see," the woman said, turning a rack with two fingers.

Before Lena replied, another voice reached across the room, low and amused, softening nothing.

"She's exactly who you want."

Lena turned.

The girl in the doorway wore ease like tailoring. Young. Luminous without trying. The kind of presence that didn't need permission. She crossed the floor with a conspirator's smile that made even the diamond woman blink.

"Don't let her taste define yours," the girl said, near enough to be kind. "Some people think the world owes them a fitting."

Lena's mouth tilted despite itself. "Hazard of the job."

"I'm Victoria." A hand offered, not flung, not forced. Simple. Certain. "Lucien's sister."

The name rang behind Lena's ribs like a bell in a crypt.

"You must be Lena," Victoria said, eyes bright as unsheathed steel. "He named you."

"He did?"

"He doesn't name people. He marks them. And Lucien never marks anything he doesn't mean to come back for."

Lena felt the mark before she understood it.

She felt the truth settle deep inside her, an echo she hadn't invited and couldn't deny.

The diamonded woman snorted, drifted away, dismissed by gravity she couldn't afford.

"What kind of room are we walking into?" Lena asked.

"Twenty-one," Victoria said, the number a threshold, not an age. "No fireworks. No crowns. I want the room to shut up before it learns my name."

A smile meant for one person, not the room.

"Barcelona next. Amalfi Coast after. He's exiling me in silk. This weekend is just one of his rooms uptown."

"So Enigma isn't the top floor."

"He owns a few places. The rest, he just walks into and people start listening."

Lena moved along the rack, fingers steady. "Big is easy to see. Power isn't."

Victoria smiled. "You'll do just fine."

They hunted in silence. Lena moved by instinct. She reached into the rack and pulled an emerald column, clean lines, simple, meant to own a room.

"This."

Victoria took it like it belonged to her bones. "Yes."

In the fitting room, the dress changed her. Throat high, back bare, restraint carved into control. She turned once. The mirror did the rest.

"Perfect."

"It teaches the room without raising its voice."

"It preaches," Victoria answered, eyes on the ghost in the glass. "Lucien was right. You see."

The glass at the front darkened, like someone blocked the sun.

Lena didn't need to look.

He entered, and the room adjusted around him.

And he looked at her like he expected her to adjust too. Like he'd already counted on it.

Black sat on him like it was made for his body. Collar open like a wound. Nothing on him begged for attention. People adjusted, instinct, not choice.

One slow turn: exits, sightlines, risk. Then his gaze found Lena. The pivot ended.

"Enjoying yourself?" he asked Victoria, eyes still on Lena.

"Very. Lena found it."

"Naturally," he said to Lena, not as praise. As fact.

Victoria twirled. Emerald carved the air like a blade through silk. "Do you see this? I'm unbearable already."

"Learn to be," he said, still not smiling.

She laughed, then vanished into the fitting room, rehearsing ascent.

Silence sat between him and Lena. He closed half the distance. When he spoke, it wasn't intimacy. It was law.

"That green. You understand legacy."

"I chose what fit," she said.

"Exactly."

His gaze swept the boutique, counting the room. When it returned, it brought everyone in it with it.

"There's a night coming. Private. Out-of-state money and trouble. I don't leave nights like that to chance."

"You want me to dress your staff," Lena said.

"I want you to dress the night," he corrected. "We'll go over what isn't negotiable. You'll handle the rest."

The words should have been flattery. They were a contract.

"I'll need two days," she said. "Sourcing. Tailors who don't ask."

"You'll have one."

She considered. "Then I'll have enough."

Something like approval passed through his eyes and was gone.

He didn't reach for her card. She offered it. His fingers took what was already his.

"My schedule's on the back," she said.

He slipped it away. "I don't keep schedules. I keep doors."

And she had the sudden, terrifying feeling she had just walked through one.

Victoria reemerged, shoes in hand, joy still expensive. "We done?"

"We're set."

He turned, and the pressure left with him.

When they were gone, the glass returned to daylight. Conversations resumed like debts coming due. Stacey's smirk soured.

Lena stood a moment longer, hand light from the card that wasn't in it. Then she returned to work.

But the marble beneath her feet still felt cold.

After work, Lena stepped onto the sidewalk. The city bled amber, the fall air sharp against her skin. She tried to leave the day behind, but Lucien's name still clung to her ribs.

Her phone buzzed. Jessica.

Ninth and Bleecker. I'll save us a booth

Lena thumbed a reply. **On my way**

The diner was a cracked relic, vinyl split like old skin, the neon OPEN sign flickering like it was running out of power. Grease stained everything, even the walls.

She pushed through the door, and the city fell away.

Inside waited jukebox static, the low hum of a broken refrigerator, and the smell of burnt coffee and old apologies.

Jessica sat in the last booth, coffee black, blonde hair slicked back, eyes sharp enough to read a lie. She didn't wave. She summoned.

Lena slid into the booth, vinyl sighing beneath her, the table tacky under her palms.

"Your pulse is in another borough," Jessica said. "Name him."

"Lucien Cole."

Jessica froze mid-sip. "Enigma Lucien Cole?"

"He sent his sister in today. I dressed her for her twenty-first."

"And that's got you starving?"

"He came in after. Asked me to dress a night for him. Private crowd. Out-of-state money that doesn't ask questions. I get one day."

Jessica leaned in. "And you think it's more?"

"It's everything." Her voice barely rose above the jukebox's dirge. "He doesn't ask. He ordains."

Jessica's eyes narrowed. "He collects women like he collects debts, Lena. You'll forgive him before you hate him."

She didn't know which would be worse.

Lena didn't argue. Not because Jessica was wrong, but because the part of her that was already unraveling didn't care.

Lena's fingers traced the cracked Formica. "Maybe I want the debt."

Jessica studied her like a doctor looking at a patient who had just chosen the disease.

Then she laid down the rule. "Then pay in blood, not hope."

The waitress dropped a fresh cup in front of Lena, bitter and steaming.

Her phone buzzed.

Change of plans. My office. 8. Don't be late

A moment later, another message followed. An address. Nothing else.

Her breath hitched, not in fear, but in the sharp, wild pull of something she'd already stepped into.

Jessica saw the screen. "Logical sense," she mocked. "Or damnation in a black suit?"

Lena didn't answer. His name was already under her skin.

She stood. Left a ten under the saucer.

"Lock your doors," Jessica called. "And your heart, while you're at it."

Outside, the night pressed against the glass.

Lena hailed a cab.

The city didn't whisper.

It waited.

So did she.

And somewhere in the city, so did he.

Chapter Seven

THE SUMMONS

By a quarter to eight, Lena stepped from the cab onto the curb in front of a tower that seemed to devour the sky.

She paused, staring up at the sleek glass facade, its edges sharp against the night.

The height of it wasn't architecture.

It was power.

His world.

She pushed through the revolving doors. Marble, steel, and silence that cost millions.

The elevator felt sealed.

No music. No mirrors.

Just her pulse counting sins against the hum of ascent.

None of them were new. They were just louder here.

The door opened to dominion, not design.

Glass walls framed Manhattan like a map he'd already conquered.

Lucien stood at the edge, one hand in his pocket, his silhouette dark against the city lights.

"You came," he said without turning. Voice low, irrefutable.

He faced her. His eyes measured her.

Lena's throat tightened. "You've got an incredible view."

"Depends what you're looking at."

He gestured to a low table, where a slim folder waited.

"Shall we?"

She crossed the room, each step heavier than the last.

Inside the folder lay logistics disguised as law.

Every rule assumed obedience without asking for it.

An unlisted gathering. Unseen. Men who didn't appear on Forbes lists because they wrote them.

Wealth that predated currency. Power that moved through invitation, not announcement.

Every element upheld the illusion of control.

Lucien outlined the vision: tone, attire, presence.

No excess. No mercy.

The air between them changed, humming with a voltage that wasn't professional.

Every time his gaze found hers, it held a beat too long, enough to make the room feel smaller.

When he finished, he leaned back, studying her. "You don't follow. You elevate. That's rare."

Rarity wasn't safety. It was exposure.

Something in his voice reached a place in her she hadn't realized was empty.

Maybe that was what unsettled her, the way his certainty made room for her in a world that never had. Around him, she didn't feel small. She felt seen.

Lena's heart betrayed her. "It's business."

He studied her for a moment. "Is that what you're praying for?"

He rose. Crossed the room. The light off the glass carved him in fire and shadow.

"I don't mix business with personal," he said. "But some lines bleed."

Lena rose slowly. "Are you always this direct?"

"Only when the risk burns clean."

A ghost of a smirk, there and gone.

Silence held. Two people circling a wound neither would name.

She hated how natural it felt, standing in his gravity, like the room wasn't complete until she was in it.

When she reached for her bag, his voice cut the hush.

"You're not leaving already, are you?"

She paused.

"It's late. I should head home."

Lucien stepped toward her. Each footfall a verdict. The air compressed, charged with unsaid things.

"There's a rooftop nearby. Private. Best view in the city. We could grab something to eat."

The offer was soft.

His eyes were not.

They were black glass over embers, promising ruin in measured doses.

Lena folded her arms, a thin shield against the pull of him.

"You don't strike me as someone who grabs dinner with just anyone."

"You're right. I don't."

He said it without vanity, which made it worse.

The simplicity of it hit harder than any flourish. No charm, no performance, just truth.

"I'm not sure it's a good idea," she said, voice fraying.

He didn't push or coax. He watched her, patient, unreadable.

Then, almost a whisper, "Most people beg for space in my world."

She arched a brow. "Yeah? Maybe you should ask one of them."

A quiet laugh, low and dangerous.

Another step, closer now.

"I never said I wanted most people."

Being chosen felt worse than being chased.

Her heart stuttered. She forced her voice steady.

"Dinner doesn't mean anything, you know."

"Not yet."

The promise in his voice tightened the air.

"If we do this," she said, "it's dinner. Conversation. No assumptions."

He nodded immediately. "Dinner. Your line, not mine."

It unsettled her how easily he accepted limits.

"You're used to getting what you want, aren't you?"

"Only when it's worth it."

"I'll meet you there."

The corner of his mouth curved, barely.

"I'll send the address."

The elevator doors closed.

Her reflection stared back, wide-eyed, breathless.

Already in deeper than she meant to be.

She told herself it was just dinner. Just curiosity.

But truth pressed against her throat. Stepping toward Lucien Cole wasn't a path she could turn back from.

Whatever happened next would leave a mark.

And she couldn't bring herself to stop.

Stepping out, she was claimed by the night, the sky a deep, endless black, dotted with the cold fire of distant stars.

Before her, the rooftop restaurant rose, understated but commanding, a hidden citadel above the city streets.

She was met instantly by a hostess whose smile was knowing, almost welcoming, as if Lena's arrival was the moment the evening had been waiting for.

She followed the hostess to a private elevator at the back. The ride was smooth and silent. At the top, a short staircase led the rest of the way, like the last few steps into another world.

She ascended, pulse quickening with each quiet step.

It was just dinner.

So why did it feel like something else entirely?

She told herself it was curiosity, nothing more.

Then why had she stood in front of the mirror longer than usual?

Get a grip, Lena.

It's a man, not a life decision.

The lie settled in her chest anyway.

The rooftop unfolded around her in warm light and shadow. Lanterns cast small pools of gold where the darkness waited beyond the glow.

The grandeur faded the second she saw him.

Lucien Cole stood at the balcony's edge, black against the city below. He didn't turn when she stepped onto the rooftop, but something in his posture shifted, as if he had felt her the second she entered his space.

Even from a distance, something dark radiated from him, leashed tight by control.

When he finally faced her, his gaze found hers and held. The air between them seemed to narrow.

"You showed."

"You invited me," she said, steadying her voice against her pulse.

He motioned to the table. The gesture was smooth, absolute.

She sat. The table was small enough that their knees nearly brushed. Lantern light traced the edge of his jaw in gold, the same shade he had chosen that first morning in her shop.

Lucien didn't open a menu. He didn't need to. A server appeared, received a single nod, and vanished.

"You're different tonight," he said, his voice low, almost amused. "Last night you fought like someone who'd been waiting for a reason to use her claws."

Her pulse jumped. The maintenance hallway flashed behind her eyes, concrete, breath hot on her neck, the snap of her mother's chain. She met his stare head-on.

"You watched the whole thing on cameras, didn't you?"

Something in his expression changed. Not guilt. Recognition.

"That building answers to me. What happens inside it is my responsibility." He leaned in slightly. "Once I decided you were leaving that hallway with me, there wasn't another outcome."

The words landed low in her stomach. Shame and heat twisted together. She hated that the memory of his voice saying, *You're safe with me*, still sent heat between her thighs.

"Why me?" she asked. "You could've walked away. Let security handle it."

"I don't let things like that happen in my world and stay unfinished," he said. "Especially when they involve a woman who looked at me the way you did in the store that morning."

Her breath caught. She straightened in her chair, trying to reclaim some distance even as heat crawled up her neck. "The way I looked at you? I was doing my job."

He didn't look away. "Don't pretend you didn't feel it. Even last night you looked at me like you were deciding whether I was going to save you or destroy you."

He let the silence sit between them.

"Maybe both."

He leaned back just enough to take her in fully. The corner of his mouth shifted, not quite a smile.

"You're thinking about last night," he said quietly. "Not the fear. The part that came after. When my hand was on your back, leading you through the crowd like you belonged there."

He watched her carefully.

"You were shaking, Lena. Not on the outside. Underneath it."

Heat flooded her face. Filthy images from her bedroom the night before rose unbidden, his hand replacing hers, his voice in her ear, the way she had come with his name trapped in her head. She forced her breathing steady.

"You like collecting broken things?" she asked.

"I don't collect broken things." His voice went lower. "I decide what belongs in my world, and I keep it there."

She set her glass down slowly. "You don't get to decide what I am."

"No," he said. "But I do decide what I let close."

Lena reached for her glass, needing something to do with her hands. "You talk like that's already a decision."

He watched her for a long moment. "You came here tonight. You're sitting across from me now, pulse racing, still trying to call this business. Tell me I'm wrong."

She wanted to. She wanted to tell him this was just dinner, just curiosity, just a bad idea she hadn't named yet.

Instead she said, "Even if you're right, I don't belong to anyone."

His mouth curved. "I would've been disappointed if you did."

The server set down their plates and disappeared. Neither of them looked away.

His eyes dropped to the untouched drink in her hand.

"Maybe you should finish your drink and go home, Lena," Lucien said. "Forget you ever met me. Your life will be quieter."

The words from the mural moved through her mind again.

Born for fire. For ruin.

She leaned forward. "Is that what you want?"

He didn't answer at first.

"No."

The question had been sitting between them all night. She finally said it out loud.

"Why am I here?"

"Because you saw me last night. You saw enough to stay away, and you came anyway."

Her pulse jumped, but she didn't look away. "Is that supposed to scare me?"

"It should."

"But it doesn't."

She held his gaze. "So don't tell me to leave."

Something dark flickered across his face, quieter than surprise, deeper than satisfaction.

"And that," he said, "is what makes you dangerous."

"To whom?"

His eyes didn't leave hers. "To both of us."

"Tell me something real."

For the first time that night, he hesitated.

"Control keeps the damage contained. Without it, I ruin things. People get hurt. I've built my entire life around not finding out how far that goes."

Something in his certainty gave way. Not weakness. Truth, stripped bare. She wasn't used to being trusted with anything that dangerous.

Men like Lucien didn't belong to anyone. She had seen that clearly enough the night before, another woman on his arm, the city at his feet. That should have made this easier. It didn't.

She lifted her glass.

"Then here's to losing control."

The hint of a smile touched his mouth. "And to whatever we find when we do."

Their glasses touched.

The silence between them changed, as if something had just crossed a line and wasn't going back.

Time drifted in low laughter and lingering glances.

Lena felt the hour first, a quiet unease beneath the wine's warmth. Work waited in the morning, but leaving felt heavier than staying. The pull between them had sharpened into something undeniable. Responsibility felt like an intrusion now.

Lucien's eyes narrowed as she muttered an apology, the chair scraping stone.

"At this hour?" His voice was quiet, edged with law. His gaze flicked to the city's sprawl below.

"I wouldn't advise hailing a cab alone. Let me take you."

"I'm fine," she began. "I know how to get home."

He raised one hand, cutting her off clean.

"Humor me. The city has a dark vein after hours. I prefer to know you got home breathing."

Not a request.

An order.

Lena felt the rush of surrender before she could name it. She nodded. Pulse hammering.

The decision felt small. It wasn't.

The ride back was silent, thick with tension.

It wasn't awkward. It felt one word away from becoming something neither of them could take back. Every time Lucien looked toward the window, he found her again in the reflection.

His profile slid across the glass, nothing soft in it. But his jaw wasn't relaxed. A muscle ticked there, small and telling.

He didn't speak.

She didn't dare.

The space between them felt charged, his cologne faint in the air, their breathing too measured.

Outside, the city slipped by in streaks of light and shadow, late-night strangers moving between storefront glow and dark corners. Sirens wailed in the distance, swallowed as fast as they came. Somewhere beyond the glass, Manhattan still bared its teeth.

She had seen those teeth up close.

A corridor. A hand clamped around her wrist. Concrete at her back. Panic tearing through her so hard it left her hollow.

Lucien had stepped into that darkness like it belonged to him more than the man who dragged her there. Since then, the city had not looked the same. Neither had men.

But inside the car, everything felt controlled, sealed in leather and the low hum of the engine.

The soft click of the turn signal.

His hand rested steady on the wheel.

At the light, she watched him shift gears, smooth and practiced, eyes fixed ahead.

Neon bled across the windshield and broke over his face in red and blue shards, like the whole city was burning itself down outside and he was driving through the ashes without flinching.

That should have terrified her.

Instead, she felt something worse.

Safe.

Somewhere between the rooftop and the ride home, the danger had changed shape.

The realization tightened low in her stomach. She turned to the window, to bodegas and scaffolding, to steam rising from grates, to people laughing too loud on corners where laughter never meant innocence. The streets still looked dangerous. The hour still looked dangerous.

The whole city looked like something that could still reach through and pull a person under.

Yet sitting beside him, she felt insulated from it in a way she didn't want to examine too closely.

"You're quiet," he said at last, voice low, eyes still on the road.

Lena swallowed. "So are you."

A faint breath left him, almost a laugh. "I'm trying to behave."

Her eyes slid to him. "Is that what this is?"

"No. This is me deciding how far I can sit this close to you and still call myself disciplined."

Her heartbeat stumbled. The city outside dissolved into color and speed. "And if you lose that discipline?"

His hands tightened slightly on the wheel. "Then I do something we'll both remember tomorrow."

She held his gaze a second too long. "And what makes you think I'd regret that?"

He glanced at her then, only once, but it landed like touch. "I didn't say you'd regret it."

The car slowed as he turned onto her street.

His voice dropped, rough with restraint. "I said we'd remember it."

Silence filled the car again, heavier now, alive with everything neither of them had said.

The car eased to the curb and went still.

The world seemed to hold its breath.

"Thank you," she whispered, her voice unsteady with him so close.

Lucien didn't answer right away.

His eyes lingered on her face, then shifted to the weathered stone of her building.

When he spoke, his tone was mild, but the undercurrent held her still.

"The pleasure was mine. Truly."

He let the quiet stretch until it belonged to him.

"I'm not ready for the night to end. Invite me in."

The question beneath his words was clear.

If she let him upstairs, this night did not stay innocent.

Lena didn't look away. "Can I ask you something?"

"You can ask."

She hesitated, then said it anyway. "Do you always arrive with a different woman on your arm, or was last night a special occasion?"

He let the question sit. Headlights from passing cars swept through the interior, casting his eyes into shadow.

"I don't lie to women. I don't make promises I don't intend to keep. And I don't bring many of them into my real life."

Lena studied him. "And which one am I?"

This time he looked at her fully. The look held, measuring, no trace of casualness left in it.

"I haven't decided yet," he said.

He let that sit between them.

"That's why I'm trying to behave."

She met him evenly. "If I invite you in, it's one drink. And we go at my pace."

He didn't hesitate. He didn't negotiate. He did not test the boundary.

And that, more than anything, undid her.

"Your pace," he said at once.

Her heart stalled, then kicked hard against her ribs.

"For a nightcap?" The words barely made it past her lips.

"Just one drink," he said.

No coaxing. No pressure.

Inevitable.

"I'd like to see your world."

Every instinct told her to draw the line.

But gravity won.

"Alright," she whispered.

Lucien's smile came slow and certain, without a trace of triumph.

"Perfect. I'll park around the corner. Go ahead. I'll meet you upstairs."

The night hit her cold and alive.

She crossed the sidewalk in a blur, traffic rumbling past, her pulse louder than any of it.

Inside, her apartment was so quiet it made her restless.

She moved fast, kicking clothes into corners, gathering glasses, shoving sketches into uneven piles. By the time she stopped, the apartment looked controlled.

She was not.

Streetlight bled through the blinds, laying fractured gold across the walls.

Her eyes kept going to the door, every few seconds, half dreading the knock, half aching for it.

Then the buzzer rang.

He hadn't hesitated.

She froze.

He's here.

A tremor passed through her fingers as she pressed the intercom.

Her voice came out thin, betraying her.

"Come on up."

The words sounded different once they left her mouth.

Like permission.
Like a mistake she already wanted.

CHAPTER EIGHT

SURRENDER TO THE NIGHT

Footsteps climbed the stairwell's spine, measured and unavoidable.

Lena steadied the tremor in her hands. She turned the lock. It opened with a precise and final click.

He stepped through. The stairwell light filtered in slanted bars, gilding his shoulders and cutting his silhouette clean from the dark.

The room felt smaller with him in it. Not cramped. Claimed. Warm walls, scattered sketches, her curated chaos, all suddenly too small for the man stepping across her threshold.

Heat climbed her throat. She braced for the scalpel of his gaze.

Instead, a half-smile. Knowing. Controlled.

"It's cozy," he said quietly, stepping farther in. His voice filled the small room until it felt impossibly close.

"It's small," she said, arms folding. "But it's mine."

She expected judgment. He gave none.

He looked at her space like it mattered because she lived in it. Something inside her shifted at the simplicity of it.

No one had ever made her small apartment feel like a world worth entering.

Her fingers grazed the bare notch of her collarbone, instinct reaching for the chain that wasn't there.

His attention slid to the half-sewn dress draped across the couch. She moved to cover it. His hand closed around her wrist with gentle iron.

"Don't." His voice softened without losing command. "It's all you."

Tension eased, quiet as a thread coming loose.

Their eyes locked. In that stillness, everything unspoken between them surged. Lena felt her pulse thicken in her throat.

"So…" Her voice dipped. "Was the drink real, or just what we're calling this?"

Lucien stepped closer. The air tightened.

"Tell me to stop." His breath grazed her lips, a question that already knew its answer.

"Don't." Her voice steadied. "I choose the fall."

And the truth hit her. She wasn't falling alone. He was already meeting her halfway.

His eyes darkened, and this time the restraint looked costly.

The world narrowed to the inch between their breaths.

He closed it.

Palm to the small of her back, he anchored her against the tide of him. His cologne filled her lungs, dark, expensive, and a little dangerous.

"You're already deeper in this than you realize," he said, hunger leashed in every syllable.

Her heart thundered, but she didn't pull away. "You make everything sound like it's already decided."

A sound, half curse, half prayer, vibrated against her mouth.

The kiss started careful and didn't stay that way.

Lena clutched his shirt, every careful thought between them burning away in a rush of heat and need.

Her spine met the wall. A muted thud, the sound of borders dissolving.

His hands framed her face, rough with a kind of reverence. She threaded her fingers through his hair, tugging the leash tighter.

His mouth moved along her throat, teeth a quiet brand, her name rough against his breath.

Doubt unraveled, thread by thread.

This wasn't surrender. It was gravity.

"Lena." His voice low against her ear. "I want every part of you tonight. No holding back."

"Then take it," she whispered. "Every inch, every thought. Take me past the point of no return."

His grip cinched her waist, tightening the moment. The kiss deepened until breath was a shared currency, rationed and devoured.

City light painted their shadows on the wall, two forms pulled into orbit.

He lifted her slowly, like restraint was leaving him by degrees. Her legs wrapped his hips by instinct, not command.

They moved toward the counter, each step tightening the pull between them. His control wavered.

He set her down. The surface was cool; his hands were not.

Fabric slipped from her shoulders like shed armor. His mouth followed the path, collarbone, sternum, each taste a mark etched in heat.

He lifted her again, swifter now, the last of his restraint giving way. Her legs locked. Shadows swallowed the kitchen's last light.

Down the hall, breath and heartbeat braided into a single cadence.

The dark received them, without mercy.

The mattress yielded beneath her, a soft surrender to the press of him.

His slacks fell away like dropped shadow. He moved with the same lethal precision she remembered from the night he saved her, but now that control was fraying at the edges. His eyes locked on hers, dark and unblinking, daring her to stop him.

She didn't.

His hands found the last barrier between them. He slid her jeans down her thighs with intent. Her own fingers moved before his could, reckless, slipping beneath the silk of her panties and circling through the slick heat already waiting for him.

A low sound tore from his chest.

"You're already soaked for me," he said, voice rough. His fingers replaced hers, sliding through her with a slowness that felt like punishment and worship at once.

He stripped the last scrap of silk away. Freed himself in the same breath. The thick length of him slid along her folds, teasing, coating himself in her, letting her feel exactly what she was choosing.

"Tell me," he said against her sternum, breath hot on her skin. "Tell me you open for no one else."

She couldn't speak. Instead she lifted her hips, pressed herself against the head of his cock, and held his gaze.

Lucien's control cracked.

He dragged his mouth down her body, skipping her lips, until his tongue found her clit in one devastating stroke. No teasing. No mercy. He licked and sucked like a man who had waited too long and was finally allowed to feast. Two fingers pushed inside her, curling, stroking the spot that made her back arch off the bed.

She cried out, thighs trembling around his shoulders.

He didn't stop. He devoured her until her moans fractured and her hands fisted in his hair, until the pleasure sharpened into something almost unbearable.

Only then did he rise over her again, trailing wet kisses up her stomach, her breasts, her throat. His hand settled there, not squeezing, just holding, claiming the exact place that still carried the faint shadow of a bruise from another man's violence.

Their eyes met.

For one heartbeat his grip tightened, and she saw the danger in him flare, the man who could ruin her if he let himself. Then he exhaled, and the grip gentled into something steadier. Something that said I have you.

"Tell me how much you need it," he whispered, voice raw with the effort of holding back.

"I need it," she breathed, hips rolling up to meet him. "All of it."

Lucien's eyes burned. He pinned her legs over his shoulders and drove into her in one full, relentless thrust.

The sound she made was half gasp, half sob. He cursed against her ear, low and broken, as if the feel of her clenching around him nearly undid him right there.

He moved hard. Every stroke measured, every retreat torturous. But she felt the tremor in his arms, the way his rhythm faltered for half a second when she clenched around him on purpose. He was right there on the edge with her.

She clawed at his back, nails digging in, pulling him closer.

"Don't stop," she gasped. "Lucien."

He rolled them without leaving her body, arm locked around her waist, keeping her pressed to his chest as he sat up. Her thighs straddled him now. He guided her hips down onto him again, slower this time, letting her feel every inch.

"Like this," he murmured against her mouth. "Take what you want from me."

She did. She rode him, reckless and hungry, while his hands roamed her back and his mouth found her throat again. When she started to tremble, close again, he slid one hand between them and circled her clit with his thumb.

She came hard, pulsing around him, crying his name like it was the only word she still knew.

He followed her over the edge moments later, holding her there as a rough, broken sound left him. His arms locked around her, holding her tight as he spilled deep inside her, hips jerking with the last helpless thrusts.

For a long moment neither of them moved.

He stayed close, forehead pressed to hers, both of them breathing the same air. The city hummed far below the window, indifferent. Inside the room there was only the heat between them, the faint tremor in his arms, and the quiet truth neither of them could take back.

This had never been casual.

And it never would be again.

Lucien eased onto his back, chest still rising in sharp intervals. The quiet stretched taut between them, sacred and dangerous.

He found his cigarettes without looking, a habit older than thought. The lighter snapped. Flame flickered, catching on the edges of him before the dark reclaimed him.

Inhale. Hold. Exhale.

Smoke curled, thinned, then vanished into the room like it had never been there.

"That," he said, voice roughened by the night, "shouldn't have happened."

He leaned in, cigarette balanced between his knuckles, and kissed her. Slow. Absolute. Smoke and salt and the taste of bad decisions.

Lucien's chest rose and fell, breath easing at last. The storm in his eyes banked to ember, but the heat remained, a low furnace behind bone.

Outside, the city whispered in its sleep, sirens threading the dark, engines prowling distant streets. Inside, the world held its breath.

Lena folded into him, cheek against his chest. His heartbeat drummed steady beneath her ear. She traced one fingertip along the line of his chest, a touch that asked for nothing. The space between them wasn't empty anymore; it held the weight of what had been said without saying a word.

His arm held her at the waist, possessive before it was tender. A claim made in the hush that followed.

She exhaled. No tremor.

Safety here was not soft. It was a blade sheathed at her spine.

He shifted. The mattress sighed. His hand slid from her hip to the base of her spine, palm flat, claiming the curve as if mapping territory no atlas would ever name.

She felt it first, the tremor in his exhale, the way his jaw unclenched by degrees. Not weakness. Surrender held at knifepoint.

The cigarette burned forgotten between his fingers, ash lengthening, threatening collapse. He didn't notice.

Lena lifted her head. Their eyes met, hers still stormglass, his now molten steel.

Neither spoke.

The ash fell, a soft gray snow on the sheet between them.

He stubbed the cigarette in the ashtray without looking, blind precision. Then both hands returned to her, one threading through her hair, the other settling at the base of her throat, his thumb resting over the pulse that still raced for him.

"Sleep," he said. Not a request. A decree.

She obeyed, not because she had to, but because the command was laced with something deeper than dominance: a promise that the dark would not touch her while he breathed.

Her lashes fluttered shut. The last thing she felt was his lips brushing her temple, once, barely there. A benediction.

Lucien did not sleep.

He watched the ceiling like it hid the blueprint of tomorrow's lies. One hand anchored her, steady and possessive.

The world beyond the glass could burn.

If it reached for her, he would strike the match.

He had broken the rule tonight.

Tomorrow, he would swear he hadn't.

The line wasn't erased.

It was ash.

The fire had done what mercy never could.

This wasn't ruin.

It was the first match struck.

Chapter Nine

INTO THE FLAMES

The next morning, sunlight worked through the blinds, gently coaxing Lena awake. Her body stirred before her mind could catch up, and for a few suspended seconds, she floated in the afterglow of a night that felt more like a fever dream than anything real.

She reached across the sheets, empty. The space where he'd been was cool. She'd half-expected he'd vanish before morning.

That the night had been something she'd wake from alone.

In his place, a single note lay folded on the pillow.

HAD TO STEP OUT EARLY. BUSINESS CALLS. CALL ME WHEN YOU WAKE UP

It wasn't reassurance. It was continuity.

She hated how her chest loosened at the note, like she'd been bracing for a disappearing act she pretended she didn't care about.

Lena stared at the words, her finger tracing the curve of his handwriting, emotion catching somewhere between her ribs. The memory of his hands, his voice, the heat of last night rushed back all at once. And yet, in the stark clarity of morning, doubt edged in with the light. Had she lost herself too quickly in something she didn't understand?

She rolled over to silence her blaring alarm, heart still tangled in the fog of thoughts, until a small red notification flashed at the top of her screen.

1 NEW MESSAGE. INSTAGRAM

Still half-asleep, Lena tapped the icon.

What opened made her stomach drop.

A photo.

Of her and Lucien.

From last night.

Taken from a distance, zoomed in from somewhere high. Across rooftops, maybe.

The frame caught them in silhouette at the rooftop table, bathed in lantern light.

It wasn't grainy. It wasn't accidental.

Someone meant this.

Whoever took it wanted her to know.

No name. No posts. No followers. Just eyes.

The account looked new. Empty. Built for one purpose.

Lena's breath caught in her throat.

This wasn't just a breach of privacy.

It was calculated.

A warning. Or a threat.

Her thumb hovered over the screen, unsure what responding would even mean. Her breath shortened.

Last night had felt private, intimate, almost safe. Seeing it through someone else's lens felt like someone had reached into the night and stolen it from her.

Her heart knew something her mind hadn't admitted yet:

Someone had decided she was worth watching.

And this, this was only the beginning.

The morning light carried a deceptive calm as Lena prepared for the day, every motion slowed by the weight of the night before and the photograph she couldn't shake. Her thoughts twisted through what-ifs and warning signs, each thread unraveling faster than she could catch it.

Then her phone buzzed.

A message from her boss flashed across the screen.

The store's gone. Vandalized. Fire. Everything's destroyed. Stay home

Her stomach dropped.

Vandalized?

The word hit like a slap. Her heart thundered. Stay home? She couldn't. Not when part of her life had just been turned to ash.

She threw on clothes she didn't even remember putting on and grabbed her phone on the way out the door. Her hands were shaking so badly she had to try twice before the app opened. By the time the car pulled up, she was already halfway into the street.

"Madison and Seventy-Third," she said, sliding into the back seat.

The driver nodded and pulled into traffic.

The city moved around her like it always did, loud, crowded, alive, completely unaware that her life had just caught fire. The driver glanced at her once in the rearview mirror, like he could tell something was wrong but didn't want to ask.

They were three avenues away when she heard the sirens.

By the next block, she saw the smoke.

By the time the car turned onto Madison, the street was already closed.

"I can drop you here," the driver said.

She nodded, already reaching for the door, her pulse thundering in her ears.

A small, stupid part of her still believed the message had to be wrong. That this was all some kind of mistake. That she would turn the corner and the boutique would still be there, windows dressed, lights warm, Donovan inside arguing about displays like always.

Then she turned the corner, and stopped cold.

The boutique was a ruin.

Glass glittered across the concrete like shrapnel, broken and impossible to ignore. Smoke still curled from the edges of scorched awnings. The front display was gone, blown out or smashed, its frame warped and blackened. Firefighters rolled up hoses while yellow tape fluttered in the morning breeze, cordoning off a stunned crowd.

People stood three deep behind the tape, half-shocked, half-hungry. Some stared at the wreckage. Some stared at her.

She didn't stop when she saw the tape. She ducked under it and went straight to the front, like she belonged there.

That was all it took.

A woman near the curb lifted her phone the second Lena stepped into view, angling for a better shot as if grief looked better with smoke behind it. Another followed. Then another.

The attention hit almost as hard as the ruin.

Not sympathy. Interest.

The kind that fed on blood as long as it belonged to someone else.

A man in a delivery jacket leaned toward the woman beside him and muttered something Lena couldn't fully hear. She caught only the shape of it.

Girl from the shop.

Poor thing.

There's more to it.

Every eye that landed on her felt like a hand she had not invited.

Lena stopped cold. The air left her lungs.

"Lena!"

Her boss stormed toward her, face pale and red-eyed.

"I told you to stay home, what the hell are you doing here?"

"I had to see it," she said softly, her voice barely a thread.

Before he could reply, a uniformed officer approached. Clipboard in hand. Expression unreadable. A pale scar split his eyebrow, giving the impression he'd already seen worse than this.

"You're Mr. Donovan?"

He nodded.

The officer's gaze shifted.

"And you are, miss?"

She hesitated, just for a second, before the words left her lips.

"Lena... Lena Hart."

"We need to show you both something."

He led them past the wreckage-strewn threshold. The air was thick with heat and smoke.

Then Lena saw it.

Paint.

Fresh. Red. Still dripping down the blackened brick.

The words stretched across the wall in jagged strokes.

LUCIEN'S WHORE

They hadn't written his name to shame him.

They'd written it to shame her.

Heat climbed her chest, not from the flames, but from the memory of his body against hers. Humiliation and fury tangled until she couldn't tell where one started.

It wasn't just the insult, it was the cruelty of it. Because for the first time in years, she'd let herself believe she might belong somewhere. That she could reach for something more and not be punished for it.

And here was the city's answer, jagged and dripping on the blackened wall: How dare you think you're worthy.

The officer turned to her, voice even but heavy.

"Do either of you know who Lucien is?"

Her mouth opened, but no sound came out.

Mr. Donovan squinted at the wall, then at her. "Lucien? That guy in the expensive suits, the high-end rides? He came in the other day looking for a dress. Said it was for someone else. I pointed him to Lena."

She felt herself disappear into the word pointed.

Like a finger had been laid on her in public.

The officer's gaze flicked to her. "He asked for her by name?"

Mr. Donovan shook his head. "No. Just wanted help picking something out."

Lena blinked hard, trying to steady herself, pulse pounding in her ears as she kept the rest buried. She didn't mention the call. Didn't mention that, just a day later, he'd phoned the store and asked for her directly. Stacey had handed her the receiver. No one else knew.

The officer stepped closer.

"Have you received any threats recently, Ms. Hart?"

"No," she lied, barely above a whisper.

Truth no longer felt like something safe enough to touch.

"Any enemies? Confrontations? Someone who might want to hurt you?"

She shook her head, a small, automatic movement.

"Have you seen this Lucien guy outside of work?"

"No. He was just a customer," she said. "He came into the store once."

Across the site, another officer looked up from a notepad. "We'll pull surveillance. Get an ID off any cameras before the feed cut."

Mr. Donovan's phone rang.

He snatched it out of his pocket so fast it nearly slipped from his hand. "Yeah. Donovan." His face tightened as he listened. "Yes, this is the owner. No, I don't have a full list yet. We just got here."

The person on the other end kept talking.

His eyes shifted once, involuntarily, toward the wall.

"No, I don't know if this was random," he snapped. "There's a name painted outside the store, what do you think?"

Another pause.

His expression changed. Not grief this time. Something uglier. Exhaustion dragged through calculation.

"What do you mean criminal association?" he said, louder now. "This is a boutique, not a cartel front."

Lena felt the words hit before she understood them.

Mr. Donovan turned away, pacing through broken glass. "No, I am not saying I know the man. I'm saying his name is on my wall. No, I can't confirm a relationship. No, I don't know what counts as targeted damage to you people. What I know is my store is burned to hell and you're already looking for a way not to pay me."

He pulled the phone from his ear for a second and stared at it like he wanted to throw it into the wreckage.

When he looked back at Lena, it wasn't accusation exactly.

It was worse.

It was distance.

Not what happened.

But what knowing her was going to cost him.

Mr. Donovan's voice cut through, raw and bitter. "My entire business is gone. You hear me? My life, ruined."

Lena didn't look at him. She couldn't.

Her stomach knotted. As much as the monotony ached, this place had been her second home for so long.

"Maybe this was my life too," she whispered.

The lead officer gave her a measured look.

"We'll need a formal statement and a number where we can reach you."

She recited it numb.

The second the officers finished with her, the cameras found her.

Not network vans. Faster than that. A local stringer with a shoulder rig. A woman with a phone held upright for a live feed. A man in a navy windbreaker with a station mic clipped to his collar pushed forward until the tape caught his thigh.

"Miss, one question. Were you the intended target?"

She froze.

Another voice, sharper, closer. "Who is Lucien?"

Her head snapped toward the sound.

The first reporter saw it and moved in. "Is the message about you? Are you involved with him?"

Flash.

White light burst across her vision.

She lifted a hand too late, turning away as another phone camera rose in front of her face.

"Is he the reason this happened?"

"Were you targeted because of Lucien?"

"We heard the officers say your name. Lena, right? Lena Hart?"

"Miss Hart, is that message about you?"

Hearing her own name from strangers did something cold to her spine.

A uniformed officer stepped between her and the cameras, one arm extended. "Back up. Now."

The reporters kept firing questions over his shoulder as he guided her forward.

The tape lifted.

The sidewalk opened.

And for the first time in her life, Lena understood what it felt like to have strangers decide who you were before you had the chance to speak.

A uniform touched her elbow, guiding her past the fluttering tape with a gentleness that felt wrong against so much ruin.

Outside the perimeter, Lena kept walking.

Only when she rounded the corner, sirens muffled, crowd out of sight, did her knees buckle. She braced against the cold brick, breath shattering into shallow bursts.

The fire still clung to her skin. The words still burned into her mind.

Her phone started vibrating in her hand.

Once.

Then again.

Then without stopping.

Texts. Notifications. A news alert from a local account she didn't follow. Someone had already posted footage from outside the store. Smoke. Sirens. Yellow tape. Her face, caught for half a second as she turned away from the cameras.

She opened the article before she could stop herself.

MESSAGE SIGNED "LUCIEN" FOUND AFTER MIDTOWN BOUTIQUE FIRE

POLICE INVESTIGATING POSSIBLE TARGETED ATTACK

Below it, another line.

EMPLOYEE QUESTIONED AFTER POSSIBLE TARGETED MESSAGE FOUND AT UPTOWN FIRE

Her stomach folded in on itself.

They had done it already.

Taken one of the worst mornings of her life and turned it into copy.

She scrolled.

The comments came fast and merciless.

SHE ASKED FOR THIS

YOU DONT GET YOUR NAME ON A WALL FOR NO REASON

WHO IS LUCIEN

THIS ISNT RANDOM

SOMEBODY KNOWS SOMETHING

FEEL BAD FOR THE OWNER

THAT GIRL KNOWS EXACTLY WHY THIS HAPPENED

MESSY

PLAY STUPID GAMES WIN STUPID PRIZES

NOT A RANDOM FIRE

LOOK AT HER FACE SHE KNOWS

One comment had a screenshot attached.

It was her.

Blurred, grainy, taken from the sidewalk thirty feet away, but unmistakably her.

Another notification slid down from the top of the screen.

A text from Stacey.

Lena please tell me this isn't about that guy

Another one.

They're saying your name in the comments

Another message came in.

Christina.

Where are you? Call me right now

She couldn't answer any of them.

Couldn't explain how a single name on a wall had reached into every corner of her life in less than an hour.

She stared at the screen until the words stopped feeling separate.

Store.

Fire.

Lucien.

Whore.

Whatever she had been before this morning, whatever version of herself still believed life could snap back into place with enough apologizing, enough distance, enough denial, that woman was gone.

The boutique had burned.

But that was not the real damage.

The real damage was this.

The police asking careful questions.

Insurance already reaching for an exit.

Strangers filming her grief.

The internet making a joke out of her name.

People deciding what she was before she had even caught her breath.

This was not a bad day.

This was not a mess she could clean up by next week.

Something had fixed itself to her life, hard and permanent.

And she knew the name attached to it.

Lucien Cole.

Lena closed her eyes.

When she opened them again, the city did not look the same.

Neither did she.

Fingers trembling, she pulled out her phone.

For one stupid second, she looked at the other names first.

Stacey.

Christina.

Jessica.

Normal people. Normal problems.

None of them belonged to the world she was standing in.

None of them could step into this and make it smaller.

Another notification lit the screen. Another comment. Another version of her life leaving her hands.

She stopped thinking.

And called the only number that made sense.

Lucien picked up on the second ring.

"Lena?"

His voice was steady, but beneath it, concern coiled tight.

"I... I need to see you," she said. "Something happened. I don't know what to do."

He didn't ask questions. Didn't hesitate.

"Where are you?"

"Near the store."

"I'll send Michael. I'm crosstown, but he'll get to you first."

He ended the call.

The world had kept moving while hers caught flames.

She stared at her screen for a second, then slowly lowered the phone. It hit her, she'd called him without thinking.

Instinct had chosen before fear could.

Because some part of her already knew: Lucien Cole doesn't run from fire. He walks into it.

And if his world meant ruin, then ruin had already learned her name.

CHAPTER TEN

MARKED BACK

Twenty minutes slipped by before a sleek black SUV eased to the curb, tires hissing on the asphalt. Lena stood still, nerves firing like live wires beneath her skin.

The tinted window slid down, revealing a composed, sharp-suited Michael. His eyes moved past her first, scanning the street, the rooftops, the reflection in the storefront glass behind her.

Only then did he look at her.

"Lena. Get in."

She gave a curt nod. Her heart kicked against her ribs in hard, uneven beats. Without a word, she climbed into the back seat. The soft thump of the door felt strangely final.

The locks clicked the second it shut. The SUV pulled away from the curb at once, smooth and deliberate, like it had never meant to stay parked.

The city slid by in silence, skyscrapers and signs smearing into a restless blur.

"Did anyone follow you when you left the scene?" Michael asked.

"I don't know."

"That's all right," he said. "We'll assume they did."

Lena turned to the window, her breathing shallow. The morning kept replaying in her head, each pass winding her tighter.

Now and then, Michael glanced at her in the rearview. Curious, maybe. Alert, definitely. But not prying.

Eventually, he spoke, voice low and measured.

"You all right, Lena?"

She opened her mouth, but her throat tightened before any sound could come out. Her eyes burned.

She swallowed, then nodded, a small, brittle lie.

Michael didn't call her on it. He only nodded once, like he had seen that lie before and knew better than to press.

No, she wasn't all right.

But words felt too small for what she carried. Saying it out loud felt too much like surrender.

The silence between them thickened. Still, one question burned at the edge of her mind, hot and unshakable.

She needed to understand what she was stepping into.

Even if she wasn't sure how much Michael would, or could, say.

Christina would panic. Jessica would judge. Lucien was the only person whose voice she could hear without falling apart.

After a beat, she drew a shaky breath.

"Does Lucien have enemies?" she whispered. "Anyone who'd hold a grudge? Or get jealous?"

Michael's gaze flicked up in the rearview mirror.

Their eyes met.

He paused. Thought about it.

"What do you think, Lena?"

The question wasn't deflection. It was calibration.

Like he was measuring how much truth she could survive.

Her stomach twisted. The way he said it, it wasn't meant to comfort her. It wasn't meant to answer. And that told her more than he ever would.

She turned back to the window, chasing calm in the blur of traffic and glass reflections streaking past.

"Is Lucien..." She hesitated. "Is he a good person?"

Michael looked back to the road.

"Lucien is many things," he said. "Depends on who you ask."

Lena waited, but he didn't fill the silence right away. The city moved in the windows, all glass and motion.

"You've known him a long time?" she asked.

Michael nodded once. "Long enough."

"From this life?"

He shook his head. "From before."

She frowned slightly. "Before what?"

Michael's eyes flicked to the mirror, then back to the road.

"Before he was who he is now."

"I was gone a few years," Michael said. "When I came back, he was already building something."

He was quiet for a moment, then added, "Coming home's the hard part. Not everybody figures out where they belong after."

Lena studied the back of his seat. "Why stay?"

Michael was quiet again.

"Some men you work for," he said. "Some men you believe in."

Lena looked down at her hands. "And Lucien?"

Michael didn't hesitate.

"Lucien changes things," he said. "That's what people don't understand. They think he wants control. He does. But control is only what he builds before the change comes."

Lena looked up.

Michael's eyes stayed on the road.

"I make sure the people around him survive it."

Lena didn't know why that answer stayed with her longer than anything else he'd said.

Outside, the city moved on, bright, buzzing, indifferent. Inside the SUV, silence wrapped around her like a second skin.

Lena hugged herself tighter, feeling the line between safety and danger vanish beneath the wheels.

She was in it now. Every mile blurred the truth a little more.

A half hour later, the black SUV eased to a halt in front of a sleek, obsidian building crowned with tall, gleaming letters: ZENITH.

One of Lucien's oldest clubs. A cornerstone of the empire he'd built long before expansion pushed him beyond New York.

Its dark glass reflected the street like a warning.

Places like this weren't built. They were claimed.

Before she could gather her composure, her phone buzzed with a new message from Lucien:

Look up

He hadn't summoned her with urgency. He'd placed her.

Exactly where he wanted her.

She raised her eyes to the third floor. There, framed by plate-glass windows, stood Lucien, watching her with an intensity that pierced the distance between them.

A second vibration quickly followed:

Come up

Her heart stuttered.

No time to think.

She slipped the phone into her pocket, squared her shoulders, and moved toward the entrance, toward him.

Lena stepped inside. Without its usual nightlife pulse, the club felt eerily tranquil in the hush of early daylight. A handful of staff moved in near silence, gathering glasses and wiping down tables, the soft chime of their work a stark contrast to the pounding music that typically reigned here.

She climbed a concrete stairwell, each step echoing off the walls.

Halfway up, Lucien's voice called down:

"Up here, Lena."

Her name sent a jolt through her, a reminder of the adrenaline still coursing through her veins.

At the top, she found herself at the threshold of a sleek private office with walls of glass overlooking the street below. Lucien stood in the doorway, his posture tense, his face set hard.

Without thinking, he reached for her, concern breaking through his control.

She jerked back on instinct, breath quickening.

Fear moved faster than trust ever could.

Her body remembered Enigma before her mind could negotiate.

His brow creased, and for a fraction of a second, he looked almost wounded, but then he gentled his tone.

"Come in," he said. "Tell me everything."

She followed him into the office. A black marble desk stood near the windows, a cut-crystal decanter gleaming on a sideboard. Lucien offered her a chair, but she remained standing, arms folded defensively across her chest. He eased himself behind the desk, never looking away from her.

"Talk to me. What happened?"

Lena inhaled, forcing down the knot of dread in her throat.

"The store was torched early this morning. Someone set it on fire. Then they left a message across the front: LUCIEN'S WHORE."

She shook her head, anger surging.

"It's disgusting, humiliating. I still can't believe it's real."

"And it's not just the fire," she continued, her voice tightening. "The police were already asking about you. Reporters were there. They were shouting your name at me like I was supposed to explain you to them."

She swallowed, forcing the words out.

"They heard my name. They filmed me. It's online already. People are commenting like they know me. Like they know what I am."

Her laugh was thin, humorless.

"My store didn't just burn, Lucien. My name is in this now."

A look of raw fury flared in Lucien's eyes. He shot to his feet, the chair scraping hard against the floor.

"They branded my name across your store and torched it?"

This wasn't about reputation.

It was about jurisdiction.

Someone had crossed a line Lucien didn't know existed until she stood on the other side of it.

His expression hardened. "Someone's sending a message."

Lena let out a bitter laugh, nerves frayed. "Yeah, well, message received. I've never felt so violated in my life."

His hands balled into fists, pacing a tight line behind the desk.

"They wanted both of us to know they can reach you. They wanted me to see my name across the ashes of where we met."

Her pulse thudded in her ears, fear warring with indignation. "Well, it worked. Now what?"

Lucien raked a hand through his hair, his expression hardening.

"Now we find out who thinks they can threaten me by targeting you, and I make them regret it."

She offered a hollow, humorless laugh. "And that's not all."

He focused on her. "Go on."

She fumbled her phone from her pocket, the phone shaking slightly in her grip.

"This morning, I got a private message. A photo of us last night, on the rooftop. Someone took it without us knowing." She swallowed. "I don't even know how they found my profile, but they did."

His face went still, his shoulders tense. "Show me."

She held out the phone. He scanned the image, the two of them locked in conversation, city lights blazing behind them.

"They want us to know they're watching," Lena whispered. "They used my store to make it crystal clear."

This wasn't surveillance anymore. It was theater.

Lucien set the phone aside, drawing a measured breath.

"This isn't random," he said quietly. "Someone is making a play to get to me."

Lena's arms tightened around her torso. "So, tell me. What kind of people are we dealing with? Who would go this far just to send a message?"

He let out a sharp exhale.

Tension sharpened the space around him.

"People with a sick notion of power. I don't know who yet. I will."

She let her anger spill out, words tumbling in a frantic rush.

"You dragged me into your life, Lucien, without warning, without explanation. Even if it was only for a moment."

Her voice caught, the threat of tears tightening her throat. "And now my livelihood is in ashes because of you. I need answers. I need to know you can protect me."

She hated how much she already believed he could.

His posture softened, the storm in his eyes shifting. He rounded the desk, stopping just short of touching her.

"I will fix this," he said. "But you need to trust me. For now, stay close."

She tensed, battling the urge to recoil from everything he represented, and the inexplicable comfort he offered.

"How close?"

"Victoria wanted you there tonight."

His voice stayed even as he reached into the drawer and pulled out a sleek black envelope.

"It's an invitation. Her party's tonight."

He held her there with a steady look. "I want you there with me."

The steadiness of it unsettled her more than a demand would have.

Because demands she knew how to fight.

This was something else. A promise that the fire would have to go through him first.

Lena stared at him, frustration rising, then looked down at the envelope, confusion mingling with the stress already twisting in her gut.

"You're kidding, right? My job just burned down, we're clearly on someone's watch list, and you think I should go to a party?"

"Tonight matters." His tone was gentle but unyielding. "It's the safest place for you right now, somewhere public, surrounded by people I trust. Until we figure out who's behind all this, I won't let you out of my sight."

Public spaces were safer. Predators preferred shadows.

Another hollow laugh escaped her, but it held no real amusement. "I'm not sure how I feel about being babysat or paraded around at a party."

Lucien's anger softened as his gaze swept over her trembling hands and haunted expression.

"I know it isn't ideal," he conceded softly. "But whoever targeted you knows we're connected. Showing up at Victoria's event, under my protection, turns their move back on them."

She clutched the gold-stamped envelope, her reality had flipped overnight into a storm of threats and secrets. Lucien might be at the center of it, but he was also her safest refuge.

She drew a slow, unsteady breath, the weight of everything pressing down on her. Fear, anger, and an odd sense of relief churned in her chest. Finally she looked up, meeting Lucien's unwavering eyes.

"Fine," she whispered. "I'll go. But not because you told me to."

Some of the strain left his face. "Good. Michael will drive you home and bring you back here tonight."

He stepped away from the desk, his posture still rigid.

A flicker of concern crossed his face.

"I'm sorry."

The words came rougher than she expected.

"You never should've been dragged into this."

Lena's composure faltered, her eyes dropping to the floor. He noticed the tremor in her stance and drew closer, placing a gentle hand against her cheek.

"Lena," he continued, "I promise, whoever is behind this will pay."

She hesitated, fear and disbelief mingling in her expression as Lucien's hand drifted to her arm, his fingers winding around hers in a slow, reassuring gesture.

"Look at me. I don't have all the answers, but you're not facing this alone."

Lucien drifted back toward the window, his attention settling on the street below. Lena watched his reflection in the glass, her own heart thrumming with a potent blend of apprehension and relief.

Her world was in ruins, and yet in the quiet force of his resolve, she sensed a promise in him that felt impossible to shake: no one threatened what he held dear without paying a price.

When he finally spoke again, it wasn't loud.

The room seemed to tighten around the words.

"They marked you to get to me." His fist clenched at his side. "I'll mark them back."

He stared out over the skyline like it was a chessboard he intended to overturn.

And in his eyes, she saw that he meant it.

CHAPTER ELEVEN

NO SAFE EXIT

Night turned the city electric. Fluorescent glare slicked across rain-soaked streets as Michael glided through congested avenues.

In the back seat, Lena's hand brushed the edges of Lucien's invitation, sleek black and gold, as elegant and commanding as the man himself. Each brush reminded her this wasn't just paper.

Zenith rose ahead of her, black and severe against the slow crawl of traffic. The white neon letters burned like a brand against the night, stark and merciless. But something had changed. The glow felt sharper now, almost hostile. No longer just a symbol of power and excess, Zenith felt like a line she could not uncross.

This wasn't a night out. This was Lucien's ground, bought with loyalty and blood, a place where fortunes rose or fell on his say-so.

As the SUV slid to a stop, Lena's pulse kicked harder. Michael stepped out and opened her door, and the night hit her all at once, bass from inside vibrating the pavement, the clash of perfume, cologne, exhaust, and ambition thick in the air. A line of guests waited along the velvet rope, catching the marquee light.

People craned for a look at whoever was being waved past the rope.

She wasn't being admitted. She was being received. And with each measured step toward Zenith's imposing doors, she felt the tension coil tighter in her chest.

She had the invitation in her hand, but it felt heavier than paper should.

The instant Lena approached the entrance, the velvet ropes parted as though expecting her arrival.

A towering security guard inclined his head, his voice calm but commanding.

"Miss Hart. This way, please."

Even the rope knew her name now.

She felt a hundred curious eyes linger on her, envy and speculation in the air.

Excitement and unease hit at the same time, neither willing to give ground.

The moment she stepped inside, Zenith was nothing like the cavernous emptiness she'd witnessed that morning. Now it blazed with life. Bodies moved with the beat, all polish on the surface, hunger underneath.

The room ran on rhythm, money, and conversations kept just low enough to matter. Overhead, chandeliers dripped with gleaming crystals, scattering shards of light across marble floors and velvet booths filled with the city's elite.

Lena exhaled carefully, fighting to steady herself. And then, between the moving bodies and the hard spill of chandelier light, she caught a glimpse of him.

For a second, the room narrowed to him, and all that remained was the man whose world she was about to plunge even deeper into.

Lucien stood near the balcony rail inside the mezzanine, framed by golden light and shadow, still enough to look staged. The chandeliers above glinted off the sharp lines of his suit, casting broken reflections across the glass behind him. He didn't just occupy the room. He controlled its weather.

He was surrounded by power-players Lena had only seen in headlines or overheard in the hushed corners of other people's conversations. But the moment he sensed her presence, the rest of the room lost definition.

She swallowed hard, fingers curling around the railing as she climbed the grand staircase. Each step brought a fresh rush of adrenaline, forcing her to acknowledge where she was, what she was wading into.

At the top, Lucien didn't immediately beckon her closer. Instead, he watched her with a stillness that felt more dangerous than movement, like he was measuring the cost of letting her closer. The space between them went taut until he finally said, "You came."

A quick rush moved through her, but she kept her voice steady.

"I said I would."

He stepped in close enough for her body to register it first, and brushed the back of his hand across her wrist.

The faintest contact, but it ran through her all the same.

"Come with me."

Victoria carried herself with effortless charm, but nothing about her felt careless. Women draped in haute couture perched in plush booths, men in razor-sharp suits sized each other up, deals taking shape behind smiles that gave nothing away.

Some looks followed Lucien with curiosity, others with wary respect. And when they trailed from him to her, Lena felt every whisper, every curious or envious glance like static clinging to her skin.

They reached a private lounge elevated above the club's pulse. Floor-to-ceiling windows revealed the city beyond, towers and traffic burning against the dark. Up here, the noise dropped to distant bass beneath candle-light and shadow.

Velvet couches, dark walls, and glimmers of gold made the room feel too controlled to be comfortable.

Amid that hush, a solitary figure waited, still and composed.

Victoria.

"Lena." The warmth in Victoria's voice was instant, her smile quick as she pulled Lena into a brief embrace. "I'm glad you came."

Lena smiled, relief flickering at the familiar presence. "Happy birthday," she said, and meant it.

Victoria carried herself with effortless charm, but nothing about her felt careless. Lena didn't miss the way her eyes cut toward Lucien, a look that said there was history there, and that Lena was only seeing the edge of it.

"Enjoy yourself tonight," Victoria said lightly, but the next words landed heavier. "Be careful. I heard what happened. My brother's world is not as controlled as he makes it look."

Lena's stomach tightened at the way the warning stayed with her, at the way Victoria's smirk faded before it became real.

Lucien noticed the strain breaking through. Instead of waiting for her to speak, he took her hand, firm but unhurried, and led her away from the watching faces and low conversation.

They moved through the private lounge, past secluded booths where people spoke low and meant it, until he pushed open a sleek black door and led her onto a quiet terrace overlooking the street below.

The night air was crisp against Lena's skin, a stark contrast to the warmth of Lucien beside her. He released her hand and turned to face her, giving nothing away.

"Tell me what's on your mind, Lena," he said. "You're holding something back."

She let out a thin laugh. "It's just... a lot."

"This world of yours," she admitted, taking in the velvet, the money, the people who smiled like knives. "It's overwhelming."

He studied her, then stepped in closer, close enough to change the air between them.

"Then stay close to me tonight," he said.

"Close how?"

"Close enough that if someone tries something, it ends fast."

Her throat tightened. "You talk like it's already happening."

"In my life, it always is."

His voice didn't rise. "The mistake is waiting to see it before it's already too close."

"That's why I don't bring people into it."

"And yet," she said.

Something in his face hardened, then eased.

"And yet."

She swallowed. "Lucien... we've known each other for five minutes."

"I know."

He stepped closer, still not touching her, letting the silence do the damage.

"I'm not asking you to trust my world. I'm asking if I can trust you to stay where I put you when it matters. Not because you're weak. Because you're not."

Lena's pulse climbed. "You want obedience."

She held his eyes. "You dress it up better than most men, but that's what it is."

His answer came without hesitation. "I want you breathing tomorrow."

It should have sounded protective. Instead, it sounded practiced.

The silence between them went taut.

"Can I trust you," he said, "the way I'd trust you with my back?"

A small tremor caught in her throat. She nodded once, slow but certain. "Yes."

That was all it took.

He moved in and kissed her, slow at first, like he was testing the edge of a line he swore he never crossed. Then it deepened, and the last of her distance burned off.

When he pulled back, his forehead stayed close to hers.

"Good," he said, and the word landed with too much weight to be casual.

As they stepped back inside from the terrace, the shift in atmosphere was immediate. The cool night air was replaced by the heat of Zenith's private lounge, the low hum of conversation, the clink of glasses, and the pulse underfoot. The room felt different now, heavier, as if something had shifted while they were outside.

Lena barely had a moment to process it before a sudden crash of glass shattered through the room. She turned sharply, just in time to see a man being dragged away by one of Lucien's security guards.

His struggling frame barely made an impact on the crowd around them. A few heads turned, but no one in the room looked surprised.

Lena swallowed hard, her fingers tightening around the edge of her dress. She looked at Lucien, searching for any sign of concern, but his expression remained unreadable. If anything, he looked almost bored.

Lucien barely spared the scene a glance before turning to her.

"Go sit at the bar," he said. "Order whatever you want. I won't be long."

His attention shifted to a small group of men standing in the far corner, their postures sharp, their conversation already underway. Without another word, he stepped away, already moving like the part of him she had not seen yet.

Lena hesitated, watching as he approached them, exchanging firm handshakes and quiet words. It was the first time she saw it, the other side of him. The one that existed beyond the polished version she had met. The one that ran this world, not just moved through it.

She made her way toward the bar, aware of the looks that kept finding her.

She slid onto one of the plush barstools, wrapping her fingers around the smooth edge of the counter, feigning ease while a tight unease settled in her chest.

Needing something to ground herself, she reached into her clutch, deciding to fill the empty space with a message to Christina. Her fingers brushed her phone, but before she could unlock it, the screen lit in her palm.

The vibration sent a small jolt through her, almost welcome, until she saw the message.

LUCIEN'S WHORE

No name. No icon. Just the words, stark and merciless.

The room kept moving around her, which made it worse.

Something tightened behind her ribs, sharp and sudden. Cold moved through her all at once, the sound around her narrowing to a thin, warped hum. Zenith kept moving, laughing, glittering, like nothing had changed.

But it had.

The message sat there like proof last night hadn't been private.

Lena hit call anyway. Panic made her reach for impossible exits.

No ring. No voicemail.

Call Failed.

She tried once more, denial clawing for a different answer.

Nothing.

The number might as well have been a ghost, unreachable by design.

Her pulse quickened. She had not even realized she'd stood up until she felt herself moving, drifting away from the bar, one step at a time, like her body was trying to hide her before her mind caught up.

When she glanced up, she saw where she'd ended up, near the entrance to the terrace, right where she and Lucien had walked back in together.

Across the open room, beyond the crowd and the chandeliers and the glint of glasses, Lucien still stood where she'd left him, deep in conversation with the same men. Suits. Watches. Faces that did not belong to the kind of life where people got to be casual.

She looked for a gap.

There wasn't one.

Power did not always raise its voice. Sometimes it simply decided where you stopped.

The men around him had tightened into a wall. They weren't blocking her. They had decided she didn't exist. Bodies angled in close, shoulders turned outward without looking like they were guarding anything. Not security. Not openly. Just presence. Ownership of space.

She took two steps toward him and stopped.

One of the men glanced up, quick and flat, then returned to the conversation like she was static.

Lucien did not look over.

From this distance, he felt unreachable, like he existed in a different layer of the room.

Was this a joke? Some bitter ex-lover, some jealous shadow trying to rattle her, something Lucien would laugh off later?

Or was it worse?

Something that knew exactly where she stood.

Her phone buzzed again.

You don't belong here

Lena's head snapped up, her gaze sweeping the sea of faces below. Strobes turned people into silhouettes, then into strangers again. The music hammered through her ribs like a warning.

The bodies swaying in rhythm, the laughter, the leaning conversations, it all looked the same.

But now everyone felt capable of anything.

Someone was watching her.

Her fingers tightened around the phone. She was about to push back through the crowd, to force her way to Lucien, when the third message came.

Leave now, or you'll regret it

A jolt of dread coiled deep in her gut, cold and immediate.

This wasn't flirting.

This wasn't jealousy.

This was instruction.

She took a shaky step back, body tensed like it expected hands to close around her. She needed Lucien, but the thought of crossing open floor with a hundred eyes on her made her throat tighten. What if they wanted her to walk into the open. What if the trap was the direct line.

Her attention caught on a dim hallway near the stairwell, a pocket of shadow at the edge of the noise. No velvet rope. No crowd. Just a staff corridor cut around the lounge.

For one second it felt safer.

Heart hammering, she slipped into it, pressing her shoulder to the cool wall. The music dulled back here, reduced to a distant throb. The temperature dropped. The silence made her hear her own breathing too clearly.

Then a hand gripped her arm.

Lena gasped and twisted.

Victoria.

"Lena," Lucien's sister said softly, urgency tightening her voice. "Are you alright? I saw you by the stairs, you looked like you'd seen a ghost."

Lena couldn't form words. She shoved her phone toward her.

Victoria read, and whatever expression she wore at parties vanished.

"That's disturbing," she murmured. "Lena, you have to be careful. People in Lucien's world don't follow the same rules most of us live by."

"So it is someone from his world," Lena whispered. "Is this serious?"

Victoria's gaze flicked toward the lounge, toward the noise, toward the places eyes could hide. "People like to play games here," she said. "But sometimes it's not a game." Her mouth tightened. "Not everyone is going to be happy about how close you're getting to him."

Lena's phone buzzed again.

You should have stayed in his shadow

Shadow meant safety. Light meant being seen.

Now I see you too clearly

Her grip tightened around her phone. The message wasn't pressure. It was timing.

Victoria leaned in, voice dropping to a blade. "Do not leave this building alone. If someone wants you frightened, they want you separated."

Lena nodded. Her balance wavered for a second.

She needed Lucien. Now.

Victoria glanced toward the lounge, jaw tight. "Stay here. I'm getting him."

"Victoria," Lena started.

But Victoria was already moving, cutting back toward the noise with the kind of speed that made panic feel official.

Alone, Lena looked down at her phone.

Her hands shook as she typed.

Can you come find me. Now. Please

She hit send.

And waited.

The club throbbed on the other side of the corridor, bass pushing through the walls. Thirty seconds. Forty. A minute.

No response.

With the music and those men in his ear, he might not have even felt his phone.

Her stomach twisted. Her breaths sharpened. She leaned out to search for him through the glass, but the lounge had changed. Darker. Thicker. A hundred silhouettes. None of them safe.

Her phone buzzed.

Not Lucien.

Last chance leave now

Her breath froze.

Another buzz.

Run

That broke her.

Everything narrowed to one choice.

For one second, leaving felt like the last decision that still belonged to her.

Lena turned toward the stairwell, weaving through bodies as quietly as she could, slipping toward the back of the club where the light died and the exits stopped being decorative.

She felt hunted. Not chased. Measured.

At the back exit, her phone buzzed again.

Good choice

Not approval.

Confirmation.

A cold certainty snapped through her, sharp enough to cut her momentum.

She shoved the door open and stepped into the cold night air.

The alleyway behind Zenith was unnervingly still, a stark contrast to the buzzing current of the club's interior. Dim streetlights cast shadows over cracked pavement, and the air carried the sharp sting of rain-soaked asphalt and distant exhaust. Somewhere far off, a siren wailed, the only proof the city still existed beyond the alley.

She exhaled, trying to steady herself.

Maybe this was the end of it.

Maybe whoever had sent those messages just wanted to scare her off.

But then she heard it.

Footsteps.

Lena's entire body stiffened.

She turned sharply.

The alley was empty.

Cold air scraped at her throat in uneven bursts.

Was it her imagination?

Or was someone actually there?

The footsteps again.

Closer.

Her heart slammed against her ribs.

Her fingers hovered over Lucien's contact.

But she hesitated.

Then her phone buzzed.

Run

Her blood turned to ice.

Hands shaking, she backed away, every hair on her body standing on end.

From the corner of her eye, she saw it.

A car.

Dark. Sleek.

Pitch-black windows.

Parked just beyond the alley.

Silent.

Waiting.

Her instincts screamed.

She took a step.

The engine roared to life.

Bile crept up her throat.

The headlights flared and pinned her where she stood.

The car didn't move.

It just watched.

Her phone buzzed again.

I'm closer than you think

Fear hit hard enough to steal the air from her.

The car revved.

She spun on her heel.

And ran.

Sound slammed too close behind her, every step echoing wrong.

Panic hit all at once and blew the scene apart.

Heels skidded across wet concrete.

Tires screeched.

The car launched forward.

Lena veered left, toward the intersection.

If she could just make it.

The roar of the engine surged behind her.

Blinding headlights bled across the rain-slick street, bleaching everything white.

Time lost its shape.

Sound warped. The bass from Zenith stretched low while the shriek of tires went thin and metallic, like someone tearing the world in half.

She saw raindrops suspended in the air, glittering like shards of broken glass. Smelled the hot sting of burning rubber. Even the stench of exhaust burned sharp in her throat.

For one heartbeat, she thought she might escape.

She understood too late that the warning had never been about fear. It had been about direction.

Then the impact came.

Violent. Merciless.

Her body lifted as if gravity had forgotten her, weightless in a moment that stretched on forever. The city tilted, the sky spun, then the pavement rose like a wall to meet her.

Pain burst through her ribs, bright and brutal.

Distant voices.

Screams.

Tires peeling away.

Her vision blurred. Darkness poured in.

And then.

Nothing.

Chapter Twelve

NO SAFE PLACE

Lena's eyes fluttered open, the sterile brightness of a hospital room slowly pulling her from unconsciousness. The first thing she registered was the rhythmic beep of the heart monitor, steady and unrelenting.

The next was pain, a dull, aching reminder of the impact that had thrown her into the void. She took a slow, shallow breath, the scent of antiseptic filling her lungs, grounding her in reality.

The truth pressed against her ribs harder than the bandages: someone wanted her gone. Not because of who she was, but because of what she was starting to mean to Lucien. And that thought, that she'd been marked for stepping into his gravity, terrified her more than the crash ever could.

Memories fought their way back. The chase. The headlights. The crash.

A voice cut through the haze, low and urgent.

"Lena."

Lucien was at her side, his hand wrapped around hers, steady enough to anchor her. His composure had been stripped down to the bone. Shirt wrinkled. Cuffs undone. Eyes red at the edges, like sleep was something he had refused.

"Thank God," he said. "You're awake."

She blinked, throat dry.

"What... happened?"

"A car hit you." His voice tightened, anger buried under fear. "They almost took you from me."

She didn't know whether that steadied or terrified her more. His words landed and kept landing.

"I thought I lost you." The confession came quieter, like it cost him.

Then he looked at her like she was the only thing in the room keeping him human.

"I watched them lift you off the pavement. I don't plan to relive that."

A shiver ran through her, not from cold.

She shifted, pain flaring across her ribs.

"I was running," she said, dragging the night back in pieces. The texts. The alley. The headlights. "Someone was following me."

Lucien's expression changed. Not shock. Recognition. Something colder settling into place.

"Victoria told me everything." His voice didn't shake, but the violence under it was unmistakable. "And I saw your message."

A small falter went through her.

"I saw it late," he went on, eyes locked to hers. "After I broke away from those men. After I finally checked my phone."

His hand tightened, controlled but close to slipping.

"I ran the second I read it." His voice lowered. "Still wasn't fast enough."

His gaze held hers, sharp, unblinking.

"Why didn't you come to me? Why did you run?"

Guilt rose like acid. The men around him had closed in like a wall. Her message had sat unanswered. The room kept moving while panic pinned her in place.

"I couldn't get to you," she said. "And I panicked."

His stare sharpened.

"I thought if I left... it would stop."

He looked like he wanted to break something he couldn't reach.

"You don't run from this." His voice stripped down to truth. "And you don't face it alone. Not anymore."

"I didn't know who to trust."

Something in him shifted. Not softer. Just heavier.

"You trust me now." Not comfort. A line drawn in stone.

Trust felt less like a choice and more like a narrowing hallway.

She tried to move. Pain flared bright. Her breath hitched.

Lucien's grip steadied her. "Don't."

"I'm not a child," she whispered.

"No."

"You're the part of me they thought they could reach with fire."

The words hit her hard.

"Whoever is behind this," he said, "they weren't trying to scare you. They were trying to move you. Separate you. Make you choose wrong."

Lena looked down at his hand over hers. It felt like an answer she hadn't earned.

"I was scared," she whispered. "I couldn't get to you."

"I understand." His voice stayed tight, aimed inward. "But you don't do that again."

"You don't get to decide that."

His eyes didn't move. "I'm deciding the part that keeps you alive."

Her breath tightened. Fury and relief collided.

"My place is across the Hudson," he said. "Away from streets. Away from cameras. Away from anyone who thinks they can reach you. Security you won't see until you need it."

"I don't want to hide."

"This isn't hiding." His voice stayed level. "This is surviving long enough to make someone pay."

"You talk like I don't have a choice."

"You have choices. You can hate me. You can fight me. You can call me a monster.

But you're not walking out of here alone."

Victoria stepped in, confidence stripped to worry. "You scared the hell out of us," she said, crossing the room. Her eyes cut to Lucien. "He's been pacing since they brought you in."

"I'm okay," Lena tried. Thin.

Victoria didn't buy it. "Whoever sent those texts doesn't feel like the type to stop at words."

"How did you know where I was?" Lena asked.

"Because I left you for one minute," Victoria said, guilt tightening her voice. "I went to get him. By the time we pushed back through, you were gone."

Lucien's hand stayed over Lena's, anchoring her.

"I told him about the messages," Victoria said. "He tried calling. You didn't answer."

"And then," Lucien said, voice flat, "one of my men saw emergency lights stacking outside Zenith. Too much movement. Too fast."

Victoria nodded. "We ran down. We saw the paramedics. Lucien followed the ambulance the whole way."

Her face tightened. "You were wrong, Lena. The club wasn't the danger. Outside was. If someone wants you frightened, they want you alone."

The weight of that hit harder than the pain.

"You won't be alone again," Lucien said. "Not while this is open."

It landed like a claim, not comfort.

"Is there anyone we can call for you?" Victoria asked.

"No," Lena said. "Not anyone who would come."

"Family?"

Lena's voice flattened. "I don't have any family."

Lucien's eyes flicked to Victoria.

Hers found his for half a second.

Something unspoken passed between them, quick and quiet, then Lucien looked back at Lena.

"Then you're not alone anymore," he said. "Not while I'm breathing."

Victoria's voice softened. "Is there anyone you want here?"

"My friends," Lena whispered. "Christina and Jessica."

"I'll get them here," Victoria said.

Lena reached toward the bedside table, wincing as pain caught in her ribs. Lucien was there before she could stretch too far, placing the phone in her hand.

She unlocked it with a trembling thumb and held it out to Victoria.

"Their numbers are in there."

Victoria took it carefully. "I'll handle it."

Lucien turned away, adjusting his cuff like he was locking something back into place.

"I'm making calls. Two men on that door. No one gets in unless I say."

"I'm making calls. Two men on that door. No one gets in unless I say."

Victoria gave Lena's hand a quick squeeze before following him out.

Lena watched them leave, too exhausted to answer.

As he stepped out, she caught a glimpse through the small window.

Lucien stood in the corridor with a man in a dark suit.

Their handshake was too brief to be friendly and too familiar to be official.

Then Lucien looked once through the glass at Lena before turning away.

The door creaked open.

The man stepped in.

"Hello, Lena."

The voice was smooth, amused, almost polite. But his eyes carried a different weight.

"Detective Raines."

He shrugged. "Or just Raines, if we're being honest."

Her stomach tightened. The scar, pale and jagged, cut from his eyebrow down toward his temple. She remembered it now, the way it had caught the light outside the store, how it had unsettled her even before she knew his name.

"You," she breathed. "You were the one on scene outside my store yesterday."

A smirk pulled at one corner of his mouth. The same cold amusement she'd seen before.

"That's right. You told me you didn't know Lucien. Funny how that changed."

Her gaze flicked toward the door.

"After how you acted, I didn't think you had any ties to him either."

Raines chuckled low, stepping closer, his shadow long against the sterile wall.

"I might wear a badge, but I don't pretend it's the badge that feeds me."

The city suddenly felt smaller.

The blood drained from her face. He didn't need to say more. She understood.

He leaned in slightly, lowering his voice. "They pulled the footage, by the way. From the store."

A cold ripple moved through her.

"Too clean," he went on. "Power cut. Cameras dead. Exterior feeds jammed. Only thing left was a grainy traffic cam two blocks away. Black car. Plates stripped. Driver masked. Surgical work."

Something dropped low in her gut.

"This wasn't random," Raines said softly. "It was a message. And not to you."

He studied her for a moment, then sighed, like he was about to say something he shouldn't.

"Your boss is going to get paid," he said. "More than the store was worth. Insurance won't fight it. Fire report will soften. Media will move on. By next week, this becomes a small article instead of a headline."

Lena stared at him.

"That's not luck," Raines said. "That's influence."

"Donovan will rebuild," Raines added. "Different name, different partners, better location. He'll land on his feet. That didn't happen because of the city."

He watched that sink in before he spoke again.

"People like you get ruined by something like this," Raines said. "People like him make a few phone calls and the world rewrites itself."

He let the silence sit for a second.

"So, officially? You got clipped crossing the street.

Unofficially? You've been marked. Which means so has he."

He studied her like he could see a future she hadn't agreed to.

"If I find anything, Lucien will know," he said. "And so will you, if you're smart enough to stay close."

And then he was gone. Just the hush of footsteps fading down the corridor, leaving her alone in the sterile room, the walls suddenly too close.

In Lucien Cole's world, distance didn't exist.
Not between streets.
Not between people.
Not between choices.
She hadn't stepped into this anymore.
It had closed around her.
Her gaze dropped to her hand, like she could still feel his grip there.
Something had shifted.
Not fear.
Something worse.
Attachment.

Chapter Thirteen

THE HOUSE ABOVE THE RIVER

A few days had passed since the hit. The bruises on Lena's body had begun to fade, but the memory clung to her like a shadow that refused to loosen, impossible to outrun.

The drive to Lucien's estate was silent. Manhattan's chaos unraveled behind them, neon bleeding into night until the world narrowed to winding roads and towering cliffs. The deeper they went, the more the landscape changed, the hum of the city replaced by the hush of old woods, their branches clawing at the night sky like ghosts that never slept.

Moonlight slicked the Hudson in black glass. A low mist curled off the ground, pale ribbons snaking across the road and coiling around the tires.

Every mile carried Lena farther from the life she recognized, and closer to the man who would unmake it.

When the SUV finally stopped, she hesitated with her hand on the door.

She had imagined grandeur. Power. Luxury.

What rose before her was something else entirely.

A fortress.

A sanctuary.

Iron and quiet threat, perched high above the river like it had been waiting for centuries. Its sharp lines gleamed silver in the moonlight, yet there was something ancient about it, a stillness that made the night air feel heavy, watching.

For one impossible second, she had the feeling this place had not been built for the man he was. It had been waiting for what he would become.

The forest stretched endlessly behind it, thick and uninviting, sealing the estate in silence. Far on the horizon, the city's glow had thinned to a faint shimmer, a memory in reverse, close enough to ache for and too far to reach.

Michael opened her door. The night air was colder here, sharper, pine and damp earth filling her lungs.

"Watch your step, Lena," he said quietly.

She stepped out.

She turned back once before walking toward the entrance.

Michael was standing by the open driver's door, watching to make sure she made it to the house.

When their eyes met, he gave a small nod, like everything that needed to be said had already been handled.

Then he got in the SUV and closed the door.

Lucien emerged from the entrance, his silhouette framed in molten gold from the light spilling behind him.

But when his eyes found hers, something unspoken shifted. The edges softened.

"Lena."

His voice carried like velvet over steel. Steady. Controlled.

"I'm glad you're here."

Something inside her went very still. "It's beautiful."

Lucien's mouth tilted, not quite a smile. He turned, beckoning her inside. "Come. You must be tired."

She followed him, footsteps hushed against cold stone.

Inside, the air was warm but unmoving. The kind of hush that clings to old churches, where every sound echoes against vaulted ceilings and secrets settle in the rafters. Nothing here felt accidental. The faint scent of leather and cedar held to the walls while gold light traced the edges of marble and dark wood.

"I had your things brought to the master bedroom," Lucien said without looking back. "You'll be more comfortable there. If you want the door closed, I'll be on the other side of it."

A sudden heat rushed through her.

The master bedroom.

This shift, this slide, it was moving faster than she could steady herself against.

"I didn't ask for the door closed," she said.

He glanced over his shoulder, and whatever answer he found in her face made the air change.

"Come. I want to show you something."

They stepped onto the balcony, and the world opened wide.

The Hudson stretched endlessly beneath them, moonlight shattering its surface into cold silver.

To the north, jagged mountains loomed under drifting night clouds; to the south, the city glimmered faintly in the dark, beautiful, unreachable, like a memory that never belonged to her.

Lucien leaned against the railing, gaze fixed on the horizon.

"This is where I come to breathe," he said. "When the weight of everything starts to close in."

There was a quiet ache in the way he said it. She recognized it. It had lived in a chamber she'd tried to seal off for years.

Lena asked, "Does it happen often?"

He paused. Then, softer: "More than I'll ever admit."

In the pale light, he looked less like the untouchable figure she'd met, more like a man haunted by the very empire he'd built.

"But here," he said, his words settling slow, "I feel like I still have a choice. Like I'm not already buried beneath everything I've done."

She studied him, the tension in his shoulders, the quiet control in his hands.

"You ever think about letting go?"

"Let go of what?"

"Everything," she whispered. "The control. The walls. The weight you carry like it's your birthright. What if, just once, you didn't?"

His eyes flicked to hers, sharp, guarded. But beneath it: something wounded.

"Men like me don't get that luxury."

"Is that because you can't?" she asked. "Or because you're afraid of what's waiting on the other side?"

For the briefest moment, something flickered across his face, not fear, but something he'd spent years refusing to feel. A truth too sharp to name.

"When you build an empire," Lucien said, his voice rough, "you hold it up, or it falls. And when it falls?"

His gaze locked onto hers, dark and unblinking.

"You find out who was only ever standing beside you because you were the one keeping the world from collapsing."

She knew that feeling, of people vanishing the moment you stopped holding the roof up. Of learning too young that love built on need collapses the second you falter.

Lena stepped closer. Her heart struck hard in her chest.

"The higher you climb," he added, "the quieter it gets. And when you fall, don't expect hands. Just eyes. Watching. Waiting."

"Then don't fall," she whispered.

His breath caught, the smallest fracture in his composure.

"I won't let you," she added.

Lucien stilled. He looked at her like he wasn't sure if she meant it, or if she didn't know what she was promising.

"You don't know what you're offering."

"Don't I?" Her voice trembled, but not from fear. "You think I can't see it? The man who won't let anyone close because he's already been cut too deep?"

His hands curled at his sides. Not in anger. In restraint.

"You make it sound so easy."

"It's not," she said. "But maybe that's the point."

A thin silence stretched between them, filled only by wind and the quiet rush of the river below.

Lena tilted her head back, throat bare to the cold, and let the sky pour into her.

"You can see everything from here," she whispered. "It's almost cruel how clear it is."

Lucien didn't look up yet. He watched her watch the stars, the way most men watched a strip of skin revealed by accident.

"Orion's bright tonight," she said.

Now he followed her gaze. The hunter burned above them, sword and belt held in ancient tension, violence frozen into light.

"I used to think he was chasing the Pleiades," Lena murmured. "Seven sisters running forever. But my mother told me a different story."

Lucien's voice caught on the edge of it. "Tell me."

"She said Orion wasn't hunting them. He was trying to keep up. They were the only light he'd ever known that didn't belong to him, didn't fear him, didn't need anything from him. So he chased them across the sky every night just to remember what it felt like to want something he couldn't own."

Something flickered across Lucien's face.

Lena stepped to the railing, fingers curling over the cold iron. "When I was nine, my father pointed at that constellation and said, 'See the three stars in a row? That's Orion's belt. One day some man's going to look at you the way Orion looks at those sisters, like you're the only thing worth chasing across every lifetime, and you'll spend the rest of yours trying to outrun him.'"

She laughed once, soft and broken. "He was drunk. Mean. But he wasn't wrong."

Lucien moved behind her, close enough that she felt the heat of him through her coat.

"And did you?" he said, close enough to brush her ear. "Outrun them all?"

"Until now."

The words hung there, small and trembling and true.

He was quiet, so still she thought he hadn't breathed. Then his hands settled on the railing on either side of hers, caging her without touching.

"Look east," he said, his attention already there.

She did. Just above the treeline, almost lost in the glare of the moon, a single star pulsed red.

"Bellatrix," he said. "Orion's left shoulder. In Latin it means female warrior. Someone told me once old soldiers swore on her before wars they knew they wouldn't come home from. They believed if you could still see Bellatrix on the night you died, she would guide you across the river."

Lena's throat tightened.

"I was eighteen the first time I killed a man. After, I came here, to this same stretch of river, long before any house stood on it. Just woods and cliffs and the water below. I stood on this exact ground while it was still wild and told Bellatrix to take me. She wouldn't. So I bought the land ten years later. Figured if she ever changed her mind, I'd already be waiting exactly where I begged."

His fingers finally brushed hers on the railing, intentional.

"I thought it meant I wasn't finished. That the world still had use for monsters. But maybe," his voice cracked slightly, "maybe she was waiting for someone worth coming back for."

Lena turned in the cage of his arms. The moonlight cut across his face like a blade, and for the first time she saw it fully: the exhaustion, the grief, the terror buried under the myth.

She reached up slowly, like he was something that might bolt, and laid her palm over his heart.

"Then let her wait a little longer," she said.

His eyes searched hers, wild, ancient, starving.

"Lena…"

"I'm not the Pleiades," she whispered. "I'm not running."

Something broke behind his gaze. Not control. Something older.

He kissed her like a drowning man breaking the surface.

Not careful. Not civilized.

He kissed her like Orion finally catching the one light he was never meant to hold and deciding the sky could burn for all he cared.

His hands shook when they slid into her hair. Hers shook harder when they fisted in his shirt and dragged him closer.

When he lifted her, her legs wrapped around his waist without thinking, and the stars wheeled overhead, forgotten.

Inside, he pressed her against the first wall he found, mouth at her throat, her name a broken prayer against her skin.

Between kisses he whispered, raw and ruined:

"I'm going to look for Bellatrix every night I'm terrified I'll lose you."

She answered by pulling him inside, toward the bedroom, toward the only war either of them was willing to surrender in.

Later, much later, tangled in sheets that still carried the cold from the open balcony doors, Lena traced the scar just under his collarbone.

"Still see her?" she asked, drowsy.

Lucien turned his head on the pillow. Through the glass, Bellatrix burned steady and red above the river.

"Yeah," he said, voice hoarse from screaming her name into the dark. "But tonight she's not guiding me anywhere."

He pressed his lips to her wrist, right over her pulse.

"Tonight she's just watching."

And for the first time in his life, Lucien Cole closed his eyes under the stars without making a single wish.

He already had her.

His breathing evened out, slow, almost peaceful, the rise and fall of a man who had finally let the sky win.

Lena stayed awake.

She listened to the quiet, felt the weight of his heart under her palm, steady for now, and watched Bellatrix hold her vigil through the glass.

His control was gone tonight, and so was hers.

Nothing about it had been careful. Nothing about it had been safe.

And maybe that was the point.

But dawn would come, cold and merciless, pulling its light across the river in a slow, unforgiving sweep.

And when it did, the armor would come back on.

Because men like Lucien Cole don't stay lost.

They find their way back to power. Always.

She pressed her face into his throat, breathing him in while she still could, and thought:

When monsters love, their kingdoms change.

But the monster always comes home.

Chapter Fourteen

ROOMS THAT REMEMBER

The next morning, Lena stirred beneath the weight of fine sheets, the scent of unfamiliar linens laced with something darker. Him.

Part of her wanted to sink into this warmth and pretend the night before was a beginning. But another part, the part that had learned not to trust comfort, whispered that beginnings didn't come with rules already set.

Her body ached with memory: last night, the crash, the hospital, the controlled command in Lucien's voice when he claimed her safety like it was his to give.

For a moment, she stayed still, eyes half-closed, suspended in warmth. Then she shifted, and caught movement in the mirror.

Lucien stood by the window. Shirtless. Slacks low on his hips. The light cut across him, leaving half in shadow, the rest hard and defined. He wasn't looking at her. He was looking out, at the skyline. At the world beneath him. At the war only he seemed to see.

But Lena didn't miss the tension in his shoulders, the way his arm held too still at his side, like a man bracing for impact long before it came.

When he turned, it wasn't abrupt. It was controlled. Slow enough to register.

Their eyes met.

"You're awake," he said, sleep roughening his voice but not the authority in it.

"I think so," she whispered, pulling the collar of his shirt tighter around herself.

It smelled clean at first, then darker, like smoke caught in fabric.

Lucien crossed the room in three slow strides and sat on the edge of the bed. His presence was a weight, steadying and suffocating.

For a moment, he only looked at her. Lena felt the measured scrutiny, the unspoken question in his gaze, like he was already there before the thought formed.

"You're safe here," he said.

It wasn't reassurance. It was decree.

"I know." The words came out softer than she intended.

He reached out, fingers brushing along her jaw in a touch so light it barely existed, and she felt it anyway.

"I covered you last night," he said. "You were cold. I handled it."

A crack entered his tone. It unsettled her more than his control ever had.

"You said you didn't have anyone," Lucien said. "Back at the hospital."

Lena went still. "I don't."

The words hung between them, unadorned and heavier for it.

She watched his face change, not with pity but with restrained curiosity. Questions he could have asked, but didn't.

Lucien didn't ask.

His hand dropped away.

"That's going to change," he said, rising.

Not a promise. A decision.

And the man she'd just kissed, the one who'd faltered, was gone again.

In his place stood the myth: precise hands, the armor he chose, silence where confession had been.

He was not harmless, only gentle by choice.

Lena watched him dress in muted awe. The ritual of it. The discipline. Like nothing in his world happened without intent.

"You think you can protect me from everything?" she said, not quite a challenge.

He didn't turn. Only adjusted his cufflinks and said, "No. But I'll handle what I can."

There was more to say. There always was. But neither reached for it.

Lucien stepped closer, phone buzzing once in his pocket, ignored.

"Stay here today," he said, gaze locked on hers. "Don't open the door for anyone but me."

"And if someone knocks?"

His eyes darkened. "They won't."

Then, softer. Almost like a secret.

"I won't be long."

He pressed his lips to her forehead, brief and claiming, and then he was gone. The door clicked shut behind him with the weight of something inevitable.

Silence followed, charged and listening.

The house seemed to wait for his footsteps to fade before it exhaled.

The warmth of his kiss still lingered on her skin. But her body had already begun to cool.

She sat up slowly, the sheets slipping off her shoulders as she swung her legs over the side of the bed. Her toes met the edge of a low rug, more for protecting the hardwood than comfort, but even that felt distant. Almost surreal.

She looked around the room, massive windows draped in thick fabric, dark wood floors, art worth more than anything that had ever belonged to her. Everything was beautiful, silent, untouchable.

It felt like stepping into someone else's life. Something impossibly perfect, like a dream designed to disappear the moment she reached for it.

Lena rose and grabbed one of his shirts from the chair, pulling it on for warmth more than comfort. It hung off her shoulders like armor borrowed from a stranger.

She crossed to the window, the fabric brushing her skin as she moved. Beyond the glass, the estate stretched out like a private kingdom, pristine gardens, stone paths, high walls. It was stunning, almost unreal, but the view left her on edge. Beautiful things always did. They never stayed beautiful for long.

She hadn't seen much of the place since arriving, just flashes between headlights and Lucien's shadow guiding her inside.

Now, in the morning light, everything looked sharp. Precise. Designed.

The air itself felt curated.

She touched the windowpane, her fingers leaving a ghostly imprint behind. The stillness tightened her chest, like the house wasn't just watching her. It was waiting.

She turned away from the view, grabbed a pair of sweatpants from the chair, and pulled them on before stepping toward the door.

She had to see more. Not because she didn't trust him. Because she didn't trust this place.

Lucien had told her to stay behind the door.

That was exactly why she opened it.

Lena stepped into the hall, her bare feet brushing polished wood, the space too still, too perfect, like a museum waiting to judge whoever walked through it. Shadows clung to the corners. The house felt alert.

She moved anyway.

The house was grand in the way old money liked to be, impressive and impersonal.

As she moved deeper, she found herself in a long corridor lined with weapons, swords, daggers, shields, even pieces of armor, all displayed with meticulous care.

Relics from other eras, forged in blood and battle. She paused at a broadsword etched with symbols that curled like smoke across the steel. It gleamed in the soft light like it had just been sharpened.

She hovered a hand over the hilt but didn't touch it. The air here felt heavy and still, as if the past were watching her.

At the end of the hallway sat a small table, out of place among the steel and stone. On it, photographs. Dozens. Unframed. Unprotected. Personal.

She picked one up with hesitant fingers.

Lucien. Younger. Softer. Standing beside a woman with dark hair and laughing eyes. She had her arm slung over his shoulder; her lips pressed to his cheek. He was smiling, truly smiling. A version of him Lena hadn't seen.

Curiosity twisted in her chest, followed by something darker.

She thumbed through the rest. The woman, always beside him. Sometimes laughing, sometimes looking at him like no one else existed.

The same face appeared again and again. And then:

"She was beautiful, wasn't she?"

Lena flinched, the photo slipping from her hands.

An older woman stood in the hallway behind her, small-framed, hands clasped tightly in front of her. Her voice was soft, but the strain beneath it was wrong.

"I didn't mean to pry," Lena started.

The woman waved her off, stepping closer. "Everyone finds those photos eventually. Mr. Cole doesn't speak of her, but the house remembers. Her name was Isabelle."

Isabelle. The name landed like a stone in her stomach.

"She was very important to him," the housekeeper continued, her voice dropping slightly. "A long time ago. But some loves leave a shadow behind. Some never really go."

"What happened to her?"

"She died," the woman said simply. "An accident. That's what they said."

A pause. Her eyes lingered on the photos, then flicked back to Lena, something unreadable swimming just beneath the surface.

"But this house has its own version of the truth," she said, voice dipping lower. "And not all of it stays buried."

Lena's pulse picked up. "I should get back to my room."

The woman tilted her head, almost kindly. "You remind me of her, you know."

Lena froze.

"She had the same eyes when she first arrived. Curious. Fragile." The woman's smile didn't reach her eyes. "Be careful, dear. Some things in this house are better left undisturbed."

The words landed too close to something her mother once told her, that the world punishes girls who reach for more than they're given. It sent a cold ripple down her spine.

She turned and walked away, her footsteps swallowed by the silence.

Lena stood there a moment longer, unsettled. Then, just as she turned to leave, she noticed a door slightly ajar, hidden in the shadows beside the table.

A faint light glowed from within.

She hesitated. Every instinct told her to walk away. But curiosity had always been her weakness.

She pushed the door open.

The room inside was small, windowless, and frigid. The walls were lined with dark wood panels, and in the center of the room sat a round table. On it, a single lit candle and an ornate music box, its lid halfway open.

It was already playing when she stepped inside. A soft, haunting tune drifted into the air, delicate and almost childlike, but wrong beneath the sweetness, dissonant, as if it had been twisted.

Lena stepped closer. Inside the box, a tiny porcelain ballerina turned slowly. Her arms raised. Her eyes blank.

Lena leaned in. The ballerina froze. The music stopped. The silence slammed down like a door.

Then she saw it. Scratched into the wood of the table, beneath the box, words carved with something sharp, the letters jagged and uneven.

I'M WATCHING YOU

A chill tore through her spine.

She backed away, heart hammering, mouth dry.

"Excuse me."

The voice came from behind her, quiet, cracked, like it had been waiting in the walls.

Lena turned.

The housekeeper stood in the doorway. Same uniform. Same posture. But her skin looked... tighter somehow. Pale and drawn, like a wax figure kept under harsh light.

Her tone was wrong. Firmer now. Hollow.

"You shouldn't be in here."

"I... I didn't know."

The woman stepped forward, slow and stiff.

Her eyes didn't blink.

"Now you do."

She tilted her head slightly, like she was listening to something Lena couldn't hear.

"Some doors," she said, almost whispering, "aren't meant to open."

Lena went rigid. The housekeeper's eyes were locked on hers, but they didn't see her. They looked through her. Past her. As if Lena had already left the room or never existed in it.

The woman stepped aside.

"You should go."

Lena didn't wait. She pushed past the housekeeper and walked fast down the corridor, the music still clinging to her long after it had stopped. She didn't look back. She didn't trust herself to.

She didn't stop until she reached the bedroom. She slammed the door behind her and pressed her back against it, trying to steady her breath. The air felt thick now, charged and watchful.

The carved words branded themselves into her mind.

I'm watching you.

She backed toward the bed without taking her eyes off the door and climbed onto the mattress like height alone might protect her.

For the first time since arriving, she wasn't sure she was safe at all.

A creak sounded in the hallway.

Drawn out. Slow. Intentional.

Lena froze, blood turning to ice. The hairs on her arms lifted, like something had passed too close without touching her.

Another creak.

Closer.

The door handle twitched.

Panic slammed against her ribs. Not loud. Careful. Too careful. A movement meant to be heard only by her.

The handle twisted.

Metal groaned like bone under strain.

Then it stopped.

Silence.

A silence so heavy it rattled inside her skull.

Lena jolted against the headboard, sheets clutched in her fists, her breath thin and sharp. Her mind screamed at her to move, but her body refused to obey. She told herself the house was settling. Old wood. Old foundations.

Something brushed over her skin. Feather-light. Unmistakably real.

Her throat locked.

The blankets tore away.

Lifted clean off her body.

Something unseen clamped around her ankles.
Her breath broke.
The world went white.

CHAPTER FIFTEEN

LOVER IN THE WALLS

She barely had time to react.

Something unseen latched onto her ankles.

Yanked.

Lena slid down the bed so fast her skin burned against the sheets. Her mind flashed white. Hospital lights. The crash. The taste of metal and medication. For one breathless second, she didn't know if she was awake or still trapped in the aftershock.

She kicked, clawed at the mattress, nails catching fabric, but the force didn't care. It lifted her.

Weightless.

Pinned.

Her wrists snapped overhead like the air had hands. Her legs were pulled apart with clinical certainty. Not rage. Control. Like she was being arranged.

She tried to scream.

No sound came.

Not even a whisper.

The room stayed quiet, and that was the worst part. Silence became its own weapon.

Hot breath touched her skin. Not human. Not warm. A mimicry of breath, shaped by something that understood the weight of contact and how to counterfeit it.

A tug shifted the air at her feet, followed by a slow, creeping slide.

Not fabric slipping away.

Something tracing the outline of her, slow and intentional, as if learning where her fear lived. The pressure climbed her legs with the calm precision of a presence that had already decided she could not stop it.

Cold prickled along her calves. A path she didn't imagine. A touch that knew where it was going.

A study, not a struggle.

A hunter mapping the places she broke.

Her chest tightened and her pulse stumbled out of rhythm. The terror rose too fast, too sharp to reason with, drowning out every excuse she tried to give it. The room stayed impossibly still, like the walls were holding their breath, waiting to see what happened next.

Whatever held her wanted her to feel it.

Every inch.

Every second.

And her body understood that before her mind did.

This was terror without shape or mercy.

Her mind reached for anything familiar. The crash, the cold, the hospital lights.

But nothing explained this.

Nothing felt distant enough to be a dream.

The fear was too sharp and too present to be imagined.

Her lungs seized. Her skin burned. Nothing about it felt imagined anymore.

The voice arrived first.

Low. Lingering. Possessive.

LUCIEN'S WHORE.

The words drifted through the dark like smoke, curling into her ears, finding every unguarded place in her mind. They spread through her like something cold poured into hot metal. The certainty of it carried the violence.

The air split.

Fabric tore. Not clean. Not accidental. A jagged rip in the quiet, too intimate in the dark to be anything the mind invented.

Lena thrashed, but the force around her didn't react. It held her with the steady weight of something certain she no longer controlled her own body.

A touch followed. Not a hand she could see. Not a mouth she could name. Only sensation. Cold pressure. Heat where there should not be heat. Something exploring the outline of her with the patience of something deciding where to hurt her most. A mocking tenderness sharpened by the fact that nothing visible produced it.

A sound tore out of her throat, but it stayed trapped behind her teeth. No air. No voice. Silence pressed into her lungs until the act of breathing felt optional.

She shook hard enough to rattle the bedframe.

Not want.

Reflex.

The body betraying the mind because terror had cornered both.

Was it the house, a nightmare, a hallucination shaped by pain and medication? The thought flickered like a light bulb about to die, then vanished under the relentless weight of the presence above her.

The voice returned. Closer this time.

As if leaning directly over her ear.

LUCIEN'S WHORE.

Her vision bent at the edges. The ceiling folded and swam. Her pulse hammered so fast the rhythm blurred into one continuous pressure behind her ribs. She fought for air like she was underwater, and the room tightened that too, narrowing her lungs to a pinhole.

The pressure climbed her body until her nerves screamed. Her muscles locked. Her back arched in a terror she could not control. Every instinct fired at once, a thousand alarms with nowhere to run.

And then it stopped.

Release.

The force withdrew with a casualness that made nausea climb her throat. Bored, almost. Like whatever had pinned her had gotten what it wanted.

Lena was thrown backward. She hit the bed hard, sheets twisting beneath her like a wave recoiling. The mattress groaned under the impact, too loud in the sudden quiet.

Her lungs seized. Light stabbed her eyes. Her breath broke into jagged pieces.

She blinked.

The room was the room.

Her clothes were still on. Every seam intact. Every button unmoved. The bed sat half dragged from its place, exactly the way it had in the dream. Her skin burned with phantom pressure. Her wrists throbbed. Her ankles ached. Her chest carried the deep, lingering pain of being held down for too long.

The air carried a faint trace of heat. Sweat. Aftermath. A presence that shouldn't exist.

The pain was real.

The bruises would be too.

And yet her mind scrambled for reasons, for rational anchors, for anything that could explain what her body remembered and the room denied.

It had happened somewhere between dream and waking, where the body kept score even when the world insisted nothing occurred.

She turned to the bedside clock.

11:47 A.M.

Her gut knotted.

She must have drifted back under after Lucien left.

The weight of it clung to her like a second skin.

She whispered, "It wasn't real."

Then, louder, "It wasn't real."

But the words fell flat.

The room swallowed them whole.

Too quiet, too still, like the air itself was listening and something in the corners had woken. Something unseen, patient, and not finished with her.

Her lungs scraped for air. For a moment she could not tell if her shaking came from the dream, or from something darker waiting on the other side of the door.

Then a sound.

A voice.

Lucien's voice.

She froze, head tilted, every nerve reaching for the slightest cue. It came from somewhere deeper in the house, low and sharp, threaded with command, a voice he had never used with her.

She crept toward the door, cracking it open just enough to hear.

Lucien's voice cut through the quiet, low and exact.

"I don't care what it takes. Handle it."

A pause. A tense reply she couldn't decipher.

Lucien exhaled, disinterested.

"Bobby Scava should've stayed gone. He got a clean exit. A life. That wasn't enough?"

Another reply. Short. Uneasy.

Lucien's tone cooled further.

"He's making noise now. Threatening to drag my name into it."

A beat of silence, razor thin.

"He knows better."

Another pause.

"Then remind him why."

No raised voice.

No theatrics.

Just precision.

"No fallout. No trail. If anyone asks?"

A soft inhale.

"It was resolved."

Lena backed away, breath catching in her throat.

She was not sure if it was fear, or the echo of that voice in her dream. The one that whispered in the dark.

Lucien's whore.

No. This was real. She had heard him.

Lena fought to steady the frantic drum in her chest as she slipped into the corridor, soft socks swallowing every footstep along the silent spine of Lucien's estate.

And then she saw it.

The hallway.

The same one from the dream.

The same shadows.

The same photos.

Lucien, younger. Softer. Smiling in a way he never did now.

And the woman. Isabelle.

Her breath caught as she stepped closer, her fingers hovering just above the frames.

It was just a nightmare.

But here it was.

She turned instinctively, expecting to see the music box room.

Nothing.

No door.

Just solid wall.

Her heart started to race.

She spun around.

And froze.

The housekeeper stood at the end of the hall.

Watching.

Lena stumbled backward, lungs seizing in tight and frantic pulls.

Was she real? Had she even spoken to her earlier?

She looked normal again, calm, ordinary, as if nothing had ever been off. As if the earlier encounter had never happened at all.

The housekeeper's face remained impassive, but her sharp, aged eyes held something knowing.

"What's the matter, dear?" she asked softly.

Lena shook her head, pressing a hand to her temple. "The room, there was a room here earlier."

The housekeeper didn't blink. "You must be mistaken."

Lena's stomach twisted. "No. I was here. I saw you. We spoke, about the pictures, about Isabelle. Then I found the room. The music box..."

The housekeeper tilted her head slightly, as if considering how much truth to allow.

"Yes," she said calmly. "We spoke. But then you went back to your room."

Lena's brows drew together. "No, I didn't..."

"Are you sure?" the woman asked gently, but there was something sharp behind the softness. "Have you been taking any medication?"

Lena's breath stalled. "What?"

"Sometimes," the housekeeper continued, her voice patient and almost too gentle, "medication and trauma can twist a dream until it feels real. Especially after an accident."

The word burrowed under her skin.

Lena's pulse thundered in her skull. "That's not,"

"Are you sure you weren't dreaming, dear?"

Lena froze.

The way she said it.

Calm. Certain. Like it was already decided for her.

"You have been taking medication though, haven't you?"

Her stomach flipped. "Wait, how do you know that?"

The housekeeper's lips curled, not unkind but tight and controlled.

"Because I've cared for someone who went through something similar years ago. After a head injury, the mind can become cruel. Dreams. Hallucinations. Things that feel real until they aren't."

She paused, studying Lena carefully.

"Mr. Cole told me you were in an accident. That you'd be staying here with us while you recovered. Sometimes the body heals faster than the mind."

Lena swallowed hard, willing herself to push past the wave of nausea twisting in her gut.

Maybe she was right.

Maybe the medication was messing with her. Maybe...

A voice cut through the moment.

"Lena."

She turned sharply.

Lucien.

Standing a few feet away, head slightly tilted, gaze unreadable in a way that made her feel even less certain of herself.

"Look at me."

Lena dragged in a ragged inhale.

Was she imagining things? She could not tell anymore.

The housekeeper gave her a final, knowing glance before drifting back into the shadows, disappearing into the vastness of the house.

Lucien's smirk didn't fade. He took a step closer, slipping an arm around her waist, pulling her against him. Warm, solid, grounding.

"You're shaking," he said.

Lena blinked up at him, lost between reality and whatever version of it she was trapped in.

His thumb traced her jaw, tilting her face upward.

"Come on, get dressed."

Lena blinked. "What?"

"Let's go for a ride."

She went still. "Now?"

A faint sound escaped him, almost a laugh but too controlled to be one.

"You need fresh air. And I want to show you something."

She didn't speak, just nodded and crossed the room in silence, the floor cool beneath her feet.

She opened the drawer beside the bed. Two prescription bottles rattled inside.

Klonopin. Tramadol.

One for the panic. One for the pain.

She stared at them for a long moment.

If the line between dream and reality was dissolving, the pills were the first thing she could control.

If the housekeeper was right, if this was her mind playing tricks, then what else could she trust? Her memory. Her body. Him. Maybe this was the only way to find out.

Without a word, she walked into the bathroom and tossed them into the trash.

The sound of them hitting the bin felt louder than it should have. Final.

She undressed with slow care, grounding herself in the small motions, then stepped into the shower, letting the water hit her skin like a reset. Not to wash the night away. Some things couldn't. But to feel something real. Controlled. Hers.

Afterward, she stood at the sink, dripping, pulse finally slowing as she stared at her reflection.

She didn't recognize the girl staring back.

But she refused to let her break.

Not now.

Not here.

She drew one last breath to anchor herself, dried off with the towel, then stepped back into the room, shaken and raw but moving anyway.

Lena fastened the final button of her jeans, her fingers trembling. The room smelled of soap and perfume now, not sweat and fear.

Lucien stood by the door, keys in hand.

"Ready?" he asked.

Not even close.

But she nodded.

He opened the door, and as she followed him into the hall, one thought returned, louder this time:

Was she waking from the dream, or walking deeper into it? Maybe she had not woken up at all. Maybe this, him, the house, the shadows in the corners of her mind, was the dream. And maybe whatever ruled it had no intention of letting her go.

Chapter Sixteen

SECRETS BENEATH THE STONES

Lucien led her through the grand hallways, his movements effortless, controlled. Lena followed without question, her body still unsteady from the dream's residue.

At the entrance, two guards stood at attention. They nodded once and opened the door.

Lucien didn't slow. "We're going for a ride to StoneHaven."

The guards exchanged a look. One spoke into his radio while Lucien kept walking.

StoneHaven?

The way he said it, quiet and reverent, sent a chill down her spine. People didn't talk about places like that. They talked about graves.

He led her down a side path toward a sleek, glass-paneled structure beside the estate. With a button press, the doors lifted, revealing eight cars lined like an exhibit: a jet-black hypercar, a deep crimson Ferrari, a silver Aston Martin polished to mirror steel.

Lucien didn't hesitate. He clicked a remote, and the black McLaren chirped awake.

He opened the passenger door. She slid in. The leather was cool, the air sharp with expensive cologne and clean metal. Lucien got behind the wheel, adjusting his grip with practiced ease.

A flick of his wrist.

The engine growled alive, low and predatory, filling the space.

Lucien's mouth twitched at her reaction. He shifted, and the car glided down the long road away from the estate.

Rolling hills spread before them, trees turning amber and crimson as the wind scattered leaves across the pavement. Morning light threaded through the canopy like molten gold.

Lucien drove with a mastery that looked instinctive. One hand on the wheel, one on the shift, posture relaxed but coiled with intent.

Lena watched the blur of color pass by, her palm pressed to the cool glass. "So... what's StoneHaven?"

He didn't look at her. "You'll see."

Not dismissive. Final.

A charged quiet settled between them, heavy with everything left unsaid.

Lucien wasn't just driving. He was somewhere else entirely. His fingers tapped once against the wheel, his gaze steady on the road, as if replaying something she couldn't see.

Memories. Or ghosts.

The farther they went, the more the landscape changed. The road narrowed, trees sharpening into older shapes, branches tangling overhead until the sunlight dimmed. Mist slid along the ground and curled against the tires.

Then she saw it.

A wrought-iron gate, massive and half-consumed by ivy. A groundskeeper in a dark coat stood beside the control box. At Lucien's approach, he pressed a button, and the gates groaned open.

Lucien eased the car forward.

The world behind them disappeared.

No birds. No wind. Only the hum of the engine and a faint whisper of air brushing stone.

Mausoleums rose like forgotten monuments, carved angels hollow-eyed, obelisks tilting toward the sky. The quiet carried weight.

Lucien parked before a black-marble crypt framed by two pillars. He cut the engine but didn't move, staring ahead as if steadying himself.

Lena's fingers tightened on the seat. She was not ready for this.

Lucien finally turned. "You asked about Isabelle."

Her breath caught. She had not asked him.

She had asked the housekeeper.

He stepped out. Lena followed into the cold stillness.

ISABELLE LAURENT

The engraved name gleamed on the marble.

A single white rose lay at its base, browning at the edges.

Not fresh. Not forgotten either.

No candles. No offerings. Only stone and silence.

Lucien stood with his hands in his pockets. "She was like you. Curious. Too curious."

Lena thought of the photographs in the hallway, the laughing woman with her mouth pressed to his cheek. Here, that same woman had been reduced to a name, a date, and a dying rose.

Lena's pulse climbed. "Did you love her?"

The question slipped out.

His mouth tightened, caught somewhere between memory and regret.

"Love is a strange word."

A breath. "I wanted to."

Another, quieter. "Maybe I did. But time did not wait for either of us."

The space between them shifted, charged.

"You want to know what happened to her," he said.

No.

But she stayed silent. Because she did.

"Then listen closely."

His knuckles grazed her jaw, light but intentional. His thumb brushed close to her lower lip, enough to steal her breath.

"She asked the right questions," he said. "But she didn't like the answers."

He held her gaze, steady and challenging.

"Are you sure you want to keep asking?"

Her fingers curled at her sides. Heat rose in her chest.

"Yes."

He studied her a moment longer, then stepped back. The air stretched thin between them.

"Then let me show you something."

He drew a brass key, turned to the door, and slid it into the lock.

The click echoed.

He pushed the door open and stepped inside without looking back.

Lena followed.

The crypt was colder than outside. Not ruined or forgotten. Perfectly kept. Marble polished smooth enough to reflect the chandelier above. The faint scent of aged wood and stone dust lingered in the air.

The chandelier flickered once, light sliding across the walls and the floor in slow, uneven bands.

Lucien walked with measured steps. She matched him, though instinct urged her to turn around.

A single sarcophagus waited at the center, floral carvings winding across the lid. No statues. No prayers. Only a name.

Isabelle Laurent.

There were no photographs in the crypt.

No smiling memories.

Only the name.

Only the dates.

Only the end.

Pressure tightened beneath Lena's ribs. This woman had been real. Loved. Lost. And Lena was standing where Lucien had come to remember her.

"It has been a few years," Lucien said.

"And in all that time, I have tried to let her go."

He exhaled.

"She was sharp. Untouchable."

His voice thinned. "Until she wasn't."

He looked at the stone.

"I told myself I would stop coming here. Take the pictures down. Throw away the key."

A humorless sound left him. "But I never did."

"So why now?" Lena whispered.

He met her eyes. "Because of you."

Her breath caught.

"Because I don't make the same mistake twice."

The warning had changed shape.

"I brought you here to show you what happens when you go too far," he said quietly. "When you step into a life that isn't built for you."

Silence sealed the room around them.

Lena sensed it. This was confession, not warning.

"What happened to her?" she asked.

Lucien looked back at the tomb before he answered.

"There was only one thing I couldn't protect her from," he said.

"Herself."

The words settled into the room and stayed there.

"She wanted this world. Wanted to understand it. Thought she could carry it."

He shook his head. "She couldn't."

He didn't elaborate.

"She left the only way she knew how," he said, voice scraped thin. "And I blame myself every damn day."

Lena felt it in the way he stood there, like this was the only place he didn't have to be Lucien Cole.

A man who never let anyone see him bleed.

And here, he was bleeding.

"Lucien..." she whispered.

His gaze snapped to hers. Cold over fire.

Dangerous, yes. But not toward her.

Toward himself.

She understood.

This was not only about keeping her safe.

It was a punishment he still carried.

Lucien had been haunted by the ghost of a woman he couldn't save.

Now he was watching another step toward the same ending.

"Tell me you won't be her," he said, low, almost a plea.

"Tell me you won't go so deep you can't find your way back."

The answer came to her, steady and unyielding.

She was already past the line.

She should lie.

She couldn't.

"You still want to know more," he said, certain.

She didn't answer.

His fingers brushed her wrist. Light. Intentional. A touch that said more than his voice ever had.

"Even after everything I told you, you're still here."

His breath touched her skin.

"Then maybe you were never as far from this world as you thought."

He turned and walked into the dark beyond the sarcophagus. No hesitation. His footsteps faded like a clock winding down.

Lena stood alone, the truth settling around her like dust. Quiet. Permanent.

She did not follow him because she was afraid. She followed because she wasn't.

Lucien stepped out of the crypt first, the stone door groaning shut behind him, as if time inside had moved differently, quicker, like the space itself refused to let go.

The autumn sky had already begun to dim, sunlight fading faster now, the treetops cast in dull gray. A wind cut through the cemetery like a silent warning, colder than before. He rolled his shoulders once, tension easing as he made his way toward the car.

And then, footsteps. Soft at first. Then certain.

Lucien went still. He knew before he even turned around.

Lena.

She stood at the entrance, hair tugged by the wind, her gaze unwavering.

She wasn't shaken. Wasn't afraid.

She had made her choice.

"I'm in," she said. "All the way."

Something in Lucien settled.

He opened the passenger door. "Get in, then."

The door closed with a sharp click.

Lucien tapped the wheel once as she settled.

"Not what you expected?"

She met his eyes. "I don't know what I expected."

He huffed a faint breath. "Good. That's how you survive."

Lena shook her head. "That's how you keep people from ever really knowing you."

Lucien tilted his head, studying her. She was bolder now.

His phone vibrated.

The smirk vanished.

He answered. "This better be good."

A voice crackled through the speaker. "We have a problem."

Lucien shifted in his seat. "Where?"

"Club downtown. You need to handle it."

"Who?"

A pause.

"Milo Corsini."

The shift in him was immediate. Lucien's posture sharpened. His breath steadied into something colder.

He ended the call.

He looked at her. A glint of dark amusement flickered beneath the harder look in his eyes.

"Guess you're getting a real introduction after all."

He glanced back at the crypt once, unreadable.

"This is the last time I ever come back here."

Whether he meant the crypt or the past, she didn't know.

He gunned the engine, and they shot forward toward whatever waited for him next.

Chapter Seventeen

THE FOOLISH PRINCE

Lucien turned onto the downtown strip, and the city shifted around them. Daylight was gone. Manhattan breathed a different kind of heat now, one made of neon glow and simmering tension. The streets pulsed under halogen haze, storefront lights flickering like a warning.

It felt less like Manhattan now and more like a city holding its breath.

The bass from the club hit before they reached the curb. It thumped against the pavement, steady and deep, like a heartbeat trapped under concrete.

Lucien stepped out of the car. Lena followed, the cold from StoneHaven still clinging to her skin.

The sign above the door glowed in polished gold.

VELOUR

Not a club. Not a bar. A territory.

And every person in line recognized him. They shifted without being told.

One of his men stepped forward from the entrance, suited, broad, eyes sharp.

"Boss. Milo and his people are in VIP."

Lucien's expression didn't change. "Uninvited."

"Correct. They're harassing the bottle girls. Running up tabs. Refusing to settle."

Lucien worked his jaw once, the motion saying more than anger ever could.

"I hate these little mafia pricks." He straightened his cuffs. "Let's go."

The music swallowed them the moment he opened the door.

Heat rushed out first, followed by perfume and bodies pressed into rhythm.

Lena followed him in, silent, taking it all in.

It wasn't just a club. It was a strip club.

Another truth of his world.

Lena blinked, momentarily thrown, then steadied herself.

This was curated chaos. Controlled indulgence.

And at the center of it all, Lucien.

He walked through the room as if it belonged to him. People shifted aside instinctively. Lena followed close, pulse threading with the music.

Upstairs, the energy twisted. Less party. More provocation.

Milo Corsini lounged on a leather couch, drink dangling from his fingers. His entourage was loud, sloppy, hands on dancers who kept professional smiles only because they had learned how to survive nights like this. The table was littered with broken glass and ash.

When Lucien stepped into the room, the noise flattened.

Milo smirked, tilting his head back with mock welcome. "Cole. Took you long enough."

Lucien's voice held no interest. "What the fuck are you doing here, Milo?"

Milo lifted his glass. "What, no hug? Thought you'd be flattered. I came by just to see you."

Lucien took in the state of the VIP section. The overturned bottle. The cracked glass. The fear behind the bottle girls' smiles.

"Your father must be disappointed."

Milo blinked. "Oh?"

"That he sent his son to play messenger instead of a man."

One of Milo's guys stiffened.

Milo laughed softly. "You talk a lot for someone operating in territory you don't own, refusing to cut percentages."

Lucien smirked. "You think I ask permission? I take what I want. If your father has a problem with that, he knows where to find me. Unless he's too old to handle his own business."

Milo's smile faded. The hit landed clean.

"Careful," Milo said. "Wouldn't want your world to collapse over poor decisions."

"The shame," Lucien replied, "is thinking you ever had a say in my world."

Milo's gaze drifted to Lena.

"Though I have to admit," he said, voice sharp, "you're slipping. Letting outsiders too close."

Lucien stilled.

Milo's smile widened. "Shame if this one breaks too."

He pointed at Lena with his glass, lazy as a man who had never been afraid a day in his life.

"Maybe this time you won't drive her to finish the job."

Lena didn't understand the whole wound, but she saw exactly where it landed.

Not on Lucien's pride.

Lower than that.

Somewhere old enough to bleed before he moved.

The bottle exploded before the final word left his mouth.

Glass tore across Milo's face in a spray of red. He jerked back, hands flying to his skin, screaming through blood and shock.

Lena flinched, not from the violence but from how effortlessly it fit him, like rage had always lived beneath his skin, waiting for an excuse.

And worse, something in her recognized it. The same part that had begun to crave the world he moved through, even when it terrified her.

His men scrambled up. One reached for the gun at his waist.

Lucien turned his head a fraction.

"Try it."

The man hesitated, grip tightening on the weapon.

No phones came out. No cameras. No one moved to stop him.

Just a held breath, and Lucien's eyes on him.

Not afraid. Not blinking. Like he already knew how this would end and was only waiting for the moment to prove it.

For the first time, doubt showed on the man's face.

His finger tightened. A tremor followed, the smallest betrayal of nerve.

And then one of Lucien's guards made the worst kind of mistake.

He lunged, locking the gunman in a chokehold without warning.

Reflex met panic.

The gun barked once.

A single shot.

Clean, brutal, decisive.

Then the club broke.

A scream tore from somewhere near the stage, high and raw.

Bodies slammed into bodies as the room lurched toward every exit at once. Perfume, sweat, and spilled liquor soured in the heat, the air thick with panic.

Dancers slid off their poles and vanished behind curtains, bare feet skidding across the glossy floor, stilettos clattering like panicked metronomes.

Someone crashed into the bar. Bottles burst against the wood, glass spraying wide.

A chair toppled. Someone went down hard.

Nobody looked back.

Nobody offered mercy.

They only looked for exits.

Milo stayed where he was, bent over himself, both hands clamped over his face like he could hold it together by force.

Blood tracked down his jaw in thick lines, warm and fast.

One eye was already swelling shut, closing by degrees.

He spat, and red streaked his teeth.

"Fucking psycho," he said, voice shredded by pain and pride.

Something shifted in Lucien's expression. Not anger. Something colder.

A hand landed on his shoulder, urgent.

"Cops are on the way."

He looked at Lena.

Her chest rose fast, not from panic, but from adrenaline finding a new home. Her eyes were wide, steady. Not fear. Not shock. She was seeing it clean, the line they'd stepped over, the door that only swung one direction.

Lucien had seen that look before. It belonged to people who understood the cost and stopped bargaining for a discount.

He turned back to Milo and moved toward him through the wreckage like the noise couldn't touch him. Calm. Measured. The kind of calm that made other men feel exposed.

He lowered himself, just enough, close enough that the words belonged only to Milo.

"You came in here like your last name still buys you air."

No heat in it. Just certainty.

"But power isn't inherited. It's proven."

Lucien caught Milo by the face and held him still. His grip wasn't rough. It was exact, like he'd found the hinge of a door.

His thumb drove straight into the split skin.

Milo's scream punched out of him, sharp and helpless, the sound of a man learning his body could be used against him.

"Next time," Lucien murmured, close enough that Milo could smell him, "send someone who matters."

He let the words sit there, heavy.

Then he leaned in a fraction more, the words landing like a private verdict, placed right on top of the pain.

"You were never going to be that guy."

He released Milo like he was nothing. Like he was already done.

Lucien turned his head and found Lena.

"Let's go."

She followed without a single hesitation. Bodies shifted aside as if clearing a path.

The doors shut behind them. The noise fell off in a clean drop.

Outside, the sidewalk was still spilling people into the night.

Cars pushed into traffic too fast, tires snapping over the pavement as drivers fled the story before it could stain them.

Clusters of people hovered under the streetlights, faces half-lit, voices low, shoulders pulled tight. They talked like a wrong sentence could drag them back inside. Others moved off quickly, heads down, throwing glances over their shoulders as if the night itself might reach out and grab them.

The air carried everything at once.

Spilled alcohol from the doorway. Heat from bodies. Sweat. That metallic edge adrenaline left behind.

Near the curb, a few stragglers stayed close to the doorway. Phones lit their cheeks, screens shaking in their hands. Recording. Replaying. Whispering to each other like they were passing contraband.

Lucien didn't acknowledge a single face.

He walked with the same even stride he had inside, jacket settled, shoulders level, the kind of composure that made the chaos feel like it had broken against him and slid away.

Lena kept close. She looked back once, only once, a quick check over her shoulder, the kind people do when they know the moment behind them is bigger than they can carry.

Then she slipped into the passenger seat, the click of the door sealing the world outside.

Lucien slid behind the wheel and started the engine. Streetlight bled across his face, then vanished as the car rolled forward.

Not rage. Not satisfaction.

Something colder.

Something inevitable.

For a moment, only the low rumble of the engine filled the car, the steady vibration under Lena's feet replacing the club's dead heartbeat.

Lena let out a slow breath. "Who the hell are the Corsinis?"

Lucien kept one hand loose on the wheel. "Old family."

"Old like... still dangerous?"

He took the next light without hurrying. "Old like the city used to lower its voice when they walked in."

She turned toward him, watching the neon slide over his cheekbone. "Used to?"

"They're living in a story that ended. The name still opens doors for them, but only because people remember the sound of it."

"And Milo?"

Traffic hissed past on wet pavement. Lucien's gaze stayed forward. "Milo's what's left when a bloodline forgets how to hunt."

Lena studied him in the dark glass and passing light. "So who hunts now?"

He glanced at her once, brief and sharp. "I do."

The city streamed around them in red lights and storefront glare.

"When you stop hunting," he said, "the world becomes someone else's."

Lena's voice dropped with the question. "Then whose world is it now?"

This time he didn't turn. "Mine."

Silence settled again, tighter now, stitched together by the motion of the car and the blur of Manhattan outside.

"You split his face with a bottle," Lena said. "What happens now?"

"Nothing."

Her head turned. "Nothing?"

"I let them keep their name. For tonight."

"Why?"

A siren wailed somewhere far off, thin against the glass. "Because they'll spend tomorrow repairing what he ruined. That's useful."

Lena narrowed her eyes. "Useful how?"

"They'll owe me air."

She gave him a look. "You call that pity?"

A faint glow from the dash lit one side of his mouth. "I call it control. They aren't a threat. They're noise. But noise can be pointed."

Lena nodded once, slow. "Wouldn't it be cleaner to end it?"

Lucien finally looked at her, long enough for the answer to land before the street took his face again. "Clean is for men who don't plan."

"And you do?"

"Always."

She watched his profile as buildings rose and vanished across the window, each flash of light cutting him into pieces and giving him back.

"So what's the plan?"

"Leverage."

"In what form?"

"A debt. A weakness. A name you can put on a table when everyone's pretending they don't have one."

The tires rolled through a shallow patch of water with a soft hiss.

"Sometimes you need a mouthpiece," he added. "Sometimes you need someone to blame who already comes with a file."

Lena kept her eyes on him. "Any tie you had with them is ash now."

His thumb traced once along the wheel. "No. It's a bruise. Bruises don't kill relationships. They remind people where the bone is."

She blinked, taking that in. "You think they'll come back after tonight?"

"I think Giancarlo will."

Her eyes lifted. "Giancarlo?"

"Milo's father."

Something in his voice reached further back now, not softer, just older.

"He and my father ran close, back when deals were done in rooms without cameras."

Lena said nothing, letting him go on while the city breathed around them.

"My father didn't build anything by being one thing," Lucien said. "He knew when to break someone, and when to let them think they walked away whole."

A red light washed through the windshield, then turned green.

"Giancarlo wasn't vicious," he added. "He wasn't brilliant. But when it mattered, he stood his ground. He didn't disappear."

"And that matters to you," Lena said.

"It matters. It just doesn't buy forgiveness."

She looked down for a second, then back at him. "So it was inheritance. Bloodline."

Lucien breathed out through his nose.

"We grew up around it. That's all. It didn't hand us power. It handed us a map."

His thumb moved once more against the leather.

"In a better world, we both would've inherited something worth the family myths. We didn't."

Lena's fingers curled in her lap.

"The difference," Lucien said, "is he accepted what he was given and called it a throne."

Outside, the city kept sliding by, endless and lit from within.

"I didn't," he said. "I built what wasn't there."

The next block passed in a wash of headlights and shadow.

"When my father stepped away," Lucien continued, "he left no crown. No safety. Just lessons."

His hand settled on the wheel, firm and final.

"And I paid for every one."

A few blocks later, red and blue washed across the rear window, bleeding forward in pulsing flashes.

Lucien's hands didn't move. His speed didn't change.

He guided the car to the curb with the patience of a man pulling into his own driveway.

No sudden brake. No panic.

Just a decision.

The patrol car settled behind them. Headlights flared across the dash, bleaching her knees.

Inside the cabin, everything shrank.

Lena's breath felt too loud.

The officer approached, flashlight sweeping once across Lena, across Lucien, across the console. He tapped the window.

Lucien lowered it.

"Mr. Cole."

"Evening."

"Mind stepping out?"

No argument. No stall.

Lucien unbuckled and opened the door.

Slow.

Measured.

Final.

He stepped out of the car, rising to his full height. The calm in him wasn't softness. It was threat held still.

The officer's balance shifted before he could stop it, a half-step back to make room for Lucien's presence.

Lucien didn't acknowledge it. He just closed the door with a quiet click and followed the officer toward the rear bumper.

Lena twisted in her seat, watching through the back window, reading the exchange by posture alone.

The officer spoke first.

"There was a disturbance at your property tonight. Shots fired. We need surveillance footage."

Lucien tipped his head. "You know the policy."

"The VIP room has no cameras?"

"Correct."

"Convenient."

Lucien's reply stayed soft.

"People don't pay for a room like that to be remembered."

"We can get a warrant."

Lucien stepped closer. Not crowding, just close enough to change the temperature of the air.

He said something low.

Lena watched the officer's spine go rigid. Watched his eyes drop, then slide past Lucien's shoulder like he suddenly remembered the kind of men who lived in this city.

Lucien added one more line, quiet and final.

Then he stepped back.

The officer swallowed. He nodded once, against his own will.

"We'll be in touch," he said, the words tasting wrong.

Lucien gave him a polite nod.

"Good night, officer."

The man walked back slower than he'd come.

Lucien returned to the driver's seat. Shut the door.

The sound landed with weight.

He shifted into drive and pulled away.

Lena studied him, her nerves still unsteady.

"You said almost nothing," she murmured. "And he let you go."

Lucien kept his eyes on the road.

"I said enough."

Her voice dipped. "What did you tell him?"

He let the question sit.

Then, with the faintest curve of his mouth, he answered.

"Men don't change their minds. They remember what they can't afford."

Career. Breath. Family. Pride.

He didn't name it.

He drove like the street was already cleared for him, the city unfolding in glass and shadow.

Lena exhaled, tension still held tight along her spine. Not fear. Something else. Her body had understood something her mind was still chasing.

The violence.

The order inside it.

The way he turned people into choices.

Lucien spoke first.

"We're staying at my place in the city tonight. I have a meeting in the morning."

Not an offer.

A decision.

"You have a place in the city?" she asked.

A flicker of amusement crossed his face.

"I have a place everywhere."

"Of course you do," she muttered, softer than she intended.

A moment passed. She tried to reach for something normal.

"While you're in your meeting, I might see if Jessica and Christina want coffee. It's been a while."

The words felt wrong in her mouth, like she was stepping into a life already slipping from her hands.

Lucien's tone didn't change, but the air did.

"Right now, you go nowhere without Michael."

She frowned. "Lucien, I don't need a bodyguard to get coffee."

"You do if you're with me."

She opened her mouth. He cut her off.

"And if you have forgotten what happened a week ago, I haven't."

The reminder tightened her throat.

Lucien dialed.

"Michael. Be at the penthouse in the morning. Escort Lena wherever she goes."

A pause.

"Stay close."

He ended the call.

Conversation closed.

Silence filled the car.

Lucien caught her watching him.

He lifted a brow. "What?"

She turned toward the window, but the corner of her mouth betrayed her.

"Something funny?" he asked, almost patient.

Lena exhaled and looked at him again, streetlight sliding over his jaw, his cheekbones, the part of him that never bent.

"I don't know if funny is the word. I think I'm still processing the fact that you can walk into a room, do almost nothing, and everyone changes shape around you."

Lucien's grip on the wheel shifted, small and unmistakable.

She didn't stop.

"And I hate that it did something to me."

His glance hit her like a challenge.

She held it.

"Watching you decide who walked out of that room was the sexiest thing I've seen in a long time."

He said nothing.

Then, finally, his voice, low enough to cut through thought:

"Show me."

Her pulse kicked. "What?"

His right hand left the wheel and found her thigh.

Heavy. Certain. Claim.

No hesitation.

No gentleness.

"Show me," he said, "how much you liked it."

His fingers traced the seam of her pants, unhurried, mapping her exactly.

She tensed. Thighs pressed together on reflex.

A soft click of his tongue. "Open."

She parted them. Just enough.

His palm settled over her through the fabric. Heat drove straight through.

He let out a low breath. "Jesus, Lena."

Her breath stuttered. Her head fell back against the seat.

He rubbed once, firm, unyielding. "You get off on me hurting people for you?"

No tease in it. Only question.

Her voice cracked. "Maybe."

He exhaled through his nose. "You're lying."

His fingers slid beneath the waistband. Knuckles grazed bare heat. His touch was steady, unhesitating.

He stroked her once, lazy, possessive, like territory he had already claimed.

She made a small sound before she could stop it.

He kept his eyes on the road.

"There's my good girl."

Her hips lifted toward his hand before she could stop them.

His voice dropped lower, calm as a blade drawn slow.

"Keep moving and I pull over. Bend you over the hood. Take you right there while the city watches. Your choice."

She went still. A shiver chased down her spine.

Lucien withdrew his hand and lifted his fingers to his mouth. He dragged her wetness across his lower lip, tasting her as he drove, his eyes never leaving the road.

"Behave," he said. "Or I edge you until you're shaking and leave you like that."

Silence pressed in. Thick. Charged.

Red light bathed the cabin.

Lucien turned his head, his gaze sliding over her and holding.

Streetlight split his face, half-lit, half-devil, all predator.

"Be careful what turns you on, Lena."

His voice was low, final.

"Some things don't let you come back from them."

She met his gaze. Chest rising and falling fast.
"Then I won't walk away."
Green.
He floored it.
The car surged forward.
Neon blurred past in wet streaks.
Every mile wound them tighter.
Thirty-three floors above the street, the penthouse waited.
Glass walls. Black sky.
A city stretched beneath it like something already surrendered.
No witnesses but the dark.
Her restraint would end in the elevator.
His control would end the moment the doors sealed.
For now, there was only the engine's low growl,
the unsteady sound of her swallowing,
and his hand at her throat when the city stopped them at a light,
his thumb pressing just hard enough to leave memory in its wake.
She smiled against his palm.
She was already gone.
And she was never coming back.

Chapter Eighteen

THE FUSE BETWEEN US

The elevator ride to the penthouse was silent. Not because there was nothing to say, but because the air was thick with everything left unsaid.

Lucien stood beside her, tension drawn tight through him, one pull from snapping. The instinct to reach for her rose and died before it could become a touch. He didn't look at her. He didn't have to. The urge to touch her was its own gravity.

Lena wasn't helping.

She leaned against the mirrored wall, lashes low, the faintest curve warming her mouth. A quiet dare. A taunt with a pulse.

And beneath the tease, there was something quieter in her eyes, something that made him want to look longer than he should.

She could still feel him on her, the ghost of his touch between her legs, the unbearable emptiness where his fingers had been before he pulled away, leaving her on edge just to watch her squirm.

Lucien exhaled once, slow, like he was holding the rest of himself back.

The elevator doors slid open.

Night spilled into the penthouse, deep and endless. Floor-to-ceiling windows cut the dark into glass shards of skyline, Manhattan glittering like a wound still healing.

The air carried the scent of aged whiskey and polished leather, threaded with something darker at the edges. Music drifted from hidden speakers, low and steady, already playing on the nightly timer.

Outside, wind brushed the glass. A helicopter circled somewhere over the city.

Lucien moved to the window, the city burning beneath him in a spread of color and noise. His reflection cut against the glass, broad shoulders, quiet breath, eyes burning low like banked coals. A man built from discipline, angles, and war.

He didn't drown in the night.

He measured it.

And right now he measured the one thing in the room he couldn't get a handle on.

Lena.

She wasn't a distraction. She was a problem he hadn't solved yet. A pressure point in his chest that refused to ease, no matter how tight he kept everything else under control. Two weeks, and she had already threaded herself into places he had kept locked down for years.

He didn't like it.

He wanted her anyway.

Worse, he wanted her in his space. In his silence. In the part of the night that had belonged to no one for a long time.

Want was easy. Taking was easier. But with her, it wasn't simple acquisition. It was something closer to hunger, the kind he had spent his entire life starving out.

He didn't understand it. Didn't try to. He wasn't the type to sit there and question impulse. He trusted his instincts, and every one of them had been dragging him toward her since the moment they met.

Across the room, she moved over the expensive floor, hair slipping over her shoulder, eyes catching the low light. Slow. Careful. Watching him like she knew exactly what she was doing to him.

He felt it.

All of it.

The heat.

The pull.

The part of him that wanted to pin her to the glass and ruin the distance between them once and for all.

His jaw tightened.

She wasn't a dream.

She wasn't a poem.

She wasn't something to cradle.

She was a fuse. Lit. Burning straight for him.

Every step she took was a dare.

Every look she gave was another spark waiting to catch.

Lucien didn't romanticize it.

He didn't soften it.

He didn't tell himself lies.

He wanted her stripped bare, voice breaking under his mouth, body giving him every answer he couldn't get with words.

And beneath that?

He wanted something he shouldn't.

Her choosing him.

Her staying.

That was the part that got under his skin.

Not taking her. Keeping her.

Waking up and finding she was still there.

Her not fucking running from the parts of him that should have sent her sprinting.

She stopped a few feet away.

The air tightened.

Her eyes met his, steady, unafraid.

That was what did it.

Not her lips.

Not her body.

Not the slow tease in her movements.

It was the look that said she knew exactly what kind of man he was, and she was still standing there.

Lucien inhaled once, slow, controlled, every muscle tightening.

Yeah.

He was already in too deep.

And he hated it.

And he wanted more.

Chapter Nineteen

NO REST BETWEEN US

Lucien's shirt dropped to the floor, revealing a body built by discipline and marked by old wars. He moved toward her slowly. He circled her once, fingers trailing the line of her spine, skimming the edge of her hip. Just enough to make her shiver.

"Look what you're making me do."

The words came out low. Not a threat. Not a confession. Something caught between the two.

Something he shouldn't have said out loud.

Velour still lived in the room with them. The shattered glass. Milo's blood. The way Lena had looked at him afterward, not horrified enough to run, not innocent enough to pretend she hadn't understood.

That was the part that had followed him into the elevator.

Not the violence.

Her seeing the order inside it.

She had watched him become the thing men feared, and instead of shrinking, something in her had opened. Lucien had felt it. Worse, he had wanted it.

They should have rattled her. Maybe once they would have. Now they just told the truth: she had gotten through him, and he hated how much he hadn't stopped her.

Lena inhaled, her chest rising, the fire in her eyes melting into something almost reverent.

Lucien's gaze dropped. Whatever control he had left snapped. He caught her by the hips, pulled her flush against him, and kissed her hard. It wasn't soft. It wasn't slow.

She answered like she had been waiting for it. Her hands slid down, found his belt, yanked it free in a single sharp pull. Leather hissed. The buckle hit the floor with a quiet clink.

He turned her toward the glass. City lights flared across the windows as he fisted her hair and pulled her head back just enough to bare her throat. He pressed her hands flat against the cool surface.

"Keep them there."

She obeyed, breath shaking, as he shoved her pants down and kicked them aside. His fingers slid into her from behind, steady and sure. He worked her until her hips jerked and a broken sound tore from her throat. Until she came hard against his hand, forehead pressed to the glass, legs trembling.

Before she could recover he turned her, lifted her, and carried her into the bedroom. He laid her on the bed, flipped her onto her stomach, and dragged her hips to the edge. When he pushed inside her she gasped at the sudden fullness. He gave her no time to adjust. He took her with long, controlled strokes, one hand planted between her shoulder blades, the other locked on her hip.

"You wanted to see what I become when I stop behaving," he said against her ear, voice rough.

She pushed back to meet him, showing him she could take what he was giving. That she wanted it.

His rhythm faltered once, then again. The tremor in his arms told her everything his silence wouldn't. He was right there on the edge with her, fighting it and losing.

When she came again, clenching tight around him, he followed with a low, ragged sound he did not try to swallow. He held himself deep as he spilled inside her, hips jerking helplessly against her.

For a long moment he stayed there, chest pressed to her back, breathing hard against her neck.

Then he pulled out, turned her over, and gathered her against him. He rolled them onto their sides, one arm locked around her waist as if the rest of the world might try to steal her while he slept. His hand moved slowly through her hair, the gentleness startling after everything that had come before.

The truth lived in the way he wrapped around her like a shield he had never offered anyone else.

His hand moved once to her ribs, careful over the places still healing from the hit. The gentleness startled her more than the violence had. He did not ask if it hurt. He already knew.

For a second, his mouth pressed to the fading bruise beneath her collarbone, not hungry now, not claiming. Just there.

Lena closed her eyes.

That was the part that scared her. Not what he took. What he noticed.

She knew she should be scared, of how fast this was happening, of how easily she was letting him in.

But fear never came.

Only want.

Want for him. For this. For whatever ruinous thing this was becoming.

Caught between heaven and hell, she did not feel lost. She felt found.

Wanted, for the first time, for every broken and burning piece of her, not just the parts she showed the world.

And some fucked-up, honest corner of her soul did not want to come back down.

Lena's eyes fluttered closed, pulse soft against his chest.

Outside, the city blurred into a smear of lights.

Lucien didn't sleep.

He stared at the ceiling, one hand still anchored on her hip.

He had let something in tonight.

He didn't name it.

He didn't dare.

But the fault line was already forming beneath his ribs.

And the night knew it before he did.

Sunlight arrived like an uninvited guest, soft and golden through the sheer curtains.

Lucien woke first, the way he always did, instincts primed even in a room that should have felt safe.

The only danger was the woman curled against his chest, her leg draped over his like she'd claimed him in her sleep.

He lay still for a moment, studying her. The quiet weight of her against him. The way she fit there without permission.

Eventually he slipped out of bed, pulled on sweatpants, and reached for the pistol on the nightstand. Not because he expected trouble. Because men like him didn't get to expect peace.

He went to the kitchen. Soon the penthouse smelled like coffee, dark and strong, cutting through the last traces of sleep.

Lena appeared a few minutes later, swallowed by one of his shirts, hair tousled, eyes still carrying the shadow of last night.

He handed her a mug. She took it with both hands, inhaled, then looked at him over the rim.

The mug was warm enough to sting her palms. She looked down into the dark coffee, then around the kitchen, all black stone, sharp lines, and impossible quiet.

"Do you actually use this place," she asked, "or does the coffee make itself out of fear?"

Lucien looked at her over his mug. For half a second, something almost human moved through his face.

"Fear helps."

A laugh slipped out of her before she could stop it. Small. Rough. Real.

The sound changed the room.

Lucien watched her like he had heard something rare and was deciding whether to keep it alive.

"You look like a man who survived a war," she said.

"I did." His voice was rough. "And I'd do it again if it ends with you here."

He stepped closer and kissed her, slow, unhurried, tasting heat and coffee and the kind of pull he should not have felt.

When he pulled back, his hand stayed at her waist, thumb tracing once along her skin. Not a promise. Just a reminder.

She leaned in, a small spark in her eyes.

"Last night... I'm still feeling it," she whispered, tone low, genuine, nothing cute about it.

Lucien's mouth curved slightly.

"Good."

She breathed out, soft, almost careful.

"I need to clean up."

He watched her.

"Join me?"

His brow lifted, a slow, wicked smirk.

"Dangerous offer."

He stepped closer.

"I accept."

He took her hand and led her into the master bathroom.

The shower stretched wide in dark-veined stone, steam curling along the glass, a bench built into the far end. It was sleek. Controlled. Like him.

Lena stepped back, untucked the towel, and let it fall. Water poured from the rainfall head in a steady, relentless rain.

Lucien watched her the way a man watches something he has already decided belongs to him.

He followed her in and sat on the marble bench, water cascading over his shoulders.

She dropped to her knees between his thighs, eyes locked on his through the steam. This wasn't submission. It was trust, quiet and dangerous in a way neither of them named.

"My turn."

Her hands slid up his thighs. She took him in slowly, every movement deliberate, water pouring over them both. Every stroke was for him. To unravel the man who made the city lower its voice.

Lucien's fingers threaded into her wet hair, anchoring her.

She looked up at him the entire time, lashes wet, eyes glassy and unafraid. When he came his hips flexed hard, a raw sound echoing off the stone as he spilled hot across her tongue. She stayed with him, swallowing what he gave her.

She rose, straddled his lap, and pressed herself against his chest. Water streamed down their bodies.

"Consider us even." Her lips brushed his. "For now."

Lucien wrapped his arms around her waist and held her there, memorizing the exact weight of her against him, wet and flushed.

When they finally stepped out, the cool air met their damp skin and pulled them back into the real world.

He wrapped her in a towel with slow, controlled hands, as if the act itself were a privilege few men would ever earn again.

Then his phone buzzed, loud and harsh, the world demanding its due.

He glanced at the screen, and the softness left him. Something colder settled in its place.

"Michael will be outside in a few minutes."

Still, he turned back to her, voice quieter now. "Get dressed."

He kissed her, slow and possessive, like he didn't know when he'd get to do it again.

He dressed in silence, layering himself back into tailored armor, but his eyes never left her.

When the elevator arrived, he pulled her in without warning and kissed her hard.

It wasn't goodbye.

Even in heels she had to reach, one hand in his hair as his grip locked around her waist.

"Go," he said against her mouth. "Before I fuck you right here."

She smirked, legs unsteady.

The doors closed, and the world took him back.

But as the elevator descended, she felt him everywhere.

The ghost of his mouth. The weight of him. The ache between her thighs.

The lobby greeted her in hushed marble and polished stone. She walked through it carrying the quiet triumph of knowing she could make a king tremble.

The glass doors parted.

The morning swallowed her whole.

Chapter Twenty

THE CALM BEFORE IT ALL
WENT DARK

The black SUV waited at the curb, silent and still.

As soon as Lena spotted it, Michael stepped out, face unreadable behind dark sunglasses. He rounded the SUV and opened the back door.

"Good morning, Lena."

Lena offered a small smile. "Morning, Michael."

She slipped into the backseat, the scent of polished leather and faint traces of Lucien clinging to the interior.

Michael shut the door behind her and slid into the driver's seat. "Where are we headed today?"

Lena pulled her phone from her bag, tapping quickly into the group chat with Christina and Jessica.

Can't wait to see you both. Be there in a few!

She glanced up as Michael adjusted the rearview mirror, waiting for her response.

"L'Appartement," she said, naming the intimate little café tucked between luxury storefronts and old brownstones.

"Just meeting some friends for coffee."

Michael gave a nod. "Got it."

The SUV pulled away smoothly, gliding into the steady flow of Manhattan traffic.

Lena leaned back against the seat, staring out at the blur of morning commuters, the rhythmic chaos of the city.

"You know," Michael said, "I've worked for Lucien a long time. I've seen him with a lot of people. None of them got rides to coffee with security."

Lena smirked, tilting her head toward him. "Is that your way of saying

I'm special?"

Michael gave the faintest breath of amusement. "It's my way of saying be smart."

Lena sighed, crossing her legs. "It's coffee, Michael. Not a drug deal."

He glanced at her, calm but direct. "Doesn't matter. Trouble doesn't always announce itself."

A flicker of unease rushed through her, sharp and sudden.

Michael glanced at her in the mirror, unreadable. "Just saying. Always be aware."

He paused, then added, "I'll be right outside."

The weight of his words settled uncomfortably in her chest.

Before she could respond, the SUV pulled up in front of L'Appartement. She stepped out, the door closing behind her.

Two familiar voices hit her at once.

"Well, well, well. Look at you, stepping out of black SUVs now."

Lena turned, a smirk tugging at her lips. Christina and Jessica stood near the entrance, arms crossed, eyes bright.

Christina reached for her hand. "How've you been, babe? You know... since the accident."

Lena opened her mouth, but the memory hit first. Running. Headlights. Glass. Then cold, blinding hospital light.

She blinked. "I'm good."

The silence held for a moment, then Christina forced it open.

Jessica smiled. "You look good. More than good."

"Yeah," Christina said, eyes narrowing slightly. "You're glowing."

"Miss Hart, your limo awaits," she added, a teasing edge in her voice.

Lena rolled her eyes and moved toward them. "Shut up."

Jessica leaned in, voice dropping. "Hi, Michael. You remember us, don't you?"

Michael nodded. "Of course. Hard night to forget."

A shadow flickered across Lena's expression, the memory of Enigma and the man who grabbed her flashing through her mind.

Jessica looped her arm through Lena's, pulling her inside. "Come on, rich girl. Coffee. Then you're telling us everything."

The café was warm and inviting, the scent of fresh espresso curling through the air. Sunlight streamed through tall windows, spilling over vintage tables and deep leather booths.

They settled into a corner booth, ordering lattes before Christina leaned forward, elbows on the table.

"Okay. Spill. What's it like?"

Lena raised a brow. "What's what like?"

Jessica scoffed. "Being with Lucien Cole."

Lena hesitated, stirring her drink. How could she even begin to explain it?

How it felt like drowning and breathing at the same time. Like being owned and worshipped all at once. Like standing at the edge of something thrilling, terrifying, inescapable.

"It's… different," she said finally.

Christina snorted. "Different? Bitch, different is a new restaurant opening on Fifth Avenue. Lucien Cole is on another level."

Jessica grinned. "Admit it. He's the best sex you've ever had."

Lena smirked behind her cup. "No comment."

Jessica groaned. "That's a yes."

Their laughter melted into the morning bustle, the clinking of cups, the quiet hum of conversation. For the first time in a while, Lena felt normal.

Then her phone buzzed.

She glanced down at the screen.

A message. Unknown Number.

Her fingers went numb around the phone.

Slowly, she swiped it open.

That coffee shop on 7th is my favorite

Lena went still.

The noise of the café dulled, the voices around her turning to static.

She gripped her phone, a hard thrum rising in her chest as her eyes darted toward the front windows. Outside, the city moved like it always did, people passing, cars idling, baristas rushing between deliveries. Normal.

Her gaze flicked across the café, scanning faces, corners, reflections in the glass.

Someone was watching her.

"Lena?"

Jessica's voice pulled her back. Both girls were staring now, brows pinched with concern.

"What's going on?" Christina asked.

"We said your name three times."

Christina forced a half laugh. "You looked possessed."

Lena swallowed, fingers tightening around her phone. Her instincts screamed at her to get up and leave, but she forced a breath.

"It's probably nothing."

Jessica leaned forward. "Bullshit. Spill."

Lena pressed her palms against the table, trying to ground herself. Maybe saying it out loud would make it sound less insane.

"Okay. The night of Lucien's sister's birthday, something weird happened."

Jessica and Christina exchanged glances before looking back at her.

"Weird how?" Christina asked.

Lena licked her lips, lowered her voice. "Someone was watching me that night. I got a text, an unknown number. It told me I didn't belong there. Then another, saying I needed to leave."

She swallowed hard, the memory pressing in like a weight on her chest.

"And then another, saying they were watching me."

She paused. Her voice dropped even lower.

"And then the accident... wasn't an accident."

Jessica's eyes widened. "Wait. All those texts came while you were still in the club?"

Lena nodded. "Yeah. They knew my every move, like they were just waiting to see what I'd do next."

Christina's expression darkened. "Jesus, Lena. That's not just weird. That's creepy."

Jessica leaned in, her voice hushed. "Did you see anyone? Anyone looking at you weird?"

Lena exhaled, shaking her head. "No. But I felt it. Like eyes on me the whole night."

A chill went through her just thinking about it.

"Lucien has his people trying to get to the bottom of it." Lena hesitated, glancing down at her phone, her pulse spiking. "But I just got another text. Right now."

Jessica's face drained of color. "Wait. Just now? While we've been sitting here?"

Lena turned her phone toward them.

The message burned on the screen.

That coffee shop on 7th is my favorite

Christina's mouth parted slightly. "Lena. Whoever this is, they're here."

Lena didn't breathe. She barely felt her fingers.

Jessica leaned forward; her voice hushed. "Okay, maybe it's some weird joke..."

Another buzz.

Lena's pulse kicked hard under her jaw.

Don't think of running out to the driver

A sharp, electric panic shot through her limbs.

She snapped her head toward the window again, scanning the street, the people, but everyone looked normal.

Her body locked. Jessica and Christina were speaking, but their voices came through wrong, muffled beneath the rush in her ears.

She needed to move. Now.

She shot up from the table, chair scraping loudly against the floor. "I have to get out of here."

Jessica and Christina jolted, eyes wide with alarm.

"Lena, Lena! Stop, think!" Jessica reached for her wrist, but Lena was already stepping back. "Maybe you should just stay here. Call Lucien!"

"You're right," Lena said.

Lena fumbled with her phone, hands shaking as she pulled up his number. She pressed the call button. One ring. Two. Three. Four.

Voicemail.

Fuck.

She tried again. Nothing.

Her chest tightened, panic creeping into her bones.

"He's not answering."

"He's in a meeting." Her voice cracked. "Fuck."

She squeezed her eyes shut, gripping her phone so tight it could crack.

"Lena, calm down," Christina urged, her voice gentler but firm. "You're safe in here. Just wait for him to call back."

"No," Jessica cut in, shaking her head. "Go to Michael, that's his job, right? To protect you? Screw whoever is texting you, just go!"

Lena swallowed hard. She looked at her phone, then at the café entrance.

Her gaze drifted to them both, heart aching. She just wanted a normal morning with her friends.

"I'm so sorry, girls."

Christina started to stand. Jessica grabbed her bag, already moving.

"Stay inside," Lena said, sharper than she meant to. "Please."

Lena shot toward the exit, forcing herself to walk fast, to keep it controlled. *Don't panic. Not yet.*

Her phone dinged, sharp, urgent.

She didn't even look. Just tightened her grip and kept moving.

Michael had moved the SUV down the block after dropping her off, tucked past the café windows where traffic could still breathe. Lena cut through the sidewalk crowd toward it, idling at the curb, windows blacked out.

She lifted a hand to wave, expecting the driver's door to pop open. Nothing.

Her pace quickened. Maybe he hadn't seen her, the tint made the cabin a mirror.

"Why isn't he getting out?" she muttered.

She tried the passenger handle, locked. The engine's low vibration thrummed under her palm.

She rapped the glass. "Michael?"

Silence.

Her skin crawled. She thumbed his contact and hit Call.

From inside the SUV, a muffled ringtone chimed. Once. Twice. Three times.

No movement. No answer.

She pressed her face closer to the glass, but the tint gave her only her own reflection. The engine was running. The doors were locked. Michael's phone was inside.

And Michael wasn't answering.

Something was wrong.

She turned in a tight circle, scanning the street, faces, doorways, reflections, heart knocking against her ribs.

Her phone dinged a third time. She looked down.

1. **Don't walk out of the café**

2. **I told you not to go to the driver**

3. **If you head back in there now, your friends die**

A slow, icy dread crept up her spine. "No, no, no."

Lena's hands trembled as she stared at the screen, her mind racing. What the hell was she supposed to do?

She typed back with shaky fingers.

Just leave me the fuck alone!!!

She hit send.

The bubble hung, then turned red.

Failed to send

Her chest seized. She couldn't reply.

Tears stung at the corners of her eyes. This wasn't just a game anymore.

She clenched her phone, teeth grinding, and before she could stop herself, she screamed into the street.

"What the fuck do you want from me?!"

Heads turned. A few pedestrians stopped, wide-eyed. A woman gripping a stroller took a cautious step aside.

Her phone dinged again.

Everything you have

Lena gasped. She ran.

The phone buzzed in her hand.

She nearly dropped it before seeing Lucien's name flash across the screen.

She answered instantly, her voice shaking. "Lucien, oh my god, it's happening again. I don't know where Michael is. He's not in the truck."

Lucien's voice sharpened; all trace of playfulness gone. "What do you mean 'it's happening again'? Where's Michael? What the fuck is going on?"

Lena's breathing turned sharp and uneven.

"The texts, Lucien. Whoever that was, they're here. Somewhere in these streets, watching me. They're after me."

Lucien didn't hesitate. "Put on your location services immediately, and tell me exactly where you are."

She moved past the café's awning, past the neighboring flower shop, barely aware of where her feet were taking her.

Her phone was pressed to her ear, her heart hammering against her ribs. "I'm, I'm still on Seventh, right outside Eden's Bloom Flower Shop. I don't know what to do."

Paranoia clung to her, thick and suffocating. Every glance, every shifting shadow, every flicker of motion felt like it had eyes.

"Make a scene, get eyes on you, and stay right where you are," Lucien ordered. "I'm sending men now."

A hard shoulder clipped her.

Lena stumbled, her phone nearly slipping from her grasp. "Shit."

A man. Mid-thirties. Bearded. Moving too fast, not making eye contact. He muttered a rushed "Sorry" as he passed.

Behind him, a white utility van with a municipal-looking seal screeched into a double-park. Two men in maintenance uniforms spilled out, clipboards in hand, city badges clipped to their vests, tools jangling from their belts. One of them carried a red responder bag slung over his shoulder. They looked like utility or security detail, the kind that made New Yorkers glance once and then look away.

She barely registered them. Until she felt it.

The presence behind her.

A hand shot out, gripping her arm.

Before she could turn, a second arm coiled around her waist, lifting her off the ground.

A gloved hand clamped over her mouth, muffling the scream that ripped from her throat.

"Medical," one of them barked, flashing a laminated badge. "Back up."

Her phone tumbled from her grasp, clattering onto the pavement.

Lucien's voice still crackled from the speaker. "Lena? Lena!"

People glanced over. A woman hesitated, frowning.

But what she saw was two uniformed men hauling a struggling girl toward a marked van. It looked like security. Or medics.

Someone overdosed. Someone drunk. Someone dangerous.

She told herself it wasn't her problem and kept walking.

Everyone did.

No hesitation. No fear of cameras or witnesses. Whoever sent them knew no one would intervene.

The van door was already open.

It happened in seconds. A second man grabbed her legs, shoving her inside with military-like precision.

She fought, thrashing, kicking, biting, but the grip was ironclad.

A sharp, acrid scent hit her nose.

A cloth pressed against her face.

Lena jerked, twisting, but the more she fought, the weaker she felt. Her limbs turned sluggish, her eyelids impossibly heavy.

The world blurred.

The last thing she saw before her vision tunneled was her phone lying face-up on the street, just shy of the curb, Lucien's name still glowing on the screen before the van door slammed shut.

Darkness swallowed her whole.

Chapter Twenty-One

AND THEN CAME THE DARK

Time fractured.

Lena drifted in and out of consciousness, never fully waking, never fully gone. Darkness pulled her under in waves, each one deeper than the last, and every time she sank, some part of her begged not to surface again.

Then reality slammed back in.

Everything hurt.

Not in one place. Everywhere. A total, blinding ache that made her body feel less like hers and more like something dragged back from a place it should not have survived.

Her wrists burned first, raw and wet against metal cuffs. Her ankles followed, bound wide, straining painfully until every small movement sent fire through her legs.

She was naked, fully exposed, her skin slick with sweat and goosebumps beneath the sterile air. Electrodes clung to her flesh. Her pulse hammered beneath them, frantic and useless, like her body was trying to warn her about something that had already happened.

A rough burlap hood smothered her vision, scratching her face with every inhale. The air inside it was hot, stale, and wrong. She couldn't see. Could barely draw breath.

But she could hear.

Somewhere beyond the hood, beyond the chair, beyond the dark she was trapped inside, a man sobbed.

Not crying. Not pleading. Sobbing in a way that sounded torn out of him, animal and broken, like agony had stripped him of everything human and left only the part that knew how to beg.

Lena froze.

Every nerve coiled.

Every breath held.

Then a mechanical wail shattered the quiet.

A chainsaw.

The shriek of metal biting air, blade spinning into a violent, manic scream. It roared forward, eating the distance between itself and the man's broken howls.

His scream rose, desperate, primal, then splintered, drowned beneath tearing flesh and cracking bone. He gurgled wetly, choking on blood, until even that fell away into thick silence.

Every muscle in Lena's body locked tight.

It wasn't torture.

It was theater.

A message.

And she understood with a cold, sinking certainty that they had waited for her to wake before letting her hear it.

Footsteps echoed closer, steady, heavy, almost calm. A voice followed, sliding through the air like smoke.

"You awake yet, sweetheart?"

She didn't answer. Didn't move. Didn't breathe.

He chuckled softly, fingers gripping her jaw through the hood. Hard enough to bruise.

"Oh, I think you are."

CRACK.

His backhand split across her face, white pain bursting through her cheek as blood pooled under her tongue.

Lena spat it out.

Calm.

Cold.

"Rise and shine," he said, leaning close enough for his lips to brush the burlap over her ear. "Here's the deal. You give us Lucien's shipment locations. Private docks. Clubs. Warehouses. Anything not on paper. Then we skip the worst parts."

Lena's mind went blank for half a second.

Shipment locations. Private docks. Warehouses.

She didn't know any of it.

She knew the weight of Lucien's hand. The sound of his voice. The shape of his world when it closed around her.

But not this.

Not the machinery beneath him.

Her voice came out steady.

"Fuck you."

A silence followed.

Then laughter.

Low. Amused. Rotten.

"Oh, that's cute. You think this is defiance?"

Fingers moved down her throat, tracing her collarbone before lingering at the electrodes fixed over her ribs.

"You have beautiful skin, Lena. Smooth. Pure."

His touch was clinical. Proprietary.

"But pure things don't last long around here."

A snap of fingers.

Electricity ripped through the pads.

Her muscles seized instantly, body arching against the restraints as agony burned through every nerve. Her jaw locked. Her lungs forgot how to work.

But she refused to scream.

When the current stopped, she slumped forward, panting.

"Now let's try again," he said. "The locations."

Her answer was silence.

He sighed. "Bring the collar."

Cold metal closed around her throat with a decisive click.

Thick. Heavy. A collar meant for ownership. A leash dangled down her chest, another calculated humiliation.

Lena went very still.

The older man took the chain between two gloved fingers and gave it a slight tug, lifting her chin.

"You feel that?" he asked softly. "That's the part of you he won't be able to save."

Lena stared into the dark beneath the hood.

"You'll die trying."

His silence changed.

Not anger.

Interest.

The hood was ripped away in one brutal jerk, the burlap scraping her skin raw as the overhead light slammed into her eyes.

When the white haze faded, the room snapped into focus.

A steel table waited beneath the single hanging bulb.

On it lay what was left of a man.

Not whole. Not recognizable. Reduced to a warning in human form.

Blood had poured off the table in heavy sheets, spreading across the concrete in a dark, shining lake. A rough pine crate sat on the floor nearby, nailed shut, dark liquid seeping from the seams.

Lena's stomach turned.

The man with the older voice leaned in, breath rasping through the filters of his matte black mask. Opaque goggles hid his eyes, but the tilt of his head carried something almost tender.

"See him?"

His voice came muffled. Distorted. Colder for how steady it stayed.

"He screamed. He begged. Told us everything he knew."

Lena lifted her gaze, eyes cold.

"Did it save him?"

The man smiled.

"No," he said softly. "But he wasn't special like you."

The room held its breath.

He gave the leash another slight pull.

"You," he said gently, almost lovingly, "I'm going to enjoy breaking very, very slowly."

Lena stared back.

"You'll die trying," she said again.

This time, his smile widened.

"Good," he whispered. "I love a challenge."

From the far wall, another voice called out. "What now?"

The older man tilted his head.

"Bring the chainsaw."

Lena's heart kicked once, hard.

The chainsaw roared to life, hungry and violent, its scream bouncing off the concrete. Blood still glistened on the teeth. It moved closer, heat spinning off the blade, rattling her cuffs.

She stayed perfectly still.

Eyes cold.

Pulse steady.

The man in the mask hovered the blade near her feet.

"Fingers first?" he shouted over the roar. "Or toes?"

"She isn't going anywhere," the older man said. "Surprise her."

The blade dipped closer.

Then the engine sputtered.

Coughed.

Died.

Silence fell like a dropped weight.

The younger man smacked the casing. "What the fuck?"

"It was fine two minutes ago," another muttered.

"Check the cord," the leader snapped.

"It's gas-powered."

"Then check the fuel."

Voices rose, uncertain now.

The only steady sound in the room was Lena's breathing.

She didn't move.

Didn't speak.

Across the concrete, the older man caught the flicker.

A smile.

Small. Calm. Unbothered.

Like she was the one holding the blade.

He stepped toward her, boots heavy on the floor.

"You think something is funny?"

Lena didn't answer.

He crouched in front of her, reached down, and with a flick of a key from his belt, unlatched the shackles around her ankles.

Metal clanked against the floor.

"You think this is a game?"

But the second the last shackle hit the ground, Lena moved.

She surged upward, shoulders low, legs coiled like a spring. Pain lit every nerve, but instinct burned hotter. She drove forward in a single vicious burst.

Two steps.

Almost three.

Clink.

The collar.

A brutal jerk yanked her backward, snapping her to a stop as the leash pulled tight.

Her head whipped back with it.

The man still had the chain.

"Where the fuck do you think you're going?"

He yanked again, dragging her off balance. Her feet scraped the concrete. She crashed back into him, chest heaving, pain flashing through her neck as his grip tightened.

He wrapped the chain twice around his hand and pulled her close, his face just behind hers.

Without warning, he spun her around and drove his fist into her mouth.

Lena's head snapped sideways. Blood sprayed across the concrete as her lip split wide.

But she didn't cry out.

Didn't fall.

She just went still.

"You run from me again," he whispered, "and I'll drag you by this fucking collar until your knees are nothing but bone."

Lena stared forward, teeth bared, blood staining them.

His hand slid up from the chain, slow and possessive, resting beneath her jaw.

"You're not in control."

But even then, even now, she didn't look away.

The older man exhaled through the mask, then tilted his head toward the far wall.

"You. Bring her up."

The tallest man in the room stepped forward. Quiet. Built like concrete. His mask showed nothing. His movements showed everything.

Too practiced.

Too precise.

Too lethal to mistake.

He came up behind her. Massive arms slid under her armpits, then locked behind her neck.

Her feet left the floor.

The chain at her throat rattled.

He hoisted her higher, suspending her in open air, arms trapped tight, spine drawn long under the strain.

"Hold her steady," the older man said.

The big man grunted.

The older man stepped in close, face inches from hers.

"Last time," he said. "Tell me what he let slip. Shipments. Clubs. Docks. Names. Anything not on the books."

Lena said nothing.

Blood trickled from her split lip.

Then, with perfect calm, she leaned forward and spat in his face.

The room went still.

The man didn't wipe it off.

The smear of blood slid down his mask.

Then he moved.

Not fast.

Not sloppy.

With the calm certainty of a man who had done this a thousand times.

He drove a fist into her stomach.

The impact stole the room from her.

Air blasted out of her lungs in a silent choke, her body folding in the big man's grip as white sparks burst behind her eyes. For one terrible second, breathing became something she remembered but could not reach.

The older man tilted his head.

"There it is."

Lena forced herself upright again, trembling, vision swimming.

Still, she didn't look away.

He leaned in slightly. "Spit on me again and I'll shut your lungs off for real."

She said nothing.

Just stared back at him.

Cold.

Steady.

He exhaled, disappointed, and nodded once.

"Bring her."

They moved quickly now.

Lena was dropped onto a second steel table, spine striking metal hard enough to flash pain through her skull. One man yanked the chain behind her neck until her head locked against the surface. Others pinned her arms. Her legs. Her body.

Exposed.

Held.

Burning with blood and humiliation.

The older man stepped forward, right between her legs, and met her eyes.

"You're going to tell us," he said calmly, "anything he told you. Anything you heard."

Stillness.

Then Lena's voice, hoarse and controlled.

"I have no fucking idea."

A man laughed from somewhere near her shoulder.

"Ahhh, she speaks."

The older man reached for his waistband, eyes still locked on hers.

That was when Lena screamed.

A raw, wild sound.

Her body snapped into motion.

Her right leg tore free just enough to swing. Her heel connected square with the center of his mask.

The impact cracked through the room.

He stumbled back with a shout, blood leaking beneath the mask as he crashed into the table behind him.

The others froze for one beat.

Just long enough.

Lena wrenched an arm loose, twisted beneath the hands still gripping her, and rolled off the table in a savage blur.

She hit the floor running.

Bare feet slapped concrete. Adrenaline burned cold through her blood. She made it halfway across the room before arms wrapped around her waist and lifted her off the ground.

She kicked.

Clawed.

Fought like something feral.

"Get the fuck off me!"

They didn't answer.

They hauled her backward like cargo and slammed her into the same cold metal chair.

A hand clamped over her mouth.

A cloth pressed hard.

Sharp chemical darkness filled her lungs again.

The room smeared.

Sound stretched.

The last thing she heard was the older man breathing through the mask, close enough to make the words feel like they were already inside her head.

"Now we find out what Lucien Cole really loves."

Then the darkness took her again.

Time passed.

She didn't know how long.

Minutes. Hours. Days.

It stretched, broke, and bled into nothing.

When her eyes opened again, she thought she was dead.

The lights were too bright. Sterile. Silent.

Like a morgue.

Then pain returned, and with it, the truth.

She was still here.

Her body ached, violated without explanation. Blood streaked her thighs, dried and dark. Her mouth was split open, throbbing and raw.

She was face-down now, arms shackled above her head. Still naked. Restrained again. Every inch of her skin felt foreign. Disconnected. Bruised. Her body shook without permission.

A tripod-mounted camera faced her, unblinking.

Red light burning.

Recording.

The lens stared back at her like an eye that had seen too much and planned to see more.

The room was quiet now.

Too quiet.

Then came the sound of boots.

Slow. Unhurried.

The door creaked open and slammed shut behind him.

The older man returned.

Alone.

She didn't lift her head.

Not for him.

He said nothing at first. He only circled her, slow and patient, like she was something left out for inspection.

Then he leaned in.

"You think you're still holding out," he said softly. "But you're just bleeding slower than the rest."

He reached up and unshackled her wrists.

Lena rolled off the table like dead weight, collapsing onto the floor, limp, shivering, too weak to stand.

He grabbed her by the hair and dragged her.

No ceremony now.

No audience.

Just punishment.

He tossed her into a nearby chair and strapped her arms down again, tight. The chain at her throat rattled with every breath.

The door creaked open again.

One by one, the other men stepped back into the room. Silent. Watching. Some leaned against the walls. One lifted his mask just enough to light a cigarette, his face lost to shadow, the ember glowing like an eye in the dark. Another tapped a baton against his leg, slow and rhythmic.

They didn't speak.

They were here to see her break.

Then he reached for something.

A firearm.

Heavy. Cold. Familiar.

He stepped forward, grip firm, gaze unreadable.

Then he held it up to her.

"Let's try this differently."

Her pulse pounded, fear and defiance burning through whatever was left of her.

"Would you die for him?"

Before she could move, cold steel pressed against her lips.

The barrel.

Her jaw went rigid.

Something primal surged inside her.

"You think he's looking for you right now?"

His tone curled with mockery, but underneath it, something darker simmered.

"Or do you think he's already replaced you?"

Lena's hands curled into fists, nails driving into her palms.

Her eyes burned.

But she didn't flinch.

"You think he'll burn the city down for you?"

He tilted the gun slightly, forcing her chin higher.

"Or cut his losses, like the rest of them?"

Her heart thundered.

Still.

The room seemed to wait for her answer.

He smiled.

Slow.

Sadistic.

"So now tell me, Lena, where is the next fucking shipment coming in?"

The barrel pressed harder.

Heavier.

Waiting.

She forced herself to breathe.

To steady the riot inside her chest.

To reach for whatever pieces of herself were not yet broken.

The man stepped closer. His voice dropped to a whisper.

"You're going to tell me in,"

Lena closed her eyes.

"Five."

The boutique. New fabric. Laughter. Ordinary things, already gone.

"Four."

Christina. Jessica. The girl she used to be.

"Three."

Lucien. His hands. His voice. The way he made her feel untouchable.

"Two."

She didn't want to die.

Not here.

Not like this.

She hated herself for wanting to live badly enough to invent something for them.

Hated that survival could make betrayal out of nothing when a gun was pressed to your mouth.

"One."

A tear slipped free.

Her lips parted, breath shaking.

She was about to lie.

The world answered.

Boom.

Boom.

CRACK.

The door exploded off its hinges in a blast of splintered steel and searing light.

A flashbang ripped through the dark, white lightning tearing the room open.

This wasn't an entrance.

It was a sentence.

A death knell.

Lena's eyes snapped open, a gasp catching in her throat as every man in the room turned, guns raised, panic unraveling beneath their twitching hands.

The smoke parted like a curtain before a final act.

And through it, he stepped in.

Lucien.

No vest. No helmet. Just a black shirt soaked in rain and war.

Backlit by chaos. Eyes like razors.

He didn't shout. He didn't run.

He just stepped forward, and with a single glance, the whole room forgot how to breathe.

Lena trembled in the chair.

Not from cold. Not from pain.

From the crashing flood of disbelief, relief, and something deeper.

Hope.

He came. Even here. Even now.

"Lucien."

It was barely air. Torn. Desperate.

"Lucien."

A sound followed. One she would never forget.

A growl, low and ruined.

The sound of a man who had already decided everyone in this room but her was going to die.

"Lena."

One word.

Grounded. Commanding. Terrifying in its promise.

All hell broke loose.

He was at her side in seconds, a blur of black and wrath.

He crouched low, hands already moving.

His touch wasn't gentle. It was urgent, almost brutal in its speed. Each motion carved from desperation and fury.

Leather straps snapped beneath his grip.

His hands shook. His breathing was ragged.

"Jesus."

A single word, ripped out of him.

"What the fuck did they do to you?"

He tore the last straps free. Wrists first. Ankles next. Freed.

Then he stripped off his jacket and put it around her shoulders, fast and rough, like the room itself had no right to keep seeing her.

His hands were all hard edges, still shaking. He couldn't stop staring. At her skin. At the marks on her wrists. At the bruises he didn't yet know the story of, but would. At her clothes crumpled on the floor, the blood on her thighs, silent witness to what she'd endured.

Only then did he reach for what was left of her clothes. Her dress. Her torn panties. Pieces of her dignity scattered like wreckage. He handed them to her gently, almost reverently.

"Get dressed."

"I've got you," he said.

One of his men slipped in behind him, gloves already on, a med kit unzipped.

"Vitals. Fluids. Nothing without her say-so," he muttered, professional and steady, his eyes staying on her face.

His calm didn't cool the rage already tightening the room.

She nodded once, her choice to be touched.

Lucien's chest rose hard, shuddering. Rage rippled beneath the surface, barely leashed.

He turned his head.

The camera sat mounted on the tripod, still pointed at the table.

Lucien walked over, slow and heavy. He brushed his hand against the edge of the table, just once, like he already knew what had happened here. He didn't bother to check the footage. He tore the camera off the mount, slammed it to the ground, and crushed it under his boot.

Then his gaze shifted.

The last man crawled across the blood-slick floor, dragging himself forward, gasping as he smeared a crimson trail in his wake. His limbs shook with the effort. His eyes, wide and frenzied, searched for a door that didn't exist.

Lucien froze.

Every inch of him wound tight, like a wire ready to snap.

"I'm going to kill him in the worst fucking way," Lucien said.

Dead quiet. Dead certain.

"He's going to pay for every mark on you."

Lena lifted her head. Tears streaked her face. Her body was wrecked.

But in her eyes, there was steel.

Something final. Something unforgiving.

"No."

Lucien turned.

Something shifted in his gaze.

Lena drew a breath, steadied.

"I want to be the one to finish this."

Silence.

Then Lucien smiled. Slow. Dark. Recognizing.

"You sure about that?"

His voice dropped.

Lena nodded.

"I want to look him in the eyes when I end this."

He reached into his holster, pulled his gun, and held it out.

"Then do it."

A flip of the grip. Handle first.

"Settle your score."

Lena took it.

Turned.

And stalked forward.

Each step was slow. Measured. Her body trembled with exhaustion, but her mind had gone terribly clear.

The man coughed, wet and broken beneath the mask. Blood leaked from the edge of it, dark against the floor.

She stood over him, looking down at what he had become.

He tried to speak.

A useless rasp.

Lena tilted her head.

Then, crack.

Her boot slammed into his ribs.

He screamed, rolling onto his back, convulsing in agony.

She lifted the gun. Aimed lower.

BANG.

A single shot. Straight through the groin.

The sound that tore out of him wasn't human. It was raw. Monstrous. Animal.

He clawed at the floor, spine arching, blood pooling beneath him in thick, black waves.

Lena crouched beside him, her voice barely more than a whisper. Calm. Ice.

"Still feel in control?"

His eyes swam with terror.

Her hands trembled as she tore the mask off.

He coughed hard, spitting blood onto the concrete. His face was a ruin. Glossy with pain. Pride had lived there once. Now there was only humiliation. Hate. Something colder.

He laughed. Not from humor. From madness. From a mind with nowhere left to go. The sound cracked halfway through, like even his voice had given up.

Lucien didn't move.

Didn't speak.

He just watched.

Lena turned to him, heart pounding.

"Lucien, who the fuck is this?"

Silence stretched.

Long. Heavy.

Lucien didn't move.

When he spoke, his voice was quiet. Cold. Final.

"Bobby Scava. Old business partner. Swore loyalty in blood, then threatened to betray me in the same breath. I spared his life. Gave him a chance to disappear. For a long time, he did."

Lucien's eyes stayed on Bobby.

"Until now."

"Yesterday morning, back at the estate, I put a bounty on him the second I heard he was back."

His voice stayed unreadable, but his eyes carried the truth.

Pure simmering violence.

Bobby grinned, if it could even be called that. A broken, blood-slick twist of a mouth on a face gone pale with shock. Sweat clung to his skin. Blood dripped steadily from his chin. His body trembled, every breath a shudder, every movement a convulsion of pain.

Still, he made a sound. Half laugh, half death rattle.

A man clawing for dignity in the final seconds of his life.

"Guess you should've just fucking killed me, huh?"

Lena stepped forward. Each footfall precise. Controlled.

The weight of everything she'd endured, the fear, the rage, the humiliation, pressed into the floor with every step.

She stopped over him. Tilted her head. Eyes like stone. Lips curling with something darker than hate.

"Guess you should've stayed the fuck gone."

BANG.

A clean shot. Right between the eyes.

His body jerked once. Then went quiet. A final, feeble spasm. Then nothing.

The gun stayed raised for one second too long.

Then Lena's arm began to shake.

Not from fear.

From the terrible knowledge that there was no going back.

Somewhere inside her, something old and frightened went quiet.

Not healed.

Not gone.

Quiet.

Silence fell, heavy and absolute.

The room felt suspended, waiting to see what came next.

Lucien didn't move.

Just watched.

Then, after a long, loaded beat, he smiled. Slow. Wicked. Proud.

Not the king rescuing the queen.

The king witnessing her coronation.

Lena turned, exhaling deeply.

"Now take me home."

Lucien stepped forward, grip firm on her waist as he pulled her in.

Their fingers locked, not gentle.

His lips brushed her temple, reverent and wrecked.

"I'll take you home. Then I'm coming back to burn this whole city clean."

They stepped outside. The sun had set.

The air was thick with the stench of oil and rust. A streetlamp flickered over cracked pavement.

Lena wrapped her arms around herself, eyes lifting to the warehouse behind them. The kind of place people vanished into and never came out.

Her voice came out raw. "Where the hell did they take me?"

Lucien lit a cigarette. He inhaled, then let the smoke drift out through his nose.

"Brooklyn."

Lena's throat tightened. "How did you even find me?"

Lucien didn't look proud. He looked focused.

"I had Michael's devices tied to my system. His watch pinged last outside L'Appartement. After that, I pulled cameras, plate readers, traffic feeds. We hunted the van."

Her breath caught. "Oh my god. Michael. Where is he?"

Lucien stopped walking.

For the first time since he found her, his face changed.

"That was Michael in there."

Lena stared at him.

"No."

His jaw worked once. "The table. The box. All of it." His voice went flat, like anything human in it had been locked away. "They made him the message."

Lena's knees threatened to give. Tears blurred the streetlamp into a smear.

"No," she whispered. "Not Michael."

Lucien stepped in, hand sliding to the back of her neck, steady and firm. A promise more than comfort.

She swallowed through the ache in her throat. "He said Michael talked.

That he told them everything."

Lucien's face went still.

"He was lying."

The answer came too fast to be comfort. It was certainty.

"Michael didn't have what they were asking you for. Not all of it. Not enough."

His jaw tightened.

"If Bobby had gotten what he wanted, he wouldn't have kept asking."

The words hit her harder than the cold.

Michael had died as bait. As punishment. As proof.

Lucien looked back at the warehouse.

"Six years. One opening. That's all it took."

Silence hung there.

"He was my best friend's brother. Family."

His throat moved. "Now they're both gone."

He looked back at her.

"He was supposed to walk you back to that car. Bring you back to me."

She remembered him in the rearview mirror.

The way he noticed everything and asked for nothing.

The way safety had sounded like his voice saying, *We'll assume they followed you.*

Lena swallowed hard. Her chest felt packed with sand.

Lucien pressed a kiss to her forehead, then kept his hand there a moment longer.

He guided her toward the car, already pulling out his phone.

A quick text. A pin drop. One word: **CLEAR**

Within the hour, the warehouse would stop being a crime scene and become an empty building again. Bleach. Plastic. Silence.

"That's why you never let them see you bleed," he said.

At the passenger side, he paused and reached into his pocket.

He held up her phone between two fingers.

"Oh. This."

Lena's eyes widened. "My phone."

"Right where you dropped it."

Lena let out a shaky breath. "Unbelievable."

Lucien leaned against the car, studying her like he was making decisions in real time.

"About today. That meeting."

She swallowed. "Right. How was it?"

He rolled his neck once, like he could feel the city closing in.

"Miami," he said. "I'm setting something up down there with an old friend."

Lena stared at him. "Miami?"

He nodded. "Two days. I fly out. You're coming with me."

It wasn't a suggestion. It was a move.

His eyes held hers. "This city is compromised. I need you somewhere I can see the walls."

Lena hesitated. Shock, fear, and the ache of Michael's name all tangled in her throat.

Then she nodded. "Okay."

Lucien's face softened, just slightly, like he'd been waiting for that.

He opened the door and they slid inside.

The warmth of the cabin wrapped around her. The engine came alive under his hand, controlled and steady. The opposite of what her body still felt.

Lena unlocked her phone, desperate for proof that the world was still normal.

Dozens of messages. Christina. Jessica. Panic. Relief.

One cut through the rest.

Answer me or I'm calling the cops

Then she saw it.

Buried between the others. Unknown number.

Her fingers went cold.

She held the phone up. Her voice barely worked.

"Lucien."

He glanced over.

On the screen was a message time-stamped just after she'd been taken.

See you soon, Lena

Lena's stomach tightened.

"Scroll," Lucien said quietly.

She frowned. "What?"

"Scroll."

Her thumb moved.

Another message sat just beneath the first.

An image.

It loaded slowly.

The screen filled with a photograph.

A man slumped in a kitchen chair, head tilted sideways, blood darkening the collar of his shirt. A badge rested on the table beside him.

The scar cut from his eyebrow to his temple.

Lena's breath vanished.

"Lucien..."

Her voice came out thin.

"That's the detective."

Lucien leaned closer, eyes narrowing as he studied the screen.

"Raines."

Silence filled the car.

Beneath the photo was a single line.

Loose ends

Lucien leaned back slowly.

"Whoever this is, they're cleaning the board."

A slow, suffocating silence settled between them.

They weren't just after her. They were eliminating anyone who got close.

Lucien's expression darkened. Something murderous settled behind his eyes.

Lena went cold.

This wasn't over.

Whoever they were, they were still watching.

Lucien glanced at her.

"In Miami, you're meeting my parents."

Lena stared.

"...What?"

Chapter Twenty-Two

LUGGAGE AND LOOSE ENDS

Two days later, Lena stood in Lucien's vast walk-in closet, fingers grazing over the smooth leather of a designer duffle as she packed. She had already layered concealer over the bruise blooming beneath her eye, dabbed makeup across her split lip, and traced the faint shadow the collar had left on her neck.

The past two days had blurred together, one decision folding into the next before she could catch her breath.

Now she was here. Back at the estate. Packing for Miami. For Lucien's business. For his family. For another part of his life she had not yet survived.

Her body still mistook silence for warning.

Lucien moved beside her. Calm. Contained. His hands folded shirts with practiced precision, but his mind was already in Miami, calculating outcomes, shifting pieces.

Miami wasn't a break. Miami was a battlefield.

The estate was quiet in a way that felt less like peace than waiting.

Lena pressed her palms against the dresser.

"What's going through that head of yours?"

Lucien didn't look up.

"Loose ends."

The words settled between them, heavy. Michael's death. The kidnapping. The threat still circling, closing in.

She swallowed hard.

"You sure we should be leaving?"

This time he lifted his gaze. Sharp. Guarded. Something dangerous sat behind it, coiled and awake.

"In a week, we'll be back. And when we are," he closed the suitcase with a hard snap, "we finish what was started."

Lena moved to sit at the edge of the bed, staring at her half-zipped suitcases. Two days since the warehouse. Since Michael. Since she pulled the trigger. And now they were heading to Miami, not to hide, not to heal, but to step deeper into his world.

Across the room, Lucien stood near the window, checking his watch. Waiting. One of his men was already on the way.

Then his phone rang.

Victoria.

Lucien answered and put it on speaker as he straightened his cufflinks. His expression tightened almost imperceptibly.

"Already on the ground?" His voice was smooth, the softness gone.

Victoria's laugh cut through the room.

"You sound surprised. I wanted to come down early. See some friends. Have a few drinks before you two get here and ruin my fun."

Lena looked down before Victoria could pull a reaction out of her, but Lucien stayed stone still.

"You landed safe?"

Not tenderness. Logistics.

"Obviously. What, did you think I would fall out of the sky just to inconvenience you?"

Lucien didn't respond immediately. Lena caught it, the slight tension in his posture, his fingers flexing at his wrist.

"Who are you staying with?"

Not where.

Who.

"With my friend Camila. You remember her, right?"

Lucien didn't react.

"Which Camila?" he asked. "The one arrested for credit card fraud or the one who crashed my boat in the Keys?"

Victoria groaned.

"Jesus, Lucien. It was a jet ski."

He didn't soften.

"And what did she crash it into?"

A pause.

"Your boat."

Lena bit the inside of her cheek.

Lucien pinched the bridge of his nose once.

"Send me Camila's address. And don't do anything that forces me to clean up after you."

Victoria sighed like she'd heard it her whole life.

"You have no faith in me."

Lucien's expression sharpened, but his eyes stayed cold.

"I have faith you'll find trouble without trying."

Lena could practically hear Victoria rolling her eyes.

"Whatever. Just hurry. Mom and Dad already know you're coming. Dad has probably been dressed for dinner since noon, rehearsing whatever speech he plans to open with."

Lucien stilled. His shoulders shifted by a fraction. The name carried weight. Old weight.

He exhaled through his nose.

"We'll be there in a few hours."

Victoria hung up.

Lucien slid his phone into his pocket. The familiar mask slid back into place. Lena had learned to fear it and trust it.

She hesitated.

"You don't seem thrilled."

He didn't answer immediately. He grabbed his suitcase. Rolled his shoulders once, like shedding something he didn't want her to see.

Then his voice went quiet and final.

"Come on. Car's outside."

And with that, they were moving.

Straight into Miami.

Into the city his parents now called home.

Into the part of his world she had never seen.

Into whatever was waiting.

Crisp autumn air met them as they stepped outside, golden leaves skimming across the stone driveway. The estate loomed behind them like something out of a dream, but today it was just a backdrop. For one dangerous second, it almost felt like they weren't walking into chaos.

Lucien rolled his suitcase behind him, one hand in his pocket, the other on the handle, moving like a man who could pack in five minutes and still look like he owned the world.

And then there was Lena, dragging five duffle bags behind her.

It wasn't really about the bags.

She knew that.

It was makeup, clothes, shoes, hair products, every stupid thing she could control because two days ago she hadn't been able to control anything.

Lucien stopped dead in his tracks, staring at the mountain of luggage behind her. The driver hesitated, like he was deciding if he needed backup.

Lucien blinked. Once. Twice. Then he dragged a hand down his face, sighing through his nose.

"Lena."

She huffed, adjusting a strap over her shoulder. "What?"

His eyes flicked from her to the bags, then back again. His voice was slow. "One week."

Lena lifted her chin. "I heard you."

Lucien's brow twitched. He gestured to the rolling monument of luggage.

"What the hell is all this? You packing for exile?"

She sighed like he was the problem. "Things."

Lucien stared at her.

"Five bags of things?"

"Necessary things."

The driver cleared his throat. "I'll, uh, start loading these in."

Lucien crossed his arms, watching bag after bag disappear into the trunk.

"Tell me," he said dryly, "what exactly do you think is going to happen in Miami?"

Lena waved him off. "You wouldn't get it."

Lucien shook his head, rolling his suitcase toward the car, muttering something she couldn't catch.

Lena climbed into the backseat and watched him rub his temple like he was fighting for patience. For one second, the normalness of it almost hurt. When he slid in beside her, the trunk slammed shut behind them.

The car eased down the driveway, slipping through the gates.

Lena watched the iron part through the tinted glass.

For one stupid second, her body got it wrong.

Opening felt too much like locking.

Her breath caught before she could stop it.

Lucien's hand settled over hers.

Not hard.

Enough.

The estate blurred behind them. Autumn bled into highway. The engine hummed, steady and low.

Lucien sat beside her, one arm draped behind her, his other hand still over hers. His watch caught the light, a quiet flash of gold, calm in a way that once unnerved her.

Now it grounded her.

She knew what that calm had cost him.

The road stretched ahead. Clean sky. Quiet leather. A man beside her who had burned his way back to her and still looked ready for the next attack.

She side-eyed him. "You're quiet."

His gaze flicked to her, sharp and calm. "I'm thinking."

Lena raised a brow. "About?"

Lucien nodded at the luggage. "What the fuck you stuffed in that fifth bag."

Lena groaned. "Let it go."

Dark amusement flickered across his face. "I've watched smugglers pack lighter."

She glared at him. "Everything in those bags is necessary."

He didn't answer right away. His eyes stayed on her.

"I felt that."

Lena blinked. "Felt what?"

Lucien finally looked at her. Really looked.

"Your breathing changed. You're back there."

Not a question.

A read.

She looked out the window. "I'm fine."

"No, you're not."

A small laugh escaped her, rougher than she meant it to be. "You always this comforting?"

"No."

"Good. I'd hate to think this was you trying."

His thumb moved once over her knuckles.

Something in her chest tightened. She forced it down.

"Honestly, I'm just preparing for your mother to hate me."

Lucien glanced over. "She won't hate you."

"You say that, but what if she's one of those high-society women who thinks anyone who wasn't born into money is a peasant?"

Lucien's mouth twitched. "You just described my father, not my mother."

Lena turned her head. "Your father?"

"He's the one you should be worrying about."

"Perfect."

"If he gives you a hard time, I'll handle it."

Lena looked at him carefully. "Handle it how?"

His gaze stayed forward. "The only way I ever handle anything."

Something cold moved through her.

She exhaled, some of the tension leaving her voice. "You're impossible."

Lucien leaned back, calm in a way that did not feel peaceful at all.

"You'll see soon enough."

The airport rose into view ahead, private hangars clean and bright under the afternoon light.

Lena stared at them. Planes. Glass. Men in suits. Open sky.

It was supposed to look like a trip.

Lucien's hand stayed over hers until the car stopped.

Lena stepped into the jet and stopped.

Lucien moved past her like he had done it a hundred times. Jacket off. Watch checked. Phone out. Men like him didn't marvel at luxury. They used it.

Lena stood there with one hand on the seat, staring at cream leather, dark wood, soft lights, a bar polished so clean it reflected the ceiling.

It should have felt beautiful.

It felt too quiet.

Her body searched for the wrong things. Concrete. Rust. A chain scraping the floor. A man breathing too close to her ear.

Instead there was carpet under her heels and warm air on her skin.

Lucien looked up.

He didn't tell her it was okay.

That would have been insulting.

"Sit down," he said.

She moved because his voice gave her somewhere to put her body.

The engines started beneath them.

The vibration crawled through the floor.

Lena's fingers clamped around the armrests.

Lucien saw it.

He always saw it.

"That sound bothering you?"

"No."

"Don't lie to me."

Her eyes snapped to his.

The words weren't cruel. That made them worse.

She looked toward the window. "I keep thinking I'm going to hear the SUV."

Lucien went still.

The cabin noise filled the space between them.

"Michael's phone," she said, quieter. "I keep hearing it ring."

His jaw shifted.

That name changed the air.

Lucien leaned forward, elbows on his knees, every polished inch of him turning into something harder.

"He was mine," he said.

Lena looked at him.

"And Bobby used him to get to you." His voice dropped. "That doesn't leave this plane with us. That stays where it belongs."

"Where?"

"With me."

Her eyes burned.

"You can't carry everything."

His stare held.

"I can carry more than you."

It should have sounded arrogant.

It didn't.

It sounded like a vow made by a man who had already decided what part of himself he was willing to burn.

The jet rolled forward.

Lena closed her eyes as the speed built. Her body braced for impact, for hands, for a door that wouldn't open.

Lucien crossed the aisle before the plane lifted.

He sat beside her, close enough that his shoulder touched hers, and placed his hand over hers on the armrest.

"Breathe."

"I am."

"No, you're surviving. Breathe."

The plane lifted.

Her stomach dropped.

Her hand turned under his and gripped him hard.

Lucien didn't move. Didn't soothe her like a child. Didn't ask her to calm down.

He let her hurt without making a spectacle of it.

The city fell away beneath them.

Lena opened her eyes.

Clouds swallowed the window.

For a while neither of them spoke.

Then she said, "What happens when we land?"

Lucien stared forward.

"We eat dinner with my family."

"That's not what I meant."

"I know."

She waited.

His thumb moved once over her knuckles.

"When we land, you stay close. You don't apologize for what you look like. You don't explain the bruises unless you want to. If my father asks the wrong question, I answer it."

"And if I answer it?"

A faint look touched his face.

"Then God help him."

Despite herself, some of the fear loosened.

The engines settled into a steady hum.

She looked at him then, really looked.

The perfect suit. The calm face. The blood still somewhere underneath all of it.

"You're different since Brooklyn."

His eyes stayed on hers.

"So are you."

That one got under her skin.

She looked away before he could see too much.

Lucien leaned back, but he kept her hand.

"Rest."

"I won't sleep."

"I didn't say sleep."

"Then what?"

His voice was low. "Sit in clean air and let nothing happen to you for one hour."

Her throat tightened.

Clean air.

No blood. No mold. No locked door. No man deciding what part of her fear amused him.

Just the low sound of the jet, Lucien beside her, and the sky holding them above everything that still wanted a piece of them.

Lena turned toward the window.

For the first time in two days, she stopped pretending to be fine.

A tear slipped loose.

Lucien saw it.

He didn't wipe it away.

He only held her hand tighter, like privacy was another thing he could protect.

The descent began. No ceremony, just gravity.

Lena shifted in her seat as the clouds thinned, revealing Miami beneath them. Sunlit rooftops. Winding waterways. The ocean flashing under the afternoon light. The city pulsed even from above, its rhythm different from New York, faster and slower at once.

Lucien's phone buzzed.

He glanced down, unsurprised.

Victoria:

Change of plans. I stayed at the airport. Thought I'd grace you both with my presence

He locked the screen.

Lena watched him. "Something I should know about?"

"Victoria's waiting at the airport."

Lena frowned. "She's been there the whole time?"

Lucien leaned back. "It's Victoria. She probably ditched her friend the second she got bored and made herself comfortable somewhere she shouldn't be."

"And she didn't tell you?"

"Victoria doesn't tell anyone anything. She just expects the world to adjust."

Lena looked away before he could catch her reaction.

Lucien was back across from her by then, arms folded, gaze lowered as the city drew closer beneath them. The humor faded from his face by degrees. He looked less like a man coming home than a man returning to something that had been waiting for him.

The wheels touched down.

A voice crackled softly over the intercom, but Lena barely heard it. Her stomach had already tightened.

She turned to him. "This is really happening."

Lucien looked at her. Calm. Certain.

"Welcome to Miami."

The jet rolled toward a private terminal, where a black SUV waited in the sun, glossy and sealed, its tinted windows hiding the world inside.

Lena stopped breathing for half a second.

Not because of Miami.

Because of the car.

Black paint. Dark glass. A door waiting to open.

New York struck through her so fast she almost reached for something to hold. Lucien's SUV. The street. The one she had run toward. The one she thought Michael was inside.

The one that changed everything.

Lucien adjusted his cuffs and stood, already moving toward the door. "Let's go."

Heat slammed into them the moment they stepped outside.

Miami air rolled over Lena, thick and bright, salt and sun layered over jet fuel, warm asphalt, and something sharper.

She slid on her sunglasses as they descended the stairs. Lucien was already scanning the airstrip, his mind somewhere ahead of his body.

They didn't make it to the SUV.

Victoria was already crossing the tarmac like she owned it, sunglasses too big, hair perfect, a laminated pass swinging from two fingers.

"Took you long enough," she called. "I had to flirt, threaten, and possibly commit a misdemeanor to get out here."

Lucien gave her a flat look. "You didn't flirt."

Victoria didn't miss a beat. "No. I threatened."

Lena almost laughed.

Then Victoria got close enough to see her face.

The performance stayed, but something behind it changed.

Her eyes moved once over the bruise beneath the makeup, the split in Lena's lip, the faint mark at her throat.

She didn't ask.

That was the first thing Lena liked about her.

Victoria turned back to Lucien, voice lighter than her eyes. "You look like shit."

Lucien didn't blink. "You look expensive."

"I am expensive. Mom says it's your fault."

"It usually is."

The driver opened the rear door.

Lena saw black paint. Dark glass. A cool interior waiting with its mouth open.

Her feet stopped.

Victoria noticed that too.

So did Lucien.

His hand found the small of Lena's back.

He wasn't pushing.

Just there.

"You're with me," he said quietly.

Lena nodded once and climbed in.

Victoria slid into the passenger seat and waited until the door shut before speaking.

"Mom wants everyone at the house before dinner."

Lucien's mouth curved without warmth. "Of course she does."

"She says she wants time with you before Dad turns the room into court."

That took the edge off him by a fraction.

Lena looked between them. "Court?"

Victoria turned back to her. "My father doesn't meet people. He cross-examines them."

Lucien looked out the window. "He starts, I finish it."

Victoria pointed at him. "See? This is why Mom is already nervous."

Lena let out a breath, almost a laugh.

"Should I be worried?"

"A little," Victoria said.

Lucien's hand settled on Lena's leg.

"No."

Victoria smiled faintly. "That's the family dynamic. He lies beautifully. I clarify."

Lucien's eyes cut to her.

She faced forward again, untouched.

The SUV pulled away from the tarmac.

Miami opened around them, too bright, too warm, too alive. Palm trees moved in the heat. Water flashed between buildings. The city looked like a vacation if you didn't know men like Lucien had business there.

Victoria leaned back, watching Lena in the mirror.

"So. Verdict?"

"On what?"

"Miami."

Lena looked through the glass. "It feels like trouble with better weather."

Victoria nodded once. "Good. You get it."

Lucien's phone buzzed.

He read the message.

Whatever ease had been in him disappeared.

Lena saw it. Victoria saw it too.

"Business?" Victoria asked.

Lucien locked the screen. "Yeah."

Victoria's face cooled. "That means blood or money."

"Usually both."

Lena turned to him.

Lucien slipped the phone away. His fingers tightened once against her knee. Grounding. A reminder. A warning to himself.

Victoria watched the gesture, then looked back out the windshield.

"Mom's excited," she said, softer. "She's been asking about you all day."

Lucien said nothing.

But something in him changed.

Small enough to miss.

Lena didn't.

The SUV carried them deeper into Miami.

The city shifted around them in clean, expensive flashes. Palm shadows across glass. Valets moving under awnings. Women in linen stepping out of cars that cost more than houses. Men in sunglasses watching sidewalks like they were paid to notice the wrong face at the wrong time.

Lena stayed quiet, looking through the tinted glass.

New York felt like it wanted to beat the truth out of you.

Miami felt like it would smile while it did it.

They veered off the highway and slipped onto waterfront roads. Sunlight broke across the bay. Yachts moved through the glittering water, white wakes trailing behind them. The air grew thicker, warmer, heavy with salt and sun.

Then the tower came into view.

Glass. Steel. Clean, hard lines cutting into the Miami sky.

The SUV rolled to the private entrance.

Lena stepped out, and the heat found her again, sinking into her skin. Salt hung in the air beneath the faint scent of flowers, sun-warmed stone, and expensive cologne drifting from somewhere near the doors.

She tipped her head back, taking in the height of the building, the tinted glass, the quiet precision of it all. Nothing here needed to announce itself. That was the point.

Lucien handed off the larger bags without slowing. The staff moved around him with practiced ease. No questions. No introductions.

He was already known here.

The lobby was cool and dim after the sun, all dark wood, soft gold, and polished stone. The silence didn't feel empty. It felt owned.

Lucien didn't stop at the desk.

He didn't have to.

The doorman gave a quiet nod and pressed the button for the private elevator.

As the doors slid shut, Lena let out a slow breath and watched the numbers climb.

The penthouse opened onto the ocean.

For a second, Lena forgot what waited below.

Sky and water stretched beyond the glass until the horizon blurred into light. Boats moved across the bay like they belonged to another life. A clean life. A life where people packed too much, met parents, drank at dinner, slept through the night.

Inside, the place held its money quietly. Ivory furniture. Dark wood. Stone counters. Nothing loud. Nothing begging to be admired.

That made it feel richer.

Lucien set his bag down near the sofa and checked the room before he looked at the view.

Lena noticed.

"You do that everywhere?"

"Do what?"

"Look for who's going to kill us."

He crossed to the bar. "Not everyone."

"Just most people?"

"Just enough."

She moved to the glass and pressed her palm against it. The cool surface steadied her.

"I've never seen anything like this."

Lucien poured a drink. "Good."

She glanced over. "That's it?"

"I was hoping it would impress you."

"The view?"

He took a slow sip, eyes on her over the glass.

"The fact that I survived long enough to buy it."

That hit differently.

The humor softened, then disappeared.

Lena turned back toward the water.

Behind her, Lucien's phone buzzed again.

He looked down.

His face gave away nothing.

That was how she knew it was bad.

"What is it?"

"Nothing you need to carry before dinner."

"I'm not glass."

"No," he said. "You're not."

He slipped the phone away.

"But you're tired. You're walking into my family with bruises and Bobby's blood still in your head. So for the next ten minutes, let me be the problem."

Her throat tightened.

Before she could answer, her phone vibrated.

Victoria.

Lena answered. "Hey, Vic."

Victoria's voice came through sharp and impatient. "Tell me you're already on your way down."

"We just walked in."

Lucien took another sip. "Tell her the elevator is slow."

"I heard him," Victoria said. "Of course it is. Change of plans. We're meeting at the restaurant. They're already there, and I'm downstairs with your driver, who looks like he was assembled in a basement by angry Russians, so move."

Lucien arched a brow. "He's very sensitive."

"He blinked once in ten minutes. I think he's charging."

Lena laughed despite herself.

It felt strange.

Not wrong.

Strange.

"Why the restaurant?" she asked.

"Dad probably didn't trust Lucien to show if they waited at the house."

Lucien's eyes cooled. "Smart man."

"Just get down here before Dad starts interrogating me like I'm responsible for your emotional damage."

Lena looked at Lucien.

He looked back.

The joke sat there, funny until it wasn't.

Victoria softened, just barely. "And Lena?"

"Yeah?"

"Wear whatever makes you feel like you can walk into a room and make people regret underestimating you."

Lena went still.

Then she smiled.

"I packed five bags. I've got options."

Victoria gasped. "Oh, I love her."

Lucien looked toward the ceiling like patience had become a religious trial.

Lena hung up and turned to him.

"Your sister is insane."

"My whole family is."

"And your father?"

Lucien picked up his keys.

"Worse."

"You're terrible at reassurance."

His eyes found hers.

"I'm coming with you, aren't I?"

One quiet line. Somehow enough.

Then he nodded toward the door.

"Come on. Before Victoria starts a felony out of boredom."

Chapter Twenty-Three

FIRST IMPRESSIONS LAST FOREVER

They glided through Miami's streets, past storefronts buzzing with nightlife, palms swaying in the humid breeze. Dusk had settled, turning the horizon violet, and the city grew louder, faster, hungrier.

Victoria, lounging in the front seat, checked her reflection in the visor mirror, then snapped it shut. "Alright, ground rules, don't be late, don't piss Dad off, and don't let Mom drown you in questions. That last one's impossible, by the way."

Lena tucked her hair behind her ear, eyes on the window. "Okay, so tell me what I need to know before we walk in."

Lucien sat back, legs stretched out, and glanced at her. "Nothing."

She scoffed. "Nothing?"

Lucien's mouth curved. "There's nothing you need to do. Just look pretty and don't run."

Victoria snorted. "Good luck with that."

Lena shot them both a look. "Comforting."

Lucien's lips twitched.

She crossed her arms. "I know you already told me your dad's the intimidating one, but I don't think I fully processed that until right now."

Lucien shrugged, his gaze on the city. "He's from another time. Built his kingdom. Made his rules."

He glanced at her, a slow grin tugging at his mouth. "Then I learned his world and built mine faster. Streets. Docks. Clubs. Men who still think blood makes them kings."

His eyes flicked back to the window.

"My father understands power. He just hates that I learned how to make it move without asking his permission."

Lena's smile faded a little.

"And the worst part?" Lucien leaned in, voice low. "You're the first thing he'll clock tonight."

Victoria cut him a look, but Lena caught it, the quick flash in her eyes.

Lena shook her head, fighting a smile. "You're exhausting."

Lucien leaned close enough that only she could hear him. "And yet you still get wet for me."

Her breath caught, but before she could answer, they pulled up to an upscale restaurant called THE MARQUIS ROOM, its name glowing in warm neon script above the doors.

Victoria huffed, fixing her hair. "Alright, deep breaths, everyone. Let's get this over with."

The driver stepped out, moving to open the door.

Lucien looked over at Lena, amusement flickering beneath something darker. "Showtime."

Something twisted low in her stomach, the weight of what this meant. These were the people who built the man she couldn't stop choosing. And for the first time, it hit her: she wasn't just meeting his family. She was stepping into the world that made him.

The three of them stepped out together, the restaurant's glossy façade under golden lights. A suited host stood at the entrance, ready to escort them inside.

The scent of grilled steak and wine lingered in the air as they were led through the dimly lit interior, the soft hum of conversation filling the space.

Lena spotted them.

Lucien's parents.

Lucien's father sat rigid and composed, carrying authority like a second skin. His salt-and-pepper hair was neatly combed, his suit a quiet display of old money.

Beside him, Lucien's mother was all elegance, her dark hair glossed with a hint of burgundy, her midnight-blue dress sharp against her warm skin.

Her gaze flicked up and landed on Lena.

Lucien's father turned his head, his sharp eyes settling on Lucien.

Then he leaned back in his chair, fingers tapping once against the table-cloth before his voice broke the silence.

"Well, well. Look who finally decided to show up."

Lucien gave a half smile and slid into the empty seat across from him.

"Wouldn't miss it for the world." His tone edged with sarcasm, the lie casual.

Victoria rolled her eyes, dropping into the chair beside their mother. "Come on, Dad, at least pretend to be happy to see him."

Lucien's mother, however, smiled warmly. "And this must be Lena."

Her gaze touched the bruise makeup hadn't fully hidden, then the careful line of Lena's mouth. She noticed. She was too graceful to show it.

Lena forced her expression steady as she met the woman's gaze. "It's nice to meet you, Mrs. Cole."

"Please," she said smoothly, tilting her head. "Call me Evelyn."

Lucien's father, however, said nothing. Just studied her with that same scrutiny before nodding once. "So, this is the girl."

Lucien's smirk sharpened. "You sound surprised."

His father reached for his glass of scotch.

"Just making an observation."

It wasn't idle. It was clinical. Measuring what in her would hold, and what would crack.

Victoria waved a hand. "Can we order already? I'm starving."

Evelyn shot her a look, but smiled. "Of course."

A waiter approached, but Lucien's father kept his attention on Lena.

She felt it then.

The test.

Lena met his gaze, spine straight, expression carefully blank, pulse roaring beneath the table.

Evelyn took a quiet sip of wine, watching with detached amusement. Victoria didn't bother hiding her smirk.

Lucien remained still beside her, unreadable, his fingers brushing Lena's knee beneath the table.

"So."

One word. Low. Measured.

Lucien's father laced his fingers together.

"You're the one who's got my son all tangled up."

His voice was smooth. Deceptively so. The kind of voice that could turn cold without warning.

Lena inhaled. She didn't shift in her seat. Didn't look away.

"Guess I am."

His eyes skimmed her face, searching for something.

Then he lifted his glass and took a slow sip.

No reaction. No approval. No disapproval.

Nothing.

He set the glass down carefully. Tilted his head.

"Do you know what you're getting yourself into?"

Something tightened in her chest, but she didn't hesitate.

"I already have."

His gaze flicked to Lucien, then back to her.

"We'll see."

Victoria's voice shattered the tension.

"Jesus Christ, Dad, do you have to be so dramatic?"

Evelyn tsked softly, sipping her wine. "Oh, let him have his fun."

Lena let out a slow breath.

Lucien's father watched her, gaze steady.

"My son doesn't bring women home. He doesn't do relationships."

Then his gaze flicked to Lucien.

"Look at this anomaly. Let's all pretend this is normal, shall we, son?"

"No, no. Tell me, Lena." He leaned forward, eyes gleaming. "What makes you so special?"

His tone wasn't mocking. It was clinical, like he'd dissect her on the spot if the answer disappointed him.

Victoria froze mid-sip of her wine. Evelyn closed her eyes briefly, already bracing.

Lucien remained stone-cold still.

Lena let it stretch.

Then she tilted her head, a slow smirk curling her lips.

"I suck his dick better than anyone else ever could."

Chaos.

Not loud.

Worse.

The kind of silence that made every fork, every breath, every shift of fabric feel guilty.

Victoria choked into her drink.

The waiter stopped mid-step.

Evelyn's lips parted, not in shock, but in recognition, something she understood.

Lucien didn't laugh.

His hand locked around Lena's thigh beneath the table, possessive and still, like the wrong reaction from anyone in that room might make him forget they were family.

Lucien's father just stared at her.

Expression unreadable.

The kind of stare that locked her spine.

Then he grinned, chuckled, and stood.

Lucien's hand shot out, gripping her wrist as he rounded the table.

"Dad," Lucien warned. Low. Dangerous.

He stopped right beside Lena, gaze flicking over her like he was seeing her for the first time.

"Stand up."

Lena's pulse spiked.

Lucien's grip on her tightened.

"Dad, what the fuck are you doing?"

His tone wasn't cruel. It was ritual. Lena understood it in the marrow of her bones. This wasn't humiliation. It was initiation.

Alexander touched Lucien's shoulder once.

"Relax, son."

Slowly, Lena pushed back her chair and stood.

The air shifted.

He reached out, gripping her jaw lightly, turning her face to the light.

Lena went still.

Not because he hurt her.

Because for one flash of a second, her body remembered another hand, another room, another man deciding what he was allowed to do with her face.

Lucien saw it.

The air around him went black.

Alexander stared at her. One second. Then another. His eyes moved over the bruise beneath the makeup, the split at her lip, the mark she couldn't quite erase.

Then he smirked.

"Welcome to the family, sweetheart."

He kissed her cheek.

Lucien stayed frozen. His father had yielded ground, not to him, but to the woman beside him.

Victoria broke the silence first, whispering under her breath. "Holy. Fucking. Shit."

Evelyn just shook her head, lifting her wine glass. "God, I need another drink."

Lucien?

He was stone-still, watching his father with murder in his eyes.

Lena sat back down, reaching for her water glass.

She hadn't blurted it. She'd aimed it.

She took a slow sip, licking her lips, then leaned toward Victoria and whispered.

"I think I passed the test."

Victoria cackled. "Passed? Bitch, you might've just become his favorite."

Lena hesitated for a moment, then turned slightly toward the head of the table.

"Mr. Cole?"

His eyes flicked to hers, amused. "Please, call me Alexander."

Lena gave a small nod, the corner of her mouth twitching. "Alexander." The name felt heavier when she said it.

Alexander's gaze lingered on her for a moment, then he turned to the waiter who arrived with drinks and a breadbasket.

"Finally," he muttered, grabbing a piece. "I was starting to think this was one of those trendy places that believes suffering sharpens the appetite."

Victoria rolled her eyes. "You didn't even look at the menu yet."

"I don't need to," he said, snapping off a corner of bread. "I already know it won't live up to my expectations."

Evelyn sipped her wine, perfectly poised. "Darling, if the food's half as dry as your sarcasm, we're all in trouble."

Alexander didn't even look at her.

Lena smirked quietly, watching the dynamic. They didn't just throw barbs. They danced with them.

Alexander turned his attention back to her. "So, Lena. Tell me. What exactly is it you do? Or are you between dreams right now?"

Lena held his stare, her tone level. "I work in fashion. Sales, for now. I'm working toward my own line."

The corner of his mouth curved, not mockery. Appraisal. He'd seen dreamers before. Most broke. Most bent. This one carried a fuse that didn't snuff, only burned hotter.

Alexander nodded once, but his silence lingered.

Lucien cut in smoothly, eyes still on his father. "And she's damn good at it."

Alexander arched a brow. "You've seen her work?"

"I would back her work. There's a difference."

Alexander folded his hands. "Interesting."

Lena leaned forward slightly. "Why? Because I'm not supposed to have dreams, or because your son's not supposed to believe in someone else's?"

Alexander grinned. "Bravo, darling. You truly aren't what I expected."

Lena returned the smile. "I tend to exceed people's expectations, Alexander."

Victoria froze.

Even Evelyn chuckled softly, lifting her glass just enough to hide it.

"She might actually survive this family after all."

Lucien sat beside her, relaxed, one arm draped behind Lena's chair, the faintest smile at his mouth. He didn't need to say it, but everyone at the table felt it:

He hadn't brought home a girl.

He'd brought home a storm.

An hour had passed, and Lena still felt the shape of Alexander's kiss on her cheek like a verdict. The once-tense atmosphere had loosened, warmer now, though the undercurrent of power still pulsed beneath every exchange. Silverware clinked, jazz drifted in the background, and the last of the wine was poured.

Evelyn lifted the bottle closest to her, tilting it, watching the final drops gather.

"Well," she said lightly, setting it down, "that seems to have disappeared."

Victoria glanced over. "Shocking. A table full of Cole blood and the wine didn't stand a chance."

Evelyn smiled faintly, the expression warm but knowing as she took a slow sip.

Lucien glanced at his watch and pushed back his chair.

"We should head out."

Alexander looked up. "What, already? Where the hell are you two going?"

"I've got something to handle." Lucien adjusted his blazer. "Victoria's staying with a friend nearby. We'll drop her off."

Evelyn's brows lifted. "Lucien, we haven't even ordered dessert."

"Not really a dessert guy."

"Shocker," Victoria muttered.

Alexander's mouth curved. "Always knew how to vanish before the bill hit the table."

"Old habits."

Victoria let out a dramatic groan. "You're so antisocial it's criminal."

Lucien didn't answer. He turned, offering Lena his hand.

Evelyn leaned in as Lena rose, her smile warm, measured. "It was truly a pleasure, darling. You're welcome at our table anytime."

"Thank you. That means a lot."

Victoria grabbed her clutch, spinning it once around her finger. "Well. Try not to miss me too much, Mom."

"Oh, sweetheart," Evelyn said lightly, "we'll survive."

Lucien faced his father. "Dad."

Alexander lifted his glass a fraction. "Lucien."

That was it. No hug. No handshake.

As they stepped away from the table and made their way toward the front doors, Victoria leaned into Lena, whispering, "You survived the lions' den."

Lena glanced at her. "You mean your family?"

Victoria grinned. "Same thing."

The air outside the restaurant was thick with Miami's late-night humidity, pulsing with the distant thump of music.

Lucien's hand rested on Lena's back as they walked toward the waiting black SUV, Victoria trailing behind, humming to herself.

Lena's phone buzzed.

She pulled it from her purse, thumb gliding across the screen.

Her heart dipped.

How's the weather down there?

No name. No number. Unknown.

Cold slid up her back. She pushed it down.

She tilted the screen toward Lucien. "You should see this."

Lucien glanced.

And then it vibrated again.

Tell Lucien to send Carter Vale my regards

Lucien stopped.

The street kept moving around them, music thumping somewhere down the block, traffic sliding past in glossy streaks of light.

Lucien didn't move with any of it.

For the first time since Lena had known him, his stillness didn't feel controlled.

It felt interrupted.

Victoria, already at the SUV, turned. "Everything good?"

Lucien didn't answer. His gaze was fixed on something in the distance, but Lena could tell, he wasn't seeing the street.

He was somewhere else.

"Lucien?" Lena pressed.

He blinked once, then twice. Slowly pocketed her phone.

"Get in the car," he said quietly.

Whatever stirred behind his eyes wasn't done.

The city blurred past outside the windows, neon washing across the glass in restless streaks. Inside the SUV, the air was quiet, not calm.

Lena couldn't stop glancing at Lucien.

He was staring straight ahead, one hand resting on his thigh, the other flexing open and closed like it was itching to reach for something. She'd never seen him like this. Controlled, yes. Dangerous, always. But not this quiet. Not like something had reached across years and put a hand on the back of his neck.

Her fingers tightened around her phone. The screen was still lit up.

Tell Lucien to send Carter Vale my regards

His expression hadn't cracked, but something inside him had shifted. She saw it. That moment where he'd stopped, eyes distant like he'd heard a ghost.

She bit her lip. "Lucien..."

He didn't answer. Just kept staring forward.

Victoria, in the passenger seat, scrolled through her phone, humming to herself.

Lena leaned closer, her words low. "Who the hell is Carter Vale?"

Lucien finally moved, just barely. His lips parted like he was about to answer, but then he stopped. Thought better of it.

Not here. Not yet.

Lena leaned back in her seat, heart hammering. She had never believed Lucien Cole feared anyone. What the fuck had just rattled him?

Victoria leaned over from the front seat as they pulled up to a sleek high-rise near the water.

"Alright, you two lovebirds enjoy the rest of your night. Try not to miss me too much."

Lucien didn't even glance at her. "Text me when you get upstairs."

"Jesus, relax. I'm not twelve."

Lena smirked. "You say that like you didn't just stomp your foot."

Victoria scoffed, halfway out the SUV. "It was one dramatic step, not a stomp. I have flair, not tantrums."

Lucien glanced up from his phone. "Whatever it was, do it again and I'm banning you from every bottle service list I control."

Victoria rolled her eyes. "You wouldn't dare."

Lucien arched a brow. "Try me."

Victoria sighed, shaking her head as she stepped onto the curb. "God, you two were made for each other. You're both insufferable."

The door slammed shut.

The SUV rolled back into motion.

Silence settled.

Then Lena glanced over at Lucien. His eyes fixed ahead again.

"So," she started, carefully, "are you gonna talk to me, or am I supposed to pretend that second text didn't just hit you?"

Lucien didn't answer right away. When he finally spoke, his voice was low. Focused.

"Carter Vale. His father ran close with mine. We grew up in the same circles. He's reckless, still sniffing coke off tables, still trying to play king without building anything. But he's useful. Smart when he wants to be."

He paused and ran a hand down his face.

"I came down here to finalize a new spot with him. The focus was expansion, moving product under the radar."

Lena frowned. "So you think Carter's behind the texts?"

Lucien shook his head. "No. Carter's a wildcard, not a ghost. He wouldn't play games like that. The text said to send him 'regards.' That's a message. A reminder. The kind only one person would send, someone who knew what we were back in those circles."

"Who?"

Lucien didn't look at her. Eyes forward.

"Someone who's supposed to be dead."

He didn't say a name, but Lena saw it anyway, the ghost behind his eyes.

"Then how the hell are they reaching us?"

Lucien didn't answer.

Lena swallowed. "So when are you going to see Carter?"

Lucien finally turned to look at her, his expression unreadable.

"Right now."

Chapter Twenty-Four

MIAMI BURNS BLACK

Miami burned after dark.

The SUV cut through the night, headlights sliding across scorched pavement. Miami didn't sleep. It sweated. Even after midnight, the city looked overdressed and half-armed.

Lena leaned back into the leather, watching neon smear across luxury cars and crooked alleys. Billboards flashed. Red lights blinked. Beneath the polish she felt it, the pulse under the skin of the city.

A predator in perfume and gold.

Lucien sat beside her, silent. One hand rested on her thigh. The other held his phone, the screen dark.

Something in him had hardened the moment that text arrived.

His stillness wasn't calm anymore.

It was control.

Her thoughts drifted back to the warehouse. Dark walls. Blood in her mouth. Lucien coming through the door without hesitation.

She still wore the bruises.

He was the reason she was breathing.

Lena tucked a strand of hair behind her ear and glanced toward the window.

"It's beautiful down here," she said quietly. "But there's something else."

Lucien didn't look up.

"You're right," he said, voice low. "What you're seeing is the façade."

He finally turned slightly, eyes cutting toward the skyline.

"Miami's a different animal."

His gaze returned to the windshield.

"International money. Cartel pipelines. Foreign banks washing cash through yachts and crypto. Syndicates wrapped in Versace and fake smiles."

"Ghosts in suits."

Lena felt her pulse quicken. He wasn't exaggerating. He was showing her the board she'd just stepped onto.

"And unlike New York," Lucien continued, "the cops down here are already bought."

A beat.

"Just not by us."

Silence filled the car for a moment.

"What about your dad?" she asked.

Lucien didn't answer right away.

"What about him."

"He's got to have pull here."

"I don't need my father."

The words landed flat. Final.

"And at this point," Lucien added quietly, "he'd probably watch me bleed before deciding whether to lift a finger."

No anger.

Just fact.

Lena studied him.

"What's Carter to you now?"

Lucien didn't hesitate.

"A decision."

His eyes stayed forward.

"One I either cash in or cut loose."

She held his gaze.

"Do you trust him?"

Lucien finally looked at her.

"I trust that he owes me."

"When we go in, you don't talk unless I pull you in. You don't wander."

He held her eyes.

"You watch."

A beat.

"And if something feels wrong..."

"You follow me."

"No questions."

Lena nodded once.

"Copy that."

Lucien looked at her a moment longer, something unreadable in his eyes.

Then he turned forward.

The building came into view.

Just like that, the air shifted. Anticipation hardened into intent.

The SUV rolled to a stop outside a gutted industrial shell, half-hidden behind sagging chain-link.

Above the entrance, a dying red neon sign buzzed in the heat.

THE VERGE

It wasn't sleek. It wasn't subtle.

It was sleaze in snakeskin.

Once it had been a warehouse.

Now it was a nightclub built for men who didn't need menus or morals.

The kind of place where names carried more weight than money.

Lucien stepped out before the driver could move.

Lena followed.

The night hit her, thick and humid. Her heels clicked against cracked concrete.

Two men stood at the steel door. Huge. Silent.

One gave a single nod.

"He's expecting you."

Lucien didn't answer.

He simply took Lena's hand.

And walked her into the dark.

The music hit like a punch to the chest.

Distorted guitars tore through the room, a wall of sound loud, dirty, unapologetic. It didn't invite you in. It dared you to stay.

The place reeked of sweat, smoke, and something metallic under the bleach. Light came in pulses. Occasional strobes. Dying neon stretched long shadows across concrete floors.

VIP booths weren't velvet sanctuaries.

They were metal cages bolted into the ground.

A few low-lives turned their heads toward the entrance, eyes tracking movement with that practiced, predatory twitch. Dirtbags in designer knockoffs nursed stolen-looking drinks.

And at the back, stretched across the only leather sofa like he owned the entire city,

Carter Vale.

Mid-thirties. Lean build. Sun-burned skin. Slicked-back hair. Expensive shirt unbuttoned too low, designer shades still on despite the darkness.

A gold chain tangled around his neck. A smear of white powder lingered beneath one nostril.

He looked like the kind of man who mistook excess for power and had survived too long doing it. The moment he spotted Lucien, he grinned and shot to his feet, already performing.

"Look who finally decided to stop pretending New York's the only city on the map."

Lucien's expression didn't change.

"Thought the greeting party would at least wipe its nose before turning up the volume."

Carter laughed and spread his arms.

"Come on, Cole. We're all friends here."

His eyes flicked past Lucien, lingering on Lena.

Lena felt the look touch the bruise beneath her makeup before it reached her eyes.

"And what did you bring me?"

Lucien stepped forward, subtle but unmistakable.

Just enough to take her out of Carter's line of sight.

"Someone whose name you don't need to know unless I tell you."

Carter's grin widened.

"Right. Right. Lucien Cole. Still keeping the cards tight to your chest. Still a tight ass."

Lucien didn't smile.

"And you're still trying too hard."

Carter barked a laugh.

"Shit. I missed you."

They exchanged a half-hug, the kind that looked friendly but felt like a negotiation.

Then Carter waved toward the booth.

"Sit. Drink. Let's talk shop."

Lena followed Lucien to the booth, quiet, like he'd told her. But her eyes stayed sharp, sweeping the room.

Carter leaned back and flagged a waitress.

"Two tequilas. One for my friend."

Then his grin crept wider.

"And one for the ghost who decided to show his face again."

Lucien didn't move.

"You wanna clarify that last part?"

Carter lifted his hands in surrender.

"Relax. Just a phrase. No need to get twitchy."

Lucien leaned forward, elbows resting lightly on the table.

His voice came out smooth.

Cold.

"Then pick better phrases."

Carter studied him for a moment.

Then leaned back.

"Damn," he muttered. "You still carry that storm around with you."

Lena felt it now, the shift in the air.

Lucien wasn't relaxed.

He was poised.

Her gaze drifted across the room.

The man at the bar who hadn't touched his drink.

The second man posted a little too conveniently beside the exit.

Lucien had seen them too. She knew it without looking.

He shifted slightly in his seat.

Just enough to keep his back clear.

Carter kept talking.

The club. The expansion. What could be done if they "played it right" down here.

But Lucien wasn't listening anymore.

He was reading the room.

What he read was simple.

This wasn't a meeting.

This was a setup.

Lucien leaned back slowly.

"You've been busy."

Carter's brow lifted.

"Yeah? You checking up on me, Cole?"

"No."

Lucien's eyes moved lazily across the room.

"Just making observations."

A pause.

"Like how you called this meeting last-minute."

His gaze drifted toward the bar.

"How the guy at the counter hasn't touched his drink."

Then toward the exit.

"And the one by the door who keeps tapping his leg like he's waiting for a signal."

Lena's pulse picked up.

Carter's smile flickered.

"You always were paranoid."

Lucien's voice dropped.

"And you were always sloppy."

A flicker crossed Carter's face.

Lucien stood.

So did Carter's men.

Two stepped forward.

Then a third peeled out from the shadows near the wall.

Lucien didn't flinch.

"This how you handle business now?"

Carter rose more slowly.

"Precaution. You show up after years, bring a girl, act like you run the city."

"I don't run this city."

Lucien's voice was ice.

"But I could."

Silence settled between them.

Lucien stepped closer.

Close enough that Carter could feel it.

"I'm going to give you one chance," he said quietly.

"One chance to fix this."

His hand slid toward his coat.

Fingers brushing the grip of his gun.

Carter's grin snapped back into place.

But it didn't reach his eyes.

The front door burst open, cutting Carter off mid-breath.

Four men stepped inside. Dressed sharp. Moving like shadows.

And at the center of them stood Alexander Cole.

Lucien's father.

The bouncers didn't hesitate. They stepped aside, not because they were told, but because they knew better.

Lucien didn't look surprised.

Just annoyed.

Alexander's gaze swept the room, landed on Carter, then drifted to Lucien, colder now.

"If you'd been down here long enough, son, you'd know this kid is a fucking amateur."

Carter's face drained of color.

Alexander let the silence settle like smoke before his attention returned to Carter.

"I heard through the grapevine you were meeting my son tonight."

He adjusted the cuff of his jacket, tone precise, disdain curling around every word.

"And unlike your father, God rest his soul, I know you're a slimy little piece of shit who can't be trusted."

Carter's smile faded. "You don't know me anymore, Alexander."

Alexander stepped forward, venomous.

"Oh, I don't?"

He leaned in just enough.

"Miami's gutter suits you. You've always belonged there."

Another step closer. Quiet force.

"I assume this little stunt was your way of reminding him who you think holds weight in this city."

Carter didn't answer.

"Let me remind you what happens when you mistake access for weight."

Alexander snapped his fingers.

Two of his men grabbed the guy by the door. Another yanked the one at the bar down by the collar.

Carter raised his hands quickly.

"Whoa, whoa, wait a minute!"

Alexander didn't blink.

"You're lucky I let you keep your fucking teeth."

Lucien stepped back, letting it unfold.

Lena watched everything. Lucien's tension. Carter sinking fast into the mess he'd made. Alexander cutting through the room like a scalpel.

And her, still right in the middle of it.

Alexander glanced at her briefly and gave a single nod.

Then he looked back to Lucien.

"We'll talk later."

And just like that, he was gone.

Taking the chaos with him.

Carter slumped back into the booth, sweat glistening on his brow.

Lucien looked down at him.

"I gave you a chance."

Then he turned to Lena.

"Let's go."

The SUV was quiet in the way a room gets quiet after a gun jams.

Lena's pulse hadn't come down yet. Her hands were knotted in her lap, knuckles drained white.

She stole a glance at him.

Lucien stared straight ahead, elbow on the armrest, two fingers pressed to his temple.

He didn't look at her.

"You knew," she said. Not a question.

His eyes stayed forward. "I knew he was weak. Didn't know he was suicidal."

She swallowed. "Your father,"

"Wasn't saving me," Lucien cut in, voice flat. "He was reminding Carter who still owns the dirt under his feet."

Lena's voice dropped to almost nothing. "I've never seen you look at anyone like that."

Lucien finally turned his head.

The look he gave her wasn't cold.

It was vacant.

The same vacancy he'd shown Carter when his hand slid inside his coat.

"He put you in the room," Lucien said. "That's a death wish with my name on it."

"You were ready to kill him back there," she whispered.

He stared out the window like the city had just insulted him.

"Ready?" he said, almost amused. "My hand was already on the grip. Two inches of fabric and one pound of pressure. That's all that was left between his heartbeat and the wall behind him."

"I stopped because my father sent his little warning first, and because the muzzle flash would've lit your face up for every shooter in the room."

He looked at her fully now, eyes flat, voice softer than the hum of the engine.

"I decided I'd rather get you home than bury you."

She stared at him.

Whatever this was had moved past love.

She couldn't tell where one ended and the other began.

Lena sank back into the leather.

The man beside her made dangerous feel like a small word.

She was sitting three inches from a storm that hadn't decided where to land.

The rest of the ride was silence, thick and electric.

Lucien never looked away from the window.

His reflection stayed locked in the glass.

She could feel him counting exits, sightlines, heartbeats.

The city sprawled outside, bright, expensive, already bleeding.

Inside the car, the only sound was the low growl of the engine and the knowledge that if the night turned, he'd burn it all down before he let it touch her.

That wasn't safety.

That was ownership.

And God help her, she didn't want out.

By the time they reached the penthouse, the silence had settled into something heavier.

Lucien opened the door, stepped inside, and walked straight to the bar. No lights. Just the glow from the skyline casting him in hard lines and darker edges.

He poured a drink without asking if she wanted one.

Lena leaned against the doorway, arms folded. "So you want to talk about it?"

Lucien took a sip, then another. "Not yet."

He stared out at the city like it had personally betrayed him.

She didn't push. She walked over and stood beside him, letting the silence stretch.

After a minute, Lucien finally spoke. "You don't build what I've built without stepping on the wrong toes. But you never expect it to be the ones you once bled with."

He turned to her.

"Carter was supposed to be clean. Dangerous in stupid ways, not in treacherous ones. Tonight told me everything I needed to know."

"I don't like loose ends, Lena. And I'm starting to think there are more down here than I planned for."

She didn't reply. Just moved closer, resting a hand against his chest.

He caught it, held it a second. Then, quietly: "I came to Miami to finalize the expansion. But now I need to start watching our backs."

Lena nodded slowly. "So what happens next?"

The city sprawled under them, bright, expensive, and already feeding someone.

"We find out who wants to die first."

Lucien's stare hardened.

Then he turned to her, voice low, steady. "Give me a few minutes. I need to make a call."

Lena nodded, watching as he crossed the room. No questions. Just trust.

The office door shut behind him with a quiet click. No lights turned on, only darkness, edged faintly by whatever ambient glow managed to slip through the glass.

He opened the drawer. Took out a burner that held no contacts, no history, just ten digits burned into the back of his skull.

Dialed. One ring.

"Speak."

The voice on the other end sounded like a chainsaw gargling bourbon: low, chewed-up, patient.

Lucien didn't waste breath on hello.

"South Beach. Carter Vale. I want every shadow he's ever stood in. Who he owes, who he's bedding, who he's selling me to. Yesterday."

Two seconds of silence sharp enough to shave with.

Then: "Already got a bead on him."

Lucien's eyes narrowed. "Since when?"

"Since the day your father stopped being useful. I don't take days off, kid."

Lucien's knuckles whitened against the glass.

"He's too comfortable," Lucien said. "Like he rehearsed this."

A dry, humorless exhale. "They always rehearse. Right up until the bullet forgets the script."

"How soon?"

"Eyes on him in eight minutes. Full dossier by the time the sun crawls out of the ocean. But listen close, Lucien."

The rasp dropped to something sub-zero.

"If this turns into a mess, I'm not digging two graves in the same week. Choose which one you want filled first."

Click.

Lucien stared at the dead phone a second longer, then closed his fist around it until the plastic creaked like bone.

He slid it into his pocket.

He didn't move. His eyes moved slowly across the horizon.

Lena appeared in the doorway, barefoot, her hair loose around her shoulders.

"You okay?"

He turned.

The look he gave her wasn't reassurance.

It was calculation wearing his face.

"We're past good," he said. "We're in the part where people disappear."

He crossed the room, stopping an inch from her without touching her. The heat off him said enough.

"You still sure you want on this ride?"

Her eyes never left his.

She didn't answer. She didn't look away.

Lucien watched her.

Then he killed the lights.

Darkness swallowed the penthouse.

Only the glow from outside carved them into silhouettes.

He shrugged out of his jacket. Let it fall where it landed.

Unbuttoned his cuffs, rolled the sleeves once, twice, exposing the faint white scars that never saw daylight.

He didn't go to the bedroom.

He went back to the bar, poured two fingers of whiskey.

Neither of them spoke again.

Eventually she walked over, took the glass from his hand, and finished it.

Then she set it down, empty, and walked past him into the bedroom.

He followed two seconds later.

No kissing.

No comforting.

No falling asleep in each other's arms.

They lay on opposite sides of a bed too large for either of them to pretend distance meant safety, eyes open, listening to the city breathe outside the glass.

Close enough that if the shooting started, he could still drag her behind him.

Far enough apart that neither of them pretended this was still safe.

It never was.

Chapter Twenty-Five

DAWN SHARPENS THE BLADE

The sun was just beginning to rise over the ocean outside the penthouse windows, pale orange dragging across glass, steel, and the white bones of the city.

Lena stirred awake. It wasn't the sun that pulled her from sleep. It was the sound. Low. Distant. The soft shift of a man who hadn't trusted the night enough to sleep through it.

She rolled out of bed and stepped into the main room.

Lucien was already up.

He stood by the floor-to-ceiling windows, shirt half-buttoned, a black mug resting untouched on the counter behind him. His watch was strapped tight, gun on the table within arm's reach. His eyes stayed fixed on the streets below.

He didn't glance at her. "I didn't sleep."

Lena walked toward him, wrapping her arms around him. "You okay?"

"I've been going over everything," he muttered. "Every minute from the second we landed."

He turned slightly. "The pieces fit too clean. That was the problem."

"Carter was never this organized."

His phone buzzed once on the counter. A black screen lit with a single encrypted line of text:

Your eyes only. 5-sec window

Lucien grabbed it, swiped, and stared.

A file. Photos. Names. One name in particular stopped him cold. He tapped. Enlarged. Studied.

His mouth tightened. "Motherfucker."

Lena stepped closer. "What is it?"

Lucien didn't answer right away. He turned the phone toward her.

A surveillance photo. Carter in a suit, leaning against a black BMW.

Standing next to him was a man in black lenses, mid-fifties, square-jawed and still in a way that made the rest of the photo feel noisy. A thin scar cut across his face. He didn't look like muscle. He looked like the man muscle answered to.

Lucien said the name under his breath.

"Victor Dresnik."

The name came out flat, but Lena felt the room change anyway.

Lena blinked. "Who the hell is that?"

Lucien's eyes didn't leave the screen. "Russian intermediary. Old world. Launders money for European syndicates. Quiet. Untouchable down here, at least."

He looked up at her, voice razor-sharp. "If Dresnik's in play, Carter isn't the problem. He's the invitation."

"Men like Dresnik don't knock unless they already own the door."

Lena's pulse jumped. "Carter's working with him?"

"Not officially yet." Lucien dropped the phone onto the counter. "This isn't about a nightclub anymore. It's leverage. Territory. A takeover."

He dumped the cold coffee and started a fresh brew, slow and methodical.

Lena leaned on the counter, her voice quieter. "What do we do?"

Before Lucien could respond, the phone rang again.

Unknown number.

Lucien stared at it. Let it ring once. Twice. Then answered.

"Yeah."

Carter's voice came through cool this time. Controlled.

"We should finish our conversation."

Lucien said nothing.

"Little Havana. Warehouse off El Prado Street. One hour. Just us. Dropping the pin now."

Lucien's face didn't move. "Sure. Just us."

The line clicked off.

He turned to Lena. "This is him forcing the board."

She searched his face, cautious. "You going?"

Lucien nodded once. "Wouldn't miss it."

She crossed her arms. "Alone?"

Lucien walked to the bedroom, threw open the closet, pulled a matte-black duffel bag from the back.

"Nobody walks into a trap empty-handed."

Then, he looked at her. "This isn't New York. You remember what I said, down here, the cops don't care who you are. They're already bought. One wrong move, and you don't just lose leverage. You get framed, or worse, you vanish."

"I wanted this clean. A fresh slate. Now I've got men down here who think a title keeps them alive."

He zipped the duffel shut and turned to her. "I want you here, away from it."

Lena tilted her chin up. "I'm not staying behind. I'm not waiting somewhere safe while you walk into it."

Lucien held her stare a moment longer than necessary. Then nodded once.

"Grab your shoes."

As she turned to go, his voice stopped her.

"If this goes sideways, you run. Don't look back."

Lena looked over her shoulder, steady.

"If it goes sideways, I start shooting."

Lucien looked at her for half a second longer.

"Then let's move."

Lucien's phone was already in his hand by the time Lena disappeared into the other room. He tapped the screen once. A name he didn't call lightly.

It rang once. Twice.

"Lucien."

Alexander's voice came through, like he'd been expecting the call.

Lucien didn't waste time. "Carter just called. Told me to meet him."

"And you're calling me why?" His father already knew the answer.

"Because it's a fucking trap."

Something shifted in the air.

"Where?"

"Some warehouse off El Prado. Little Havana."

"That area's old ground. One of the first areas we took when we came south."

Lucien's tone hardened.

"Not anymore. Not since he started making side deals."

"Are you asking for backup?"

"Figured I'd give you a heads up before it hits."

Alexander exhaled, soft and slow.

"I'll send a few men to keep it contained."

Lucien didn't say thank you. Alexander didn't expect him to.

Just before the line went dead, Alexander spoke again.

"Be smart, son. Don't lose yourself down here trying to prove you're better than me."

A pause.

"You already are, Lucien."

Lucien lowered the phone.

For a second, he didn't move.

He grabbed the burner.

Dialed the next number.

One click.

"Talk." The gravel rasp of Ghost's voice.

Lucien didn't flinch. "Little Havana. Warehouse off El Prado. I want eyes there before I even see the fucking building."

"Already have three angles. Working on the fourth. You going in armed?"

"I'm not going in to talk."

"Then you'll need cleanup."

Lucien's voice was like steel. "Only if there's anything left."

Ghost paused. "What about Lena?"

Lucien didn't hesitate. "She's with me."

Another pause. A colder tone. "Then she gets two shadows of her own. Let me know when it starts."

The line went dead.

Lucien turned toward the hallway just as Lena stepped out, leather boots laced, eyes sharp.

"You ready?" he asked.

She took one long look at him, then nodded.

"Let's go."

Outside, Miami was already moving. Traffic. Heat. Church bells somewhere in the distance. In Little Havana, the warehouse waited.

Chapter Twenty-Six

CHECKMATE MOVES ONLY

They moved quickly through the building's lower level, the air cooling as they descended into the private garage beneath the tower. Concrete floors. Motion sensors blinking awake overhead. The kind of silence money buys.

Lena glanced around, heels echoing. "What are we doing down here?"

Lucien didn't look back. "I keep one vehicle down here. Always."

He stopped beside a matte-black AMG coupe, dark trim, red brake calipers visible through the spokes. The car sat low and predatory, built for speed and silence.

"I'm driving us there myself," Lucien said, sliding the key from his pocket. "I want control."

The car slid through the city in long, controlled bursts of speed. No convoy. Just the two of them and whatever waited at the end of this stretch of Miami asphalt.

Lena watched him, his hands steady on the wheel, eyes fixed far down the road. There was something about the way he drove, controlled, ready to swerve at a moment's notice. She'd seen that look before in men who expected the road to turn on them.

"So..." she said carefully, her voice breaking the silence. "Who was the second man on the phone?"

Lucien didn't take his eyes off the road. "Ghost."

Lena blinked. "That's a name?"

Lucien smirked, just barely. "Not a name. A fact."

She waited.

"Back when everything was paper, he was my father's shadow. Former special forces, the kind erased from rosters. Black-bag, off-book. He can erase a man, bury a phone, pull plates before the cops know a camera caught them, and put eyes where no one admits cameras exist."

He paused, tone colder now. "I watched him hack a federal surveillance grid using nothing but a burner phone."

Lena stared.

Lucien's voice never shifted. Flat. Final. "He doesn't exist. No past. No prints. No weakness. Countries hire ghosts. I call him."

Lena leaned back slightly, eyes narrowed. "And you trust him?"

Lucien's fingers flexed on the wheel. "With my life. He's been off the grid for a while, but he's never missed a call from me."

A beat.

"If he's in, we've got eyes everywhere."

She didn't say anything. Just turned back toward the window. Lucien had backups for his backups. If he was calling Ghost, this wasn't a meeting anymore.

Lena's gaze drifted to the side mirror. A dark vehicle had been following them for several blocks, two cars back, never too close, holding the lane. She kept her voice even.

"We've had company since 27th."

Lucien didn't glance over. "Copy. Ours, Ghost's, two back. Dark SUV."

She turned to him, brows raised.

"There are already a few planted near the warehouse," he added. "And a couple trailing us, keeping distance." His tone was calm, but there was steel under it.

"You think we'll need them?" Lena asked.

Lucien's fingers flexed around the wheel. "I plan like we will."

Her breath caught, not in fear, but in awe. He wasn't paranoid. He was prepared.

He spoke again, voice low. "If Carter's still breathing after all this, it's because I let him. And if there's any deal left on the table, it's mine. My terms. My number. Or he disappears."

She didn't respond. She didn't have to.

The car slowed as they turned off the main road, sunlight cutting sharp lines across the dash. The city fell away behind them, storefronts and palm trees replaced by the stark, abandoned sprawl of Miami's industrial outskirts. The kind of place that held secrets and buried them deep.

Ahead, the warehouse emerged, low and concrete, forgotten by time. Rust ran down the corrugated walls in long stains. No signs. No names. Just a patch of asphalt and too much silence.

Lucien leaned forward. "That's the spot."

Lena sat straighter, every nerve on alert. Her heart wasn't racing, but it was awake.

Parked near the loading dock, two vehicles faced the lot like they'd been there a while, legal plates, windows dark enough to hide behind, and just enough distance to feel wrong.

Lucien scoffed. "Two cars, staggered. Nobody sits like that without a second play."

Lena followed his gaze. "What about Ghost's guys? The ones tailing us?"

"They peeled off a mile back," Lucien said. "Can't be seen with us, I'm holding up my end like we agreed." His tone dropped. "Got a few even closer for immediate backup if it goes south."

"Should we let Ghost know?"

Lucien's mouth twitched. "Trust me. He's already watching."

Lucien's gaze flicked once. No reaction. Just a slow breath.

"We're early," Lena said quietly.

Lucien's lips curved, not a smile, something sharper. "There's no early in rooms like this. Just the ones who walk in blind and the ones who leave breathing."

They came to a slow stop. The engine cut. Heat shimmered on the pavement, warning them to turn back.

Lucien didn't move right away. Instead, he turned to her. Eyes locked.

"You stay to my right. You don't move unless I move. Understand?"

She nodded once, calm and clear.

He reached into the glovebox, pulled a compact matte-black piece, and placed it in her palm.

"No hesitation."

Lena's fingers curled around it, her grip steady.

Outside, the heat waited. They stepped out together, no fear, no doubt, walking side by side straight into the lion's mouth.

The moment Lucien and Lena stepped out, the driver-side door of the lead vehicle creaked open.

Carter Vale stepped out wearing Ray-Bans, a gold chain, and the same smug weight he always carried.

From the second car, another man emerged, unhurried, carrying the kind of calm that usually meant someone else was about to die.

Victor Dresnik. Lucien clocked him instantly.

Ghost's file had called him "a professional with no affiliations."

Carter spread his arms like they were old friends running into each other on vacation.

"Lucien. Thought you might have ghosted me after last night."

Lucien didn't answer. Just stared. Carter's grin didn't falter. He motioned toward the warehouse behind him.

"No need to stand out here like we're plotting a coup. C'mon inside. It's cooler in there. Victor hates waiting."

Victor's face didn't move. He was already watching Lena. Like a man assessing whether she was arm candy or armed.

Lucien stepped forward. Not fast, but not like he was waiting on a fucking invitation, either.

"I said I'd come. I'm here. Talk."

Carter laughed, too loud for the space between them.

"Same old Lucien. No drinks, no handshake, just straight to business."

Lucien's tone was flat. "It stopped being business the second you brought backup."

Carter's smile faltered. Barely. Victor shifted his weight.

Lena didn't move, staying just behind Lucien's shoulder. Her hand hovered near the compact piece tucked against her side. Just in case.

Carter looked at her. "She doesn't say much, huh?"

Lucien didn't blink. "She doesn't need to."

That shut Carter up for a beat. Then he motioned to the warehouse doors, stepping back.

"Alright then. Come inside. We'll talk. Just us." His smile thinned. "Scout's honor."

Lucien didn't move. He glanced at Lena. Then nodded.

They stepped forward together, into the mouth of the building, the heavy doors creaking open as they stepped inside.

Behind them, nothing moved. No wind. No witnesses. Just old steel and silence.

The inside of the warehouse was worse than outside, hot, stale, and stinking of dust and oil. Light filtered through broken windows above, casting long, fractured shadows across the concrete.

Lucien's eyes adjusted instantly.

Victor moved first, stepping in behind Carter but keeping to the side. Strategic. Calculated. The kind of movement professionals made when they weren't sure if it was a deal or a kill box.

Carter stopped near the center of the space, turning with that same shit-eating grin.

"Alright. Let's talk."

Lucien didn't budge. "Start talking, then."

Carter chuckled, but it didn't reach his eyes.

"That deal we were finalizing? The one you flew down here for?" His smile vanished. "It's dead."

Lena stayed still.

Lucien didn't flinch. "So what is this?"

Carter paced, turning like he was showing them around a showroom.

"Thought maybe we could still clear the air. You know, before things got messy."

His hand dipped into his coat, smooth, practiced, and came out with a gun already half-raised.

Lucien's voice dropped. "I should've fucking killed you last night."

Carter chuckled again. Hollow. "C'mon, don't be like that, man. We came up together. Built half the East Coast buzz back in our twenties. You and me, same grind, different fathers."

Lucien's face didn't change. "That supposed to mean something to me?"

Carter's grin faded. "I've been hearing whispers," he said. "City's talking. Cole blood making moves down here. Not your old man. You."

He shrugged. Eyes sharp. "Me? I'm not looking to burn in your fire. So I figured, why not be the one known for putting it out?"

Lucien stepped forward like the decision had already been made.

"Correction," he said. "I'm not making moves. I'm taking ground."

Carter's smirk flickered. "Yeah, see, that's the thing. Down here? There's already a table."

Lucien's eyes stayed on him. "Good. I'll take the head of it."

Carter's smile thinned. "And everyone seated at it has sharp teeth and long memories. You show up uninvited, start making noise, people might wonder if you forgot how this game is played."

Lucien stepped forward again.

Cold.

Calm.

"I didn't forget the game."

A pause.

"I just stopped asking for a seat."

He leaned in.

"Move."

Victor moved, fluid and fast, drawing his weapon and leveling it at Lucien's head. Carter's swung across and locked on Lena.

"Hands where I can see them," Victor said.

Lucien didn't move.

A small red dot appeared on Carter's chest.

Then another touched Victor's throat.

Carter froze. "You've gotta be fucking kidding me."

Ghost's voice rasped through Lucien's earpiece. "I have the room."

The warehouse doors slammed open.

Bright daylight poured in behind five more armed men.

And in the center, Alexander Cole. Impeccably dressed. Hands in his pockets. Not surprised. Not rushed. Just there to make sure the room remembered whose history it was standing in.

The walkie crackled again. "Alexander?" Ghost's voice asked.

Alexander smiled. "Ahh. Ghost, my old friend. Watching over my boy, are you?"

Ghost's voice crackled over the radio. "There's a price for everything in this world."

Carter stared at the scene, his hand still raised, gun still out, but his confidence slipping fast.

He let out a sharp, unhinged laugh. "Jesus Christ. It's a goddamn family reunion in here!"

Lucien took a step forward now, locked on Carter. The game had just flipped. And Carter knew it.

He spun slowly in place, eyes jumping from Ghost's men to Alexander's, to Lucien, and finally back to Victor, his voice rising into a jittery blend of bravado and desperation.

"Oh, come the fuck on," he barked. "This is bullshit! You all brought backup? You brought your daddy?" He gestured wildly at Lucien. "You think this makes you look strong? Nah, man. It makes you look scared."

No one answered. Carter's face flushed, his composure cracking under the weight of every rifle now pointed at him.

"You think Miami's gonna let you run it like New York? You think this little pissing contest ends here? There are bigger names watching, bigger pockets funding all of this, and none of them are gonna kneel to some pretty-boy prince and his fucking armed babysitters!"

His hands shook. The gun he held was still aimed at Lena, but it was slipping. Just slightly. He didn't even notice.

Victor noticed.

Carter turned to him, eyes wide. "Back me up, man. We talked about this. You said we were good. You said..."

Victor turned his gun to him.

"Victor," Carter said, his voice cracking. "Victor, what the fuck are you doing!?"

Victor didn't answer. He stepped forward once. Calm. Cold.

Carter flinched. "No, wait, wait, wait."

The shot cracked through the warehouse like a thunderclap.

Carter dropped instantly, blood spraying across the concrete.

His body collapsed before the echo finished rolling through the rafters, limbs twitching once before going still.

Victor stood there, arm extended, barrel still smoking.

Then, without looking at anyone, he muttered, "He was never going to survive this room."

Lucien didn't move. Alexander didn't blink. Ghost's men didn't lower their weapons.

Lena exhaled, her heart pounding, blood singing in her ears.

Victor finally looked up, eyes landing on Lucien. "Let's talk," he said calmly. "Just the two of us."

Lucien didn't look at Lena.

"Why don't you stay outside with my father?"

Lena's brow twitched, but she nodded.

Alexander, hands still in his pockets, turned to her with a half-smile. "Come on, sweetheart. Let's go have ourselves a little chat while the boys talk business."

As they stepped out, Lucien's eyes lifted to the man on the catwalk, his walkie clipped back on his shoulder.

"The money's wired. Should hit within the hour," Lucien said.

Ghost's voice cut through the static. "Funds received. Extraction in progress."

The shadows folded. One by one, the operatives disappeared back into the dark like they were never there.

Outside, the warehouse doors closed with a hollow thud, sealing Lucien and Victor inside.

Heat rolled off the pavement in waves. The air smelled like sun-baked rubber and dust. Miami kept breathing like nothing had happened.

Alexander stood with his hands in his pockets, posture loose, eyes fixed on the door. Not worried. Just waiting, like he'd waited his whole life.

Lena watched him.

Then she found her voice. "You're not worried?"

Alexander's mouth twitched, not quite a smile. "I don't have to. He doesn't lose."

"And if he does?"

Alexander finally looked at her. The look had no softness in it.

"Then he won't come back out."

The words sat between them. No drama. No threat. A rule.

Lena swallowed. The warehouse door felt louder now, heavier. Like it held a storm behind it.

She stepped closer anyway, lowering her voice as if the concrete could hear.

"What happened to him?" she asked. "It's like there's something under everything he says. Something he never lets anyone touch."

For a few seconds, he didn't answer at all. Cicadas buzzed in the distance. A car passed somewhere far off and never mattered.

Then he spoke, quiet.

"You ever see the moment a boy disappears?"

Lena didn't move.

Alexander kept his eyes on the warehouse door.

"When Lucien was thirteen, the feds were closing in. Evelyn and I had to vanish for a while. I left him with a man I trusted."

His jaw worked once.

"That is the sentence I've been paying for ever since."

The heat pressed around them. Cicadas screamed in the distance.

Alexander swallowed, but his voice stayed even.

"That man had a clean house. Clean shoes. Clean hands when I shook them. That's what still gets me." His eyes went colder. "Everything about him looked safe."

Lena's stomach tightened.

"He wasn't."

Alexander's fingers curled inside his pockets.

"When I came back, Lucien wasn't the same boy."

"He didn't run to Evelyn. Didn't cry. Didn't ask where we had been. He just stood in the hallway with a bag in his hand, like he'd packed himself away before we ever opened the door."

Lena's breath caught.

"He had bruises he tried to hide. Marks he lied about. And eyes," Alexander said, his voice thinning at the edges, "God help me, those eyes. They weren't scared anymore. Scared would have been mercy."

He looked down at the pavement.

"They were empty."

Alexander kept going because stopping would have broken something.

"I asked him what happened. He said nothing. I asked again. He said he fell. Thirteen years old, standing there like a little soldier, protecting the monster because he thought if he said the words out loud, it would become real."

The warehouse door stayed shut.

"Then Evelyn touched his face."

His voice changed.

Barely.

But Lena heard the fracture in it.

"He flinched from his own mother."

"When I found out," Alexander said, "I went quiet. Real quiet. The kind of quiet men mistake for mercy."

He lifted his gaze again.

"I tracked him down."

Lena didn't ask what happened.

Alexander told her anyway.

"I didn't bring a gun."

A beat.

"Guns are too generous."

The cicadas screamed in the heat.

"I made him understand every second he stole from my son. Then I buried what was left of him somewhere the earth won't give back."

Lena's throat burned.

Alexander didn't look proud.

He looked like a man who had done the only thing left and knew it still hadn't been enough.

"But killing him didn't give Lucien back what he took."

His eyes returned to the warehouse door.

"That's the part no one tells you. You can put a man in the ground. You can erase his name. You can burn every room he ever stood in. But you can't walk into your son's chest and drag the boy out alive."

Lena wiped nothing. The tear slipped down her cheek anyway.

Alexander saw it and gave her no comfort.

He had not brought her there for comfort.

"And seven years later," he said, "Lucien woke up and found his best friend dead on our living room floor."

The words hit different.

Not sharper.

Deeper.

"Blue lips. Foam at the mouth. Eyes open."

Lena's stomach turned.

"He tried to save him."

Alexander's voice dropped.

"He was twenty, but the sound that came out of him wasn't a man. It was the boy again. The one I thought was gone."

He looked at her then.

Really looked.

"He screamed for me. Like I could fix it. Like I was still allowed to be his father in that room."

Lena could barely breathe.

"He did CPR until his arms gave out. He kept saying his name. Over and over. Begging him like the dead negotiate if you love them enough."

Alexander's mouth tightened.

"I pulled him back and he fought me. Fought me like I was the one killing him. He had blood on his hands from where his knuckles split against the floor. He kept trying to crawl back to him."

"And when it was over, when the ambulance lights were gone and Evelyn was upstairs crying into a towel so he wouldn't hear her, Lucien sat on that floor until sunrise."

Alexander's voice went almost flat.

"He didn't say a word."

Lena stared at him.

"At thirteen, he learned the world could touch him anywhere. At twenty, he learned love doesn't save what it holds."

Alexander stepped closer.

Not invading.

Making sure she heard him.

"So when you look at him and think calm, you're wrong."

His eyes cut toward the warehouse.

"You're looking at a locked door."

Lena's pulse thudded in her ears.

"He built that control with his bare hands because if he ever let himself feel everything at once, there wouldn't be a city left standing around him."

Alexander's voice hardened.

"They took his mercy first. Then they took his trust. After that, all he had left was teeth."

Lena looked back at the closed warehouse door.

For the first time, she didn't just see Lucien's violence.

She saw the shape of the wound underneath it.

Alexander's voice lowered.

"If you love him," he said, "you don't get to love the polished parts. You don't get to choose the version that opens doors, wears suits, and makes you feel safe."

He held her there with his stare.

"You take all of him."

The cicadas screamed.

"And if you can't," Alexander said, "leave him alone."

He looked back at the warehouse.

"Because he doesn't survive it a third time."

Silence.

No closure. No mercy. Just heat, truth, and a closed door.

Back inside, it was just Lucien and Victor now, standing in the center of the warehouse, dust still settling, the silence heavier than the heat.

No more shadows. No more backup. Just two men.

The bottom line.

Victor adjusted his stance, watching Lucien with the cool steadiness of someone who'd been on both sides of a barrel.

"Hell of a way to say hello," he muttered.

Lucien didn't smile. "You're lucky that's all it was."

He took a slow step forward, eyes drifting to the trail of blood, brain matter, and skull fragments spilling from Carter's head across the concrete, then back to Victor.

The silence stretched.

Long enough to matter.

Then Lucien broke it.

"So what now, Victor? You playing diplomat? Or just waiting for my back to turn?"

"I didn't come here to play anything," Victor said. "I came to offer you a partnership."

Lucien's gaze flicked again to the blood seeping into the cracks of the concrete. His voice stayed dry.

"Interesting pitch, considering your last partner's brains are decorating the floor."

Victor didn't budge.

"He was a liability. An embarrassment. All flash, no discipline. He never grew up. Never grasped what this life actually demanded."

He closed the distance.

"This city doesn't bow to boys pretending to be wolves. It feeds on them. There's no seat for that kind of chaos at the table being built here."

A beat.

"Carter wasn't a partner. He was a jester in a room full of kings, a loose cannon that couldn't be trusted."

Lucien's tone dipped colder. "Hard to talk trust when the man talking to me had a gun aimed at my head five minutes ago."

Victor gave a single nod. "Fair."

Then he added, "But sometimes you have to play the role just long enough to survive the board. Then you make your real move."

Lucien's eyes narrowed, his patience thinning.

"Alright. Enough theater. Why am I still standing here?"

Victor's tone sharpened now.

Less pitch.

More truth.

"You have the reach. The control. But your empire's loud. Public. Flashy."

He motioned to the stale air of the warehouse.

"I deal in silence. Old-world syndicates. Eastern Europe. Russia. Money that doesn't want to be seen, only cleaned and sent home. My clients move oil, arms, diamonds, whatever keeps their countries running and their enemies poor. But they need clean passage. Stateside fronts.

"I have the channels. What I don't have is scale outside Miami.

"I move money through shell corporations, property chains, crypto, art, hospitality. But I need volume. Liquidity. Flow."

Victor met Lucien's eyes.

"Your empire has that."

He spread a hand slightly.

"We streamline it. Your heat, my ghost-hand. We build a clean pipeline through nightlife, hospitality, art dealing, even offshore ventures."

Lucien finally spoke. "Why now?"

Victor smirked. "Because the ones I work for are circling. If I don't offer them something sustainable here, they'll find someone else. Someone stupid. Someone who'll bring feds to the front door in a week."

Lucien stepped in closer, eyes narrowing. "And why me?"

Victor took another step.

"Your clubs? Perfect surface. High volume, high-end clientele. You already move product in and out. You know how to bury heat under lifestyle. But I've got something you don't."

Lucien tilted his head. "Enlighten me."

Victor's smile barely curled.

"Four clubs. Eight total businesses. All down here. Each one with clean books, vetted staff, and just enough ties to local officials who owe me favors. My network's built for discretion. Not flash. But it's airtight."

He paused, voice dropping lower.

"You're fighting to keep Miami clean while your people keep the New York veins pumping. But you've got overflow. Cash that needs to vanish. Product that needs to pass quieter."

Victor went on, tone clinical now.

"We flip the stream. I run a few quiet channels up to you. You run your overflow down to me. Your dirty gets washed in my clean. My ghosts stay ghosts. And your feds? They keep chasing ghosts in suits who don't exist."

Lucien considered that.

"You cross me, your European friends won't find your fucking ashes."

Victor smiled and extended a hand.

"That's the language I speak."

They shook once.

Firm.

No warmth, just wartime respect.

Victor's eyes flashed.

"Let's build something neither coast can touch."

The warehouse doors creaked open, flooding the air with heavy heat and blinding sun. Lucien and Victor stepped into it, shoulders squared, the weight of what just happened trailing behind them like smoke after a blast.

Alexander leaned against his truck, arms folded, his men now gone, like they'd never been there. Lena stood beside him, chin lifted, eyes scanning the two men as they emerged.

Lucien's gaze found her first.

No words.

Just a look.

One that said: We're clear.

Lena held his gaze longer than she normally would. Not because she doubted him, but because now, she understood the quiet war behind his eyes.

And for the first time, she saw the boy still fighting underneath the man.

Alexander raised a brow. "So? You boys hug it out in there?"

Victor didn't miss a beat. "Wrapped up Carter's retirement. Closed casket."

Alexander smirked, pushing off the SUV. "Bit messy for a sendoff."

Victor's eyes flicked to the blood drying on his sleeve. "He was never big on clean exits."

Lucien opened the passenger door for Lena. She slid in, quiet but alert. Eyes on Victor now, studying him like a second exam.

Victor stepped toward his own car but paused just before reaching the door.

"One more thing," he said over his shoulder. "There's a fundraiser this evening. Downtown. Governor's circle. Real suits. Real money. I'll be hosting."

Lucien narrowed his eyes. "You want me to play politician now?"

Victor turned, half a grin. "I want you to show face. Make a generous contribution. Let them see you in a room where no one bleeds."

He paused, then added, "Black tie. Real donors. Real judges. Don't bring the storm, bring the weather."

He adjusted his cuff. "You do that, and some very important people in this city will start to see you less like a threat and more like an ally."

Alexander chuckled, dry. "And here I thought you weren't the political type."

Victor looked over at him. "Men like you built the rules. We learned how to survive them."

Lucien didn't respond right away. He stared at Victor for a long second, then gave the smallest nod.

"I'll be there."

Victor slipped into the back seat of his car. "Good. Just don't forget, it's all face value tonight. Shake the right hands. Don't take your finger off the trigger."

The door shut behind him. The engine turned over.

Lucien watched the car disappear down the road, then turned back to his father.

Alexander stood there, arms crossed, eyes narrowed, not with judgment, but calculation.

"This partnership sitting right with you?" he asked.

"For now," Lucien said. "It's the only move that makes sense."

Alexander gave a slow nod. "I'll have eyes at the fundraiser. Quiet ones."

Lucien turned and slid into the car beside Lena.

"Where to now?" she asked.

Lucien stared out the windshield.

Then his voice came low, dry, and razor-edged.

"We clean up."

"Then we shake hands."

CHAPTER TWENTY-SEVEN
THE ART OF CONTROL

The penthouse doors shut behind them with a soft click. High above the city, Miami fell away, leaving only silence and tension in clean air and glass.

Lucien tossed his jacket onto the nearest chair, his movements slower now. Measured. The energy he'd carried into the warehouse was still there, buried beneath something heavier.

Lena watched him cross the room. He didn't say a word.

He stopped near the windows, staring out over the skyline like he was already ahead of whatever came next.

She stepped closer, quiet at first. "How are you really doing?"

Lucien didn't look back. "It's handled."

"But handling it and carrying it are two different things."

That made him pause.

She reached for him, fingers brushing the back of his arm. "You've got people who'd burn the world for you. You don't always have to carry it alone."

Lucien finally turned, his gaze finding hers, less guarded. Not soft. Just open enough to matter.

"Everyone has a weakness. Even kings."

Lena took his face in her hands. "Then you better stay close to yours."

He kissed her like a man still fighting for something worth surviving for.

Lena looked up at him, then swallowed. "Can I ask you something?"

Lucien didn't move. "What is it?"

"How do you shake the hand that nearly pulled the trigger on you?"

He stepped in. Not rushed. Not angry. Controlled.

The air tightened around him, like static before a strike.

"Are you questioning my decisions, Lena? How I choose to handle business?"

She instinctively backed up, her spine brushing the edge of the counter. "I... I just assumed that was survival. Not business."

Lucien didn't stop until he was inches from her, close enough to feel the heat rolling off his body.

His mouth brushed her ear as he spoke. "That was dominance, disguised as forgiveness."

Lena's breath caught in her throat.

He wasn't touching her yet, but the tension had already stripped the air between them bare.

Lena didn't move. Not out of fear. Out of gravity.

The kind he pulled her into without touching her.

His breath lingered at her ear, warm.

A threat, soft as silk.

She tilted her head, not shying away. "And what about this?" she whispered. "What are you hiding behind it?"

Lucien didn't answer right away. He looked at her the way he looked at enemies across polished tables and glass walls, like he already knew how this would end.

"Nothing. That's what should scare you."

His hand found her waist with the same precision he brought to everything else.

Lena's breath caught as his thumb skimmed her ribs, pausing on the fabric of her dress like he was testing its threshold.

Her body stayed still, caught between resistance and surrender.

He didn't rush. He never did. His mouth hovered just above hers, close enough to taste the decision hanging between them.

"Tell me to stop," he whispered.

But she didn't. Couldn't. Wouldn't.

And still, he didn't take. Not yet.

Lucien's forehead dropped gently against hers, a quiet exhale threading between them. For one suspended second, he let the mask slip.

His control didn't slip. If anything, it hardened.

"You want answers. You'll get them. But not like this."

Lena searched his eyes, looking for softness.

She found restraint. The kind that burned hotter than indulgence.

Lena blinked up at him, dazed. "So what now?"

He stepped back, not far, just enough to let the air cool between them. Just enough that she felt it.

Lucien straightened the cuffs of his shirt like he hadn't just brought her to the edge of something she didn't have words for.

"We get dressed. Smile for the cameras. Make sure the right people see us together tonight."

"We're not walking in as a question mark. We're walking in as a fact."

She watched him, still catching her breath. "You mean at the fundraiser?"

He glanced at her over his shoulder, gaze sharp but unreadable.

"In rooms like this, appearances write the rules. Standing next to the right person is currency. Silence trades like gold."

He didn't look at her.

"You won't owe anyone. But they'll believe you do. That's the point."

Lena swallowed. "And you're okay with that?"

Lucien gave her the faintest smile, humorless, controlled.

"I'm not here to be okay. I'm here to win."

"Then let's win," she whispered.

Then, without another word, he turned and disappeared down the hall, leaving Lena alone with the tension still coiled beneath her skin, and the sense that whatever he was protecting her from had already started.

The sky burned gold, streaked with pink and smoke as the sun began its slow descent into the ocean. From up here, the world looked quiet. But Lena had learned, quiet never meant safe.

In the bedroom, the air held the faint imprint of Lucien's cologne, sharp, clean, and quietly dominant.

She stood by the vanity, slipping earrings through her lobes, her reflection steadier than she felt.

The dress Lucien had sent was sleek, black, and unforgiving.

She hadn't asked how he knew her size. Precision was part of his nature.

Behind her, his voice cut through the hush.

"Turn," he said.

And she did, without question.

Lucien stood a few feet away, tuxedo cut to perfection, his eyes moving over her like a man assessing both armor and weakness.

In his hands, he held a necklace, delicate, diamond-edged, a piece that whispered legacy and quiet intent.

He stepped forward and fastened it around her throat with careful fingers.

His touch never lingered.

It didn't have to.

The heat it left behind said enough.

His breath warned against her neck. "This isn't just a party. It's performance. Every move you make is a message."

She met his gaze in the mirror.

"What message am I sending?"

He looked at her like she was a loaded weapon.

"That you belong to no one, but you're already spoken for."

She didn't know how to respond to that.

But her pulse did.

Lucien checked his watch, then leaned in, brushing his lips against the shell of her ear.

"It's time."

He didn't offer his arm, but when they stepped into the elevator, he stood close enough that the whole city could've burned and she wouldn't have noticed.

The car curved through a palm-lined drive, its engine a whisper compared to the waves crashing just beyond the mansion walls.

Governor's Circle didn't have street signs, just polished stone markers and iron gates that only opened for the already powerful or the dangerously persistent.

As they approached, the gates parted without a word, revealing a beachfront mansion carved in glass, marble, and intent.

The kind of place built not just to impress, but to remind you who couldn't be touched.

Lucien didn't speak. He never did right before walking into a room like this.

Lena sat in stillness beside him, the scent of leather and sea air drifting through the open windows.

Her hand rested on her lap, steady on the outside, fire underneath.

She hadn't asked where they were going.

He hadn't told her.

But somehow, she knew this wasn't like the other nights.

Tonight was a different kind of war.

The car stopped beneath a grand overhang lit by low, golden sconces.

Uniformed valet approached, heads slightly bowed.

Lucien stepped out first, smoothing the front of his jacket with the practiced grace of a man used to being watched.

Then he turned and extended a hand to her.

Not a date.

Not a gesture.

A command dressed in silk.

Lena took it.

As they moved up the steps, the sound of ocean mingled with string music pouring from inside, violins overlaid with the dull thump of deep bass, like a symphony laid over a heartbeat.

Inside, the mansion opened like a cathedral, all high ceilings, endless glass, and people dressed like gods.

Politicians.

Heirs.

Men with perfect smiles and dead eyes.

Women in dresses sharp enough to wound.

Heads turned as Lucien entered.

No introduction.

No announcement.

Just a shift in the atmosphere, subtle but immediate, like gravity adjusting to something heavier.

Lena's heels clicked against polished stone as she moved beside him, her chin high, eyes scanning.

Everyone looked.

No one dared approach.

Not yet.

Lucien leaned in slightly, his voice only for her. "These people don't network. They maneuver."

She didn't respond. She didn't have to. The tension between them spoke loud enough.

Victor spotted them first, raising a glass from across the room.

Lucien nodded once.

"Remember. You're here for show. They'll wonder if it's more."

Lena arched a brow, cool and unshaken. "Isn't it?"

Lucien's lips curved, just slightly. "That's what makes it dangerous."

Lucien's hand lingered at the small of her back as they moved deeper into the mansion, past glittering chandeliers and waiters in black. The music pulsed, low and tasteful, like a heartbeat under the floor.

He kept his eyes forward, scanning the room with the still focus of a predator. Every nod, every glance, every shift in posture logged behind his eyes. Calculated.

A man in a dark suit stepped from the shadows near the marble staircase. Lean build, gray temples, eyes that didn't blink often.

Lucien stopped mid-stride.

The man didn't raise his voice. Just said, "Five minutes."

Lucien held his stare a beat, then nodded once.

He turned to Lena, voice low. "Give me a moment."

She frowned. "With who?"

Lucien's eyes didn't leave the man. "Someone who prefers silence to spectacle."

Then, he looked at her. Only briefly. But it was enough.

"Stay where I can see you."

And just like that, he was gone.

Lena stood alone in a palace of power, every eye that hadn't dared meet Lucien's now slowly turning toward her.

A woman approached first.

Early sixties, raven hair streaked with silver and swept into a polished knot. Her emerald dress held to a frame shaped by privilege, discipline, and time.

Wealth clung to her like perfume, and her smile was far too pleasant to be safe.

"You must be the one. Lucien's latest?"

Lena blinked.

"Excuse me?"

The woman laughed lightly, like it was all a joke, like the walls didn't have ears.

Or maybe she owned them.

"I mean no offense. He's always so controlled, it's fascinating when someone breaks through. I've known him since he was a boy, you know. Lucien was never easily rattled. Not even then."

Lena kept her expression composed, her voice even.

"Or maybe I'm not the one breaking through. Maybe he is."

That drew another smile, cooler now, more precise.

"Oh, darling. Everyone in this room is aware you have. That's why they're watching."

Lena felt it then.

The pressure.

The eyes.

The weight of every glance held too long. Every crystal glass gripped a little too tightly.

The woman took a half step closer, her voice dropping, almost intimate.

"Careful who you stand beside in a place like this. Power looks glamorous until it marks you."

"And Lucien's power?"

She tilted her head slightly.

"It doesn't fade. It scars."

She lingered just long enough to let the words settle, then turned to go.

"Tell him Celeste Moreau sends her love. I'm sure Evelyn would be so pleased he's finally brought someone home."

Her heels echoed across the marble as she slipped back into the crowd, leaving Lena standing in a room full of people.

Suddenly, completely alone.

Lena stood perfectly still, refusing to show it, but something inside her tightened.

From across the room, Lucien's eyes met hers again. Steady. Sharp.

His gaze said one thing.

You're still mine.

But her pulse said something else.

Then come claim me, she thought, just as the crowd began to part, like it already understood the answer.

He didn't force it.

He didn't have to.

His presence carved space without asking for it.

He reached Lena in seconds, but didn't speak right away.

His hand brushed her back, just lightly.

But the effect was grounding.

Claiming.

His eyes lingered on the spot where Celeste had stood, then swept across the rest of the room, calculating.

"You're shaking," he said quietly.

"I'm not," Lena answered, even though she was.

Lucien didn't smile. But something flickered in his eyes, approval, maybe. Or something darker. Pride in her stillness.

"Good. You should know how it feels to be watched. Judged. To circle power without blinking."

She looked up at him. "Is that what I'm doing?"

He tilted his head slightly, just enough to lean in without touching. "No. You're walking through it."

Before she could respond, another presence approached.

Victor.

His grin was wide, easy, meant for public consumption, but his eyes were razor-sharp.

He wore a white tux with a loosened bowtie and held two glasses of champagne like a man who never carried anything he didn't intend to weaponize.

Victor handed one glass to Lucien. "Well. Look who finally stopped hunting shadows long enough to make an appearance."

Lucien accepted the drink but didn't sip.

"Funny," he replied. "I thought I was the shadow."

Victor's smile widened.

"Not tonight. Tonight, you're the king of the room. Verdict's in. The ones who matter are impressed."

Lucien glanced at Lena, then back at him.

"I didn't come here to be crowned."

Victor lifted his glass. "No. You came to win."

He clinked it gently against Lucien's.

"And you did."

Something unspoken passed between them.

Lena felt it.

An invisible shift.

Lucien hadn't just made an appearance tonight.

He'd taken a piece off the board.

Maybe more than one.

Victor turned to her, eyes gleaming. "And you. You wear silence well."

Lena matched his gaze. "Better than champagne."

Victor laughed, sharp and brief. "She's dangerous."

Lucien's voice was quieter now, but final. "I know."

A third man joined them, older, broad-shouldered, dressed immaculately in midnight navy. His watch flashed as he extended a hand, not for show, but with the ease of a man used to being recognized.

Victor leaned in, amused. "Lucien, meet Thomas Graye. If something moved in Miami politics in the nineties, it was either on his payroll, or in his pocket."

The man offered his hand.

"Lucien Cole. Haven't seen you since you were half this height and all sharp edges. I did a lot of business with your father back in the day."

Lucien took the hand without hesitation. His grip was firm. Unhurried.

"I've heard your name more times than I've said my own. Though I'm sure the files read: handle with caution."

That drew a chuckle. Deep. Genuine. The man liked him already.

Graye studied him, pleased. "You've done well for yourself. Different style than your father. But the reach? It's starting to feel familiar."

Lucien's smile edged sharper. "I'm not my father."

Graye raised a brow, more intrigued than offended. "That a good thing?"

Lucien didn't flinch. "Depends on who you ask."

A beat of tension passed between them, weighty, not hostile.

Then Graye laughed, clapping a hand on Lucien's shoulder like passing a torch.

"Spoken like a man who knows when to burn the blueprint. We should talk soon, there's opportunity coming. And I'd rather see your name on contracts than your competitors'."

He handed Lucien a discreet black card. Just a symbol. But everyone who saw it understood what it meant.

Graye gave Lena a small nod. "And this one?"

Lucien didn't even glance her way. "Mine."

No further questions.

As Graye disappeared into the crowd, Victor exhaled and chuckled under his breath.

"Well, fuck. He likes you. You just bought yourself a pipeline to half the city."

Lucien looked at the card, then passed it off to Victor. "Hold it."

Victor raised a brow. "Since when do I carry your keepsakes?"

But Lucien was already watching the room, his eyes narrowing toward the gallery entrance as a hush settled.

A soft chime rang out.

Then a voice:

"Ladies and gentlemen," the announcer said smoothly, "we now begin the charity art auction benefitting the Armitage Foundation. All proceeds will go directly to rebuilding coastal infrastructure following this past season's hurricane."

A pause.

"Every piece you see tonight was personally donated by world-renowned artist Adrien Vescari, whose work continues to challenge and define modern political expression through abstraction and tension. He'll be joining us shortly to say a few words before we begin."

Victor nudged Lucien. "You staying for this?"

Before he could answer, the announcer's voice returned.

"And now, please welcome the man behind tonight's collection, the incomparable Adrien Vescari."

Spotlights cut across the room.

At the far end of the gallery, a sleek platform rose beneath a wall of canvases, each one draped in velvet, waiting to be unveiled like secrets dressed as art.

Adrien Vescari stepped into the light. All black. No tie. No pretense. Just presence. The kind you couldn't fake.

He approached the mic, and didn't begin with a greeting.

He began with truth.

"The mind of a creator is not polished. It's not clean. It's not safe.

It's painted with beauty, shaped by chaos, marked by shadows, and lit by flashes of madness.

It's the echo of every failure, the hum of every sleepless night, the flicker of a dream refusing to die.

It's building kingdoms out of breakdowns and symphonies out of silence.

People think we make art from inspiration, but sometimes we make it just to breathe.

Just to survive.

Just to prove to the universe that even in the depths of despair, we are still here.

Still burning.

Still creating.

Because that's what we do.

We suffer loud so others can heal quietly.

And maybe, just maybe, the most beautiful masterpieces are the ones born when no one's watching, no one's listening, and the world has already counted us out.

That's what these pieces are tonight.

And I think you'll recognize parts of yourself in every one, if you're willing to see them."

Silence. Not the hollow kind. The holy kind.

Then, the applause. It came in waves. Controlled, elegant, reverent.

As Adrien stepped offstage, the velvet was pulled from the first canvas.

Then the second. And the third.

Gasps stirred through the room, soft, startled.

Each piece more brutal than the last.

Bold strokes. Sharp lines. Color schemes that didn't seduce so much as confront.

There was nothing soft about this art. No safety. No compromise.

And then:

One canvas stopped the room.

It wasn't the biggest. Or the brightest.

But it bled.

Dark reds streaked across fractured whites, layered over what looked like a body, curled in silhouette, barely visible beneath the chaos.

A storm, trapped inside a frame.

The auctioneer's voice sliced the silence.

"Opening bid: fifty thousand."

A paddle lifted. Then another.

The number jumped, $75,000. Then $90,000.

The crowd began to chatter, not from excitement, but from discomfort.

The painting wasn't beautiful. It was honest. And honesty like that made people itch.

Across the gallery, a man raised his hand. Older. Commanding. Tux crisp. Cufflinks matte black.

His expression didn't change, just a slow, practiced nod.

"One hundred and fifty thousand."

The air tightened.

Victor leaned toward Lucien, voice low. "That's Harlan Caldridge. Old money. Old world. Doesn't lose."

Silence.

Lucien raised his hand. One motion. Fluid. Final.

"Two hundred."

A ripple moved through the crowd.

Not shock, respectful unease.

Like watching someone play with fire and knowing he wouldn't burn.

Across the space, Harlan's jaw tightened.

He raised his hand, barely. Not to be outdone.

"Two twenty-five."

Victor glanced sideways.

"You trying to win the painting or the message?"

Lucien didn't answer. He raised his hand again, smooth as breath.

"Two-fifty."

Not a cent more. Not a hint of hesitation.

The way you close a door someone forgot was still open.

The auctioneer hesitated.

Harlan didn't move. His hand rested on the chair's edge, clenched, unmoving.

For a second, it looked like he might raise it again.

"Sold. For two hundred and fifty thousand dollars."

Applause rose. But not like before.

This time, it was controlled. Intentional. Respectful.

Not for the art. For the man who claimed it.

Lucien said nothing. Didn't look around. Didn't nod.

He stepped back into the crowd, calm as a pulled trigger.

Victor let out a breath he hadn't realized he was holding.

"That wasn't a bid," he muttered. "That was a warning."

Lucien turned to Lena.

"Now we're done here."

Chapter Twenty-Eight

LEAVE NOTHING HIDDEN

They stepped out through the tall glass doors, the air warm with jasmine, cigar smoke, and the distant hush of the ocean.

Laughter still echoed behind them, faint now, like a party happening in someone else's life.

The valet pulled the car around beneath the lights.

Lucien opened the passenger door for Lena without a word.

She slid in, every movement measured, like the night was still holding its breath.

By the time he joined her on the driver's side and pulled onto the coastal road, the city dimmed around them. Still present, but quieter now, like it had stepped back to give them space.

Then, finally, he spoke.

"You held your ground in there tonight."

Lena glanced over, surprised by the break in quiet.

"Is that your version of a compliment?"

Lucien's mouth curved, barely. "It's my version of respect."

She let that settle. Then: "From Victor? From the donors? Or from the woman who tried to psych me out five minutes after you walked away?"

"All of them. But mostly me."

Lena looked ahead, watching the road curve toward the edge of the coastline.

"You really didn't think I'd survive that room, did you?"

Lucien didn't answer right away.

Then, he reached across the console, found her hand, and brought it to his lips.

For a man who once swore he'd never need anyone, the gesture was heavier than any vow.

"I hoped you would."

His mouth brushed her skin, slow. Reverent.

Then he held her hand like he meant to keep it.

"You didn't just survive. You changed the room."

Lena's breath caught. But her voice stayed level.

"So where are we going now, Mr. Cole? A throne room? A rooftop deal? Another war in silk?"

His hand closed a little tighter around hers.

"None of that. Just somewhere quiet."

"Why?"

"Because I want to show you something."

That silenced her, not from fear but from knowing he meant it.

She didn't ask another question. Didn't press for details. She just let him drive.

The drive slowed. The road narrowed, gravel overtaking pavement; thick palms closing in, fencing that didn't guide, only warned: YOU DON'T BELONG HERE

Lucien pulled to the shoulder beside a rusted iron gate.

No signs. No lights.

Just a sliver of moonlight caught on wet sand beyond the tree line.

He killed the engine, stepped out, and moved around to the trunk without a word.

Lena followed.

Her heels clicked once, then crunched against the gravel, sharp. Jarring.

She rounded the car to meet him.

The trunk popped with a soft click.

Lucien lifted it with one hand and reached inside, pulling out a gun.

Cold. Silent.

He checked the chamber once, then tucked it beneath his jacket like it was a watch or a wallet.

Routine.

Lena stiffened. "Lucien."

He didn't look at her. Just smirked. "Relax."

Then he reached in again and pulled out a towel.

Unease twisted low in her stomach. "No, seriously. What is this?"

"Relax, sweetheart. I'm not taking chances."

He pulled out a bottle next, dark green glass, the label worn like it had a story. Two heavy crystal tumblers followed, wrapped in cloth.

He shut the trunk. Quiet. Final.

Then turned to her.

"Come on. You'll like this."

He started forward.

After a few steps, glanced back. "Pull off your heels, and hold on to me if you need to. You won't make it down this path in those."

She didn't argue. Just bent, unfastened the straps, and curled the heels in one hand.

The gravel beneath her feet was cool, sharp. But she didn't react.

She caught up and pressed a hand lightly to his back, not for balance but for presence.

Lucien didn't look at her. He just moved.

Through the narrow, overgrown path, dune grass licked their legs, palms whispered above.

The sound of the ocean grew louder. And louder. Until it drowned out the world.

No cars. No voices. No city. Just pulse and tide.

Then the trees opened, and the world changed.

The beach unfurled before them, white sand untouched, the moon high and full, casting silver fire across black water.

Waves crashed slow and deep, a rhythm that didn't belong to them.

No lights. No footprints. Just space, air, and them.

Lucien stopped at the edge of the dune. His eyes locked on the horizon.

"No one comes here at this time. Tonight, it's ours."

Then he looked at her. And that was it.

The moment didn't ask for permission. It shifted.

They didn't go all the way to the shoreline. Just halfway down the sand, close enough for the ocean's whisper to drown everything else, far enough that the waves wouldn't reach them.

Lucien set the towel down without a word, crouched, uncorked the bottle, the pop muted in the quiet.

He poured two fingers into each tumbler, crystal catching the moon like a blade catching light.

He handed one to Lena, then sat close, legs stretched, jacket open, the ocean's dark moving in his eyes.

From inside his jacket he drew a small black case, clicked it open, and lifted a joint between two fingers.

"When in Miami," he murmured, a private joke the night understood and nobody else would.

Lena raised a brow. "Seriously?"

Lucien didn't blink. He lit it with an unhurried flick, drew in once, deep and steady, then sent the smoke up to the stars like it belonged there.

"It's not for the high. It's for the silence."

He offered it to her, not pushing, just placing the door within reach.

Lena paused, not afraid, curious about him, about what it meant to be let this close.

"I don't usually smoke."

"I know."

No pressure. Only an invitation that could be taken or left.

She took it, brought it to her lips, and drew slow.

She coughed once, startled more by the intimacy than the burn. Lucien gave a soft, private laugh. "You're good. You'll feel it."

They sat without searching for words. Breathing. Listening.

Waves. Wind. The first clean warmth in her chest, something inside loosening.

Lena tilted her head back, eyes tracing the sky. "You can still see Orion," she said softly. "Even here."

Lucien followed her gaze. "Still aiming," he murmured.

She smiled faintly. "Still missing."

"Maybe that's mercy. The world's already full of things that don't miss."

A quiet passed, warm, steady. The surf broke close enough to taste.

She pointed higher. "There's the Dipper."

Lucien leaned back on his elbows. "Still pointing home?"

"Always," she said.

He looked over, the faintest smile. "Then maybe that's ours."

"A promise?"

"A direction. For when the world tries to make us forget."

"You think it would?" she asked.

"The world always does."

He watched her for a long moment. The same stars. A different silence.

The joint had burned out between his fingers, just a thin curl of smoke trailing off the tip. He thumbed his lighter, flame catching with a low hiss.

He drew once, slow, the ember flaring against the dark. "Do you want to know the hardest part of power?"

He didn't wait. "Most people don't want it. They want the feeling of control. The costume. The crowd. They want the noise that lets them sleep."

Another drag. Smoke threaded between them before he offered it back.

"The moment you stop acting like you need that noise, they decide what you are."

His eyes stayed on hers.

"They either kneel, or they come for your throat."

Silence fell, different now. Wider. Deeper.

Then, as if the thought had come from someplace beyond himself:

"You know, sometimes I wonder if there's a God, a creator, a source behind all this, or if life is nothing more than a chain of evolutionary coincidences, random, indifferent, unfeeling."

His eyes never left the water. His voice stayed low, steady, like he was speaking to the tide instead of her.

"Who built the universe. Who struck the first spark that became time. Who hung the moon where it never falls. Who carved the heavens into patterns we pretend we understand. Who poured the ocean into its basin and taught it to return. Who laid the sand beneath our feet grain by grain, who sculpted mountains with pressure and patience, who breathed life into oceans, who gave us air and then gave our lungs the instinct to keep taking it."

He paused, not for drama, for gravity. The waves answered for him, slow and deep.

"Look at it. Beauty everywhere, and none of it crafted by human hands. If it's all random, why does it feel arranged? If it's all chemical, why does it bruise the heart? Where did it come from? What was here before we had names for anything? Was there something before this life, and is there something after?"

The glass in his hand caught a sliver of moonlight, then dimmed again.

"I question my own mortality sometimes. I think about the day my body stops listening. The day the world keeps moving without my permission. And I wonder what I am in the end.

Am I something that actually lasts? Something bigger than this life?

Or am I nothing, a brief flare between birth and oblivion, a flicker the dark doesn't even notice?"

Lena didn't rush to answer. She sat beside him, legs curled beneath her, glass resting in her hands like something ancient, fragile. The wind moved through her hair. Salt clung to the air. The horizon held its line like a promise no one could cash.

Finally, she gazed at the same water, not trying to fix him, only meeting him where he stood.

"I don't know the answers," she said. "I don't even know if we're meant to." Her voice stayed soft, but it didn't waver. "Maybe that's the point.

Maybe the questions are where the truth lives. Maybe it's in the asking, the doubting, the wondering that we touch something bigger than ourselves."

She shifted closer, shoulder to shoulder, as if to make one thing certain with her body.

"And maybe that's enough, my love. Not certainty. Not control. Just the courage to look into the dark and still keep reaching."

Lucien turned and met her gaze.

Soft, raw, unguarded.

"Maybe."

The word left him like smoke and lingered between them.

Lena kept her voice careful, like she was touching a bruise.

"Do you think you'll ever find peace, Lucien?"

He took a slow breath and let it settle in his chest before he answered.

"I wasn't built for peace." His eyes stayed on hers. "Some of us have war in our blood. Not the kind fought with guns. The quiet kind. The kind that wakes up when the world gets too still."

He looked back to the water for a second, like it knew him better than he wanted her to.

"Even when things are good, my mind hunts for what could go wrong. I count exits. I watch shadows. I listen for the change in a room before anyone admits it shifted."

His voice stayed even, but the truth underneath it shook.

"I love like there's a blade hidden somewhere, just in case."

He swallowed, and when he spoke again it was softer, stripped down.

"But under all of that, the scars, the armor, the fire, I still want what everyone wants."

A quiet exhale.

"To be understood. To sit somewhere without scanning the room. To have one place, one person, where the war can finally rest."

He turned fully to her then. No performance. No mask. Nothing between them but the night.

"And I'm starting to find that with you, Lena."

She didn't answer with words.

She answered with movement.

Softly, she shifted closer, rising onto her knees and slipping into the space between his legs.

Like she belonged there. Like the decision had already been made somewhere deeper than thought.

Her hand lifted to his face, fingertips finding his jaw, tracing the line of it with a care that felt almost dangerous.

Then her palm rested against his cheek.

Lucien didn't move.

He let her.

He let himself be seen.

Her voice came steady when she spoke, quiet but certain, like the words had been waiting for their moment.

"Before I met you, I was tired in ways I couldn't name."

Her thumb moved slowly along his cheekbone.

"Not exhausted or frustrated. Just worn down by the same days wearing different clothes. The routines. The polite smiles. People who talked and never said anything real."

She watched his face as if she was memorizing it, as if she was learning the truth of him by touch.

"And deep down, I knew something was coming. Something that would crack the pattern."

A small breath.

"I didn't know what. I didn't know who. But when you walked into that boutique, part of me recognized you."

She leaned closer until their foreheads nearly touched, her breath warm at his mouth.

"I don't know if we're souls bound through lifetimes or just a collision the universe couldn't resist."

Her eyes held his with a fierce tenderness that didn't apologize.

"But the moment we met, it felt like we'd known each other for eons."

Her fingers slid into his hair at the base of his skull, not pulling, just anchoring him.

"And no matter how insane things have become, not once have I doubted it."

The ocean kept coming behind them, heavy and endless. The wine sat forgotten in the sand. The night held its breath like it was listening too.

Lena's gaze didn't waver.

"I think you've been mine for a very long time."

Lucien stared at her like he'd been holding his breath for years and only now remembered he was allowed to let it go. Something in his face broke open, not weak, not small, just human.

When he spoke, his voice was wrecked and reverent all at once.

"Then take what's already yours."

For a second she moved.

Then his hand slid along her thigh.

And Lena froze.

241

Not visibly. Not dramatically. Just a stillness so small most men would have missed it.

But Lucien wasn't most men.

His hand stopped instantly.

The ocean kept moving behind them, waves folding into the dark like nothing had happened.

He studied her face.

"Lena."

She blinked, breath catching as if her body had remembered something her mind hadn't invited back.

For half a heartbeat she wasn't on the beach anymore.

Rough hands.

Cold concrete.

A door slamming somewhere in the dark.

Lucien didn't ask what she saw.

He already knew enough about the world to understand.

His voice dropped, steady and calm.

"Hey."

His fingers lifted her chin until her eyes found his.

"You're here with me."

No urgency. No pressure. Just truth.

"No one touches you tonight unless you want them to."

The words settled into her like warmth after a long winter.

Lucien didn't move. Didn't try again. Didn't reach for her.

He waited.

And after a moment, Lena's breath steadied.

Her hand slid into his hair at the base of his neck.

This time she pulled him closer.

"I want you," she whispered.

She didn't hesitate. She climbed onto him, her thighs bracketing his hips as she settled into his lap. No teasing. No testing. Just heat, weight, and gravity taking what it wanted.

Lucien's hands closed around her waist, hard, like the last of his restraint was turning brittle. His eyes stayed on her face.

"I'm not letting you go tonight. Not after the way you looked at me, like you saw through everything."

Lena's breath caught. She leaned in until her lips brushed the corner of his mouth, almost a kiss, almost a dare.

Her voice fell to a whisper, laced with truth.

"Then stop hiding."

Lucien kissed her like the decision had already been made. Nothing gentle. No careful pace. Not a kiss, a claim, an ache, the answer of a man who had waited for her to choose him and then followed her under. His grip tightened, like he needed proof she was real.

She broke away only a fraction, just enough to meet his eyes.

"I want all of it."

Lucien leaned back slightly, just enough to speak, the heat between them thrumming, undiminished.

His voice was rough with hunger. "Then take what you want. But know I'm taking you right back."

Lena didn't move.

"Look at me." She did.

There was no fear in her eyes. No hesitation. Just heat. Just possession.

Lucien's gaze locked with hers, something raw flashing between them, unspoken but undeniable.

"You want this?"

She nodded once.

"Then show me."

The tension crackled, hot, electric, undeniable.

She moved, her hand sliding down to curl around him, claiming what was hers.

Lucien's jaw locked, his breath catching as he leaned in, mouth grazing her throat, teeth dragging just enough to make her shiver, lips pressing a mark beneath her ear.

"I've been careful with you, Lena," he whispered. "I don't know if I can be gentle tonight."

She smiled against his mouth, breathless. "Then don't."

And that was all it took.

His hand slid down until it caught the hem of her dress. He pulled, unhurried. Fabric climbed her hips, skimmed her back, then vanished, leaving the air suddenly aware of her skin.

Her bra followed. One quiet snap and it fell away. His finger hooked her panties and drew them down her thighs, slow, his eyes never leaving hers. What mattered wasn't what he was removing, but what he was seeing.

Her hands were already at his waist. The belt gave. The button popped. The zipper yielded. She pushed his pants down his hips, freeing him, and he watched her with a stillness stretched tight.

She opened his shirt, button by button, then dragged her nails down his chest.

Then he moved.

Lucien turned her onto her back in one smooth, controlled motion, his body settling over hers with command.

The sand gave beneath them, the tides crashing louder now, like the ocean itself recognized what was about to happen.

His mouth found hers again. And this time, it wasn't tender. It was hunger. Possession. A vow sealed in skin and breath.

His kiss was bruising. His hands were everywhere, gripping her hips, fisting in her hair, dragging his mouth across her collarbone as he pressed his body fully against hers.

And just like that, the moment tipped over the edge, from restraint to ruin.

The sky above them stretched black and endless, the waves crashing in slow, primal rhythm.

But all Lucien saw was her.

Lena.

Naked on the towel, legs open, wet for him, moonlight washing her in silver, claiming her the way night claims its own.

"Look at you," he rasped, his grip tightening as if that alone might keep him steady.

She bit her lip, arching for him like an offering. "What are you waiting for?"

He didn't answer. He drew her to him and took what she was already offering, close enough that there was nowhere for the sound to go but into his chest.

Her nails carved red into his back, her thighs locking tight around his hips as he drove into her like every stroke was a sin waiting to be committed. Like every thrust was a confession, a scream, a war he'd finally stopped fighting.

Their bodies slammed together, sweat-soaked and coated in sand, the towel twisted beneath them. Her moans turned feral when he started talking.

His voice was rough. "Been thinking about you all night."

"The way you taste. The way you take me. You fucking ruin me."

He bent down and bit her lip hard enough to pull a cry from her throat, his mouth dragging across her chest as he kept driving into her.

His voice roughened. "You want to be filled? Want me to come inside you, right here under the stars?"

"God, yes. Lucien, yes."

He gripped her jaw, made her look up at him while he railed her into the earth.

Then he pulled back and spread her thighs wider, watching her for a moment before pushing into her again with a low groan, burying himself deep.

"I want you waking up tomorrow still feeling me. Still knowing exactly who had you under the stars."

Her orgasm ripped through her, violent and untamed.

Her body convulsed beneath him, legs shaking, back arching, and he snapped.

He pulled out and repositioned her without ceremony, drawing her hips up before pressing back into her from behind.

"Not done. Not fucking done."

The force of him sent heat through them both, their skin slick with sweat, their bodies raw and animal under the moon.

The stars watched. The waves kept breaking. But Lucien didn't stop to feel poetic. He was too far gone. Too deep in her.

He gripped the back of her neck and slammed into her again, hard enough that the world narrowed to his body and the sand beneath her hands.

"You take me like you chose every inch of this."

Her second orgasm hit even harder, a scream into the towel, legs giving out as her body sagged beneath the weight of it.

He caught her, held her there, riding out the last shuddering aftershocks until she went slack against him.

Then he drew her up, rolled onto his back, kissed her deep and hungry, and let her settle over him, her rhythm finding its own.

"Ride me."

She stayed there, raw, shaking, destroyed, and started to move. Slow at first. Then harder. Desperate. Fucking herself on him like she couldn't get deep enough, like her body craved everything he hadn't given yet.

He held her hips, watching her ride him, sweat running down his chest. She was unhinged, moaning, dragging her nails down his stomach, her body moving hard against his with every slap of skin.

"This what you wanted?" she panted, eyes wild. "You buried so deep I can't fucking breathe?"

Lucien cursed, sitting up, arms tight around her, mouth at her throat. "You're gonna make me come."

"Then do it," she whispered. "Fucking drown me in it."

He gripped her sides and slammed her down, once, twice, dragging her up and down on him.

Then he came.

Exploded inside her, shaking, clutching her like she might dissolve in his arms.

Like he'd poured the last of himself into her.

They collapsed together, tangled and panting beneath the universe. Her cheek on his chest. His arms around her. The waves still crashing in the distance like applause.

But nothing else existed. Not the city. Not the family. Not the past.

Just the sound of their breath. The taste of sweat and salt.

And the impossible truth that somehow, in all that chaos, they had found something real.

Lucien's voice broke the silence.

"I don't know what the fuck that was."

Lena rested her cheek against his chest, eyes closed, her voice soft.

"That was us, seeing each other in our truest forms."

A pause. The ocean exhaled.

"For the first time."

Lucien stared up at the sky, chest still heaving. The waves rolled in and broke, rolled in and broke, like they were carrying their names out into the dark.

And for the first time in his life, he didn't care if the night remembered him. She already did.

Chapter Twenty-Nine

WHEN GOD BLINKED

The sky was pale lavender with the first hint of dawn spreading over it. The waves rolled in slowly, brushing the shoreline in a steady hush.

Lucien sat upright, bare feet in the sand, elbows resting on his knees, a cigarette burning low between his fingers. He stared out at the horizon, shirtless and still, the wind moving through his hair. The storm in him had quieted, but the silence still carried weight.

Behind him, tangled in the crumpled remains of a towel, Lena stirred. A low, aching groan escaped her, drawing Lucien's glance back.

"You alive?"

His voice was rough from smoke and not enough sleep.

She opened one eye. "Barely."

He raised a brow, lips twitching with amusement. "You okay?"

She shifted, winced, and gave a half-laugh. "Just a little sore."

Lucien smirked. "A little?"

She rolled onto her back with a dramatic sigh, the sand sticking to every inch of her bare skin. "Okay, maybe more than a little."

Lucien chuckled, indulgent. "I did warn you I wasn't feeling gentle."

She smiled at the sky. "And I said don't."

For a while, neither of them moved.

Then, from the corner of her eye, Lena caught movement. A pelican soared across the water, sudden, sharp, then dove, slicing into the sea and surfacing with a fish trapped in its beak.

Lucien watched it too. "Everything in nature either hunts or survives. That's all it knows."

Lena turned to him, brushing a strand of hair from her cheek. "We've both been surviving. Maybe it's time we start hunting for something better."

Lucien looked at her then, really looked. No masks. No armor. And for the first time in his life, he didn't feel alone in the dark. He felt like he had finally found someone who could stand in it with him.

For a few seconds, the world left them alone.

Then Lucien's phone buzzed against the sand. His gaze dropped to the screen. His expression hardened at the name.

Victor.

The cigarette burned to the filter between his fingers. He didn't notice.

He answered. "Yeah."

Pause.

Something in his expression changed. The calm in his eyes vanished.

Lena sat up the second the change moved through him.

Lucien's eyes stayed on the ascending sun as he spoke into the phone. "Alright. Send the location. I'll meet you there."

He ended the call without another word.

"Well. Peace just died."

Whatever had settled in him got buried before it could last.

"What happened?"

He didn't look at her right away. Just stared out toward the horizon.

"Victor wants us at his place. Now."

He turned to her then. "Says we've got a problem."

Lucien and Lena approached along a narrow drive, royal palms standing on either side. To the right, the ocean stretched wide and silent. Beyond the gates, Victor's beachside mansion emerged, low and sprawling, all stone and glass, with windows thrown open to the sea. Sleek and modern, with a silence that felt staged.

Lucien pulled up. Tires crunched over white gravel.

Lena shifted in her seat. The buzz of adrenaline hadn't worn off. She was still barefoot, her dress back on, Lucien's jacket draped around her shoulders. Her hair had fallen into loose waves after a night in the sand and ocean air. The salt hadn't left her skin. The night hadn't left her bones.

Victor was already waiting. He stood on the marble steps, shirt unbuttoned, espresso in hand, like it was just another day. But the tension in his posture betrayed the calm.

So did the two armed men flanking the front doors.

Lucien stepped out first. The second his shoes hit the stone, Victor nodded once and turned without a greeting.

"Inside."

Lena followed, staying close to Lucien as they moved through a sun-drenched atrium and into a living room staged for wealth instead of comfort: slabs of imported limestone, a suspended fireplace, leather furniture untouched by time or guests.

But none of it softened the room.

The ocean was still visible through the glass, but it no longer reached them.

Victor sat.

Lucien didn't.

"We've got an issue."

He set the espresso down without sipping it.

It had gone cold.

"My spot." He paused. "Our spot."

That last word landed heavier than he meant.

"Midnight Club went dark three hours ago. Down in SoFi. Power's out. Cameras offline. No signal. Not a goddamn whisper from security."

His jaw worked once.

"Those guys don't miss calls."

Lucien watched him. "When?"

"Main feed went static at three twelve a.m. Not a flicker since."

Victor leaned forward slightly.

"I sent a runner down half an hour ago. He should've checked in by now. I don't walk into haunted houses unless I know who's haunting them."

Lucien didn't blink. "You think it's a hit?"

"I think it's coordinated."

Victor's words left no room for denial.

He leaned back slightly, eyes fixed on Lucien.

"I've owned clubs down here for over a decade. Not once has anything like this happened."

He paused.

The meaning settled in.

"Only thing that's changed is us. So I figured I'd fill you in before we step into it."

Lena didn't look at either of them. Just the table, like she was trying to hold the room still.

Before Lucien could say another word, his phone buzzed.

He checked the screen.

One of his men up north.

He answered. "Yeah."

"Boss," the voice came fast. "The shipment got rerouted last minute. Quiet. Clean. Someone scrubbed the records. But the feds were waiting. They intercepted the truck outside Newark. Half the product's already in evidence. The rest got moved to a federal site."

Lucien's expression didn't change. "You think someone inside gave them the route?"

"Had to be. No way they find that truck otherwise."

Lucien ended the call.

"It's not just Midnight."

Victor studied him. "Talk."

"Midnight Club's dark. And the feds just grabbed half our shipment outside Newark."

Victor's eyes sharpened. "Same night?"

"Same hour."

Not coincidence.

Timing.

Lena's eyes moved between them.

Victor was angry.

Lucien wasn't.

That was worse.

Victor exhaled slowly. "Someone's taking a swing."

Lucien didn't blink. "No."

Victor looked at him.

"They're not swinging," Lucien said. "They already hit."

Victor's phone lit up on the table.

Unknown number.

Lucien's gaze dropped to the screen. "Answer it."

Victor pressed accept and lifted it to his ear.

No voice came through.

Only breathing.

Wet.

Thin.

Then the line clicked dead.

A second later, the phone lit again.

One image.

Victor opened it, and the color drained from his face.

Lena saw enough before he turned the screen away.

Concrete floor.

A body.

Too much red.

Then Victor turned the phone toward Lucien.

The runner lay on a stained floor in a room none of them recognized. Cinderblock walls. Bare bulb overhead. Water pooled beneath one shoulder. His eyes were open, fixed past the camera.

His shirt had been cut away.

Across his chest, carved deep and ugly into the skin, was one word.

MIDNIGHT

Lucien stared at the image.

No shock.

No visible rage.

Only that dead, terrible stillness Lena was beginning to understand.

Victor's voice came out low. "That's Marco."

His thumb dragged once across the edge of the phone.

"He has a wife."

Then another message appeared beneath the photo.

COME SEE THE REST

Victor's face twisted.

He hurled the phone across the room.

It hit the limestone wall and shattered.

One of the guards reached for his weapon.

Lucien looked at him.

The guard froze.

Victor stood, breathing hard. "I'm going to tear that club apart."

"No," Lucien said.

Victor turned on him. "No?"

Lucien stepped closer.

"If they wanted you dead, they wouldn't send a picture first."

Victor's chest rose and fell.

Lena looked toward the shattered phone.

"They're not warning us."

Lucien's eyes stayed on Victor. "No. They're aiming us."

Victor looked like he might break something with his bare hands.

"They want you angry," Lucien said. "So we don't give them that. We go in clean, see what they left, then decide who bleeds."

Victor stared at him, the room balanced on the edge of violence.

Then he grabbed his keys.

His hand shook. Not from fear. From restraint.

"Come on."

Lucien looked at Lena.
She was pale, but she didn't step back.
Victor was already moving for the door.
"We'll take my car."
Whatever this was, it had already started.
And now it had a name.

Chapter Thirty

MIDNIGHT MASS

Victor's Rolls-Royce idled at the curb outside the Midnight Club. Sleek black paint caught the dull light of a sky turning grim, storm clouds rolling in thick over the Miami skyline. What had started as a golden sunrise was now a canvas of charcoal and steel.

Three doors opened at once.

Victor stepped out first, eyes already locked on the darkened facade.

"We run brunch out of this place every Saturday and Sunday. Always packed."

He stared at the dead doors.

"Not like this."

It wasn't fear in his face.

It was offense.

Lucien and Lena joined him at the curb. The neon signage was dead. Doors closed. Windows blacked out. The club looked hollowed out.

There was no staff. No valet. No music bleeding through the walls. Just silence.

Lena could still see the photo every time she blinked.

Lucien kept his eyes on the entrance. "Locked?"

Victor shook his head. "Shouldn't be."

Lucien pulled the door. It eased open. They stepped inside.

The club was drenched in darkness. Not even emergency lights flickered. The usual hum of electricity, the quiet, invisible heartbeat of the place, was gone.

Victor looked toward the upstairs office. "I'm checking the system." He turned, disappearing up the back staircase.

Lucien and Lena moved through the main floor together. The air was stale, tinged with old perfume and something else, something faintly metallic. At first glance, everything looked untouched. Bottles behind the bar still lined the shelves. Tables were upright. Chairs pushed in. Nothing broken. No signs of struggle.

Then Lena stopped cold.

Her hand found his arm. "Lucien..."

He followed her gaze. The stage curtain. It had been defaced, spray-painted in violent red strokes that ran down the fabric:

NO KINGS. NO CURTAINS. NO COLE

Lena felt it before either of them said a word. This wasn't vandalism. It was staging.

Lucien's body went still.

Then, just before the stage, half-shrouded in shadow, lay the bodies.

At least two dozen. Scattered across the back end of the club.

Bartenders. Security. Hosts. Waitresses. Staff from last night's shift, still in uniform. All of them dead.

Some were slumped over tables, drinks spilled beside them. Others lay collapsed behind the bar or halfway down the aisles, caught mid-shift, mid-breath, like death moved through the room before anyone could react. One girl still had a tray beneath her arm, like she hadn't even seen it coming.

One of the waitresses still wore a cheap gold birthday sash, half buried beneath her.

The massacre hadn't been loud. It had been clinical. Silent. Precise. No time to scream. No one left to hear it. Just ghosts now.

Lena staggered back a step. Her breath caught. Her eyes welled.

Lucien turned to her, quiet, composed, but seething beneath the surface. "Go get Victor."

She didn't argue. She ran. And Lucien stood alone, surrounded by the stillness of the dead, staring at the message on the curtain with eyes that promised only one thing: Retribution.

Lena returned with Victor seconds later.

The moment he saw the carnage, his body locked.

Then he moved. Fast. Past Lucien. Past Lena.

"No." His voice cracked.

He stepped over bodies, eyes wide, bloodshot. His breathing turned ragged. He dropped to a knee beside one of the hostesses.

"She couldn't have been more than twenty-five." She was face up; name tag still pinned to her black blouse.

Victor's hand shook as he reached for her wrist, as if there might still be a pulse.

Lucien's voice cut hard. "Wait. Don't touch her, Victor. Fingerprints. You know better."

"Motherfucker!" Victor's voice trembled, fury drowning every word.

Lucien watched from a few steps back, silent and steady, fists clenched at his sides.

Victor stood slowly, eyes glassy, tears mixing with rage. "Half of them were just kids. Just trying to make a living. My fucking staff, Lucien."

Lucien didn't speak. He didn't have to.

Victor wiped his face with a trembling hand. "Power's completely out. Couldn't get anything on upstairs. Let's check the circuit breakers."

He turned and stormed toward a utility door behind the stage, one most patrons never saw. It hung slightly open.

They pushed through.

A hallway stretched before them, narrow and industrial. Bare walls. Exposed pipes. The kind of corridor meant only for staff. They moved slowly, eyes tracking every corner, every shadow.

Then they smelled it. Burned plastic. Melted wiring. Something had been torched back here, intentionally. The door to the electrical panel was already hanging open, wires pulled, systems dead.

Victor stared at the mess. Then he leaned in. "What the fuck is this?"

Lucien stepped closer, and they both saw it.

Written in black marker, scrawled inside the metal casing where no one would've looked unless they opened it themselves:

BURN THEM BOTH

Lucien's eyes narrowed.

Victor's face went blank. Then flushed red. "This wasn't just for you, Lucien. This hit was for both of us."

Lucien went to speak, but his phone buzzed in his pocket. He pulled it out. No name. No number. Just UNKNOWN on a blank screen, and a sick feeling in his gut.

Victor noticed. "Who is it?"

Lucien didn't speak. Just pressed accept and lifted it to his ear.

Silence.

Then.

A voice. Distorted. Calm.

"Ten seconds."

Click.

The line went dead.

Lucien lowered the phone slowly.

Victor stepped in. "What'd they say?"

Lena was already backing up, eyes darting.

"Ten seconds," Lucien said.

Whoever had called knew exactly where they were standing.

Victor blinked. "Ten seconds for what?"

BOOM.

Outside, tires screeched.

Then: a voice over a megaphone.

"THIS IS THE MIAMI PD. WE HAVE THE BUILDING SUR-ROUNDED. EXIT WITH YOUR HANDS ABOVE YOUR HEAD. DO IT NOW. SLOWLY. NO SUDDEN MOVEMENTS."

Red and blue lights exploded through the front windows, strobing the club into hell.

This wasn't law arriving. It was a signal.

Lucien's eyes narrowed. "You've gotta be fucking kidding me."

Victor slammed a fist against the wall. "Goddamn it!"

Lena backed up another step. "They set us up."

Lucien turned slowly toward the front of the club.

"No." He paused. "They started a fucking war."

The sirens outside howled louder now, urgent, suffocating. Emergency lights bled through the cracks in the blackout windows, casting the darkened interior in pulses of panic. Victor stepped toward the entrance, rage etched into every line of his face.

"Lena's right. It's a goddamn setup," he growled. "They're framing us. Making it look like we wiped out my fucking staff."

Lena understood then that the bodies were only half the message. The rest was waiting outside with lights on it.

Lucien didn't move. His phone was still in his hand, the screen black, the line dead. His expression stayed eerily calm, too calm.

Lena backed away from the front, breath catching. "What do we do?"

Victor spun. "We can use the kitchen exit. Service stairs in the back."

"No." Lucien's voice cut through the chaos.

Victor froze. "No?"

Lucien didn't move. "We don't run from this."

Victor stepped toward him. "Lucien."

"If we run, we're guilty. That's what they want. They want panic. Disor-der. They want a fucking headline by noon."

Outside, the megaphone crackled again.

"I REPEAT, THIS IS THE MIAMI POLICE DEPARTMENT. THE BUILDING IS SURROUNDED. EXIT THE BUILDING NOW WITH YOUR HANDS ABOVE YOUR HEAD. DO IT SLOWLY. NO SUD-DEN MOVEMENTS."

Sirens and shouting collapsed into a dull roar around Lena.

"Lucien."

He finally looked at her.

"They're watching," Lucien said. "Cameras. Chopper. Body cams. We run, they pull the trigger."

Victor cursed under his breath, pacing like a caged animal.

Lucien opened the burner and punched in Ghost's number.

Typed two words.

Need air

Then hit send.

Then locked the screen and slid it into his pocket.

Victor watched him. "What was that?"

"Insurance."

Victor frowned. "What kind?"

"Off the books. Counterintel. The kind of man who can make a report disappear."

Victor glanced toward the flashing lights outside. "And he's going to handle this?"

"He's already on it. If this goes sideways, the paperwork won't survive the morning."

The phone buzzed once.

Lucien glanced down.

One new message:

Delay in progress. Two minutes, max

Victor stared at him. "You had this guy the whole time?"

Lucien's voice stayed level. "You think I got this far without a Ghost in my corner?"

Outside, footsteps gathered. Heavy boots. Orders shouted.

Lena's hands trembled. When Lucien reached for her, she didn't pull away. His fingers laced with hers.

He looked at Victor. "We walk out. Heads up. Hands visible. Don't twitch. Don't talk. Let the attorneys do their jobs."

Victor gave a sharp nod.

"If this goes wrong,"

Lucien cut him off. "It won't."

Lucien exhaled and turned toward the front doors.

The three of them moved in unison, bathed in the strobing light of what the world would see as villains.

But they weren't running. They were walking into the fire.

They already knew. Whoever tried to frame them would regret not finishing the job.

The doors creaked open, metal scraping against silence.

And the world outside erupted.

Two dozen squad cars lined the block, their doors flung open like wings, officers crouched behind them with rifles aimed center mass. Somewhere above the storm clouds, a helicopter circled, invisible, but everyone on the street could feel it watching.

The sun fought through the clouds and lost, leaving the street in a dull, gray glare.

"Hands above your heads! Step forward! Slowly!"

Lucien stepped out first, Lena at his side, Victor just behind. Their hands raised high.

The second their feet hit the pavement, the line of rifles shifted, fingers tightening on triggers.

Lena blinked against the daylight, heart hammering. Her legs felt unsteady, but Lucien's grip on her fingers never wavered.

They didn't flinch.

Didn't run.

Because they knew this was all part of the show.

From across the line of police, a higher-ranking officer stepped forward. Kevlar vest. Hard stare. A hand raised, signal to hold fire.

"Identify yourselves!"

Lucien's voice cut through the tension like a blade.

"Lucien Cole. Victor Dresnik. Lena Hart."

A pause. Murmurs behind the shielded cruisers. Officers speaking into radios. Wind tightening the air.

An unmarked black SUV rolled through the police line like it had been waved in long before the uniforms arrived.

The driver's door opened. A man stepped out between the cruisers, moving like the space already belonged to him. Navy suit. FBI badge clipped to his belt.

He took a few steps forward, eyes moving once over the scene.

"Stand down. Lower the weapons."

The rifles lowered, not fast, but fast enough.

He stopped a few feet in front of Lucien.

"I'm Special Agent Hall," he said. "You're coming with me."

Victor stiffened. "On what charge?"

The agent didn't even blink. "We'll talk downtown."

Lucien didn't move. "We want our attorneys."

"You'll have them. But until then." He signaled.

Handcuffs clicked behind their backs.

Lucien met Lena's eyes, calm and unreadable, and leaned in just enough to say:

"They're walking us into their playbook."

Lena's breath trembled. "Then burn every page."

The van doors sealed with a metallic finality, shutting them into a box of steel and reinforced glass. Outside, the world became nothing but a muffled blur of sirens and cameras.

Lena sat between them in the back of the transport van, Lucien on her left, Victor on her right. No one spoke at first. Just sirens. Just the rhythmic scream of something already being written wrong.

Victor stared straight ahead, his expression locked in place. A faint smear of red still marked his hand from brushing a bloodstained tray on the way in.

Lucien's wrists were cuffed behind his back, but his spine stayed straight, his gaze fixed on the slit of reinforced glass as if the van itself couldn't cage him.

"Two dozen bodies," Victor finally muttered. "No security footage. No entry logs. Just us, and the perfect fucking narrative."

Lena looked down at her cuffed hands. "They wanted a fall. We just walked into it."

Lucien didn't blink. "We didn't fall. We were pushed."

The van turned a sharp corner. The city rolled by, indifferent, beautiful and brutal at the same time.

Victor scoffed under his breath. "You think your guy can keep us out of the headlines?"

Lucien kept his eyes forward. "He's not here to stop headlines."

Lena met his gaze. "Then what is he here for?"

Lucien leaned back against the seat. "To rewrite them."

Victor looked at him then, not like a partner, but like a man realizing how much of Lucien existed off the map.

The van slowed. It rolled past the sign for Miami PD headquarters, an older building from the seventies dressed up in modern armor, security cams, bulletproof glass, concrete barriers out front.

Reporters were already gathering. Cameras clicked. Hands slapped the hood as they pulled into the private intake lane.

Lucien didn't look at them. Neither did Victor.

Lena did, just once. One glimpse out the window.

Flashbulbs. Cell phones. Eyes hungry for blood.

They didn't even know what they were looking at yet.

The door opened.

"Out," an officer barked.

They stepped into the sun like criminals being unveiled, wrists bound, surrounded by uniforms.

But Lucien held his head high. So did Victor.

Lena lifted her head and followed.

Inside, the booking process was methodical. Cold.

Photos. Fingerprints. Inventory of belongings.

Lena flinched when they reached for her necklace, Lucien's necklace, the one he'd clasped around her throat yesterday.

Another hand flashed through her mind. Rough. Unwanted. Her mother's chain ripped away.

Lucien clocked it. Said nothing.

Just stared, hard enough to make the officer hesitate mid-motion.

The man blinked, cleared his throat, and slowly dropped the chain into an evidence envelope.

For the first time that morning, someone in uniform looked unsure of himself.

"She can have it back after processing," he muttered.

They were separated briefly, Lena down one hallway, Lucien and Victor down another.

For the first time since it happened, she was alone.

And that's when the fury hit her.

Someone had orchestrated this. Framed them.

Walked them into a trap with every camera in the city watching.

And the truth she already knew, now undeniable, ignited inside her.

They had no idea who they'd just tried to bury.

Because Lena wasn't the girl from the boutique anymore.

Lucien Cole didn't kneel.

And now, neither would she.

Chapter Thirty-One

ON THE RECORD, OFF THE LEASH

The door buzzed open.

Lucien stepped through first, cuffs tight behind his back, flanked by two officers who walked like they didn't trust what was between them.

Lena followed, Victor just behind her.

The intake hall was cement and echoes, lit by the cold hum of fluorescent lights.

Two detectives waited by the doors ahead, badges around their necks, watching them.

An older one with salt-and-pepper stubble glanced at the clipboard in his hand. "Lucien Cole. Lena Hart. Victor Dresnik."

Lucien didn't flinch. Didn't look.

The younger detective tilted toward Lena. "Rough morning?"

Lucien's stare shifted just enough to freeze the man where he stood.

The older detective straightened. "Alright, separate rooms."

Lucien cut in. "No."

Both detectives looked at him like he'd lost his mind.

Lucien kept going. "You want answers? You don't separate us."

No one moved.

Then, from the back, another voice entered the hallway. Smooth. Calm. Controlled.

"I agree."

Everyone turned.

Agent Hall stepped into the room.

The same sharp-eyed Fed from outside the club. Only now, the adrenaline was gone.

What remained was colder. More calculated.

His suit was untouched. His badge flashed briefly as he approached, but Lucien didn't need to read it again.

He already knew the name.

"I'll be taking point on this. Bureau directive."

The detectives blinked. "You're Bureau?"

Hall nodded once. "And you're lucky I got here before someone let this leak."

He turned to Lucien. "We'll talk. Not in there."

Lucien's eyes narrowed. "Then where?"

Hall gave a small, calculated smile. "Somewhere quieter."

They moved him through the back corridors of the precinct, past rows of closed doors and flickering lights. The kind of sterile hush that meant decisions were being made somewhere else.

The guards didn't speak. Lucien wasn't a suspect anymore. He was a situation.

And somewhere between those two things, the room had already been chosen for him.

Inside the room, fluorescent lights buzzed faintly, the kind of sound that wormed into your skull and made silence impossible.

Lucien sat cuffed to the steel table, posture relaxed, eyes sharp and unreadable.

A predator in a cage. Still a predator.

Hall knew it too. That was why he hadn't brought a tape recorder.

Agent Hall stood by the door, flipping through a slim file. Every movement was measured. Lucien didn't trust quiet men. Quiet men made decisions.

Hall finally sat, dropping the file on the table between them.

"Over two dozen dead."

"No usable cameras. No witnesses. Every feed in the building was fried, backups wiped clean off the cloud. You and your two companions walk in minutes before the cops arrive. That's the kind of scene that makes headlines. And handcuffs."

Lucien didn't respond. His wrists remained bound, but his stare didn't flinch.

Hall leaned in slightly, lowering his voice. "You're calm. I don't like that. Makes me wonder what you're waiting for."

Lucien let the question sit. Men like Hall revealed themselves through what unsettled them.

Lucien's mouth curved. Just barely. "You'll know when it happens."

Hall studied him a second longer, then slid a folded piece of paper across the table.

"Ballistics matched two victims to a Glock recovered at the scene. Not your prints, but that won't matter to the press. Or to the ones looking to make a name off this. Isn't that right, Mr. Cole?"

Lucien's eyes flicked once to the paper. Then back to him.

Hall continued, voice even. "That's right. The truck seized outside Newark? Your truck. The reroute? Yours too. Someone handed them a full manifest, shipping codes, crate IDs, backend trail. All of it leads back to a shell company flagged under a Cayman account tied to one of your off-books trusts."

He let that hang for a moment.

"Someone knew the route. They used your own pipeline against you. They didn't want the product. They wanted to weaponize the narrative. And now you're in Miami. Worst place, worst possible time. Not to take from you, but to make the world watch you lose it."

Lucien didn't touch the paper. Just glanced up, toward the corner of the ceiling, where the red light on the surveillance camera had gone dark.

Hall noticed. His brows twitched. "What the hell?"

The lights flickered.

Then steadied.

Lucien finally spoke. "You're not the only one with friends in high places."

Somewhere out in the world, Ghost sat in the dark.

A bank of monitors glowed in front of him.

With a single tap, the live camera inside Lucien's room died.

Red light, gone.

Audio, dead.

Ghost spoke into a comm line no agency on record could trace. "Room's dark. He's clear. Six minutes max."

Back inside, Hall stiffened. He understood.

"You brought a spook."

For the first time since he entered the room, Hall looked less like the government, more like a man recalculating.

Lucien held his gaze. "I brought the fucking storm."

Hall believed him. That was the problem.

He didn't speak again. Not right away. Sat there, staring across the table at a man whose hands were cuffed, but who clearly wasn't the one trapped.

Then the fluorescent lights overhead blinked again, twice this time. Not a power issue. A signal.

Lucien leaned back slightly. "Let's skip the performance."

Hall narrowed his eyes. "You want off-book? Fine. Let's go off-book."

He pulled a second folder from his briefcase. This one thinner. No labels. Just a black clip holding down pages that weren't meant to exist.

He slid it forward. "Alistair Royce."

"We've had eyes on him longer than you've been in this game. You think this was just a warning? He's not warning you. He's making a move."

And if Hall was saying his name out loud in a room like this, then the board was already further gone than most men in this city would survive.

"Your partner's club hit here in Miami. The seized shipment in Newark. The bodies. That wasn't a power play. It was a setup. And you walked into it exactly the way he wanted."

"And yet you're not here to arrest me."

Hall met his gaze. "Because some of us want the real target. And we know you're the one most likely to draw him out."

Not stop him. Not expose him. Draw him out. Hall had already decided what Lucien was useful for.

Outside the room, footsteps echoed faintly. Doors opened and closed down distant halls. But inside this room, it was just two men playing a much older game.

Lucien nodded once. "So what's your angle?"

Hall lowered his voice. "I keep you out of the system. For now. But you give me Royce. I don't care how. I don't care when. Just make sure when the dust settles, he's bleeding in the spotlight."

Lucien smirked. "Say I hand this asshole to you on a silver platter, what do I get in return?"

Hall leaned forward, voice steady. "Your freedom."

Lucien didn't blink. "Bullshit. I want everything wiped. Miami. Newark. Lena. Victor. All of it. Charges vanish like they never existed."

"That's not how the Bureau works."

The edge of a grin tugged at Lucien's lips. "No. But it's how power works. And you're not here because you like rules."

Hall stared at him for a long beat, calculating. Then, slowly, he slid the file off the table and stood. "I'll make the call. But if you're playing me, you'll regret it."

Lucien almost smiled. Men always mistook recognition for risk.

Lucien leaned forward, the chains at his wrists clinking softly as he met Hall's gaze head-on. "I don't bluff."

Lucien leaned back, cuffs clinking softly. Hall watched him without blinking. But he nodded once, like two predators acknowledging each other.

He slid the file back into his briefcase, snapping the clasp shut with finality. "Enjoy holding, Mr. Cole. I'm sure your lawyers are already at war with my inbox."

At the door, Hall paused. Glanced back. "Be ready when I call. If we're going to bring Royce down," Hall narrowed his eyes, "we'll need to take a few more pieces off the board."

A pause.

"Give me Royce, and I'll bury the rest. But I need you alive to deliver."

Silence.

"I can't walk you out that door yet. But I'll start greasing the wheels. You'll be out before the press finishes their first headline, if your spook keeps things quiet."

Lucien gave the faintest nod, as if to say, Get your pieces ready. I'll deliver him.

Hall tapped his wrist subtly, a silent signal for whoever was watching.

Ghost's fingers moved again.

Mic back online.

Camera live again.

The red light blinked back on in the corner of the ceiling.

Lucien looked toward the camera.

"And now we're back on the record."

Hall knocked twice. The door clicked. Unlocked from the outside.

No guard entered. No announcement made.

Just the silence of something, someone, working the system from behind the curtain.

Then the door shut behind him, slow. Final.

Lucien sat alone in the quiet that followed, the fluorescent lights buzzing like a low, mocking drone.

He exhaled through his nose.

This wasn't survival anymore.

This was the start of the hunt.

The prey had a name.

Royce.

Chapter Thirty-Two

CUT LOOSE, WAR BOUND

The door clicked open again. This time it wasn't Hall.

A uniformed officer stepped in, gloves on. "Let's go. Holding."

Lucien turned without a word. The cuffs stayed on until they reached holding, but his spine stayed straight, eyes sharp.

The hallway outside buzzed with motion, officers moving, urgent calls, the distant clatter of booking. They walked him through it all like he wasn't the most dangerous man in the building. But everyone could feel it.

Something coiled beneath his calm.

An edge.

As they reached the holding area, the officer unlocked the door and nodded toward the cell. "In you go."

The officer uncuffed him, shoved him inside, and locked the door.

The setup was too clean. Even the cage had been arranged for him.

Three men were already there. Big. Scarred. Tattoos crawling up their necks. One was seated; arms folded. The other two stood, pacing like caged dogs.

Lucien said nothing. Just walked to the corner and leaned against the wall, calm, composed, eyes on the floor.

The door clanged shut behind him.

Stillness settled over the cell.

Until one of them chuckled. Low. Nasty.

"Well, well. Cole in the flesh."

Lucien didn't look up. "Took you long enough."

Another one shifted. "He's cocky."

"No." Lucien raised his head slowly, locking eyes with the tallest one. "I'm just not afraid of dead men."

Tension cut the air.

Lucien stepped forward once. Just enough to let them know the distance between them didn't matter. Then he looked straight at the one closest to him, the one whose leg twitched ever so slightly with anticipation.

"You think I didn't notice?"

"The way your left hand shakes when you breathe. The way your knee taps every time you look at me. You're not just nervous, you're timing something."

The man froze.

Lucien looked at him. "You think I don't know you three jerkoffs were planted here?"

He didn't say it like a guess. He said it like a man already counting who had signed off on the attempt.

His voice dropped. "I've got four words for you."

Lucien held his stare.

"I. Fucking. Dare. You."

The other two barely had time to react.

Lucien moved first, fast, clean, brutal.

Not rage. Not impulse. A decision.

His fist cracked against the biggest guy's jaw with a sickening snap, dropping him cold. No warning. No second punch.

Just lights out.

The other two froze mid-step.

Lucien straightened. "Yeah. Sit the fuck down."

They did.

Silence reclaimed the cell. Seconds later, an officer walked by, paused at the bars, eyes narrowing on the unconscious body on the floor. "What the hell happened to him?"

The two men glanced at each other, staying quiet.

That told Lucien more than panic would have.

Lucien shrugged, deadpan. "I think he was dehydrated."

The officer gave him a look. "Uh-huh."

He waved over another cop. "Bring him here," he said, gesturing to the hallway behind him.

A moment later, they shoved Victor into the cell. The door clanged shut behind him.

Victor looked down at the guy laid out cold, then back up at Lucien. "The fuck happened to him?"

Lucien didn't miss a beat. "Tripped on my patience."

Victor blinked, then chuckled under his breath. "You're a real piece of work, you know that?"

Lucien didn't respond. Just tilted his head, that faint smirk still playing at his mouth, like he already knew how this ended.

Lucien's gaze stayed locked on the twitchy one, the leader of the three. Sweat gathered at the man's brow, eyes darting like a cornered animal trying to find a way out.

Lucien stepped forward. "You're scared? That's not fear in your eyes. That's realization. You finally understand you're in the cage with the thing you thought you were cornering."

The man flinched.

"I've peeled men apart for less than what you three just pulled. And I didn't leave their bodies hidden. I left them where people would find them. Because that was the fucking message."

He sank lower, eyes locked on the man's. "You think I don't know who sent you?"

Lucien let it hang.

"You think Royce sent you here to win his favor?" He gave a slow shake of his head. "No. He sent you here to die slow. You're not a soldier. You're a fucking receipt, proof of purchase for a war he's too much of a coward to fight himself."

Lucien's gaze stayed on him.

"And judging by the three of you, and the kind of man he clearly is, my guess? It wasn't even Royce who made the call. He let someone beneath him handle it. Because that's all you are. Not soldiers. Not trusted. Bodies for hire. Disposable. Forgettable."

The man's throat bobbed. "You don't know shit about us," he rasped. "And you sure as hell don't know shit about Royce." But it barely came out.

Lucien tilted his head. "No. But you do. And you're going to tell me everything."

A long beat stretched thin as piano wire.

"He's not here," the man gasped. "He's out. Out of the country. No one knows where."

Lucien didn't blink. "Who does?"

"There's a contact," the man said. "Goes by Finch. He runs point for him here in the states. He's up in Atlantic City."

There it was. Not the king. The nerve ending.

Lucien didn't waver. "Where in Atlantic City?"

"Ocean Club Condos," the man blurted. "Big place. Right on the beach."

Lucien stepped closer, patience thinning, temper coiled tight beneath his calm. "What. Fucking. Room?"

The man's head shook violently. "We, we don't know. No one does. It's all burner calls, and dead drops. He's careful. Paranoid."

Lucien's stare narrowed.

The man swallowed, fast. "They never gave us a fail-safe. In case anything went sideways."

Lucien waited.

"All we know is, he hits the gym in the building. Every morning. Eight a.m. sharp. Doesn't trust anyone else. Doesn't meet in his own unit. That's where he is anytime we ever got a call."

Lucien stared down at him, like he was looking at a man already marked for the morgue. "Then I guess we know where to start."

Lucien rose, slow and dangerous. He looked down at the man, voice stripped of mercy, hollowed of anything human.

"You don't tell Finch I'm coming."

He leaned in.

"You don't warn him. You don't whisper my name. You disappear."

"Because when I arrive, I'm not coming for power. I'm not coming for fucking deals."

He leaned closer.

"I'm coming to leave him screaming."

He straightened, glanced to Victor. "You ever rip a man's legacy out by the roots?"

Victor grinned through his rage. "Shit, I thought that was the job description."

Lucien turned back one last time. "If he's watching, tell him hell's not hot enough."

A second later, the cell door buzzed. The captain stepped in, broad-shouldered, the kind of man whose authority didn't need to raise its voice.

Irritation was carved deep into the lines of his face. He didn't look at Lucien right away.

"As much as I'd love to leave you assholes in here to rot," he muttered, voice flat, "I just got a call from people way above my pay grade. Said to cut you loose."

Victor raised a brow. "Define 'loose.'"

The captain's eyes cut to him. "You're not cleared. You're not safe. You're just, free. For now."

He turned and left without waiting for a response.

Lucien rose first, like he'd been expecting this moment since the cuffs went on.

Victor stood slower, cracking his neck with a roll of his shoulders. "Feels like we should be thanking someone."

Lucien didn't answer. He just turned his head to the three men, eyes unreadable, voice low. "I'll be seeing you three again real soon."

Not a threat.

A promise.

They were led down a long corridor, past officers who wouldn't meet their eyes. Past desks and lockers and flickering lights. Past the bullpen. Past the front entrance, where reporters pressed against the glass like wolves scenting blood, flashes popping, microphones raised.

And then the doors opened.

And there he was.

Alexander Cole.

Standing at the bottom of the station steps.

No coat. No umbrella. Just a tailored black suit, the shoulders dusted with the promise of a rain that hadn't started yet.

Hands behind his back. Eyes sharp. Unmoving.

Beside him, Lena.

She turned the instant she saw Lucien. Their eyes locked, and she didn't wait. She ran. Up the steps. Across the space between them. Into his arms.

"I missed you," she whispered, voice raw. "Are you okay?"

Lucien held her tighter than words would allow. He kissed her temple, his voice low against her hair.

"I'm fine," he whispered. "But tonight, we pack. Tomorrow, we go to New Jersey."

Lena pulled back just enough to look at him, eyes flickering with emotion. "New Jersey?"

Lucien nodded once. "We've got business in Atlantic City."

Below them, Alexander didn't speak. Didn't move. Just watched. Like a man who'd seen enough blood spilled in his life to know when the war had truly begun.

He looked less like a father waiting outside a station and more like an old king measuring the first true shot of a war.

Then Alexander's voice cut through it, calm, cool, carrying a gravity that pulled all of them toward it. "Come on. Let's go sit down."

The backroom of Alexander's private poker spot wasn't marked. No signs.

No windows. Just reinforced walls, velvet-lined tables, and a stillness that felt older than the building itself. The kind of room built for secrets and war councils.

They gathered there now, Lucien, Victor, Alexander, and Lena.

The air was cool. The scent of old cigar smoke clung to the leather chairs like memory. A single light hung above each table, casting long shadows over green felt and scattered chips. The rest of the room stayed buried in dim, whispered darkness.

Alexander sat at one of the tables, a cigar smoldering between his fingers. He let the smoke drift from his lips, slow and deliberate, like it was part of the conversation.

Lucien stood near the edge of the room, arms crossed, posture carved from stone. He'd been cuffed earlier. Not anymore. Now he was free. And somehow, the stillness around him felt more dangerous than anything that came before.

Victor moved behind the bar and poured himself a drink. Two cubes of ice clinked into crystal. The sound rang out like glass under pressure. He stared into the amber liquid for a moment.

"It makes sense now."

He said it like a man finally seeing the architecture instead of just the damage.

Lucien looked up, eyes narrowed, focused.

Victor turned to face the room, the overhead light catching in his eyes. "Alistair Royce."

The name landed like a loaded gun.

"Of course it's him. He sees your rise as a threat. You consolidated cities. He saw you lining up with me, reaching into Miami, and that's when he moved. The Midnight Club hit wasn't to scare you. It was a message."

Alexander nodded slowly, his eyes cutting through the haze toward Victor. "Cutting power. Killing surveillance. That was Royce saying, 'You're not untouchable.'"

He looked at Lucien. "Next, he hits your shipment in Newark, feeds it to the feds. And just like that, Hall's sniffing around. And Hall doesn't just show up unless someone's whispering in his ear."

Lucien's arms stayed crossed, eyes locked in a slow burn. What followed wasn't hesitation, it was calculation.

"He's sniffing, but he's not biting." He glanced toward his father. "Hall's taking our side. Quietly. Willing to bite the hand that fed him, because he knows it wasn't the hand of innocence."

Lucien didn't look away.

"It was the hand of something bigger."

His tone didn't rise. It didn't need to. "He's giving us time. Enough rope to pull Royce out of the shadows before we string him up with it."

Then Lena stepped forward, voice low and tight. "Holy shit. I don't think this morning was the beginning of Royce's plan."

Lena paused, the name catching in her throat.

"Bobby Scava. When they took me, he didn't ask for money. Didn't even mention the past."

She looked at Lucien. "He just kept asking the same question, over and over, 'Where's the next shipment coming in?'"

Lucien's eyes met hers, slow and sharp.

"That's what they were after," she continued. "The whole time. Your next move."

"That's not random," Victor said. "This Scava guy you knew vanished for years. And then suddenly he resurfaces right as Royce starts pulling strings?"

Victor went still, something clicking into place.

"And now I'm thinking about Carter."

His voice cooled. "The way he flipped. After all those years. Talking about how you came down here uninvited, acting like you disrupted some grand plan he had lined up with you. Something changed between the moment you left New York and the moment you touched down in Miami."

"I think Royce was in his ear too. Feeding him fear. Turning him into another pawn."

Alexander let out a grim breath and tapped ash into a crystal tray.

"You're not wrong. Giancarlo Corsini called me last night. Apologized for some mess Milo caused at your club earlier this week. Said someone had been filling his son's head. Talking about honoring the family name. About not letting you set up shop without kicking something up."

Alexander leaned back in his chair.

"Sounds like Royce again."

The air in the room thickened. The kind that made you feel the weight of ghosts.

Alexander's voice darkened. "And now you've got three guys magically planted in your holding cell? The same day you're arrested? One of them name-drops Finch like he's reading from a script? That's not coincidence."

Victor lowered himself into one of the leather chairs.

"That's coordination."

Lena's voice cut through the room.

"It's him. Every piece leads back to him."

Victor nodded slowly. "This guy's been running a war from every angle.

Streets. Courts. Feds. Jail."

"He's not trying to hit you. He's trying to erase you."

The words sank like poison into the air.

"Erase us now."

Lucien didn't flinch.

Then Lena spoke again. "Maybe he's the one behind the texts."

Alexander narrowed his eyes. "What texts?"

Lucien didn't hesitate. "No. That wasn't him."

He looked to Alexander.

"Someone's been stalking her since we got together. Texts from an un-known number. Watching her. Tracking her. Started back in New York."

The room shifted at that, not from shock, from math. That meant there was another hand in play.

His eyes flicked to Lena. Then back.

"They torched her store too. Middle of the night. No warning. No sus-pects."

Alexander shook his head. "No. Royce wouldn't stoop to burner texts and small-time intimidation. That's not his theater. He orchestrates from the shadows. If he wanted to rattle you with a crude trick, he'd have done it himself."

"He'd use someone close. Or worse, he wouldn't bother rattling you at all. You'd already be dead."

Victor scoffed, setting his drink down. "How the hell do you even know him?"

"He was part of our generation. Backed Carter Vale's father in bad real estate deals. Always the silent partner in dirt that never made headlines. Bankrolled every lawyer who kept Corsini from rotting in a cell."

He took a slow drag from his cigar, the cherry glowing red in the dim.

"Royce doesn't move through street corners. He moves through signa-tures. Through handshakes. Through private planes."

"He's got judges. Agents. Politicians in his pocket. Ghosts in suits."

He flicked ash from his cigar.

"And rumor has it he's been tied to something much bigger."

Silence fell again, final this time.

Then Alexander leaned forward, elbows on the felt. The weight of his gaze landed on Lucien like a crown being placed.

"He's been watching you, Lucien. Every step. Studying. Waiting."

He paused. The only sound was the soft hiss of the cigar burning down.

"His mistake," he murmured, "was letting the young lion eat."

He crushed the cigar into the tray.

"Because once a lion tastes blood, he doesn't stop until the whole pride bows.

Until he's king of the fucking jungle."

No one moved. Not Victor. Not Lena.

Lucien didn't blink.

Alexander sat back. "You want to beat Royce? You don't chase him. You hunt what he hides behind. You burn his systems. Cut off his logistics. Make his own people wonder if the devil they know is worth dying for."

He exhaled slowly.

"And when he finally comes out of hiding?"

He looked at Lucien.

"You don't strike first."

A pause.

"You let him crawl to you."

Lucien nodded once.

"Then we start with Finch."

Chapter Thirty-Three

OASIS ON THE EDGE

The tarmac steamed under the early sun, heat clinging to the asphalt. Lucien's matte black jet waited at the edge of the runway, sleek. Private. Silent. The SUV that brought them still idled nearby, its engine low beneath the building tension.

Lucien stood beside it, a phone pressed to his ear, eyes fixed somewhere beyond the jet, beyond the skyline, beyond the moment itself.

Lena sat on the SUV's back bumper, elbows on her knees, staring at the concrete like it might answer her.

Victor paced a few feet away, one hand curled around a cup of black coffee, the other drifting toward his sidearm out of habit.

The call didn't last.

When it ended, Lucien pocketed the phone and turned toward them. "That was Hall. The feds are running silent for now. He bought us a few days. Media blackout. Pressure on the captain to delay internal reports. But that clock is already ticking."

Victor scoffed. "Two dozen of our own workers, murdered in our place, and we're supposed to pretend like it didn't happen for now?"

"I'm not pretending anything. Payouts are already moving, quietly, through third parties. Your team's handling the families. Ghost is handling the press, the leaks, the heat. It won't undo what happened, but it buys us time to hit back."

Lena finally looked up. "You're compensating the families?"

Lucien nodded once. "Of course we are."

Her voice stayed quiet. "But that's blood money."

Victor exhaled through his nose. "Yeah, and they won't refuse it, either."

Lucien walked to her slowly and crouched in front of her, his voice lowering with him. "It's the cost of war, Lena. A war we didn't start."

He paused.

"This is the mess we were dragged into. I'm cleaning what I can."

She looked at him then, really looked. Her eyes rimmed with fatigue. Her fingers clenched. But she nodded. "So that's it?" she said. "We're just leaving?"

Lucien stood. "We're not leaving. We're repositioning. Royce wanted noise. We'll hunt him from the dark instead."

Victor tilted his head. "And Jersey's the next shadow?"

Lucien gave a slight nod. "Finch. Ocean Club Condos. I want to be waiting for him when he least expects it."

Lena rose, glancing toward the jet. "What about here? What about everything we're leaving behind?"

"We're not leaving it behind. We're setting the trap somewhere else."

She hesitated, then added, "And your family? Your mother? Victoria? Do they know what's happening?"

"No. But it won't stay buried much longer."

Lena's voice cracked. "Why does life keep fucking us?"

Lucien turned toward her, voice steady, a slow burn beneath every word.

"Because life doesn't care who you are. It only cares what you do when it tries to bury you."

He stepped closer.

"It'll strip you. Starve you. Take everyone you love. Just to see if there's anything left worth saving."

His voice lowered.

"The rest learn to bleed with purpose."

His eyes held hers.

"Pain isn't the enemy, Lena. It's the test."

She blinked slowly and swallowed. No words came, just a nod, like something fragile inside her had just been set on fire and reforged into steel.

Lucien kissed her temple. "Come on."

Victor gave them a slow clap. "Bravo. That was fucking beautiful. Who knew the devil had such a soft side?"

Lucien didn't even look back. "You keep thinking he does, Victor. That's your first mistake."

Victor grinned. "Duly noted."

Lucien looked past them both, toward the jet, toward the sky beyond it. For a moment he said nothing. Then he nodded once.

Lena stepped forward first, her hand brushing his as she passed.

Lucien followed, eyes lingering on her back before climbing the stairs behind her.

Victor took one last drag of his coffee, tossed the cup, and muttered, "I guess somebody better tell Jersey we're coming."

The jet engines purred low in the background, steady and waiting.

Two hours later, the hum of the jet had softened to a low vibration beneath their feet.

The pilot's voice crackled through the overhead speaker, all business, and entirely too soon. "Preparing for descent into Atlantic City International."

Lucien stirred from light sleep, eyes opening slowly as he scanned the cabin.

Lena sat beside him, hair tousled, the blanket slipping from her lap as she rubbed her eyes.

The jet sliced through clouds glowing gold at the edges.

She blinked, shoulders tense, her body still stiff from the awkward way she'd slept.

For a moment, she forgot where they were.

Then it came back.

Miami already felt distant. The humidity, the noise, the chaos.

Up here, it was different.

Ahead waited the bite of late fall, cold air sharp enough to wake old memories.

This was closer.

Closer to the place it all began.

Closer to the fire she'd been forged in.

The pilot's voice came again. "Touchdown in approximately five minutes."

Victor stirred across the aisle, rubbing the sleep from his face. "Can't believe I missed the champagne."

Lena glanced at Lucien. "Do we have a car waiting?"

"Yeah. I've got someone meeting us."

Victor arched a brow. "Anyone we trust?"

Lucien looked toward the window, the gold-edged clouds sliding past. "Young guy. Been putting in work this past year. Loyal. Hungry."

A pause.

"He'll be filling a seat that shouldn't be empty."

Lena's gaze dropped.

Michael.

No one said the name.

Lucien looked ahead again. "We'll see how he does. For now, we use what we have."

The wheels touched down with a low groan, jolting the cabin just enough to pull them fully back to reality.

Outside the window, the marshlands carved thin channels through the earth, raw and living, glass-green and gold beneath the morning sun. Saltwater glistened in shallow pockets across the meadows, the tide creeping over the edges like it had nowhere else to go.

The runway sat nestled at the heart of it all, surrounded by salt flats and silence. A strange kind of calm for a place about to shake their world awake.

Beyond it, the skyline lay distant and worn. Faded casinos. Crooked silhouettes of once-grand hotels. Hollow towers clinging to the coast like relics of forgotten empires.

A final chapter the world had abandoned before it could end.

Victor yawned. "Jersey always looked better from the sky."

Lucien didn't answer. He was already standing.

The cabin door opened with a hiss. A rush of crisp, briny air flooded in, cooler than Miami but alive in its own way. A different kind of edge. One you couldn't fake.

Lena paused in the doorway. Her eyes swept the horizon, the marshes, the open sky stretching toward something that felt at once familiar and utterly unknown.

At the base of the stairs, the black SUV waited, engine idling low like it had been holding its breath.

The same vehicle that had carried Lena and Michael into a nightmare, one she survived and he didn't.

Clean. Silent. Still breathing ghosts.

A young man leaned against the driver's side, mid-twenties, lean, coiled with quiet strength.

Something in his posture was rigid. Ready. Not the brash arrogance of a kid, but the contained energy of someone who'd seen real war.

Maybe not overseas, but in alleys and cages where you either learned to survive or didn't.

He wore a navy bomber and dark jeans, but it was his eyes that caught Lena's attention.

Focused. Calm. Lethal.

Like a soldier with no uniform.

Lucien approached. "Logan."

The young man straightened immediately. "Boss."

No hesitation. No questions.

Victor gave him a once-over. Lean frame. Quiet posture. Eyes that stayed put.

He nodded, half-impressed. "Kid's got the hunger in his eyes."

"He's been tested," Lucien said. "Hasn't failed yet."

"Good. Let's hope he doesn't start today."

Logan opened the back door. "Ocean Club's prepped. Straight shot from here. Twenty minutes."

Lucien's eyes lingered on the horizon.

"No detours."

He slid into the backseat. Lena followed.

Victor climbed in last, one hand near his gun as the door shut behind them.

The SUV rolled forward.

Atlantic City waited.

The SUV came off the Atlantic City Expressway and slipped into the rising pulse of the city. Morning light flashed across the windshield as towers of glass and steel rose around them, casinos gleaming with promise, profit, and illusion.

Everything felt like it was holding its breath.

Money. Movement. Memory.

All of it packed into a coastline that never slept.

Victor leaned back in the front seat, sunglasses pushed into his hair. "We're really gonna come all the way to Atlantic City and not enjoy ourselves? Come on, let's grab the penthouse at the Trop. Gamble, eat, fuck, live a little before we hunt down this piece of shit."

Lucien's eyes stayed fixed on the road beyond Logan's shoulder.

"We didn't come here to play."

Calm. Measured. All business.

Victor snorted. "No, but we are kings, and even kings need a crown for a night."

Lucien was about to shut him down, but then he glanced sideways.

Lena sat quietly, looking down, fingers working at the hem of her dress. She didn't seem to realize she was doing it.

Something in him gave.

The part of him born in ash and sharpened by war wanted momentum. Move. Strike. Crush the inconvenience under his heel.

But the man who loved her saw the ghost of Miami still in her eyes.

He felt it too.

"One night," Lucien said. "Then we get back to war."

Victor turned just enough for the corner of his mouth to lift. "Now you're speaking my language."

He looked at Logan and pushed his sunglasses back over his eyes.

"Make a right up here."

Then he checked his phone, thumb scrolling once.

"We'll stay at the Tropicana. Right next to the Ocean Club."

The SUV veered southbound down Pacific Avenue. The Tropicana rose in the distance, bold, towering, alive even in daylight.

They cut left at Brighton Avenue and Pacific, pulling beneath the valet canopy.

When they rolled to a stop, a uniformed attendant stepped forward just as Logan shifted the vehicle into park and stepped out.

"Handle it with care," Logan said flatly, handing over the keys without making eye contact. His tone was calm but edged, the kind carried by a man used to weight behind his words.

Lucien stepped out a moment later. He slipped the valet a folded hundred with no ceremony. "Take your time. Don't scratch it."

The valet nodded quickly, understanding exactly what kind of men stood before him.

Lena grabbed one of the sleek black travel bags from the trunk. They had brought a half dozen from Miami, but she chose to carry her own. As she turned, she caught the quiet gesture.

Lucien tipping without ego, without expectation.

Just respect.

She noticed that.

Then the Tropicana's revolving doors parted, pulling them into softly chilled air tinged with polished brass and freshly cleaned floors.

Lucien led. Lena beside him.

Logan and Victor followed, casual, unreadable, Victor still wearing his sunglasses indoors.

At the front desk, a young concierge greeted them with a practiced smile.

"Welcome to the Tropicana. Do you have a reservation?"

"No." Lucien slid his card onto the counter. "I'm looking for a penthouse suite. Just for tonight."

Her fingers hovered over the keyboard. "Penthouse suites usually require advance reservation, but... let me check."

Her tone shifted mid-sentence. Something about him had her typing faster.

She scanned the screen, then looked up with a flicker of surprise. "As it happens, we just had a last-minute early departure. The Park Avenue Suite. Fiftieth floor, West Tower. Multiple bedrooms. Sweeping views."

"Whatever it is, charge it. I want access to that floor restricted."

She dipped her head. "The fiftieth is keycard only. You'll have privacy."

"That's fine."

She typed quickly, fully attentive now. "Housekeeping's finishing the suite. It'll be ready when you get there."

She slid two keycards across the counter and gestured toward the rear of the lobby.

"Up the escalator, left through the casino, then past the fountain. West Tower elevators will be on your left. Room 5006."

Victor leaned in, pleased. "Now this is more like it."

They made their way toward the escalators, riding up into the heart of the Tropicana. The main casino floor opened before them, quieter than it would be by nightfall, but still alive. Slot machines blinked like lullabies, soft melodies chiming beneath the low current of morning movement.

Guests wandered down from their rooms, some bleary-eyed and hungover, others smiling like they'd left their luck on the table and planned to come back for it later. Waitresses moved between tables. Laughter mixed with the clink of chips. Somewhere in the background, Sinatra drifted through the room.

They passed the fountain, water dancing in rhythmic arcs beneath a glass ceiling, and stepped into the shopping promenade. Marble floors. Boutique storefronts glowing behind glass.

Victor glanced over as they passed one of the higher-end stores. "Careful, kid. Let her start eyeballing accessories and we're not making it to the elevators."

Lucien didn't reply, but his eyes flicked sideways.

Lena slowed.

Then stopped.

In one of the windows, a pocketbook sat alone on a pedestal. Midnight black. Soft leather. Gold trim. Elegant. Perfect.

She stared for a moment.

Not because she wanted it.

Because she wasn't sure she was allowed to.

"You okay?"

She blinked, then let out a soft chuckle, rubbing the back of her neck. "Yes. Sorry."

She walked past him, cheeks faintly flushed.

Lucien didn't move right away. His eyes lingered on the window. On the bag. On the way she'd looked at it like she never expected something like that to be hers.

Then he turned and followed them down the corridor.

They reached the elevator to the West Tower. The doors slid open, and they stepped inside.

Lucien pulled a second keycard from his wallet and handed it to Lena. "I'm going to grab a coffee. Make a quick call."

His voice softened just enough to reach her beneath the noise. "I'll be right up."

She nodded, fingers brushing his as she took the card. The doors closed on her, Victor, and Logan.

Lucien turned back through the shopping promenade, retracing their steps to the window where she'd stopped.

The bag was still there.

Black lambskin. Gold hardware. Iconic curves.

A Chanel Classic Flap.

He didn't hesitate.

He stepped inside.

Upstairs, the elevator opened with a soft chime, and Lena stepped out first, followed by Victor and Logan. The hallway was silent, plush carpet underfoot, warm ambient lighting overhead. She found the room number etched in gold.

5006.

Lena handed the keycard to Victor, who gave a small nod and slid it through the reader. A soft beep. The light turned green. The lock clicked, and he turned the handle.

They stepped into a world made for people who never checked prices.

White marble floors stretched beneath their feet, black veins running through the stone. Dark counters. Heavy curtains framing windows that went floor to ceiling.

A grand piano sat near the far wall, more decoration than instrument, set on a deep red rug. Behind it, the windows opened up to the whole city, and Lena stopped without meaning to.

One side showed the bay, boats drifting through the inlet. Another showed the ocean and the boardwalk. The third looked back over Atlantic City, casinos and towers lined up along the coast.

The place was all glass, marble, and money.

The bathrooms were bigger than her old apartment, all black tile and deep tubs.

It didn't feel real. It felt like somewhere she wasn't supposed to be.

And somehow, for tonight, it was hers.

Victor had already closed the door behind them, his eyes sweeping the suite with visible approval. Without a word, he and Logan both unholstered their weapons and set them on the entryway table like gunslingers stepping into town after a long night.

Victor eyed Logan's sidearm with interest. "Damn. What is this?" He picked it up, turning it in his hand like he was handling art.

"Hudson H9," Logan said flatly. "Nine-mil. Striker-fired. 1911 trigger system. Low bore axis for recoil control."

Victor gave an impressed nod. "Yeah. Poetry with recoil."

Lena raised an eyebrow as she passed by, one hand gripping the handle of her suitcase. "Boys will be boys."

Victor grinned. "Hey, some girls carry lip gloss. We carry judgment."

Lena rolled her eyes, smirking as she grabbed her suitcase and walked toward the master bedroom. "I'm going to shower. Try not to blow each other."

Victor called after her. "No promises."

She shook her head, laughing to herself as she stepped into the master bedroom and set her suitcase gently on the bed. Lena unzipped her bag and peeled off her clothes piece by piece, until nothing was left between her and the world but bare skin and scars.

She walked into the bathroom, the light spilling over stone and glass, casting soft gold across her figure. She stood in front of the mirror, completely naked. Silent. Still.

Her eyes met her own.

A few months ago, she'd been dressing mannequins in five-figure gowns and curating window displays at one of Manhattan's elite boutiques, clocking out to microwave dinners and empty subway rides home.

Then came the man in the shadows. The hit-and-run. The night everything turned. The blindfold. The screams. Michael's voice. Blood on the floor. A bullet meant for her skull.

Saved by a man who had just begun to love her, who saw something in her no one else had.

Miami came next. Business meetings wrapped in threats. Carter Vale's skull split open by Victor's bullet. The massacre at the Midnight Club. The bodies. The message. The weight.

And now, somewhere between the blindfold and bloodstains, she had stopped being afraid of who she was becoming.

Now she stood in a borrowed kingdom, bare, breathing, unbroken.

She inhaled deeply, staring at the woman in the glass.

Not broken. Not lost. Changed. Hardened. Awake.

Not the woman who survived it.

The one who walked out of it carrying something back.

She was Lucien's partner now, not just in body, but in blood and fire. His equal.

She stepped into the shower. The water hit her like rain against stone, sliding over her skin as if it could wash away what the world had carved into her. But she didn't want it gone. It had made her.

She didn't cry. Didn't speak.

Just stood there, letting the weight drip off her inch by inch, the heat anchoring her to something solid.

When she finally stepped out, the steam wrapped around her like silk, thick, warm, almost holy. She dried off slowly, ran her fingers through her damp hair, and opened the bathroom door.

Lucien stood by the window, shirtless, slacks still on, looking down from a penthouse that wasn't his, over a city that wasn't home.

Cities didn't belong to men.

Men took them.

One hand was in his pocket. The other held a glass of something dark.

He didn't turn around when she entered.

Her eyes fell to the bed.

There, perfectly placed against the cream duvet, sat the black Chanel bag. Still in its box, tissue paper tucked neatly. A single silent offering, an answer to a question she hadn't dared to ask out loud.

Lucien spoke without looking at her. "It caught your eye."

Lena froze, her throat tightening, not with fear, but with something tender and sharp all at once.

"I used to look at things like that through glass and keep walking."

He took a slow sip from the glass, still facing the window. "You don't have to walk past things anymore."

Something inside her finally stopped bracing.

She crossed the room barefoot, steam still trailing off her skin, and ran her fingers lightly across the box. This wasn't just a gift. It was proof he saw her.

She stepped behind him, watching the tension in his shoulders, the quiet fire in the way he stared out over the city like it owed him something.

Then she reached up and touched his back. Warm, taut, familiar.

He turned to face her. No words. Just the space between them shrinking like it had a gravity of its own.

Their lips met, slow at first, searching, then hungry.

Lucien's hand gripped her hip, the other tangled in her damp hair.

Her breath caught. Her body pressed into his. It was everything. Too much. Almost too much.

And then, CRASH. Glass. Somewhere out in the suite. Followed by muffled voices.

Victor's voice, sharp: "Logan, are you kidding me?"

Logan didn't flinch. "It slipped."

Lucien exhaled through his nose, half sigh, half laugh, and leaned his forehead against hers.

"Later," he whispered, brushing his thumb across her cheek.

Lena smirked, breath still uneven. "I think your new partner has a crush. They were practically comparing barrel sizes in the living room before."

Lucien smiled like a man who could kill for her and kiss her in the same breath, and believe both were sacred.

Then, without a word, they slipped beneath the covers together.

Sleep came quickly. Not from weakness, but from the weight of the last twenty-four hours.

CHAPTER THIRTY-FOUR

HOUSE MONEY, HOLY SIN

The sun was already dipping when Lucien opened his eyes.

Lena was curled against him, bare and warm beneath the linen sheets, her hair a quiet tangle on the pillow, her breathing steady. Calm.

They had slept the whole afternoon away.

He sat up slowly, letting the silence stretch, the kind of quiet you could only buy.

He slipped out of bed, pulled on his slacks, and crossed the carpet without a sound.

He opened the door.

And froze.

Victor and Logan sat on opposite ends of the velvet couch, cleaning their weapons like wolves killing time. An empty pizza box sat on the coffee table. A muted documentary about the psychology of slot machine addiction played on the massive flat screen.

"I'm telling you," Victor said, not looking up, "hold it sideways and you might as well tattoo 'gangster' on your forehead and save the coroner some work."

Logan didn't look up, checking the chamber out of habit. "It's not about how you shoot it. It's about when."

"Logan, you talk like that and people are gonna think you mean it."

Lucien watched them for a moment, then shook his head. "Children."

Victor looked up, grinning like a shark. "There he is. Thought you died in there."

He gestured at Logan with a dramatic wave. "Man, I love this fucking kid. He's like the son I never wanted."

Logan racked the slide once, smooth and absentminded. "That's probably for the best. I'd have put you in a home by now."

Victor blinked, then laughed like he'd been slapped.

Lucien pressed a palm to his face. "We're going to dinner in an hour. Don't burn the place down."

The next hour passed in quiet rhythm, each of them retreating into their corners of the suite, the last calm before the night.

Victor slipped back into his black-on-black suit from earlier that morning, adjusted his collar in the mirror, then cracked open a bottle of bourbon from the minibar. He sipped it like water, half-watching a segment on casino crime rings while throwing jabs at Logan about close-quarters combat.

Logan pulled on his fitted jacket, checked the weight of the pistol at his back, and adjusted it once. No expression. Just movements honed by discipline and war. The kind of man who never got comfortable, not even in a penthouse.

Lena stood in front of the mirror in the master bathroom, tying the thin straps of her silk dress behind her neck, one thigh bared by a high slit, the back barely there. She moved like a storm in slow motion. A touch of gloss. No perfume. Just the scent of hot water and something on her Lucien couldn't name.

Lucien stepped into tailored slacks and open-collared white shirt, the black suit jacket slung over one arm, then sat at the edge of the bed to fasten his cufflinks. No tie. No words. Just the watch, the posture, the weight of a man who owned every room he stepped into.

The Chanel bag was already on her shoulder.

When they finally stepped out of Room 5006, it wasn't just four people heading to dinner. It was power dressed to kill, moving through marble like they'd already been invited.

The elevator doors slid shut with a soft whisper. The four of them stood there, dressed in black. The air inside was cool and still, no music, no distractions. Just the hum of motion and the tension of men used to owning rooms.

Victor broke the silence first. "Where we eating, boss?"

Lucien didn't look over. "Carmine's. I made a reservation."

Victor's grin spread. "Big portions. Good music. Giant meatballs. I like it."

Logan didn't miss a beat. "Sounds like your eHarmony bio."

"Please. That's a line I save for my Silver Singles account."

"I'm sure women love hearing about your meatballs."

Victor turned, unfazed. "You wish you had my meatballs, kid."

Lena bit back a laugh.

Lucien kept his eyes on the numbers glowing above the door. "Figured we keep it simple tonight. Eat like kings. Leave like thieves."

Victor tapped the elevator wall with two fingers, as if toasting it.

"And drink like tomorrow's a rumor."

The elevator chimed. The doors slid open.

They stepped out onto the main floor like they belonged there.

They made their way down the corridor, the lights dimming as they entered The Quarter. The air shifted, warmer, heavier, laced with wine and the slow throb of indulgence.

The first and second floors curved around them in a ring of restaurants, each with its own flavor, its own story, alive with conversation and soft music. People poured in from self-parking above, a steady tide of the well-dressed drifting toward shops, restaurants, and whatever called to them.

Ahead, Carmine's sat beneath its deep red awning, warm light spilling from inside. The scent of roasted garlic and crushed tomatoes drifted into the hallway, an invitation written in steam and spice. A pair of host stands waited at the entrance, flanked by potted ivy and soft laughter.

Lucien approached the host stand first.

The host looked up from his screen, the way people do when they think you're just another table.

"Reservation name?"

"Lucien Cole. Party of four."

A few taps. Then the host looked up, pausing just a second longer than usual.

"Right this way, sir."

They were led inside, past crowded tables and wood-paneled walls covered in black-and-white photos, oil portraits, and menu boards that hadn't changed in years. The place was loud in the best kind of way, clinking plates, overlapping conversations, laughter bouncing off the walls.

The chandeliers cast a warm, even glow over everything, nothing fancy, just old-school and steady.

Their table was tucked near the back, round and semi-secluded, draped in white linen, the kind of table where people made deals and stayed too long.

Victor pulled out a chair with a sigh of dramatic relief. "I love this place. They don't serve portions, they serve consequences."

Logan took his seat without a word, adjusting his napkin like he was about to field-strip a rifle.

Lena slid in beside Lucien, the soft black of her dress catching the overhead light just enough to turn heads.

Lucien didn't bother with the menu. He looked up at the waiter. "Start us with fried zucchini, calamari, and two bottles of Amarone. We'll order mains after."

The waiter nodded like he'd just been handed orders from a general and slipped away.

Victor raised an eyebrow. "Ordering for all of us without even asking? Ice cold."

Lucien smirked. "You'll survive."

Victor leaned back in his chair, grabbing a piece of bread from the basket and tearing it in half with unnecessary aggression. "So, tomorrow morning. Ocean Club's right next door. We walk out, cut a right, we're in the lobby in five."

His eyes sharpened under the soft glow. "We get him. Clean. Precise."

Lucien gave a slight nod. "No noise. In and out."

Logan said nothing. Just reached for his water and kept listening, calm, watchful, like he'd already mapped five exits and two fallback points.

Lena watched Lucien a second longer.

Business was never far. Even here. Even now.

But tonight still belonged to them.

The appetizers came fast, platter after platter, a small parade of waitstaff setting the table with practiced urgency. Fried zucchini, golden and crisp. Calamari, still sizzling. Bowls of red sauce thick enough to cling to the spoon.

Then the wine.

Two bottles of Amarone, already uncorked, the kind of service that came without asking when your name carried weight.

Victor grabbed a piece of zucchini before anyone else could. "Now this is foreplay."

Logan stabbed a piece of calamari with surgical precision, never looking up. "You should really work on your phrasing."

Victor pointed at him with his fork. "Don't act like you're not impressed. You eat like a monk. It's unhealthy."

Lena reached for her glass, amused. "You two bicker like an old married couple."

Lucien, already sipping from his own glass, spoke without looking up. "They're bonding. It's disgusting."

"It's called camaraderie, partner. You should try it sometime."

Lucien smirked. "I have a better vice."

His hand found Lena's thigh under the table, slow and certain. She didn't flinch, but her eyes met his over the rim of her wineglass. Dark. Knowing.

The waiter returned, pen in hand and a napkin draped over his arm. "Any ideas for dinner, or should I give you a few minutes?"

Lucien didn't miss a beat. He glanced at Victor, wineglass still in hand. "Go ahead. Tell him what we want."

Victor lit up. "Oh, we're doing this."

He threw a look at Logan. "See? That's how democracy works. Not one guy ordering squid for everyone like a fascist."

Lucien raised an eyebrow. "Careful. I can still take it back."

Victor turned to the waiter. "Chicken scarpariello, rigatoni alla vodka, double veal parm, and a porterhouse for the table, medium rare. And bring extra garlic bread. Don't play with me."

The waiter nodded, scribbling fast.

Victor leaned back, triumphant. "Now that's dinner."

Logan finally spoke, calm and even. "If we survive tomorrow, it'll be in spite of your cholesterol."

Victor raised his glass. "I'll die full and happy. That's the dream."

Another basket of garlic bread landed on the table like an answered prayer.

Victor didn't wait. He tore off a piece and dragged it through the marinara like it was his last meal. "This is how people end up in food comas and bad marriages."

Lena sipped her wine. "You say that like we make good decisions."

Logan reached across for a piece, dipping without a word.

Victor stared. "Did you just take the last corner piece?"

Logan didn't even look up. "You hesitated."

Lucien leaned back in his chair, watching them from the center of the noise.

The overhead lights were soft, golden, catching the shine of Lena's dress and the glint in Victor's eyes.

Under the table, his hand brushed Lena's. Just once.

A quiet reminder that even here, even now, they were still tethered beneath it all.

Victor raised his glass. "To carbs, chaos, and clean kills."

Lena raised hers. "And nights that feel like they belong to us."

They clinked glasses.

Not loud, not dramatic, just four people wrapped in silk and shadows, stealing a few quiet hours from a world that didn't usually give them any.

A cast-iron skillet of chicken scarpariello hit the table with a hiss, lemon and garlic cutting through the air.

Then the rigatoni.

Then two veal parms, big enough to share but no one planned to.

And finally, the porterhouse, still sizzling when it hit the table.

Lucien watched it all arrive like a man used to being brought things.

Victor's eyes widened. "This is what heaven smells like. Garlic, meat, and money."

Logan picked up his fork. "You left out gunpowder."

Lena laughed softly, reaching for the rigatoni. "No business talk at dinner."

Victor threw up a hand. "Thank you. Finally, someone understands me."

Lucien served her first, rigatoni and veal, portioned with care, then filled his own plate.

The wine kept flowing, deep, red, bottomless.

Every bite was good. Every moment louder, warmer. Like they'd stolen the night and were spending it fast. For a while, there was only laughter, full mouths, shared glances, forks tapping heavy plates. They didn't talk about tomorrow. Not yet. Tonight, they just ate, drank, and let the world wait.

By the time the second bottle of Amarone ran dry, half the dishes still sat untouched, victims of full stomachs and good conversation.

Victor leaned back, one hand over his gut. "I swear, I need a stretcher."

Lena nodded, sipping the last of her wine. "I don't think I'll ever eat again."

Even Logan looked mildly affected, his jacket unbuttoned, fork resting on the edge of his plate like a surrender flag.

The waiter returned with a hopeful smile, notepad in hand. "Any interest in dessert? Coffee, perhaps?"

All four answered at once:

"No."

"Absolutely not."

"Not even close."

Lucien just shook his head.

The waiter chuckled, already backing away. "Understood."

He reached for the checkbook, but before he could set it down, Victor raised a hand. "No. I got this tonight."

Lucien raised an eyebrow but didn't argue. Logan muttered something that sounded suspiciously like a bet being settled.

Victor waved the waiter off and stood, pushing back from the table with exaggerated effort. "Alright. Let's go spend money somewhere dumber."

They stepped out of Carmine's and into the buzz of The Quarter, re-freshed, overfed, and dressed like trouble.

Then they turned toward the casino floor, where the night was still wait-ing to be spent.

For now, it was theirs.

Lucien broke from the group and headed for the casino cage. Polished glass and chrome shimmered under the overhead lights, the low buzz of mon-ey moving all around him, cards swiping, chips clinking, voices rising and falling.

He stepped up to the window, calm and direct. "I need twenty-five thou-sand in chips."

The cashier looked up. "Cash or card?"

"Card."

She nodded toward the machine behind her. "We'll have to process it as a cash advance. There's a fee. I'll need ID."

Lucien handed both over without pause. "Run what you can."

A few quiet moments passed. A supervisor was called. One swipe. Then another. Approvals. Nods. Receipts printed and torn away.

Minutes later, a black velvet pouch slid across the counter, heavy with chips stacked in clean rows. Lucien took it without blinking and turned back toward the floor.

A few feet away, Victor was punching buttons on the ATM with one hand and rubbing his stomach with the other. "Just grabbed five. Gonna start slow. Maybe hit some slots. Get the luck going."

Logan stood nearby, arms crossed, expression unreadable.

Lucien reached into his jacket, pulled out a thick envelope, and handed it to him. "Take a week's pay early. If you want to play, play."

Logan shook his head. "I'm not a gambler. I'm just here to keep an eye out and hang back."

Lucien gave a quiet nod, and the night divided around them.

Victor veered left into the glow of the slot machines. Logan drifted after him at a distance, less interested in the machines than the exits. Lucien didn't bother with the slots. He moved straight to the high-limit blackjack tables near the back, where the lighting dimmed just enough to feel expensive and the minimum bets were high enough to scare off the amateurs. No ropes. No velvet. Just pressure. You could feel it in the way the dealers handled the cards and the players handled their liquor.

Lucien took his seat at a table with a clear view of the pit, dropped a clean stack of chips on the felt, and gave the dealer a nod. Lena stood behind him, one hand resting lightly on his shoulder.

The first few hands went steady, small wins, smaller losses. Just a warm-up.

Then Lucien turned slightly and looked up at her. "Your call. Hit or stay."

Lena hesitated, then smirked. "Hit."

The dealer flipped a card, Queen of Spades.

Twenty-one.

Lucien looked pleased.

Two hands later, he turned to her again. "What now?"

She leaned in, eyes sharp. "Double down."

He did.

The next card hit the felt with a crisp flick. Another win, a big one.

The dealer pushed a fresh stack of chips across the felt.

Victor showed up mid-win, sipping something brown. "I leave for ten minutes and you two are rewriting the odds?"

Lucien didn't look away from Lena. "She's on a streak."

Lena gave him a sideways look. "Or maybe you're just finally listening to me."

Lucien grinned, dragging the chips toward him. "Same result."

The wins kept coming.

Not every hand. Not every call. Enough to turn heads. Enough for the pit boss to start watching. Enough for nearby players to edge in, hoping the luck might rub off.

Lena stood closer now, her hand on Lucien's shoulder like she was tethering him there. Her attention moved between the cards and his face, every decision an unspoken dare.

He slid another stack forward.

"Call it."

"Split."

The dealer hesitated. Glanced up. Then executed the move with machine-like precision.

Double win.

The stack grew again.

Victor let out a low whistle. "Jesus. You two should be illegal."

Lucien glanced up at the digital readout, buy-in vs. total. He was up nearly forty grand.

Lena leaned in, lips brushing his ear. "You could walk away right now."

"I could."

She smiled faintly, voice low. Certain. "But you won't."

Lucien's smirk was slow. Dangerous. "Not until the table bleeds."

A passing waiter swept by with a tray of drinks. Victor grabbed one without asking. "I'm hitting roulette. I feel like losing something expensive."

Lucien didn't look up. "Don't bring back an STD."

Victor grinned. "No promises."

As he disappeared into the lights and noise, Logan took his place behind Lena, calm and silent as ever.

Lucien played on. Two more hands. Another spike of chips. The crowd thickened. Strangers now, watching, whispering, leaning in. The streak drew attention like blood in the water.

Lena stepped in behind him, both arms wrapping around his shoulders, chin brushing his neck. "This isn't luck anymore," she whispered. "This is all you."

Lucien didn't answer. He doubled down again. And won. Again.

The dealer pushed the chips across the felt like an offering.

Lucien's stack rose, tall, sharp, precise. A skyline of money.

The air shifted around the table. Not just awe now. Not just envy. Attention.

Lena's arms stayed around him, her voice velvet in his ear. "If you were anyone else, they'd be panicking."

Lucien didn't respond. Because they were.

A moment later, a man stepped into the edge of the circle.

Mid-40s. Sharp suit. Tighter haircut.

A floor supervisor, professional and polite, with eyes that said nothing in here surprised him anymore.

He didn't interrupt the play. Just waited until Lucien glanced his way.

Then he smiled. "Hell of a run you're on tonight, sir."

Lucien didn't blink. "That a problem?"

"Not at all. Just wanted to introduce myself. I'm Marcus, floor supervisor."

A nod. Respectful. Controlled. "If there's anything you need tonight. Drinks, food, something quieter. Let me know. You're in good standing with us."

Lucien leaned back in his chair. Measured. Calm. "Good to know."

Marcus's smile didn't move. "Of course. You keep playing smart, we'll keep watching close."

He said it like a compliment. But Lena felt the shift immediately.

Marcus turned and walked off, smooth, efficient, already scanning another table.

Lucien looked up at the dealer. Then back at the cards.

He didn't say a word. Something in him sharpened.

The next hand looked harmless. Almost too harmless.

He barely glanced at the cards. Then slid a fresh stack forward, heavier than any before.

Twenty-five grand. A single bet.

The dealer didn't speak. Just nodded. And dealt.

An eight and a three.

The dealer showed a seven.

Lena leaned in, close. Her lips brushed his cheek, then found his mouth, slow, firm, certain.

Mid-kiss, Lucien lifted one hand off the felt and flicked two fingers forward, clean, controlled.

"Hit."

The dealer laid down a Queen.

Twenty-one.

Lucien didn't smile. Didn't blink. Didn't move. He simply turned his head from the kiss, eyes sharp and unreadable.

The table lost it.

A gasp.

A low "holy shit" from across the way.

A few phones started to lift before staff moved in to shut it down. Chips clinked across the felt.

The dealer pushed the win forward.

Victor stepped in just in time to see the stack hit the felt. Fresh drink in one hand. Tie half-loosened. A smudge of lipstick on his collar.

He took one look at the pile and whistled. "That little prick of a pit boss is really eyeing you now."

Lucien stood. Lena beside him. Victory all through her posture.

She looked at him. "How much?"

He adjusted his cuffs. Didn't count. "Sixty-five."

Victor shook his head. "I'd say cash out before they start asking for blood types."

Lucien didn't answer. He was already moving, cutting across the casino floor like a storm in tailored silence.

The weight of the night pressed into his jacket, chips stacked in the velvet pouch.

Lena stayed beside him, silent but charged, her eyes catching flashes of color off the slot machines as they passed.

Logan moved behind them, quiet, scanning the floor.

They reached the cage. Lucien set the pouch on the counter with quiet finality. No words. Just presence.

The cashier opened it and began counting, each chip tapped against the next in clean rhythm, every move under surveillance.

A moment later, she looked up. "That'll be sixty-five even. You'd like that in cash?"

Lucien nodded once. "All of it."

She didn't flinch. Just turned to the safe and began laying it out.

Ten thousand.

Ten thousand.

Ten thousand.

Ten thousand.

Ten thousand.

Ten thousand.

Five thousand.

Each banded stack hit the counter like a period.

She counted it again, out loud.

Lucien didn't blink.

A supervisor stepped closer, watching quietly from the side. "Would you like a soft case or an escort to the elevator, sir?"

Lucien took the stacks, compact bricks of hundreds, and slid them into his jacket one by one. Clean. Efficient. Like a man who'd handled cash before. "No."

He turned to Lena. "Let's go."

They didn't have to look far for Victor.

Lucien, Lena, and Logan were crossing the floor when Victor appeared through the crowd like a one-man parade.

Drink in one hand. Half-lit cigarette in the other.

Two women on his arms like he'd picked them off a roulette wheel.

One blonde. One brunette.

Both stunning. Both trouble.

Victor spotted them, smoke trailing from his mouth. "There he is. My lucky fucking charm."

He took one last drag, then snuffed the cigarette out in a tall chrome ashtray near the slots without breaking stride. The blonde leaned in, whispered something that made him smirk wider.

"Elevators?" he asked.

Lucien gave a single nod, already turning toward the West Tower.

Victor grinned wide. "So these two honeys are coming up with me. One for me. One for the kid."

Logan raised an eyebrow. "Hard pass."

Victor shrugged. "Suit yourself. More cardio for me."

Lucien hit the button for the elevator, calm as gravity. He looked at Victor. Then the girls. Then back at Victor.

"I don't care what you do tonight. Just don't knock on my bedroom door unless someone's dead, or you need a place to hide the body."

One of the women giggled.

The elevator doors parted with a soft hiss.

They all stepped inside, Lucien, Lena, Victor, Logan, and Victor's new entourage, the kind of mix that made tourists stare and security reconsider their pay grade.

Victor raised his glass as the doors began to slide shut.

"Fair warning. You're missing the afterparty of the century."

Lucien didn't look back. He slipped an arm around Lena's waist and let the doors seal the night behind them.

The elevator rose fast and smooth, a gold-lit ascent to the fiftieth floor.

When the chime sounded, Victor stepped out first, still talking, one arm around the blonde, the other carrying a half-finished drink like a badge of honor.

Logan followed, quiet and steady, a counterweight to Victor's chaos.

They walked down the hall to Room 5006.

Lucien pulled out the keycard and slid it through the reader.

Victor gave Logan a little nudge. "If I die tonight, bury me face down."

Logan didn't blink. "If you die, I'm just rolling you under the couch."

The door swung open, and the suite greeted them in all its quiet glory.

Lucien stepped inside and gave a single nod to Victor and Logan. "Seven A.M., sharp. Tomorrow, we hunt."

Victor raised his glass in a half-salute, but the two women were already halfway to the bar, laughing over something no one would remember by morning.

Lucien closed the bedroom door behind him and Lena. The latch caught with a quiet click.

Inside, the world slowed.

Lena spun toward him, eyes wide, giddy and glowing from the wine, the lights, the win.

"Oh my God. Sixty-five thousand dollars."

She shook her head, smiling. "You killed it tonight."

Lucien stepped in, pulled her close, and kissed her, slow, claiming.

"We killed it."

She smiled, eyes locked with his.

Then he leaned in, voice low against her ear. "You ever fucked on a shitload of money?"

Her smirk was instant.

Dangerous.

Lucien stepped back, reached into his jacket, and pulled out the thick stacks, banded and heavy.

One by one, he tore off the bands and sent them flying.

Hundreds rained down over the bed like a storm of sin and power.

Cash hit the silk in waves, some falling soft, others smacking like promises.

He set his gun on the dresser, handle turned away from the bed.

Then they reached for each other, smiling, undressing, already burning before skin ever touched skin.

They didn't make it to the center of the mattress.

Lucien had her up against the edge, dress shoved high, her back arching into a sea of money.

His mouth crashed into hers, hot, breathless, hungry.

A hundred-dollar bill clung to the curve of her ass as he gripped her thighs and pulled her into him.

She moaned, voice muffled by his neck, her fingers clawing through his hair.

The money stuck to their skin, slick with sweat, wrinkling beneath them with every thrust.

His hand found her throat.

Her legs locked around his waist.

The bed creaked beneath them, money crumpling under the heat of it.

They moved like they were trying to outrun tomorrow.

When it was over, they collapsed into it, bodies and bills, soaked in sweat, the city outside flickering like it knew.

Lena turned toward him, smiling through the high of it, a hundred-dollar bill pressed between her lips.

"I don't want diamonds," she whispered. "I want to be fucked in hundreds."

Lucien laughed once, under his breath. The sound of a man who'd give her the world just to watch her ruin it.

He pulled her into his chest and kissed her temple.

"Then you'll never run out."

Chapter Thirty-Five

ENEMIES IN THE GARDEN

Morning came like a gun cocking.

The alarm cracked through the dark at six thirty.

Lucien stirred first, bare chest rising slow, four hours of sleep heavy in his bones. He reached for the nightstand, killed the alarm, and let the quiet settle for just a second.

Beside him, Lena groaned. "Already?"

Lucien smirked. "Time to hunt."

She rolled to the edge of the bed, grabbed gray sweats and tugged on a tank top from her bag. Her hair was a mess. Eyes half-closed. Voice still dusted with sleep.

"I need iced coffee or I'm not even human." She reached down, grabbed a loose hundred-dollar bill off the bed, and waved it like a flag. "Breakfast money."

Lucien sat up, rubbing his jaw. "Grab three black coffees too. Cream and sugar on the side. I'm sure the guys will need it." He glanced toward the suite door and muttered, "God, I can only imagine what it looks like out there."

Lena laughed under her breath, slipped on her slides, and grabbed her keycard from the dresser.

She opened the door and stopped.

Victor was sprawled out naked on top of the blonde in the middle of the living room carpet, like he'd fallen from heaven and forgot to land properly. Logan sat upright on the couch, fully clothed, out cold. The brunette was passed out in the corner, an empty bottle of Prosecco clutched to her chest like a teddy bear.

Lena blinked. "Jesus Christ."

She grabbed her phone and took a picture, already knowing exactly when she'd use it, then closed the door slowly behind her and went to get coffee.

The hallway was colder than she expected. Or maybe it was just the contrast, the crisp, clinical quiet of early morning crashing against the heat and haze they'd just crawled out of.

Lena moved through the hotel in a daze. Hoodie up. Oversized sunglasses on, more armor than accessory. She looked like a billionaire's daughter doing the walk of shame, minus the shame.

The Quarter was half-awake. A few guests shuffled through in silence. Casino workers cleaned up the wreckage of the night shift. Someone vacuumed near the fountain like the night before hadn't happened.

She reached the coffee shop just as the overhead sign blinked to life.

The girl behind the counter looked like she regretted every life choice that had led her to this shift.

Lena stepped up and dropped the hundred. "Large iced coffee with oat milk, one sugar. And three black coffees. Cream and sugar on the side."

The cashier blinked, taking in Lena's tank top, sweats, and still-flushed glow. "Rough night?"

"You should see the suite."

The girl had no idea how to respond. Lena just smiled, took the drinks, and walked out like a woman who knew exactly what the rest of her day held.

Ten minutes later, she stepped back into the room, balancing the tray as the door clicked shut behind her.

Logan was just waking up, rubbing his eyes like a man caught sleeping mid-battle. He squinted, scanned the disaster zone, then looked down at Victor, still naked and draped across the blonde like a human blanket.

"Coffee's here," Lena said, setting the tray on the counter.

Logan stared at Victor.

"Jesus Christ. I wish I woke up blind."

"Weren't you supposed to roll him under the couch if he died?"

Logan yawned, stretching. "I would've, if he'd died before I passed out. Honestly, I'm just as shocked as you."

Lena sipped her iced coffee.

Just then, Lucien stepped out of the bedroom, dressed head to toe in black, watch already strapped to his wrist.

He stopped in the doorway. "What the fuck am I looking at?"

No one answered.

Lucien pointed. "Get him up."

Logan walked over and nudged Victor's shoulder with the toe of his boot. Victor groaned and blinked like a man confused why the room wasn't clapping.

"Morning already? Felt like I just closed my eyes."

Lucien didn't smile. "Then open them. Get up. Get these girls out of here.

We move in thirty minutes."

Victor squinted, still flat on the floor. "Let me find my pants, and maybe my will to live."

The next half hour passed in a blur of black coffee, hot showers, and quiet tension.

Lucien gathered the bills, loose now, scattered from the night before, and stacked them back into order. One by one, he slipped them into the inside pocket of his jacket.

They sat heavy against his chest.

The kind of weight only power could buy.

The girls were gone. The suite stripped down to what mattered, the mission, the crew, what came next.

Logan checked his pistol at the kitchen counter, racked it once, then holstered it without a word.

Victor sat hunched on the edge of the couch, cradling his coffee like it was the only thing tethering him to life. He'd managed to button his shirt. That was the extent of his accomplishments so far.

Lena stepped out from the master bathroom, dressed and ready, tight black jeans, black boots, a fitted black tank beneath a leather jacket. No makeup. No gloss. Just sharpened edges.

Lucien looked at her for a beat. Took in the steadiness in her eyes. The quiet fire under the caffeine. He didn't ask if she was coming. He didn't have to.

He just gave a nod and pulled open the door. "Finch is supposed to be a paranoid little weasel. Let's not spook him before we have to."

Lena smirked. "You mean don't let Victor speak?"

Victor raised his cup. "You wound me."

He stood, holstered his sidearm, and shook off the last remnants of sleep.

Then he looked at them. Lucien, Lena, Logan.

"Look at this crew. Real presidential."

Lucien didn't smile. He stepped into the hallway. "Come on. Let's go."

They followed, four deep.

No formation.

No commands.

Just presence.

That was enough.

The casino doors swung open.

The world shifted.

Warm, recycled air gave way to a crisp fall morning. Fresh. Bright. A little too calm for what lay ahead.

Lena stepped out first, the ocean breeze brushing across her face like a warning. She pulled her jacket tighter and looked left.

Down the boardwalk, casinos rose like monuments to a hundred broken dreams and the few that cashed out clean.

Glass towers caught the early light, gleaming in pinks and golds. Seagulls carved through the air above them.

Somewhere in the distance, the ocean murmured, a low, endless hush beneath the rhythm of early joggers pounding the boards.

For a moment, it didn't feel like a war was coming.

It just felt alive.

Atlantic City had always known how to dress rot in light.

Lucien walked beside her, calm, unreadable. Logan trailed a few paces back, hands in his pockets, watching everything. Victor was already muttering about his hangover, but no one answered.

Lucien's phone buzzed in his jacket. He glanced at the screen, sighed, and answered without breaking stride.

"What?"

Agent Hall's voice came in hot. "Are you out of your fucking mind? I've got alerts on your accounts while I'm keeping you off the books, and I'm watching your card activity in real time, ten grand plus tax at a casino and a twenty-five-thousand-dollar cash advance. You weren't supposed to leave Miami. Do you have any idea the weight of the strings I'm pulling over here?"

Lucien stayed calm. "If you want this to work, you'll work with us. And as a matter of fact, I could use your help."

"Weird timing to be asking for favors, don't you think?"

Lucien didn't miss a step. "Unless Royce stopped being your target, I suggest you listen to what I have to say."

Hall went quiet.

"Go on."

"Back in Miami, Royce planted three goons in the cell with Victor and me. Thought they'd finish the job. They talked. Said Royce is out of the country but still running things here. His stateside ops go through a guy named Finch. Ocean Club in Atlantic City. That's all I got."

"You have a full name?"

"No. That's where you come in. All I've got is a handle and a schedule. He hits the gym there like clockwork. Every morning. Eight a.m. sharp."

"And what, you're just walking in?"

"I don't have an angle on him yet. But if I'm walking into that building, I need to know who I'm walking into."

Hall exhaled hard. "I'll see what I can find. But if Atlantic City turns into another Miami, make sure the flames burn the right people."

Lucien hung up.

Five minutes passed. His phone buzzed again.

"You're in luck. Real name's Derek Fincher. Forty-eight. Lives on the 12th floor. Resident of the Ocean Club since 2021. No criminal record. Ex-Navy. Might not be as soft as he looks."

Lucien ended the call and slid the phone into his jacket. Just enough to keep the Fed useful.

He tapped open a new thread and fired a message to the only man he trusted to deliver what Hall never could.

Change of plans. Need eyes. Real name's Derek Fincher. What can you get me?

A minute later, Ghost replied. Not a question. A statement.

Everything

Another ping followed seconds later, clean and precise.

Background checks. Utility accounts. Wi-Fi associations. Cell patterns. I'll have his last twenty Amazon orders, his dry cleaner, and his go-to coffee spot before your next breath. If he so much as searched 'how to disappear,' I'll see it

Lucien read it in silence. The wind curled off the water. Somewhere in the distance, a gull screamed and vanished.

That's why he didn't need a full task force. He had Ghost, and Ghost had the dark.

Another ping.

Fincher leaves the building daily around 9:00 a.m. Walks three blocks up to a café called Cleo's Corner on North Montpelier Avenue. Orders a black coffee and an everything bagel. Sits by the window. Same table. Same seat. Same routine

More data followed.

Amazon orders, resistance bands. Protein powder. Tactical gloves. Espresso pods. Beard trimmer. Last six months, nothing personal. Nothing impulsive. Guy's tight. Predictable

Another.

No family in-state. Two out-of-state sisters. One ex from five years ago. Restraining order on her. She vanished after that. No pets. No kids. No regular visitors

Lucien's phone lit again, each line colder than the last.

Phone stays on him. Always. One burner registered to a fake name, bought from a kiosk two weeks ago. I cracked the IMEI. Last text sent three days ago, "All quiet. Routine holds."

Final ping.

He's not a soldier. He's a signal tower. Royce trusts him to sit still and watch. That's the job. Even statues crack if you hit the right angle

Lucien stared at the screen and didn't answer.

He slipped the phone back into his jacket and turned toward the group.

"His gym routine isn't the only pattern."

Victor raised a brow. "Meaning?"

"Ghost says he hits a place called Cleo's Corner on North Montpelier every morning."

Logan's attention sharpened. "That's public. He's exposed there."

"Exactly."

Lucien glanced toward the street, then back to the crew. "He leaves Ocean Club around nine, walks up to Cleo's, orders a black coffee and an everything bagel. Same table. Same seat. Same routine."

Victor smirked. "Creature of habit. I love that in a target."

Lucien didn't smile. "We check out, grab the truck, and park across the street before he shows. We stay inside, watch him go in, let him settle. Then I go in alone."

Lena narrowed her eyes. "You sure he won't recognize your face?"

Lucien shook his head once. "He's not looking for faces. He's looking for patterns. Eyes in the back of the room. Angles. Mirrors. We don't give him any."

Logan nodded. "What do you want us doing while you're in there?"

"You sit tight and watch the block. If he bolts, you follow him. No scene, no noise. Just track him."

He turned to Lena, his tone softening slightly. "You stay in the truck no matter what. Keep eyes on the whole block. If I signal, Logan rolls up the street. Victor intercepts from the corner."

She nodded.

Victor rolled his shoulders. "Just coffee and a bagel, huh?"

Lucien's voice dropped. "That's the routine. I'm about to break it."

He looked at them. "Lena and I will go up, grab our things, and check out. You two head for valet. I want the truck out front, engine running, by the time we hit the doors."

No hesitation.

No confusion.

Just motion.

The sliding glass doors whispered closed behind them.

Lucien and Lena stepped into the valet bay, dim and enclosed, the air thick with exhaust and the stale bite of cigarette smoke. Fluorescent lights hummed overhead. Engines idled. Doors slammed. A stream of people came and went. Some arriving in heels. Others leaving in regret.

Logan and Victor waited near the curb as the SUV pulled around.

The vehicle rolled to a stop. Logan took the driver's seat. Victor slid in beside him. Lucien and Lena climbed into the back.

No one spoke as they pulled away from the canopy. Tropicana shrank behind them. Cracked pavement and shuttered storefronts slid past the glass.

Lucien checked his watch.

8:58 A.M.

They turned onto North Montpelier, the quiet street giving them a clean view of Cleo's Corner up ahead. Modest signage. Fogged windows. Not crowded. Not empty. Just enough faces to study.

Victor leaned forward. "So how do we know who the fuck he is? We've never seen this asshole."

Lucien kept his eyes on the café. "We don't. Let's see who walks in like they've done it a hundred times."

Logan, steady at the wheel, nodded toward the sidewalk. "Boss. Take a look."

The man was mid-forties, buzzed hair, military shoulders, uncomfortable in civilian skin.

Victor didn't wait. "Yeah. That's him."

Lucien watched the man cross to the café, unhurried and efficient. He stepped inside and ordered without looking at the menu.

Bagel, coffee, window seat.

Right on time.

"Unreal," Lucien said. "Like clockwork."

He opened the door and stepped out, no rush, no weight in his stride. Just calm.

From the SUV, Fincher looked almost ordinary. That was always the danger.

The bell above the café door gave a soft, innocent chime.

Warm air carried the scent of fresh coffee and burnt toast. Music drifted from ceiling speakers, barely louder than a whisper. Someone coughed. Another stirred their drink with a plastic stick, the faint tap cutting through the hush.

Then the room felt him.

Not loudly, not all at once. Just a shift. Like gravity changing its mind.

Lucien scanned the tables. One man alone near the window, black coffee, everything bagel, zero expression. Just like Ghost said.

Their eyes met.

Fincher didn't move, but he straightened by a fraction, like his body remembered old habits.

The kind of stillness men learned in places where moving first got you killed.

Lucien walked to the counter, calm, no urgency.

"Large black coffee," he told the girl behind the register, who looked like she hadn't yet decided if he was trouble or not.

She nodded and started the order.

Lucien didn't look at her. He watched Fincher in the reflection of the pastry case glass.

The coffee came hot and fresh, with a clean white lid and a stamped sleeve. Lucien took it without a word.

He crossed the café and sat down at Fincher's table without asking.

No permission. No warmth. Just control.

Lucien placed the cup on the table and rested both hands beside it.

He leaned in. "We're going to talk. You're going to listen."

Fincher shifted his chair a few degrees, just enough to keep the door in his peripheral without turning his head.

He just stared. "I figured I had about a week left before someone like you showed up."

Lucien smiled without warmth. "I'm flattered. Let's make the most of it."

Fincher reached for his coffee, eyes never leaving Lucien. He took a sip and set it down.

"You with the FBI?"

Lucien leaned back. "Do I look like the Bureau?"

A half nod. "No. You look like who they call when the Bureau's too slow."

Lucien let the silence stretch.

Fincher studied him. "You're not here to threaten me. Not in daylight. Which means you need something."

Lucien nodded. "Smart. Let's keep that momentum going."

Fincher exhaled. "Royce said this might happen."

That was the first real tell. Royce wasn't just reacting to Lucien. He was planning around him.

Lucien raised a brow. "Royce talks a lot for a man in hiding."

Fincher gave the ghost of a smile. "He doesn't hide. He watches. Builds. Waits. You think just because you rattle one cage, the whole structure falls?"

Lucien didn't blink. "No. But sometimes you don't need to bring down the whole building. Sometimes you just kill the electrician. Then everything goes dark."

Fincher stiffened.

Lucien leaned in. "I'm not asking you to betray him. I'm giving you a chance to survive him."

Fincher's eyes sharpened. "You think Royce doesn't know you're here? You think he hasn't planned for this?"

Lucien shrugged slightly. "If he had, we wouldn't be talking. And you wouldn't look like you're deciding whether to run or comply."

Fincher's grip tightened on the cup. "You don't know what kind of man he is."

Lucien's voice cut clean. "I know what kind of men he uses."

For the first time, Fincher looked away.

"He's not in the country. That's all I'll give."

Lucien nodded slowly. "You just said enough."

Fincher's eyes flicked back. "You think you can get to him?"

"I don't need to get to him. I just need to make him bleed long enough for the sharks to smell it."

Fincher didn't reply.

Lucien didn't press. He let time do what pressure didn't need to anymore.

Fincher wanted to say something else but couldn't find a version that didn't ruin him.

Lucien sipped his coffee once, watching him over the rim, calm and unhurried.

"Let me guess," Lucien said. "Royce sends you money in intervals. Small amounts. Dirty accounts. Just enough to keep you quiet and just barely protected."

Lucien went on. "You've been a loyal shadow. Eyes on the street. But you haven't heard from him in how long? A week? Ten days? And suddenly I'm here. Which means he knows you're vulnerable, and he's willing to let you burn first."

Fincher's fingers tapped the side of his cup, anxious rhythm trying to pass for composure. "What exactly do you want from me?"

Lucien smiled faintly, not kind. "Just a name."

Fincher looked up. "A name?"

Lucien nodded. "Not a list. Not a file. Just one person Royce trusts. Someone still on this side of the water. Someone closer to his spine."

He held Fincher's gaze. "Give me that, and you disappear clean. I'll make sure the right people forget you exist. You go back to your bagels, your black coffee, your little routines."

Lucien leaned in just slightly. "Or you don't. And the next person who sits across from you won't be offering choices."

The silence stretched between them.

Then Fincher spoke.

"There's a guy. Mercer. Quiet. No profile. Handles cash, movement, off-books stuff. Royce only uses him when it matters. Moves like a ghost."

Lucien blinked once. "Where?"

"North Jersey. Runs out of some private airstrip," Fincher said. "Not sure where exactly, but I've heard talk of a warehouse off the Route 46 corridor. That's all I know."

Mercer wasn't the prize. He was the first artery close enough to cut.

Lucien sat with it long enough to know he wasn't bluffing. Then he stood. No handshake. No thank you.

"Enjoy your bagel."

Lucien stepped out of the café.

He didn't look back.

The SUV waited across the street, engine idling. Logan in the driver's seat. Victor riding shotgun. Lena watching him through the tinted glass.

Lucien climbed in and closed the door behind him. "Pull away."

Logan didn't ask questions.

He eased back into the flow of early morning traffic.

Lucien pulled his phone from his jacket and thumbed Ghost's thread.

Two rings. Then Ghost picked up.

"Talk to me."

Lucien kept his voice low. "Mercer. No first name. Royce's logistics guy. Quiet. Trusted. The kind you only meet if you're a problem, or a solution. Private airstrip in North Jersey. And a warehouse somewhere around the Route 46 corridor."

Static hummed faintly. Then Ghost came back clean. "Alright. I'll map every warehouse that touches 46, and every private strip within a workable radius. Cross-check it against hangar leases, shell companies, and anything Royce ever whispered into a burner phone. Give me an hour."

"Do it in thirty and I'll add twenty percent to the payment."

A pause. Then Ghost came back.

"Copy that. Check back in."

The call ended.

Lucien slid the phone back into his coat and stared out the window, already calculating the next move.

"One name down," he said quietly. "Now let's see what the fuck he's guarding."

A half hour passed in near silence. The SUV pushed north on the Parkway, swallowed by long stretches of marsh that bled into dense green, miles of nothing stretching quiet and endless.

Lena lay sideways across the back seat, her head in Lucien's lap. One hand clutched the hem of his jacket. The other curled under her chin like a child mid-dream. Lucien held her gently, fingers cradling the edge of her jaw, thumb tracing slow lines down her cheek.

Then his phone buzzed.

The vibration cut sharp through the silence.

Victor turned slightly in the passenger seat, glancing back over his shoulder. Logan's eyes flicked to the rearview, unreadable but alert.

Lucien didn't move at first. He just looked down at Lena, still asleep.

Then he answered on speaker. "Yeah."

Ghost's voice came through. "Warehouse in Belleville. Back lot off Route 7, near the 46 corridor. Between a trucking depot and an abandoned lot. Not listed on any current leases. Shell company out of Panama. No signage. No real digital footprint."

Lucien's gaze drifted to the trees beyond the highway. "How long's it been hot?"

"Movement ramped up three weeks ago. Overnight deliveries. Black SUVs, no plates. One rolled in last night at 2:37 a.m. I pulled a nearby traffic cam."

A pause, like Ghost was already two layers deeper.

"The airstrip's in Linden," he continued. "Private. Restricted. Nothing filed officially in months. But I pinged a Gulfstream G550 that's shown up on satellite three times in the last ten days. Lands without logs. Leaves the same way. Guess who owns it."

"Royce," Lucien said flatly.

"One of his banks, through three layers of cutouts. But yeah."

Lucien sat back, thumb returning to Lena's cheek as she shifted slightly in her sleep. "Anyone on-site?"

"Thermal reads show six to eight inside. Armed. Disciplined. And there's a motion-triggered perimeter net. This isn't street muscle. This is containment."

Victor turned fully now, brows raised. "They know we're coming?"

Lucien didn't answer him. He stayed with Ghost. "How long till you can get me schematics?"

"Fifteen minutes. I'll send thermal overlays and exit routes. And Lucien, this isn't a trap house. This is an operating room. Whoever's in there matters."

They weren't guarding product. They were guarding process.

"Good. Then they'll bleed clean."

Lucien ended the call.

The SUV rolled on for a stretch. Pine trees thickened on both sides, shadows slanting across the highway like prison bars.

Victor finally spoke, but his tone was different now. Lower. No grin. No quip. Just weight.

"I've got ties in North Jersey. Russian side. People I don't call unless it matters."

Lucien glanced up once. No surprise. Just acknowledgment.

Victor kept going. "They've got gear. No questions. No mess. Move like ghosts and bury what needs to stay buried."

A pause.

"You make a call. I'll make a call. We meet at the warehouse."

No one spoke. Because when Victor stopped joking, everyone remembered exactly who he was.

Lucien's phone pinged.

He looked down, a secured message from Ghost. Encrypted. No preview.

Just a blinking prompt.

He opened it.

Blueprints.

"Back entrance is fenced. East side's blind," Lucien muttered, eyes on the schematic. "No cameras in the loading bay. One office. Two exits. Eight warm bodies tracked inside."

He held the phone up between the seats so Victor could see. Victor turned, looking over his shoulder, eyes narrowing as he studied the layout.

"They're boxed in," Victor said.

Lucien nodded once. "Then we seal it shut."

He pulled out his phone and dialed a number by memory.

One ring.

"Warehouse in Belleville. I'll send the pin. I need two men with thermals. Suppressed. No comms. One high. One low. Watch the exits. No noise unless a body drops."

"On it," the voice replied. The line went dead.

Victor was already on his own call, speaking low. No charm. No grin. Just clipped commands, sharp and final.

He hung up, eyes flat again. "My guys will take the north wall. Lock down the alley. Wait for us to move first."

Lucien nodded once, voice calm. "Then let's go knock."

No one in the truck corrected the lie.

Chapter Thirty-Six

PULL THE THREAD

The SUV veered off the main road and rolled onto a narrow service path that twisted behind a row of rusted shipping containers. Gravel crunched under the tires. Ahead, the warehouse came into view. Unmarked. Windowless. Still in the way bad places are still.

Lucien sat forward slightly, eyes fixed.

It wasn't big. It was built for endings. Faded brick. Steel doors. A ring of perimeter cameras, now looped, courtesy of Ghost. The sun hung just off its peak, casting hard shadows across the lot.

Victor adjusted the cuffs of his shirt, calm as a man about to break something. Logan stayed focused, both hands on the wheel. Lena said nothing in the backseat. She knew what this was.

Two black sedans were already parked nearby, low to the ground, their engines idling. Shadows moved inside. Lucien's men.

Victor's phone lit once. He checked the screen, his expression settling.

"My side's in position. Back alley's covered."

Lucien checked his watch. "Three minutes."

He reached for his phone. One text already waiting from Ghost:

PERIMETER NET CONFIRMED, short-range IR grid
Jamming the uplink on the next reset cycle
Thirty-second window. No second chances
Entry in two-fourteen. Wait for my green

Lucien looked back to the warehouse, already seeing where it would break.

He turned to Logan and caught the eagerness in the kid's posture.

"You stay back."

Logan blinked. "You serious? I can help on the entry."

Lucien cut him off.

"You protect her. Everything else is secondary. Back it up into that corner.

No line of sight from the front. If anyone who isn't me or Victor comes near this vehicle, you crush them with the front bumper. Don't wait for confirmation. You take off. Hard. No thinking. No hesitation."

Logan didn't argue. There was no offense in his eyes. Just purpose.

Lucien turned to Lena, brushing her hand once, brief but firm.

"When I come back through that door, you're the first thing I want in my sight."

Lena didn't smile. She nodded.

Lucien stepped out.

The door clicked shut behind him.

Victor followed, quieter than expected for a man his size. His jacket was open just enough to show the grip of a suppressed sidearm tucked low. They moved in sync.

Lena watched Lucien cross the lot like a man the world had failed to kill too many times.

Dust hung in the air. Gravel cracked under their boots.

Two men stepped out from the parked sedans down the lot. All black. Tactical. Calm. One of them nodded once and drifted off, vanishing behind a stack of containers toward the roof. The other disappeared around the building, already gone.

Victor scanned the lot. "We're set."

They crossed the distance without hurry. The building seemed to rise as they closed on it, sealed up and waiting.

They reached the loading dock, no sound but the buzz of a distant highway and the thud of Victor's fist against the steel door.

Lucien reached into his coat and drew his piece.

Three seconds stretched into four.

The door opened halfway, creaking like it hadn't moved in years.

Victor stepped in first, slow and low, gun up. Pure motion.

Lucien followed, eyes sharp.

The warehouse swallowed them.

The door slammed shut behind them.

Outside, nothing moved.

In the backseat, Lena kept her eyes on the warehouse door.

The silence around it felt wrong, too complete, like violence had learned how to pray.

Slats of light spilled through warped vents near the roofline. Dust held in the light. The air smelled of oil, rubber, and something metallic. Blood, maybe. Or something about to be.

One of Lucien's men was already inside, up in the rafters, rifle trained downward, covering their movement without a sound. Another shadow moved along the far wall, Victor's call, tracking angles.

They swept past a stack of crates, through a corridor of tarped pallets, the floor groaning under their weight.

Shipping labels clung to the sides. Rotterdam. Lagos. Singapore. None of it was real.

A folding table nearby was buried in burner phones and satellite trackers, blinking softly in the dim.

Then Mercer stepped into it.

Mid-forties. Buzzed hair. Tactical vest. He stood at the folding table like the room answered to him. Two men flanked him, one with a submachine gun, the other barely old enough to shave. Three more lingered around the room, spread along the pallets and crates, watching the door. Two others stood near the rear loading bay, half-buried in shadow.

Guns came up as Lucien and Victor stepped into the light.

They didn't stop.

They walked until the only thing between them was space, and whatever God these men prayed to.

Victor's gun was up. Lucien matched him, but no one fired. Not yet.

Lucien looked Mercer dead in the eyes.

"You get one chance to leave this room still answering to your own name."

Mercer held his ground. "Who sent you?"

Victor didn't look at him. "Wrong question."

"You're not cops."

"No."

Mercer glanced between them, something shifting behind his eyes.

"You walked in blind."

Lucien gave the faintest nod toward the dark.

The first shot popped.

The boy on Mercer's right folded as a round tore through his skull. The other jerked as a second round punched through his neck.

No scream, just silence, just two suppressed cracks whispering from the rafters.

Then the floor broke.

Victor's men moved, one from the shadows, one from the blindside. Another shot snapped from behind a stack of crates. A fourth man dropped before he could turn.

Lucien's second man came out of the far aisle, already firing. One more body hit the concrete hard.

Three more bodies dropped, weapons clattering across the floor.

Ten seconds. Seven men down.

Now it was just Lucien, Victor, and Mercer.

Lucien stepped forward. "You were saying?"

Mercer's voice cracked. "You think this changes anything?"

Lucien didn't even glance at the bodies.

"No. It leaves you alone."

Mercer exhaled. "You think this ends with me?"

Lucien let him sit in it.

Mercer steadied, then met his eyes.

"You don't know how deep this goes."

Victor watched him. "Royce?"

Mercer didn't move.

Lucien's smile was thin.

"That's exactly why we're here."

He stepped closer.

"You leaked my shipment."

Mercer didn't answer.

"Newark."

Lucien watched his face.

"That wasn't random. That was a message from Royce."

Lucien stepped closer.

"And now I'm here at your fucking door."

"Royce has been flying in and out of Linden. My guy pulled the pattern. Same jet. Same pilot. Same schedule. Three times in the last ten days."

Lucien held Mercer's stare.

"You know who he's meeting when he lands?"

Mercer said nothing.

Lucien's voice dropped.

"Neither do I. That's the only reason you're still standing."

Victor shifted beside him, coiled.

Lucien kept his gaze locked on Mercer's.

"You hold the ground while Royce moves above it."

Mercer watched him. "You don't know the game you just stepped into."

Lucien didn't smile. "Good. Then I'll burn it from the inside out."

Mercer hesitated.

A twitch. A breath. Like silence might still save him.

Then Victor moved.

Fast. Violent.

He slammed Mercer back against the folding table, one arm across his chest, the other across his throat. The edge of the table dug into Mercer's spine. Air left him in a gasp.

"You weren't the one who touched Miami," Victor growled. "But you're tied to the hand that did."

He leaned in, close enough that Mercer couldn't look away.

"Different room. Same hand on the throat."

Lucien watched without a word.

"Two dozen of mine died down there," Victor said, tightening his grip. "So tell me who else is carrying orders for Royce."

Mercer choked, breath catching in his throat.

Victor eased the pressure just enough to keep him conscious.

Lucien stepped in.

"We already know who you are."

Mercer's breath rasped in Victor's grip.

"You helped seize my shipment."

His eyes stayed locked on Mercer's.

"You weren't the architect. But the orders ran through you."

Lucien leaned closer.

"So now you're going to give me something else."

Mercer wheezed, voice raw.

"You already got what you came for."

Lucien cut him off.

"No. I came here so Royce never hears your name again. Ever."

His voice dropped, almost quiet enough to miss.

"So tell me who's next."

Another step.

"Who else has a hand in this?"

The warehouse held its breath.

"You're standing in the last seconds of a life I haven't bothered to take yet."

He flicked a glance at the rafters.

A faint red dot danced on Mercer's chest.

"In five seconds, my guy in the dark back there sends you off this earth. I want a real answer. Right now. Give me enough, and you walk out of here."

Mercer looked at him. For a moment, it almost seemed like he was going to choose death.

Then something in his eyes broke.

"Okay," he rasped. "Okay... alright."

"Royce doesn't hide in the dark. He hides where power looks legitimate."

Lucien said nothing. Just listened.

"Upscale office complex in Kearny. Corner suite. Fourth floor. It's registered as Summit Transit Group, looks like a legit logistics firm. No sign on the door. Just tinted glass and silence."

Victor stepped in a little.

Encouragement or threat.

"That office is his second skin. Backups. Accounts. Names. If Royce ever had to vanish, that's where he'd leave himself behind. He's not there, but his fingerprints are. Everything he's ever moved, everyone he's ever owned, it's all in that office."

Lucien's jaw flexed. "And how does he get in and out?"

"Linden Airport. Private terminal. Twenty minutes south. Same pilot. Same Gulfstream. He's flown in three times this month. Doesn't linger. But you knew that already. He has someone open the office, transfer the data, lock it down again. Then he's gone. In and out like smoke."

Lucien filed it away.

"There aren't guards. Not like you're thinking. It's protocol. Codes. Rotating access. No cameras inside. No staff. Just biometric locks. Changing codes. And one guy who shows up when something moves. Wren. No one sees Royce. Not even him. It's all signals. You pull the wrong thread in that place, the whole system collapses."

Lucien narrowed his eyes. "Who's Wren?"

"His accountant. Keeper of the codes. No online profile. Never shows his face. But he handles Royce's movements. You want to get to Royce? That office is where the leash connects."

Mercer looked at them both. Face pale. Voice shaking.

"That's everything. I swear it. I gave you the real play. You said I'd walk out."

Lucien stepped forward, calm as ever.

"No. I said you'd walk out if the answer was enough."

He raised the gun.

"You gave me leverage."

One shot.

Mercer dropped.

Lucien gave the slightest nod toward the rafters.

The red dot disappeared.

Lucien holstered his weapon and turned, walking out of the warehouse with Victor beside him.

They didn't speak. The room was already finished.

At the edge of the lot, Lucien lifted his phone, pressed one button, and held it to his ear.

"Did you get all that?"

A moment of static.

"Every word. File's already compiling."

Lucien lowered the phone and kept walking, the next move already set.

A few steps later, Ghost's message hit.

Summit runs on silence. Give me 30 minutes. I'll own the locks

The black SUV waited just ahead. Logan behind the wheel. Lena still in the backseat, alert, watching.

Victor reached the front passenger door and climbed in. Lucien slid in beside Lena.

As the door shut, she turned slightly, eyes locked on him. "Everything okay?"

Lucien stared ahead like saying it out loud would make the next fire real.

"Mercer cracked. Gave us a location. Kearny."

Victor picked it up.

"Royce's vault."

Lucien kept his eyes ahead. "Linden Airport. That's how he moves. Same jet. Same pilot. In and out."

They pulled away from the warehouse, the horizon ahead turning into concrete, steel, and clouds.

Ghost sent the rest before they hit the main road.

Rotating entry codes confirmed. Biometric lock

Access logs tied to Wren only

Mapping now. Breach window: thirty seconds

Coordinates, timers, and kill-switch en route

Every word was a warning.

Logan pressed the accelerator, merging into open highway, Jersey flashing by in concrete and wire.

"I guess it's happening," he muttered.

Victor rolled his neck, eyes locked ahead. "No. It's already begun."

Chapter Thirty-Seven

SEVER THE HEAD, BURN THE CROWN

They eased to a stop just shy of the intersection, tucked into the corner of an industrial side street near the Kearny waterfront. Summit Transit Group sat dead ahead. Four stories of brushed steel and tinted glass, quiet, sterile, built to disappear.

The kind of building that looked innocent until you understood how much death it could hold.

Lucien raised his phone and fired off a single text.

Two minutes out

Ghost replied almost instantly.

Understood. You'll have a thirty-second breach window. I'm staging the kill-switch protocol now

Another ping followed, longer this time.

I can get you in, but I can't destroy it from here. Royce built it that way

The core systems are closed-loop. No remote failsafe

Once you're inside, you'll hit the primary node. I mapped the server room through old utility blueprints and internal access logs. Top of the rack, far wall, left of the desk. You'll see a blinking amber LED. That's your target

Lucien read it once. Then again. Then nodded to himself.

What happens after we hit it?

Power will surge. Drives will heat. You'll have ten minutes from activation to walk out clean. After that, everything turns to ash

He lowered the phone and looked forward, eyes narrowing on the glass building beyond the windshield.

"Let's erase him."

Not the man, not yet. First the shadow he hid inside.

The SUV rolled forward and slipped into a loading zone behind the building. No marked cameras. No signs of life. Just a keypad entry at a plain steel side door, humming faintly with power.

Lucien stepped out first. Victor followed, tightening the strap on his shoulder rig.

Lena touched Lucien's wrist just before he shut the door behind him. "Be careful."

For a second, the war fell away. There was only her hand on his wrist, and the life in him that still answered to it.

Lucien looked at her, gaze locked. No bravado. Just promise. "Ten minutes. Then we're out."

He closed the door and turned toward the entrance.

His phone vibrated once.

You're green. Access unlocked. Breach window starts now

Lucien pressed the keypad.

A soft click. The door eased open like it had been waiting, like Royce had built the whole place assuming no one alive would ever reach this far.

Lucien glanced at Victor. Then they stepped inside.

No alarms. No echo. Just the hush of climate-controlled air moving through the walls.

The hallway was sterile. Gray floors. White walls. Silent recessed lights.

Victor moved left. Lucien right. Each checking corners. Each step calculated.

The silence felt wrong.

They passed ordinary-looking office doors, glass partitions, a half-lit reception space, a printer still warm from someone who never really existed.

Everything was too clean. Too untouched to be real.

They reached the double doors at the end of the hall. A red swipe reader sat flush beside the handle.

Lucien held up his phone again.

Override engaged. You've got ten minutes. Starts the moment you breach

He pushed the door open.

The server room blinked to life in rows of steel and cold LEDs.

Floor-to-ceiling racks. Blades humming. Routers breathing like sleeping machines.

A low blue wash lit the space like the inside of something alive.

Far wall.

Left of the desk.

Amber LED.

Lucien crossed the room in five strides.

Victor stayed near the door, eyes scanning, pistol drawn and loose in his hand.

Lucien's phone buzzed again.

Check the top-left drawer under the desk

According to an old asset log I intercepted, there's an encrypted SSD stored there. Black. Unmarked

You'll know it's the right one. No serial. Just weight

Plug it into the far-right port on the tower

It'll pull core logs, transfers, comms, blackmail indexes

Once it flashes green, yank it and walk. Hall can use that. It's everything he needs to bury him

Lucien reached the desk and pulled the drawer open.

There it was, matte black, no markings.

A small drive that looked like nothing, but carried everything.

Entire lives had probably been ruined by less.

He crossed back to the server tower and found the port, far right, tucked beneath a nest of cables. He plugged it in.

The LED blinked red.

Then yellow.

Lucien waited.

Green.

He pulled it free and slid it into his jacket.

"We've got it. The whole empire in one flash. Hall gets it."

Then he turned to the primary node, pressed the kill command, and watched the purge begin.

The LED blinked once.

Twice.

Then turned red.

A quiet click sounded beneath the floor, like a circuit locking into finality.

Somewhere deep in the walls, Royce's kingdom had started eating itself alive.

A single message flashed across the nearest screen: *FAILSAFE TRIG-GERED. DATA PURGE INITIATED*

The hum deepened, like the building was holding its breath.

Drives heated. Server racks glowed with sudden urgency.

Fans kicked in. Lights dimmed. A slow internal heartbeat began, one final countdown.

Lucien's phone buzzed again.

Timer's live. Ten minutes to clear

Lucien stepped back, watching the data spine of Royce's empire collapse from the inside.

He turned to Victor, voice calm, already moving.

"Let's go."

They moved fast, but not rushed.

Lucien led, eyes steady. Victor behind him, watching every shadow like it might flinch.

The corridor was still empty, still quiet, but something in the air had changed.

Tension moved beneath the lights, as if the building had finally realized its own time was running out.

They passed the glass doors, the ghost offices, the fake desks, and the disconnected phones.

Everything that had once felt invincible now felt hollow.

At the end of the hall, the exit keypad blinked green, still under Ghost's control.

The door started to swing inward.

Lucien stopped.

A man stepped through the glass doors. Mid-forties. Suit. Thin leather case in one hand.

He froze when he saw them.

His eyes flicked past them toward the server floor.

Toward the dying lights.

Color drained from his face.

"What the fuck did you two do?"

Victor's gun was already up.

The man stumbled backward toward the door.

"Do you have any idea what you just,"

Victor fired.

The suppressed round punched through the man's thigh. He collapsed hard, screaming, clutching his leg.

Lucien stepped forward.

The man fumbled inside his jacket, shaking.

Lucien's eyes dropped to his hand.

"Don't."

Victor narrowed his eyes.

"What the hell is that?"

The man pulled a small black fob free, blood streaked across his hand. He laughed once through the pain.

"Panic button, asshole."

Lucien didn't even look impressed.

The gun came up.

One shot.

The man dropped.

Lucien glanced at the fob on the floor.

"Clock's running."

Victor stepped over the body.

They pushed through the door.

The air hit them hard, real and alive, nothing like the oxygen-pumped cold of machines.

This was the open breath of the world.

Across the lot, the SUV idled. Logan behind the wheel.

Lena leaned forward the second she saw them, eyes scanning, pulse visible in her neck.

Lucien slid into the back seat. Victor shut the door behind him.

"It's done."

Logan pulled away from the curb, turning without a word.

Behind them, Summit Transit Group stood quiet.

No alarms. No explosions. No final act of destruction.

But inside, everything was dying.

Drives melted. Files collapsed. Every thread Royce had ever pulled burned down in the dark.

An empire didn't always fall with sirens. Sometimes it died in silence, one severed nerve at a time.

Lucien glanced out the window.

"We didn't just hit him. We cut the root."

Lena looked back at the building one last time, then at him.

"So what now?"

Lucien's eyes stayed on the road ahead.

"Now?"

A pause.

"We wait."

Because dying kings were predictable, but wounded ones were dangerous.

His voice dropped slightly.

"His head's been severed. The crown just hasn't fallen yet."

The words hung in the air.

"That should be enough to draw him out."

He reached for his phone, thumb already moving.

"I'm calling Hall. Time he gets up to speed."

Lucien scrolled to Hall's number and hit call.

The line picked up fast. Tension coiled in the silence before Hall's voice came through.

"You said you'd keep me in the loop. This better be worth the silence."

Lucien's voice stayed calm. "We didn't go dark. We went surgical."

Silence on the other end.

"Summit Transit Group. Kearny, New Jersey. Fourth floor. Looked like a logistics firm, but it was the vault. Bank accounts. Identities. Leverage. All of it gone."

"Jesus Christ," Hall muttered.

"Royce built it without guards. No cameras. Rotating biometric protocols. A ghost named Wren holding the codes."

Lucien watched the city slide past the window. "My guy got us in. We triggered the purge. What's left in that building now is ash."

Another moment passed.

"He wasn't there, was he?"

"Didn't need him to be."

Lucien's gaze stayed on the road ahead. "That building wasn't about catching him. It was about breaking him. We snapped the spine of his operation. And he's going to feel it."

Hall exhaled slowly. "So what's next?"

"He comes back stateside. It's the only move left. When he does, we'll be ready."

Lucien reached into his jacket and tapped the encrypted SSD in his inner pocket. "And I've got a gift for you. Pulled the core logs before the purge. One SSD. Transfers, comms, shell accounts."

A beat.

"Everything. Enough to bury him and scorch the earth around him."

Hall exhaled long and rough. "You're sure this draws him out?"

Lucien's eyes hardened. "We didn't just knock on the door, Hall. We set fire to the house."

And somewhere out there, Lucien could already feel the smoke reaching him.

"Alright," Hall said. "But this is it. If he surfaces, I don't want red tape. I want intercept. Clean. Legal. Final."

Lucien's voice dropped to ice. "Then keep the trigger warm."

A pause stretched between them before Hall spoke again.

"When he steps out of the shadows, we end it."

Lucien ended the call.

No goodbye.
No ceremony.
The war had already shifted.

Chapter Thirty-Eight

VICTORY WAKES THE WOLVES

The night air rolled cool across the harbor, brushing Lucien's skin as he guided the yacht into open water.

The yacht was a sleek, low-slung beauty he'd rented for the night, no crew, no noise, just the two of them and the city lights sliding past in scattered gold.

Behind them, Manhattan gleamed, towers etched in metal and firelight, reflections breaking across black water.

For once, there was no war to fight.

No blood to spill.

No clocks ticking down to betrayal.

Victor was handling business uptown.

Logan was on standby, somewhere in the city shadows.

Ghost monitored the wires from his own corner of the dark.

And Lucien, for tonight, allowed himself the cruelty of peace.

Peace never came to men like him clean. It came stolen, dressed in silk, already carrying a knife.

He throttled forward, the yacht slicing a clean path across the black water, the engine a low, steady heartbeat beneath their feet.

Lena leaned against the rail, her hair caught in the salt air, her eyes reflecting the skyline.

There was a quiet about her tonight, a softness Lucien rarely let himself believe he could still touch.

She looked less like something made for this world than something heaven had dropped into it by mistake.

Men like Lucien weren't built to keep holy things. They were built to ruin them, or die trying not to.

For a few stolen minutes, there was no kingdom to defend. No empire of ghosts breathing down his neck. No city waiting to collect interest in blood. No Royce lurking in the shadows.

Just the night.

Just the water.

Just her.

Lucien kept one hand steady on the wheel, the other loose at his side, the weight in his bones easing with every slow turn.

Above them, the sky hung cloudless and black, scattered with hard points of starlight..

Lena drifted closer, her hand brushing his jacket as she leaned in to watch the city slide by.

She didn't say anything.

She didn't need to.

Lucien eased back the throttle, letting the boat drift.

Freedom, for a moment, wasn't a lie. It moved around them like a rumor, fragile enough to vanish if either of them spoke too loud.

It lived in the way she stood there, in the quiet she brought with her, in the way his chest didn't feel so heavy when she was near.

Even the decay along the edges, a ferry abandoned at the dock, a warehouse with shattered windows, looked softened tonight, because she was in it, and he was still breathing.

Lucien studied her.

Not a weapon. Not a shield. Not another pawn in a war he never wanted.

Just Lena.

Not the woman the war kept reaching for. Not the future men like Royce would gut just to prove they still had teeth.

Just here.

He wondered what it would feel like to keep going. Not back to the ghosts he left behind. Not back to the life that never stopped demanding blood.

Just forward, into the black.

Into peace.

Into her.

Something in his mouth almost broke into a smile when she turned and caught him staring.

"What?" Her voice was teasing, soft.

Lucien shook his head, the corner of his mouth twitching. "Nothing."

And he meant it.

Because right now, for once, nothing was wrong. Nothing needed fixing. There was only breath, stillness, and the impossible weightlessness of being alive.

He wasn't a king. He wasn't a killer. He wasn't a ghost.

Just a man.

Alive.

Which was always the most dangerous thing he could let himself be.

The war could wait. Royce could wait. The world could burn for all he cared.

Tonight was hers.

Tonight was theirs.

Lucien Cole let himself believe survival could be more than breathing.

The yacht drifted, the city unspooling around them in gold and glass.

Lucien shifted, resting his hand against Lena's lower back as she leaned into him.

An unconscious touch, steady, grounding, like if he let go, he might lose not just her, but himself.

Lena smiled, soft and private, and turned her gaze back to the water.

Lucien exhaled a breath he hadn't realized he'd been holding.

And then the burner buzzed against his chest, sharp and precise.

Lucien went still.

Not tense. Not panicked.

He stopped moving completely, the way a predator goes still when it smells something wrong on the wind.

Lena caught the shift immediately, her body tightening beside him.

Lucien pulled the phone from his jacket and saw the number flash across the screen.

He answered without a sound.

The harbor dropped out.

The night collapsed to nothing.

Ghost's voice came through low, knife-tight.

"He moved."

He didn't soften the rest.

"There's a bounty out. Ten million. Dead or alive."

It wasn't just money. It was permission. A citywide blessing for every coward with a gun and every scavenger born hungry.

For a split second, everything froze.

The water.

The boat.

The fucking skyline.

Across the harbor, a small fishing boat slowed, its lone occupant lifting a phone and pointing it toward the yacht.

Lucien moved calmly, steadying the wheel as the boat drifted farther into the harbor.

Lena stepped closer without thinking, reading the shift in him before the words even came.

Lucien broke the silence.

"Who knows?"

Ghost didn't hesitate.

"Everyone. Crews, freelancers, junkies with a death wish. You're live game now."

Lucien's fingers tightened around the phone until the plastic creaked.

"Timeline?"

Ghost's answer was a scalpel.

"Already started. The bounty's moving."

Lucien closed his eyes for half a breath.

Of course.

Of course Royce wouldn't crawl back to be caught.

Of course he would turn the city into a fucking weapon.

Lucien opened his eyes, fixing them on the far line of Manhattan. The lights still pretty. Still soft. Still lying.

Lucien looked over at Lena, steady, already bracing.

"Call Logan. Tell him to get the truck ready."

Lena nodded, already pulling her phone from her jacket.

Lucien put the burner back to his ear.

"Scramble the channels," he said, voice dropping colder.

He glanced at Lena as she pressed the call through, her hands steady even though her face had gone pale under the harbor lights.

"If they're coming," he said, "then we're hunting too."

Ghost didn't argue. Didn't ask questions.

The line clicked dead.

Lucien slid the burner back into his jacket.

He turned the wheel hard, swinging the yacht back toward Manhattan, toward the lights and the blood waiting in the streets.

The night was over.

Peace had lasted exactly long enough to remind Lucien what could be taken.

The war had found them again.

Lucien Cole wasn't planning to survive this. He was planning to end it.

Lena studied him. "What's happening?"

Lucien didn't look at her. "Ten million."

She frowned. "What?"

"That's the price that just went on my head."

He kept his eyes on the water. "Every killer, crew, and lunatic in the city is looking for me tonight."

The wind moved across the deck.

Lena stepped closer. "Lucien."

"We can't stay out here," he said quietly. "Open water's a coffin."

As the lights of the city grew sharper, swelling in front of them, the illusion of peace dissolved.

Too loud. Too bright. Too alive for what had just been set into motion.

The skyline loomed over the water.

Every tower felt hostile now, like behind every window someone was already aiming.

Lucien pulled the throttle back as the marina came into view, a regular slip tucked between yachts twice as flashy and half as dangerous.

He guided the yacht in smooth and clean. The hull kissed the dock.

Lucien killed the engine in one clean motion, then stood and offered his hand.

Lena stepped down first, her boots landing hard on the wooden planks.

Only once she was steady did Lucien follow, silent, eyes already scanning the dock.

The air changed, thinner and sharper.

The black SUV rolled up fast to the edge of the marina.

Logan was behind the wheel, headlights low.

Lucien took Lena's hand, not tender, not soft, just steady.

They moved.

Logan jumped out as they closed the distance. "What's going on?"

Lucien yanked open the rear door and nodded once at Lena.

She climbed in without hesitation.

Lucien slid in after her and slammed the door.

Logan was already moving, rounding the front of the SUV at a run and throwing himself back behind the wheel.

"Drive," Lucien said.

Logan punched the gas.

The SUV lunged into traffic, cutting hard into the late-night flow.

Lucien leaned forward between the seats. "Royce didn't take the hit like a man. He took it like a fucking coward. Ten million, dead or alive."

Logan glanced at him in the mirror. "Christ."

"We're exposed," Lucien said. "Every block in this city is a loaded gun now. Get us out of Manhattan."

Logan nodded, shifting lanes hard. "Where to?"

"The estate," Lucien said. "We regroup and plan. We're not getting picked off in the open."

As they hit 12th Street, Lena turned her head toward the window.

Her heart pounded in a rhythm that didn't feel human.

The city looked different tonight.

Every face, every corner, every stretch of light looked wrong.

The city no longer felt like a place. It felt like a mouth opening.

The people on the corners no longer looked like people. They looked like masks, as if the whole island had put on a human face just to get close enough to bite.

She could feel it, the entire city shifting half a step to the left.

Like they were being watched by eyes that shouldn't have been there at all.

Lucien scanned the windows, tracking every alley mouth, every rooftop, every figure moving too slow or standing too still.

"Pick up speed."

"I'm trying," Logan muttered, weaving past a food delivery van and gunning the engine.

The street ahead went quiet.

Too quiet.

A man on the corner stopped walking.

Another lifted his phone.

And every instinct in Lucien's body went cold.

The sound was small and clean, out of place. A ping of metal against metal.

A second later, the top of the SUV sparked.

Bullets.

Before the shock could register, a second shot ripped through the side window, glass exploding into Logan's lap.

"Shit!" Logan veered hard. Tires shrieked as they skidded sideways, nearly clipping a fire hydrant.

Lena screamed and ducked as safety glass sprayed backward, peppering her legs.

Lucien didn't flinch.

"CUT LEFT!" he barked.

"Crosstown. Get to the west side."

Logan swung the wheel. The SUV barreled through a yellow light as horns exploded from every direction.

Lucien's voice stayed cold.

"Use the West Side Highway. Take it straight to the G.W. We're getting the fuck out of the kill zone."

Another shot cracked from ahead, front-left.

The windshield spidered, then collapsed in a violent spray of glass, fragments scattering across the dash like diamonds under pressure.

Lena ducked as Logan swerved, tires screaming.

Gunfire ripped through a parked car, sparks shearing off its frame as they flew past.

Pedestrians screamed, scattering in every direction. A couple hit the ground. Others ran blind into traffic.

Even at this hour, the streets were packed, people moving in panic, human obstacles everywhere.

She twisted to look back as they passed the shooters.

A silhouette ducked into a stairwell.

Another slipped between two cars.

They weren't amateurs.

They were already waiting.

The bounty hadn't just spread. It had rooted fast, ugly, and deep.

Logan's eyes locked on the mirrors. "Windshield's gone. We take another hit, we're wide open."

Lucien leaned back, calm, like he'd already calculated the ending.

"We won't."

He glanced at Lena, then forward again.

"Not tonight."

They tore down the dark arteries of Manhattan, cold air ripping through the shattered windshield.

Lucien leaned forward slightly, eyes on the rearview mirror.

No headlights.

No obvious tail.

But something didn't sit right.

Too coordinated.

Too clean.

Lena looked from the road to him. "How did they find us that fast?"

"They knew the route," he murmured, almost to himself.

The skyline faded behind them in the mirror.

And hell came with it.

The SUV roared up the on-ramp, the George Washington Bridge looming ahead, a steel skeleton slicing through the black sky.

Lucien sat forward, his focus cutting through the road ahead, the city lights bleeding away behind them.

He pulled his phone from his jacket and glanced at the screen.

No missed calls. No new messages.

He tapped Victor's number.

The line rang. Once. Twice.

Dead silence.

Lucien ended the call and tried again. Still nothing.

Beside him, Lena shifted, small enough to miss, but Lucien caught it. Logan glanced in the rearview, catching the shift in Lucien's face.

No one spoke. The bridge rose around them, steel beams flashing past like the ticking of a slow, merciless clock.

Lucien tried again.

Ring.

Ring.

Voicemail.

He let the screen go dark and stared into the night.

Victor's silence felt wrong, cold and coiling in Lucien's gut, deeper than instinct, heavier than fear.

This wasn't panic. Panic was for men who still believed chaos had rules.

They were almost across when the phone buzzed in his hand, the Jersey cliffside rising jagged against the dark.

Incoming FaceTime call.

Victor's number.

Lucien's jaw tightened.

Without hesitation, he answered.

The screen opened.

Not Victor's face.

Three masked men.

Black tactical gear. Balaclavas pulled tight over their faces. Eyes glinting beneath the harsh light of a rotting room.

In the background, Victor sat zip-tied to a steel chair. Blood trickled from a cut above his brow.

Breathing.

Alive.

But hurt.

One of the masked men stepped closer to the camera and tilted his head, studying Lucien through the screen. A combat knife rested against the back of Victor's hand.

The blade tapped slowly.

Tap.

Tap.

Tap.

Then the voice came, muffled but clear enough.

"Tick tock."

Tap.

"Every minute you wait, he loses another piece."

Tap.

"Bring yourself, King."

A pause.

"The clock's not the only thing bleeding."

The call cut to black.

Lucien's thumb hovered over the screen for a moment.

Then the phone buzzed again.

A new text.

No words. Just a pinned address from Victor's number.

A breadcrumb soaked in blood.

The Upper Bronx.

Not abandoned. Forgotten.

A place where the city had given up and the dark had moved in.

Logan glanced at him in the rearview mirror. "Boss?"

Lucien's voice cut in. "Step on it."

Logan's foot dropped.

The SUV surged forward into the night.

In the backseat, Lena's fists pressed against her legs. Her gaze fixed on the black ribbon of road ahead as she forced the panic back down her throat.

This wasn't a fight anymore.

It was a bloodletting waiting to happen.

Lucien Cole had just been given a choice.

Run.

Or bleed for family.

For him, that had never been a choice. Only a direction.

Chapter Thirty-Nine

BEHOLD A BLACK HORSE

The SUV pulled off the main highway, tires crunching onto the narrow private road that wound up the Palisades, climbing into darkness.

The estate waited where it always had, set back from the world, fortified behind a half-mile of thick trees.

Below the cliffs, the Hudson stretched black and endless, cutting through the shadows like something old and watching.

It had seen empires rise, fall, and drown without ever changing its course.

Tonight, it felt closer, heavier, like the dark itself had shifted to meet him.

Lucien stared out the window as Logan glanced at the dashboard, where the estate's address still glowed on the screen, a digital trail leading straight to them.

The estate felt less like home and more like a command post.

Homes were for men who believed tomorrow was guaranteed. This place was built for men who planned for war.

The gates appeared ahead, towering black steel lined with floodlights and reinforced fencing.

Logan tapped in the code Lucien gave him. The gates hissed open, slow and mechanical.

They rolled down the long driveway, passing the cold lawn and rows of security lights.

The main house stood dead ahead, a fortress built to keep ghosts in, not out.

To the left sat the converted carriage house, Lucien's glass-walled garage now sealed behind reinforced blast doors.

Logan killed the engine outside.

Lucien stepped out first, the night air cold against his skin.

He motioned to Lena. "Inside. Both of you."

Lucien pulled a black security fob from his jacket and pressed once.

The doors shuddered, then slowly rolled up.

Fluorescent lights snapped to life.

They moved together on instinct, stepping over the line like crossing into a different world, where hesitation got buried and decisions stayed dead.

No words. No second thoughts. Just the low hum of electricity and the cold taste of preparation waiting inside.

Parked dead center between the rest of his cars sat something new, a matte-black monster carved from armored steel and built for impact.

Logan froze mid-step. "Holy shit."

Lucien stepped up beside him, eyes on the beast.

"Ordered it a while back. For Michael to run point. Paid extra to expedite. Still took forever." A quiet moment passed. "Guess it showed up right on time."

Everything did when the clock ran out.

He turned to Logan.

"Meet your new office."

Lena stood just behind them, arms folded tight across her chest, silent, wary, watching the thing like it had teeth under the hood.

Lucien didn't slow or smile. He just walked toward it like the decision had already been made.

It wasn't a truck.

It was a statement.

And statements like this weren't meant to be read. They were meant to land.

Rezvani Vengeance.

Eight hundred ten horses beneath a 6.2-liter supercharged V8. Level 7 ballistic armor. Thermal night vision. Run-flat tires. Underside explosive protection. Strobe and blinding light arrays. Steel ram bumpers built to fold lesser machines in half.

Even the mirrors carried concealed pepper spray.

Lucien stepped up beside it and laid a hand on the armored hood, like he was checking a weapon, like it already belonged to the war.

"She's got EMP shielding, reinforced suspension, magnetic deadbolts, and a 24/7 cloud recording system. We get hit, we'll know who, how, and where they breathe."

Logan walked a slow circle around it, then another, silent and reverent.

Behind them, Lena shook her head once, almost under her breath.

"It's a goddamn war machine."

Lucien's voice cut through the air without turning. "That's the idea."

Peace had already been taken off the table.

He tossed the keys over his shoulder.

Logan caught them on instinct, still staring like the thing had chosen him for something bigger than a drive.

Lucien circled to the passenger side and climbed in.

Logan slid into the driver's seat, running his fingers over the wheel like he was gripping something bigger than himself.

Lucien gestured toward the tactical switchboard above them.

"Here, smoke screen.

Here, anti-pursuit spikes. Anyone dumb enough to follow gets crippled. Their tires won't survive it."

Logan turned in his seat, glancing into the rear.

"Jesus..."

Lucien nodded once. "Rear cabin. Ballistic glass. Reinforced partition. Space for extra gear and a locked console for another sidearm."

Logan sat back slowly, his face caught somewhere between adrenaline and reverence.

Tears welled behind the bravado, but he blinked them away hard.

"This for me, boss?"

Lucien turned his head. Eyes sharp. Cold. Calculated.

"No."

A pause.

"It's for me. You're just driving."

Logan smirked, then tapped the ignition once.

The Vengeance roared awake, a deep, guttural snarl that rattled the steel walls around them.

It didn't sound like a machine. It sounded like permission.

Outside, the night pressed in, hungry and listening.

Inside, the war finally had something built for the kind of man who wasn't planning to survive.

The engine settled into a low growl beneath them, like a caged animal waiting for the gate.

Lucien sat motionless in the passenger seat, the cold blue wash of the dash turning his features into carved stone.

The phone rested in his palm, silent and waiting.

He scrolled through the encrypted contact list, rows of names.

Men he'd built with, fought beside, bled for.

But now?

Every name felt like a gun pointed at his back.

Trust wasn't currency anymore. It was a liability.

Logan settled into the driver's seat, watching him.

"You calling in the troops?" he asked.

Lucien's thumb hovered over the screen.

He didn't look up.

"I don't need them."

Lucien exhaled, pushing the ghosts down.

"Armies are built for numbers. For intimidation. For power."

He finally turned his head toward Logan, eyes cold and unreadable.

"But numbers turn when the wind changes. Loyalty bought with fear dies with fear."

He scrolled, quiet and methodical, then began deleting. Name after name. No hesitation.

"I don't need soldiers who flinch when the price gets high. I need wolves. Men who'd burn the city before they'd sell my name."

From the backseat, Lena said nothing. Her eyes stayed on Lucien, absorbing the brutal clarity in every word.

Lucien scrolled slower now, stopped on a single name, and pressed call.

The line rang once.

Twice.

A gravel-thick voice answered:

"Boss."

Lucien muttered, "Get ready to kill."

The line went dead. A silent confirmation.

Lucien hit another name. And another.

Each call was short, brutal, final.

Three men. That was it.

Enough to start a war. Not enough to lose control of one.

Three names he trusted, not because of what they ever said, but because of what they'd already bled to prove.

He fired off the location to each one, the pinned address from the masked call.

No instructions. No explanations.

Men like that didn't need either.

Just coordinates. A silent promise that blood would follow.

When it was done, Lucien slid the phone back inside his jacket, close and alive.

He turned back to Logan and Lena.

"No mass calls. No rallying cries. No banners. We move silent."

Logan nodded once, a grim spark catching behind his eyes.

Lena squared her shoulders, bracing for the blood that was coming.

Lucien stared out across the yawning dark beyond the garage doors.

The city was out there, alive, rotting, waiting.

And now Lucien was riding out, not with an army to shield him, but with wolves sharpened by blood, not promises.

Chapter Forty

AND HELL FOLLOWED
WITH HIM

The Rezvani tore through the New Jersey backroads, tires biting into the cold asphalt.

Logan drove with no hesitation, no doubt, just raw focus.

Lucien sat silent in the passenger seat, body still, mind stripped to the bone.

Lena sat in the back, eyes flicking between them, a quiet storm building in her chest. But she trusted him. She trusted what this meant. Whatever waited ahead, they would face it together.

The GPS on the dash blinked like a warning.

Lucien slid his thumb across the encrypted screen.

No need for words.

The location, sent from Victor's number, burned in his mind.

Not a name. Not a plea. Just numbers, just bait.

The kind of bait meant for men who would crawl through hell if family was tied at the other end.

And Lucien took it.

Ghost had sent the details minutes earlier, cold and stripped to the bone.

You're heading into a cage

Old metal structure. Minimal cover

Abandoned in '98

Drone thermals show at least twelve warm bodies

Two snipers posted overwatch

Heat cluster west wing, third floor

Intercepted comms say Victor's still breathing, condition unknown

Lucien didn't blink.

Perfect. A clean trap was still a cage. It just meant the killing would be organized.

No distractions. No mistakes. Just the kill box.

They hit the G.W. Bridge again. This time like pack animals under a full moon, chasing the scent of war.

No one in the truck said it, but they all felt it, the night had already chosen what it wanted from them.

Manhattan rose to the south, glittering, buzzing, oblivious.

But they didn't stop.

They veered north, the city bleeding away into colder sprawl, forgotten neighborhoods, crumbling brick, and broken-windowed ghosts.

The streets narrowed, the houses faded out, and the air went colder.

Then there it was.

An old asylum waited ahead, its sign half torn, the name ST. GER-MAINE'S barely visible beneath rust.

It stood like a carcass under the night sky, three stories of peeling white paint, boarded windows, and rusted fire escapes.

Chain-link fencing hung half-collapsed around the grounds.

A shattered ambulance sat to the side near the back entrance, stripped down to its bones.

The world felt wrong here, like too much pain had soaked into the concrete and never dried. The place had swallowed screams and never given them back.

Logan had killed the lights two blocks out.

Lucien's voice came calm as death.

"Two-minute walk. Back entrance."

Logan cracked his knuckles once on the steering wheel, then killed the engine.

The sudden silence was suffocating.

Lucien reached back without looking and pressed a compact pistol into Lena's hand.

"Safety's on," he said.

Lena adjusted her grip on the sidearm, tension rolling off her in waves.

Lucien reached back, squeezed her knee once, firm and anchoring, then grabbed the tactical bag.

Suppressors.

Extra mags.

Blades.

Hard gloves.

Night-vision lenses.

War prep.

Just another night in hell.

The only difference was whose name the violence answered.

"Stay sharp," Lucien said quietly, checking his gear. "They're not trying to trade Victor."

He glanced toward the asylum.

"They're trying to bait me."

Logan pulled a suppressed Glock from under his jacket and checked the chamber.

"They won't get the chance."

Lucien let a faint smirk cross his face.

Good.

Let them believe it.

He wasn't coming to negotiate.

He was coming to burn the fucking earth.

Some men arrived with terms. Lucien arrived with consequences.

They stepped out into the dark.

Boots crunched dead leaves.

Their breath misted in the cold night air.

The asylum stood ahead of them, broken, empty, and waiting to be filled with screams again.

Buildings remembered certain kinds of suffering. This one had never forgotten.

Only this time, they wouldn't belong to patients.

Lucien gave a low hand signal.

Logan moved first, smooth, silent, clearing the side alley that snaked toward the shattered ambulance bay.

Lena followed, her pulse hammering low in her ears.

The air smelled like rot and old rain.

They moved fast, a ghost unit, hugging the crumbling walls, slipping through a breach in the fence.

Up ahead, the main doors stood open like a mouth of black.

Lucien paused at the threshold and listened.

Only the hollow groan of wind through broken glass.

He gave a hand signal.

Logan peeled right, sweeping the perimeter.

Lena moved with him.

Lucien stayed a step behind her, guiding her forward with small hand signals.

They moved again, silent and tight, as Lucien pushed them across the entry floor.

Every step felt like a countdown.

Like the whole building was measuring the distance between breath and blood.

They reached a dark junction, a cracked corridor breaking off to the right, the main hall stretching left into deeper shadows.

Lucien stopped.

Body coiled.

His eyes locked left, toward Ghost's recon point: west wing, third floor.

He raised a hand.

Silent command.

Stack left.

Lena stepped in behind him, gun high.

Logan moved to the rear, smooth, composed, eyes sweeping everything.

Just as Lucien began moving, Lena glanced back to check the flank, and caught it.

Logan.

A flick of his hand.

Right. East.

Not where Ghost said Victor was.

Not where Lucien was going.

Just a twitch.

One finger.

Gone.

Almost nothing.

But it lodged in her brain.

Why?

Ghost's thermals were clear: west wing, third floor, heat barely holding.

Lucien didn't slow or turn.

He pressed forward, carving into the dark.

Lena followed.

Logan brought up the rear, quiet, unreadable.

The knot in her gut didn't fade.

But she buried it.

Because Lucien was leading them.

And whatever waited ahead, he wasn't walking into it alone.

They moved deeper into the dead bones of the building.

Moonlight slipped through broken windows, scattering jagged shadows across the floor.

Debris crunched underfoot.

Each creak of old metal sounded too loud.

Lucien led them down a narrow hall, pistol tight to his chest.

They reached the stairwell.

A steel door hung crooked on its hinges.

Lucien paused, listened, swept the darkness.

Then he moved.

Up the stairs.

Second floor.

Third.

A faint buzz tickled the edge of Lena's hearing.

Radios.

They were close.

Lucien lifted a hand.

Stack. Lucien took point. Lena stayed second. Logan covered the rear.

They reached the third-floor landing and peeled left into the west wing, where Ghost had flagged a thermal profile consistent with Victor.

Each step tightened the air.

Ahead, past a set of cracked double doors, something waited.

Victor.

Alive.

Close enough.

Lucien tightened his grip on the pistol.

One door. One room. One move.

He turned slightly. Lena at his flank. Logan just behind.

His eyes cut through the dark.

"Hard and clean. If he's breathing, we get him out. If he's not..."

He left it there.

Then he shifted forward, low, fast, controlled.

Shoulder to the door. One glance to Lena. Three fingers.

"Three. Two. One."

He breached.

The doors exploded inward, hinges shrieking as the darkness inside erupted.

Victor sat slumped in a steel chair, hands zip-tied behind him, blood dried across his jaw like war paint.

His left eye was swollen shut. The skin on his face blistered in patches, like someone had tested heat across him inch by inch. His hands were wrapped in gauze, but blood still soaked through the nail beds, ten tiny acts of war.

Still breathing.

Barely.

No guards. No movement.

Just Victor.

And the heavy silence of a setup.

Lucien's pistol swept the room, clearing the corners, eyes cutting across everything.

Lena dropped low beside Victor, already cutting the ties.

"He's alive," she said, voice tight. "Pulse is weak, but he's here."

Lucien exhaled once, relief buried fast under instinct.

Then, crack.

A sharp sound above them. Metal on metal.

Something shifted in the ceiling.

Lucien's head snapped up.

Logan shouted, "Above!"

Too late.

Smoke poured through the vents, thick and oily.

Gunfire tore down the hallway behind them, automatic and controlled.

They were surrounded.

Lucien yanked Victor upright, slinging his weight across his shoulder.

"MOVE!" he barked.

Lena covered the hall, firing through the fog. Her hands trembled. Her aim didn't.

Logan returned fire with calm precision.

They backed into the stairwell, third-floor smoke swallowing everything.

The hallway lights snapped on, not the dim rot of an abandoned building, but fresh power, red pulses washing the walls.

This place had been prepped, powered, waiting.

This wasn't a reaction force.

This was the trap.

Not the sloppy kind built on rage. The expensive kind. The patient kind.

Lucien kicked open the second-floor landing door, gunfire chasing his heels as he dragged Victor across the threshold.

"Back entrance!" he snapped. "Now!"

But the exits were already locked down.

More fire down the halls.

Voices shouted in foreign tongues.

Not street crews. Mercs. Royce hadn't sent hitters. He'd hired soldiers.

Which meant this had gone beyond revenge. This was procurement. Strategy. Budgeted violence.

The cadence of their commands was clean. Disciplined. Eastern European, maybe.

Lucien knew the type.

"They're professionals," he snapped, dragging Victor deeper into cover. "Ex-military or private contract."

They ducked into a half-collapsed nurses' station, drywall ripped open like a wound.

Lucien set Victor against the wall and slammed a fresh mag into the pistol.

Blood stained his collar.

His hands didn't shake.

Not once.

He looked to Logan. "My guys are en route. The wolves are coming."

Wolves were different from armies. They didn't need permission to turn a place into meat and ruin.

Logan hesitated.

Just a breath.

But it was there.

A flicker.

Lena caught it and said nothing.

Then shouting from above.

"Targets acquired. Rooftop secured. South exit clear on your mark."

Lucien didn't smile.

He stood with his gun raised.

"They thought they were building a trap. We're about to turn it into a fucking graveyard."

Smoke choked the hallway.

Victor slumped half-conscious beside him.

Behind them, Lena braced the stairwell with one hand, gun raised, the other gripping Victor's collar to drag him when the moment came.

Logan stayed near the landing, calm.

Wrong calm.

A voice echoed down the corridor.

"West flank sealed. Roof overwatch in position. Three tangos neutralized near generator bay. You're green."

Shapes began moving through the fog.

Not enemies.

Lucien's men.

Black-clad and silent, they appeared out of the smoke like ghosts.

Not saviors. Not heroes. Just Lucien's answer to the dark.

One dropped from a ceiling beam.

Another slipped past a broken window, blade flashing once across a throat.

Suppressors hissed in the dark.

Down the opposite hall, the enemy opened fire.

Lucien's overwatch snipers dropped three shooters before they could even reset.

Bodies slammed against the cracked linoleum.

In the chaos, Logan's voice cut through. "I thought we only had three men covering us."

Lucien didn't look at him. He just stepped forward, weapon raised.

"I never show my real hand until it's too late to stop it."

That was how men like him stayed alive.

Two shots. Clean. Lethal.

A voice shouted from the stairwell. "South stairwell clear!"

Another followed. "Moving to breach eastern ward!"

Lucien turned to Logan. "We move now. Take him."

Logan grabbed Victor under one arm.

Lena took the other.

Lucien covered the rear.

They moved clean, not fast, through smoke and blood. Down two halls. Left. Right.

Two of Lucien's men slid in behind them, rifles up.

A flashbang detonated somewhere above. White light ripped through the stairwell.

A scream.

Then silence.

They burst through the side exit.

Outside, cold air ripped into their lungs.

Smoke from the vents curled into the dead sky.

A black tactical van idled just beyond the ambulance bay, side doors open.

The Rezvani crouched in the side alley past it, low under a dead floodlight, engine cold, blacked out and waiting.

Lucien waved them forward.

Logan loaded Victor into the van with two of Lucien's men.

Lena stayed with Lucien.

Lucien stepped to the front passenger window and handed the driver a small slip of paper, crisp and folded tight.

"This is where you're going. No stops. No chatter. No fucking deviations."

Then he circled to the rear, yanked the door halfway closed, and grabbed Logan by the shoulder.

His voice dropped low, lethal.

"You stay with him. Don't let him out of your sight. If anything feels off, anything, you act before you think."

Logan nodded, quick, clean, no questions.

But Lucien's eyes lingered a moment longer, reading him, weighing him.

Then he slammed the door shut.

The van peeled off first, tires spitting gravel, headlights slicing through the black.

Lucien turned to Lena and motioned sharply toward the truck. "Come on."

They ran, boots hammering cracked asphalt, and climbed in.

Lucien hit the ignition, and the engine snarled awake like it had been waiting to kill.

Tires ripped through the debris-streaked alley as he cut hard onto the main road, heading south, leaving St. Germaine's burning behind them like a page torn from a blood ledger.

Lena sat beside him, eyes on the rearview, watching the last of the smoke fade into the dark.

Lucien thumbed open his encrypted screen, pulling up the location: a blacklisted trauma clinic buried off-record, clean, clinical, built for ghosts.

The kind that paid in cash and left before sunrise.

No names. No questions.

Just blood, sutures, and silence.

The burner buzzed inside his jacket.

GHOST.

Lucien answered without slowing the truck.

One hand stayed on the wheel, the other clenched tight.

"Talk."

Ghost didn't soften the entry.

"Something's wrong."

Lucien's jaw tightened.

"You were marked back at the marina when you got in with Logan. Somebody pinged the truck. Low-level darknet trace. Didn't go public. Didn't hit the bounty boards."

"But the tag stuck."

The Rezvani howled as Lucien blasted through a yellow light and cut across two lanes.

"You cleaning it?"

"Trying," Ghost said. "But it's bad."

A short beat.

"Second ping just came through. Outside the asylum perimeter."

Lucien's eyes flicked to the mirrors.

"Explain."

"Shortwave bounce. Private relay. Not forums. Not bounty hunters."

"Private. Exact."

Lucien didn't hesitate. "How close?"

Ghost answered instantly.

"Close enough to smell you."

The words sat between them.

"If you're not being followed yet," Ghost added, "you will be."

Lucien's grip tightened on the wheel.

"Find the leak."

Silence stretched across the line. Then Ghost said, "Already on it."

His voice dropped cold enough to make the truth sound inevitable.

"But kid... if you trust who you're riding with..."

A pause.

"Trust carefully."

Click.

The line went dead.

Lucien stared straight ahead. The glow of Manhattan rose in the distance like a warning.

He didn't say a word.

Just drove.

Beside him, Lena slowly turned her head, watching him like she was trying to see past the silence into the war behind his eyes.

"Talk to me," she said. "What's going on?"

Lucien didn't answer right away.

Manhattan loomed ahead, glass, steel, and concrete stacked into the clouds.

The truck hugged the East River, carving down the FDR like a shadow stitched to black water.

When he finally spoke, his voice was low and flat.

"Ghost just called."

Lena straightened.

"We got pinged," Lucien said. "First at the docks. Then again near the asylum."

He switched lanes.

"Not public. Not bounty chatter. Encrypted channels. Private relays."

Road noise filled the silence.

"Someone's tracing proximity, not location. Means it's not dumb heat.

It's measured. Intentional."

Lena processed it the best she could.

"They're following us?"

"Not yet. But they're hunting smart. Ghost said if we're not being followed already, we will be."

Lucien cut hard onto the Brooklyn Bridge ramp, headlights chasing steel as the skyline shifted behind them.

Silence settled heavy in the cab.

"Who do you think it is?" Her voice was hesitant.

Lucien's hands tightened slightly on the wheel. Not enough to betray doubt. Just enough to show he was thinking.

"We'll know soon. And when we do, it ends."

Not with a warning. With a body.

Chapter Forty-One

THE ENEMY ALREADY INSIDE

The clinic didn't look like salvation.

It looked like a bunker where surgery replaced mercy.

The kind of place built for men too dangerous to die in public.

Tucked beneath the underbelly of a condemned parking structure in Red Hook, Brooklyn, the entrance was nothing but a rusted freight elevator masked behind a locked panel and a biometric pad that didn't ask for names. Just thumbprints from ghosts no one officially remembered.

The city buried places like this the same way it buried bodies, off-record and useful.

The truck coasted into the underground lane, tires hissing over cracked concrete.

Lucien said nothing.

Lena didn't press.

The freight gate lifted with a hydraulic groan, revealing a short tunnel lined with floodlights and silence. No guards. No welcome. Just antiseptic and cold metal.

Safety didn't live here. Only function did.

They pulled to a stop near the service entrance.

Logan had arrived in the black van minutes earlier.

Victor was already inside. Unconscious. Still bleeding.

Still breathing.

Lucien stepped out first.

He said nothing, just scanned the corridor.

His eyes didn't move fast. They settled into everything.

A medic in surgical blacks met them at the door.

No words. Just a nod.

Lucien returned it.

Inside, the place unfolded like a vault, gleaming white walls, glass partitions, and custom medical rigs humming with AI triage.

Not a hospital. Not a battlefield. Something in between.

The sort of room where pain got managed, not forgiven.

Victor was already on the table, shirt buttons open, EKG pads stuck to his chest, oxygen tubing hooked under his nose.

Two specialists worked in silence.

One tracked vitals on a flickering monitor.

The other flushed IV lines and checked for internal bleeding.

Logan stood near the back of the room, arms crossed, face unreadable, all discipline.

He hadn't left Victor's side since the van ride.

He didn't speak or move, just waited like a man fulfilling orders without question.

Lucien clocked his position without even turning his head.

Lena stayed near the door, weight forward, eyes moving across the room. She didn't trust it. Not this place. Not the quiet.

Lucien stood near the foot of the table.

Still. Watching.

Victor's hand twitched.

Just once, and Lucien caught it.

Then Victor's eyes opened, bloodshot, dazed, but awake.

Lucien leaned in, voice low. "You're good. You're out. You're safe."

His breath rattled, lips cracked and trembling, as he caught Lucien's sleeve and drew him closer.

A whisper.

"You didn't leave me."

Another breath.

"They said you weren't coming."

Lucien didn't flinch. Didn't blink. Didn't say a word.

But something shifted in him, a silence heavier than rage.

Something cold and brutal settled behind his eyes, like he was measuring the distance between pain and punishment and deciding how much of the city he was willing to drag through both.

His phone buzzed. One line from Ghost.

They got your location

He rose fast, turned to the medic.

"We're done. Patch him to move."

The medic blinked. "He's stable, but,"

"Sixty seconds," Lucien said, his tone closing the room.

He wasn't asking for medicine anymore. He was asking for movement.

The medic didn't argue. He grabbed a black injector from the tray.

The needle punched into Victor's thigh.

Victor's back arched as the drugs hit his bloodstream.

His pupils blew wide.

"Epinephrine. Ketamine. Clotting agent," the medic said, already stepping away.

"He'll be able to move. Pain won't stop him."

The medic stripped off his gloves and dropped them into the tray.

"But he's still broken."

Lena was already moving, helping to peel off the EKG pads, tightening the wrappings, sliding an arm behind Victor to help him upright.

He winced, but didn't resist.

He was weak, but he could move.

Lucien turned to Logan. "Truck. Now."

Buried in the lower level of the garage, the truck waited, dark and still, coiled like muscle under skin.

Lucien opened the rear door. Lena helped Victor into the backseat, careful but quick.

Logan slid behind the wheel without a word, calm as ever. Lucien shut the door, circled around, and climbed into the passenger seat.

He said nothing, just stared forward as the truck rumbled to life.

The truck rolled back into the shadows of the city.

Inside, the silence was thick, the kind that knew violence was still coming, like a fifth passenger in the cab.

Victor's head rested against the window, eyes half-open, breathing slow and heavy.

Lena's eyes stayed on him.

Lucien stayed still, gaze locked forward, unreadable.

Then the burner went off in his jacket.

Lucien answered.

Ghost came through sharp. "I got something."

Lucien said nothing.

"The pings weren't tracking your movement. They were mirroring it." A pause, then the faint sound of fingers typing. "It's not just bounty chatter. These hits came through private encrypted channels. Shortwave. Targeted."

His voice dipped lower.

"The first signal didn't come from outside. It came from inside your vehicle."

A long, quiet breath.

"So whoever it is, they've been close."

Lucien hung up and scanned the cabin.

Victor's chest rose and fell, weak and steady.

Logan's eyes flicked toward him a second too long.

Lena leaned forward, sensing the shift in him.

But Lucien didn't turn. Didn't speak. Didn't give anything away.

The Rezvani cut through the black.

But inside, Lucien was already building the next move in his head.

The war hadn't followed them.

It had been riding with them the whole time.

That was the thing about betrayal. It never chased from behind if it could sit beside you instead.

The road unfurled ahead, slick and dark under the incoming storm.

Lucien shifted slightly in his seat, just enough to unlock the burner buzzing in his lap without drawing attention.

The screen flared low. One unread message.

Third ping just went live. Same relay pattern

Lucien's pulse didn't change.

He tapped out a response beneath the angle of his jacket.

Can you isolate origin?

The reply came fast.

Not yet. But it's not coming from the vehicle itself. It's coming from the person carrying it

Not a reaction force

Proximity-enabled intent

BLE signal. Ultra-short-range. Ten, maybe twenty meters max

Precise shit. Could be in a watch. Gear. Clothing. Even skin

Somebody near you lights up the grid every time you move

Lucien stared at the screen for a long moment.

His thumb moved again.

Leak a false ping. Loud. Somewhere that'll draw attention

A moment later, Ghost replied.

West Side. Meatpacking. Near the old rail yard

I'll stage it as a bounty flare-up. Just went live

You'll know who it is within twenty minutes

Lucien locked the screen and slid the phone back into his coat.

He didn't move. Didn't speak.

Stillness was where Lucien did some of his worst thinking.

He leaned forward and tapped the nav on the dashboard.

The route recalculated instantly, pulling them away from the outbound highway. The vehicle glided through the industrial stretch of Red Hook, past rusted fences and shuttered loading docks, before dropping into the Battery Tunnel, two miles of concrete silence carved beneath the East River.

When they emerged into Lower Manhattan, steel pressed in around them.

The West Side rose ahead.

Logan eased the truck forward.

"There," Lucien said, pointing.

A cracked lot opened beside an old loading dock. A rusted rail crane leaned sideways over the site like it was waiting to fall.

Logan pulled in slow, eyes sweeping the area. "You want me to circle or post?"

"Post," Lucien said. "Engine off. Lights out."

The truck idled for a beat, then fell quiet. Buried in the dark.

No one spoke.

Lucien tapped the center console. The screen flipped into tactical mode, a military-grade thermal overlay blooming across the dash like infrared fire.

Every corner of the lot lit up in gradients of heat. No more blind spots. The truck saw everything, or close enough to make hiding expensive.

He stepped out, boots crunching gravel, and moved toward the front of the truck. From a crouch behind a concrete divider, he narrowed his eyes and locked on the far side of the lot, instinct sharpening his vision.

Across the windshield behind him, the thermal overlay flickered, heat signatures glowing like ghosts on glass. But Lucien didn't need the screen. He was already dialed in.

Nothing at first. Just rust, water, and silence.

Then, movement.

A figure. Distant. Half-shadowed near the upper scaffolding of a warehouse roof.

No markings. No flashlight. No fumble.

Too smooth for a scavenger. Too quiet for a cop.

Lucien's eyes narrowed.

He stepped back inside, eyes locked ahead, and let the thermal overlay confirm it, one heat signature, holding steady.

Not a trick of light.

Not imagination.

He clicked the burner once and texted Ghost.

How long since the flare went live?

Ghost's reply came back almost instantly.

Twelve minutes. Got two signals. One spoofed from Astoria. The other's real, thirty meters from you

Lucien lowered his gaze toward the roofline.

Thirty meters.

He'd drawn something out.

Lucien stepped back inside and settled into the seat, staring through the windshield at the broken lot, the leaning crane, the rusted bones of a trap that hadn't closed yet.

They weren't biting. They were watching. Waiting.

His thumb moved.

Watcher confirmed

They're still on us

If they want a war, we pick the ground

He opened Ghost's encrypted thread and dropped a set of coordinates. Nothing else.

Seconds later, Ghost replied:

Copy

City's already moving

The bounty buys a long line of killers

Lucien locked the screen. "Get us out of here."

Logan shifted in his seat. "Where?"

Lucien didn't look at him. "Location's on the dash."

He settled back in his seat, eyes fixed ahead. "Let's see who shows up to kill me first."

Whether they came wearing an enemy's face or a friend's.

Chapter Forty-Two

TONIGHT WE FIGHT IN HEAVEN

The street was dead when they pulled up.

Just past two in the morning, Fifth Avenue should've still been alive. Instead it felt gutted, like the city had already backed away from whatever was about to happen here.

No headlights. No voices.

Just scaffolding stacked like bones around a dark tower of glass and failed ambition, four stories tall, half-wrapped in plastic sheeting and construction netting that whipped in the wind like a shroud.

The name still clung to the front in tarnished gold.

HEAVEN ON 5TH

Half-faded. Half-forgotten.

Beneath it:

OPENING SOON

But it never did.

They rolled to a stop along the curb.

Headlights died.

Lena glanced up from the backseat.

Lucien sat forward, head bowed, writing in a black notebook braced on one knee. He didn't speak. Just wrote, like the words weighed more than the war waiting outside.

Logan killed the engine.

Lucien was already stepping out.

Boots hit pavement.

Above them, storm clouds rolled low and heavy, the moon fighting to stay visible behind them.

The wind picked up, hard and restless.

Lucien looked up at the building.

Not the walls.

The ghosts they held.

Lena stepped out behind him. Logan followed, eyes sweeping the street with quiet precision.

Behind them, blacked-out SUVs rolled in and stopped. Doors opened. Men stepped out.

Lucien's wolves.

Armored. Silent. Ready.

Lucien didn't acknowledge them.

He walked straight to the entrance.

The access panel beside the doors was still dusted with construction grit, the screen smeared by weather and time.

He keyed in a six-digit code from memory.

Click.

Steel shifted somewhere inside the frame.

The doors unlocked with a slow mechanical shudder.

Not welcoming them. Waking up like a vault opening for the first time.

Not to protect what was inside. To witness it.

Victor followed behind them, slower but upright.

Bandages peeked beneath the collar of his coat, darkening slowly where the stitching pulled. One eye still swollen. The pain hadn't left him.

But the fight was still in him.

He lit a cigarette, fingers stiff beneath the gauze, and took a drag like pain had never taught him anything else. Then he followed them in, scanning the building like a man already expecting violence.

Silence met them at the threshold.

Raw concrete. Exposed rebar. Black marble floors still covered in construction sheeting. Tools abandoned. Wiring half-run.

Staircases climbed into darkness.

Even unfinished, the place had weight.

Some buildings knew what they were before the first night ever crowned them.

It already knew what it would become.

A monument.

Lena stepped in behind him, eyes sweeping the vast, hollow space.

Her voice was a whisper.

"What is this place?"

Lucien stood still in the center of it all.

Didn't turn.

"This was supposed to be the crown. Three floors. Mezzanine. Rooftop glass. Deals made here. Empires born here. Heaven on earth."

He turned to face her now.

"But tonight, we turn it into hell."

Not by accident. By design.

The words settled into the room. No one answered.

Lucien stood in the center of the unfinished floor, shoulders square, eyes moving over what remained.

The outline of the bar, still unplumbed.

Taped diagrams curling off the concrete.

Cracked renderings scattered across a folding table.

The DJ booth that never rose.

The elevated tables that were supposed to hang above the dance floor like a balcony for the untouchable.

And everywhere, the version of it that never came to life.

Glass. Light. Power.

Laughter spilling across a city he already ruled, whether the world liked it or not.

But it never happened.

The storm came fast.

The blood came first.

And the dream?

Left frozen in place, somewhere between vision and aftermath.

Lucien exhaled slowly.

He turned.

His eyes landed on Lena.

She wasn't speaking.

She wasn't posturing.

She was just there.

Shoulders squared. Jaw tight. Fire still in her eyes, but something deeper beneath it. Exhaustion. Grief. Loyalty stronger than most men deserved.

She'd given everything for this.

She'd bled for it. Killed for it.

She'd held him together through the worst of it.

He hadn't just dragged her into this world.

He'd rewritten her in its language.

He didn't know what she saw when she looked at him now.

But he knew what he saw when he looked at her:

The last good thing that hadn't rotted.

Which was why the world kept trying to drag her into the same grave it built for him.

Lucien turned back to the room.

To the dream, half-born and half-buried.

His voice came low. Controlled. "I need air."

Nobody stopped him.

He climbed the stairs slow, footsteps echoing through steel and shadow, until the rooftop doors appeared ahead.

The wind was louder here.

And behind it, the city waiting.

The skyline bled light against the night. Beautiful the way a wound is from far enough away. A thousand broken promises flickering in neon.

Lucien stepped onto the rooftop. The wind cut hard against his skin. Cold. Angry.

Out in the distance Manhattan moved like a restless animal. Cars honking. Sirens wailing. Shadows moving through alleyways.

The city had smelled blood.

His blood.

And a city full of starving men always moved faster when the king was suddenly worth money.

He could feel them circling, waiting to tear the king from his throne.

The rain started. Thin. Cold. Washing the city, but not him.

There wasn't enough water in the world to clean him.

Some stains didn't wash. They answered when called.

Lucien exhaled ragged, steam rising in the cold.

He stared into the endless black skyline, fists clenching at his sides.

The world had crowned him.

But no one told him the crown was also the gallows.

That power and punishment had always been cut from the same metal.

That every ounce of power he clawed from the dirt tightened the noose.

He slammed his fists into the steel railing.

Once.

Twice.

A third time until the skin split and blood slicked the metal.

The pain wasn't enough to quiet the fire inside.

No audience. No enemy. No mercy.

Just Lucien Cole and the weight of everything he buried to become him.

He squeezed his eyes shut and saw them: ruined lives, brothers who died believing a lie, innocents shredded by a war they never chose.

"This isn't a war," he whispered.

"It's a reckoning."

Wars still pretended there were sides. Reckonings only cared who was left standing.

For the first time, he admitted the truth.

"I am not the king. I am the executioner. This throne is my cross."

His chest heaved, breath half sob, half curse.

The bounty. The betrayals. The monsters he fought. The thing he became.

All the blood spilled. All the men buried. All the nights he traded pieces of himself for one more sunrise.

All of it led here.

For what?

He wanted to scream, to rip the fucking sky open and demand why it was never enough.

Instead, he lowered his head and whispered to the boy he used to be.

"You built the kingdom they told you to. You became the monster they forced you to be. And now they want your head for it."

The rain fell harder, cold and dirty, washing ghosts off the streets but leaving them caked in his bones.

"Let them come."

He straightened. No armor. No illusions. Just the storm inside him, coiled and starved.

And the world was about to find out what a man with nothing left to lose could do.

His boots scraped across the soaked rooftop, puddles forming like bruises.

The rain slicked his hair back and streamed down the sharp angles of his face.

Let it fall. Let it drown whatever was left of the man he used to be.

He didn't wipe it away.

The world wanted a monster?

He'd give them a goddamn apocalypse.

Not the kind from scripture. The kind a man made for himself.

Sirens screamed beneath him, engines roared, and a thousand desperate heartbeats seemed to pound through the concrete.

He could feel them.

The bounty hunters.

The broken men.

The scavengers coming to feed.

They weren't coming for justice.

They were coming for a fucking payday.

And Lucien Cole was going to bury them all.

He stalked toward the stairwell door, every step heavy, like even the roof should have feared carrying him.

Back inside, the hallway was alive with motion.

Victor barked orders to the crew. Logan checked weapons. One of Lucien's men worked the monitors, syncing feeds with Ghost's remote systems.

Data poured across the screens, tracking movement across boroughs, bouncing between servers like it smelled blood.

It all faded into white noise the moment Lucien stepped inside.

Lena saw him first.

She froze mid-conversation, her body recognizing the shift before her mind caught up.

Lucien's eyes were different.

Not the simmering heat she knew.

Not the cold calculation he showed the world.

Something deeper lived there now.

Something buried and trying to claw its way out.

She moved toward him without thinking. Around them, voices died one by one as the others noticed him too.

Lucien shrugged off his soaked jacket. The leather hit the floor with a wet thud.

His shirt clung to him, rain-soaked, streaked with blood. He looked cut from war. Like the storm had finished something the city started years ago.

No words passed between them.

Lena felt it.

The fracture.

The surrender to the storm.

Her chest tightened, not from fear, but from the brutal ache of watching the man she loved stand there and let him carry the weight alone.

She stepped closer.

Slow. Careful. Like approaching something wounded enough to collapse into her arms or kill her where she stood.

Lucien didn't move.

Lena lifted her hand. Her fingertips brushed the edge of his wrist.

He flinched once.

Barely.

But he didn't pull away.

"I see you," she whispered, soft enough that only he could hear.

"Not the king. Not the killer. Not the ghost."

Her fingers slid down, wrapping gently around his scarred hand.

"I see the man. And I'm not fucking leaving him."

Lucien's breath shuddered.

A sound so raw it split her heart in two.

He said nothing, standing there like a monument built from blood and regret.

But his hand closed around hers.

Tight. Desperate. Alive.

And somewhere behind those dark eyes, something flickered.

Not forgiveness.

Not salvation.

Something harder.

Hope wrapped in barbed wire.

Ugly. Painful. Real enough to survive this world.

The kind of hope that only knew one thing:

We fight or we die trying.

Lucien didn't let go.

He pulled her closer.

No words.

No hesitation.

Their mouths crashed together.

Not gentle. Not careful. A kiss that devoured.

Deep. Fierce. Final.

Lena's fingers knotted in his collar.

Lucien's hand slid into her hair.

They kissed like the world had already ended.

Tires screamed outside.

Boots. Voices. Weapons moving fast.

"They're here!" someone shouted from the stairwell.

Lucien didn't move.

Lena met him harder.

Another voice:

"Multiple vehicles. They're breaching the lower floor!"

The kiss broke long enough to breathe, long enough to look at each other.

Victor's voice cut through the room.

"They're in the goddamn building!"

Still Lucien held her.

Pulled her tighter.

"Ready weapons! Get high ground!"

"Fuck, we've got dozens. Dozens!" the tech specialist barked.

"They're spreading across all floors!"

Lucien finally pulled back.

Only inches from Lena's face.

His lips were warm. His breath slow.

He looked at her like she was the last thing in the world worth believing in.

His hands closed around her cheeks.

"See you on the other side."

Victor shouted again.

"Here they come!"

Lucien turned toward the stairwell.

The door hung open like a mouth waiting to scream.

The first man hit the threshold.

Lucien drew and fired in one smooth motion.

.45 hollow point, center of the forehead.

Bone, blood, wall.

The body folded before it hit the floor.

Lucien let go of Lena. Not gently. Not roughly. Just final.

"Positions."

The room erupted.

Boots thundered. Fresh magazines slammed home.

Shouts cracked like gunfire as the crew scrambled for cover.

Victor barked orders from the mezzanine, a black rifle slung over one shoulder, pain in every step, rage in every word.

"Two teams! Left stairwell! Freight lift center! Push them back!"

Logan dropped behind a column of unfinished steel, already firing short bursts into the stairwell as shadows spilled through it.

The second hostile hit the third floor and took two rounds from Victor before he could aim.

The third never made it.

One of Lucien's men split his jaw with a shotgun blast, painting the scaffolding behind him red.

Lucien moved differently.

Not frantic. Not panicked. Surgical. Precise. Lethal.

Like the decision to become this had already been made somewhere higher than pain.

He moved through gunfire like it couldn't touch him, dropping two hostiles with chest-high shots that landed like verdicts.

"This is still mine."

A grenade clinked across the floor.

One of Lucien's men dove, snatched it mid-roll, and hurled it back through the stairwell.

Lucien was already moving, clearing the space before the echo of the blast reached them.

Boom.

The wall trembled.

Dust. Screams. Silence.

Then another wave hit.

Shadows surged from the smoke, automatic fire shredding drywall and sparking off steel.

Lucien dropped low behind an unfinished column, returned two clean shots.

One man dropped. Another staggered, clutching his thigh before Victor finished the job with a shot to the temple.

"Southwest stairwell! Two more!"

A hostile lunged at Lena.

She fired.

Click.

Empty.

She ducked, grabbed a steel pipe fitting off the floor, and swung with everything she had, snapping his knee sideways.

The man screamed and dropped.

Before he could recover, she stepped in and drove the steel into his chest.

He stopped moving.

"I'm sick of this!" she screamed, voice ragged and raw.

She stared down at him, chest heaving.

Logan fired a burst toward the scaffolding. Suppressive fire.

Something about it felt off.

Lucien didn't see it yet.

But Victor did.

Back near the surveillance rig, one of Lucien's techs yelled. "Movement patterns are wrong."

"They're not breaching. They're funneling us!"

Lucien's head snapped toward him.

"Say again."

"Schematics. They're herding us to the upper floor. Ghost says the building's been mapped. This is coordinated."

Lucien's voice dropped.

"This isn't chaos."

"It's control."

Which meant the hand behind it was closer than blood on the floor.

Then it happened.

An enemy hit the floor hard, body riddled with bullets.

His comm unit still hissed.

Victor stepped over it and froze.

Crackling, faint, but unmistakable:

"The son is there. Keep him alive. Do not engage."

Victor's eyes flicked up.

Across the room, Logan stood near the north side windows.

Firing again.

Too controlled.

Victor's jaw locked.

Didn't say a word.

Just kept watching.

Then the room turned red.

A flashbang popped off near the east wing.

Lucien turned, dropped two more targets with precision, but not fast enough to stop what came next.

A scream.

Domingo, one of Lucien's men, stayed close to Lena and took two rounds to the chest blocking a flanking shot.

He dropped instantly. Gasping.

Lena caught him before he hit the marble.

"Stay with me," she said. "Stay with me."

Blood spilled from his mouth.

Lucien saw the pain fold in her chest.

Didn't flinch.

But his hand tightened around the trigger.

Final bodies dropped.

The last invader tried to climb the balcony rail and escape. Victor put a round in his spine.

Silence fell, broken only by the static hiss of radios and Lena's ragged breathing.

Logan's voice cut through, too loud, too clean. "We fucking did it!"

He turned toward the center of the room, smiling, wiping sweat off his face, weapon lowered.

Victor stepped forward.

No smile.

No reply.

Just one clean motion.

Crack.

Gun handle to the back of Logan's skull.

Logan dropped like a brick.

Lucien turned.

"Tie him up."

No one asked why.

They just obeyed.

Two of the men grabbed Logan by the arms and dragged him toward the far corner. Zip ties. Reinforced tape. A rifle leveled at his chest, even unconscious.

Silence followed.

Not peace. The silence violence leaves behind.

Victor limped across the floor, breathing hard, eyes sweeping the bodies.

Lena stood still, blood on her hands, her chest rising too fast.

Not from panic. From finally seeing what this war kept taking from her.

Lucien just watched.

Then, his burner buzzed.

He pulled it from his coat pocket, screen cracked, blood-smeared.

Ghost's voice came in fast and urgent.

"You woke the neighborhood. Got an ocean of five-oh heading your way."

Lucien slid the phone back into his pocket and stared out toward the shattered glass windows overlooking the street.

In the distance, sirens rose.

Soft at first.

Then swelling.

Like the city had finally decided to collect.

And Heaven on Fifth was about to learn what kind of altar it had really become.

Chapter Forty-Three

THE JUDAS CLAUSE

Sirens bloomed through the night like a warning shot from God.

The city was finally waking up to the smell of what they'd done.

Lucien didn't react.

Just turned toward the shattered lobby doors and nodded once.

"Move."

Victor and two men dragged Logan out, zip-tied, barely conscious, his head cocked back from the blow.

Still breathing.

Still useful.

In this world, usefulness was the last mercy a traitor ever got.

Outside, the street filled with shadows, blacked-out SUVs idling as men peeled off toward exfiltration routes, vanishing into the dark.

Lucien's burner buzzed.

Ghost:

You've got ninety seconds before that place is swarming with blue. Westbound route is clear

Drop onto Gansevoort and cut up Eleventh. I'll thread you through the district

Don't miss the window

Lucien was already moving.

"Victor, backseat. Gun on Logan. Lena, front. I'm driving."

They loaded Logan into the rear seat, his head rolling, wrists zip-tied.

Victor circled around and slid in next to him, pistol already drawn and resting on his thigh.

Lena took position, breath sharp, eyes scanning the mirrors.

Lucien hit the ignition.

The engine didn't roar.

It growled low and patient.

Like it already knew the difference between escape and war.

"Hold on."

They peeled off the curb, tires biting into soaked asphalt.

Ghost's map glowed on Lucien's phone, turning the truck's dash into a war grid, every turn a countdown.

The city had become geometry now. Angles. Timing. Survival measured in blocks.

Behind them, Heaven on 5th vanished into the dark.

And somewhere deeper in the city, the sirens were rising.

They surged west, the truck's military tires chewing through the pavement without mercy.

No one spoke at first.

The city outside blurred, rain-slick streets, red flashes, shadows darting between alleys. Every block burned another second.

Lena checked the mirror. "You think we'll make it out clean?"

Lucien kept his eyes on the road, one hand steady on the wheel.

"We make it out. Clean's a luxury."

From the backseat, Victor's voice cut through.

"If they had more hitters staged, we'd be leaking by now."

Lucien nodded.

"Whoever sent them, they weren't ready. They'll be regrouping."

A low groan came from Logan's side.

He was waking.

Victor didn't hesitate. He pressed the muzzle of the pistol to Logan's ribs.

"Try something. Please."

Logan's eyes blinked open, dazed. Blood at his temple. His breath shallow.

"What the fuck..."

Lucien didn't look back.

"You'll get your answers. We'll get ours first."

They cut onto Gansevoort.

On the dash, Ghost's tracker pulsed red. One more turn.

Behind them, sirens flared again, closer now. Two intersections back.

Lena checked the rearview monitor, the high-def feed washing the cabin in blue.

Flashing cruisers filled the frame.

"We have a tail," Lena said.

Lucien's thumb flipped the first switch.

"Smoke."

A valve opened somewhere beneath the chassis.

The night behind them collapsed into fog.

Not cover. Punishment.

Thick smoke poured from the rear vents, swallowing the lane in seconds. In the red wash of the cruisers' lights, it turned the street into a rolling wall of darkness, spreading behind them like spilled ink.

The cruisers drove straight into it.

For half a breath, everything went quiet.

Then brakes shrieked.

Metal slammed.

A siren warped into a dying howl.

Lena flinched.

Victor didn't look up from Logan.

"Good. Let them choke on it."

Lucien's voice stayed calm.

"Blinders."

Lena's hand moved before the word finished.

The rear system ignited.

White light detonated inside the fog bank, a violent burst that turned the street behind them into a burning cloud.

Headlights bounced wild inside it.

Shapes collided.

A cruiser fishtailed through the glare and smashed into a hydrant hard enough to shear the bumper off.

Another slammed its brakes too late.

Steel folded.

Glass erupted.

Lucien didn't glance back.

"Now the tacks."

Lena hit the final switch.

A sharp metallic hiss answered.

Hundreds of hardened spikes scattered across the asphalt behind them, skittering like a swarm of knives.

The fog swallowed them.

The next cruiser burst through the smoke at full speed.

Then:

Pop.

Pop pop pop.

Tires detonated.

Rubber shredded.

The vehicle lurched sideways and slammed into a row of parked cars hard enough to flip one onto its side.

Another unit tried to cut around the wreckage.

Too late.

Spikes ripped through both front tires.

The cruiser slewed across the street and buried its hood into a delivery truck with a hollow boom.

Sirens strangled mid-wail.

The rest of the chase dissolved into chaos behind them.

Lucien didn't react.

Didn't smile.

Didn't slow.

He drove.

Headlights off.

Hands steady on the wheel while Ghost's route burned quietly across the dash.

The Rezvani slid through the next intersection like a shadow peeling free of the city.

Lena checked the rear monitor again.

Red and blue strobes flashed through the fog bank, distant now, tangled in wreckage.

"No pursuit."

Victor's pistol never left Logan.

Logan was awake now.

Very awake.

And very quiet.

Victor spoke without looking at him.

"Keep it that way."

Lucien's voice cut through the cabin.

"We're not clear."

His eyes stayed on the road ahead.

"One wrong move and this whole city comes down on us."

The truck slipped back into the grid of Manhattan streets.

Black.

Silent.

Moving like it had never touched the street at all.

Outside, the city pulled the noise back into itself.

For the first time in miles, it felt like New York was holding its breath.

Getting answers out of Logan was the next move.

They didn't go back to the estate.

Didn't risk the penthouse.

Lucien took them somewhere colder, quieter, and forgotten.

An old shell property tucked behind a condemned bodega near the edge of the West Side, nothing but concrete walls, dust, and silence.

The kind of place that didn't ask questions.

The kind of place built for ghosts, and for the things ghosts did when there was no one left to lie to.

Victor dragged Logan from the truck. Zip-tied. Bloodied. His head hung like a puppet with its strings cut.

They entered through the back.

The block was dead, no lights, no neighbors, no eyes on it.

Inside, the place looked dead: stripped floors, one hanging bulb, a folding table with two bullet holes and a burn ring at the center.

Lucien had been here before. When his world was smaller. Dirtier. Paid in blood.

Tonight, he brought none of that. Only the weight.

Logan hit the chair hard. Didn't scream. Didn't beg. Just grunted somewhere between pain and defiance.

Victor stayed behind him. Pistol out. Cold eyes forward.

Lucien stepped in last.

Didn't sit.

Didn't blink.

He just stared at Logan, like the truth was hiding somewhere behind his eyes.

Logan blinked, trying to steady his vision, blood crusted in his hairline, neck stiff, wrists swollen from the zip ties. He looked up, tired but steady.

His voice came out hoarse, laced with dry defiance.

"Go ahead. Break me. End me. You're no better than the ones you kill."

Lucien didn't answer.

Victor stepped forward.

The pistol didn't rise.

It didn't have to.

"You sold us out," Victor said. "The docks. The asylum. The fucking clinic. Heaven on 5th. That was you."

Logan looked up, just enough to flash a crooked smile.

"I didn't set the fire. I just passed the match."

That was always the language of cowards, pretending the hand that helped ruin something wasn't theirs.

Victor kicked the chair back.

Metal shrieked across the floor.

"You think this is a fucking joke?"

Logan tensed, chest heaving.

"I didn't have a choice."

Lucien tilted his head slightly.

"You always have a choice."

"Not when you're born into it," Logan spat.

Victor's eyes narrowed.

He grabbed the front of Logan's jacket and yanked him forward so fast the chair legs scraped the floor.

"I heard it," Victor snarled. "On their comms. 'The son is there. Keep him alive.'"

Logan tried to look away.

Victor slapped him. Open palm. Fast. Precise. Not to injure. To shock.

"We know it was you they meant."

"Whose son?" Victor demanded.

Logan didn't answer.

Victor slammed him back again.

"Whose son, motherfucker?! Speak!"

Lucien finally spoke, calm, low, dangerous.

"I already know. I've known."

He stared at Logan like he was looking straight through him.

"But I want to hear him say it."

Victor raised the pistol, slow and quiet, and pressed it to Logan's kneecap.

"Say it, or I'll rip the truth out through the bone."

After a long pause, the answer came broken and bitter, forced through clenched teeth.

"Royce is my father."

The truth didn't explode. It sank, heavy and filthy, into every corner of the room.

No one moved.

Victor stared.

Lucien stood still.

Logan looked down, because there was no more hiding left.

Victor's voice cut through the silence.

"You little piece of shit. You sold out the only people who didn't treat you like a fucking asset."

Logan didn't answer.

Lucien stepped closer, slow, like a sentence already passed.

He crouched, not to plead but to study, his face shadowed by the single bulb.

He pulled a cigarette from his coat, struck a match, and let the flame linger a moment before touching it to the tip.

Smoke curled upward, thin and steady as wire.

He let the moment thicken until the air itself leaned in.

"You think control is a fist. You think force is the final word."

He drew once, the ember flaring.

"That's the cheap play. Violence wakes people up. It makes them fight. It makes them remember who they are."

He leaned in, close enough for Logan to smell the smoke and the heat rising off his skin.

"The deadliest thing isn't the bullet you see. It's the thought you believe is yours. A whisper that sounds like memory. A doubt that wears your face. Suggestion slides in dressed as desire, and by the time you notice, it's already steering your hands."

Logan's pulse stuttered.

Lucien's voice thinned, sharp enough to cut.

"People are patterns. Hit the right place, they fold the same way every time."

He stayed close, eyes locked on Logan.

"We don't break them to make them weaker. We make them believe they chose their chains. That's how you own a man without ever touching him again."

He straightened slowly, voice colder now.

"Leverage is slow mercy. You can end a life and be done with it. Or you can hold a life and watch it drag a king across a map."

He smiled. There was nothing warm in it.

"Which one feeds us for longer?"

Logan's hands flexed against the zip ties.

He wanted to scoff. He wanted to argue.

But the room already knew where Lucien's patience led.

Lucien rose and let the question hang.

"You want to live? Then help us pull him out of hiding."

Logan scoffed.

"He's not stupid. He won't walk into a war zone just because I say so."

"He won't come for you," Lucien said. "But he will come for your body."

Logan's brow furrowed.

"We leak that we found the traitor. That we killed him. Make it loud. Make it stick."

Victor's eyes gleamed.

"You. Hooded. Duct-taped. Laid out like a trophy."

"To the feds, it'll look like underworld payback."

Lucien nodded.

"But to Royce? It'll scream blood. He'll come himself."

Logan looked down, like he was staring into his own grave.

"So I'm bait."

"You already picked your side," Lucien said. "Now you get to pay the toll."

Logan's voice came bitter.

"You want me to sell out my own blood?"

Lucien leaned in, eyes like ice.

"You already did. Us."

Logan exhaled, slow and shaking.

"Fine. But when this ends, it ends."

Lucien straightened.

"The Judas Clause."

He turned to Victor.

"Let's bury the king."

Victor looked at Logan, not with rage but with something colder.

Disgust.

The kind reserved for traitors who wore your colors while bleeding you dry.

Lucien stood there, staring at Logan like he wasn't looking at a person, but at the last piece of a truth he'd hoped was wrong.

He stepped into the hall and pulled the burner from his jacket.

Ghost answered immediately.

"You get what you needed?"

Lucien didn't waste breath.

"You were right. The leak was on our side. It was Logan."

A pause.

Then Ghost's voice came back.

"Knew it. Everything lined up too clean around him."

Lucien's tone didn't waver.

"He's Royce's son. A mole from the beginning."

Static filled the line.

"What's the move?"

Lucien stared into the dark hallway like he could see the entire endgame from there.

"We fake his death. Make it loud. Blood, photo, the whole thing. I want his body wrapped like a cartel hit and dumped in a burn lot, somewhere no one walks without a piece."

Ghost didn't hesitate.

"I'll push it. Low-tier bounty channels, encrypted group threads. Won't take long to reach the right ears."

"Make it stick," Lucien said. "I want Royce convinced his son's been butchered."

"Copy," Ghost said. "Send the photo when it's staged. I'll have it moving inside the hour."

"You looping Hall?"

Lucien answered without hesitation.

"I'll handle Hall. He's my deal, my leverage. Royce steps back on U.S. soil, I deliver him. That was the deal."

Silence on Ghost's end.

"You think Royce comes himself?"

Lucien didn't blink.

"He won't trust anyone else with his son's corpse. He'll come to see it with his own eyes."

Ghost's voice dipped colder.

"Then it's done."

The line went dead.

Lucien turned back into the room.

Victor stood near the wall, reloading calmly.

Lena crouched beside a duffel, fingers moving through boxes of ammo, not with skill but just to keep busy.

Her eyes flicked up as Lucien stepped inside.

Logan was still in the chair, breathing shallow, head dropped forward, face empty.

Lucien looked at him now like a chess piece that had finally flipped.

"Get him cleaned up. We're staging a kill and selling death. Royce only buys precision hits."

Victor gave a nod.

Lucien moved to the table, placed his burner down, and unzipped a matte black case.

Inside, the SSD. The digital imprint of Royce's entire empire.

Not just money. Not just leverage. A map of every rot he ever planted and called power.

Lucien slid it forward slightly, just enough for everyone in the room to feel the weight of it.

"Everything he's built is in here," he said. "Every account. Every bribe. Every body he buried."

Lena stared.

Victor stepped closer.

Lucien's voice dropped to steel.

"This ends with him. No deals. No mercy."

Not as a symbol.

As a weapon.

Then Lucien looked from Lena to Victor.

"All of it leads to this."

He zipped the case shut.

Lucien stood in the middle of the room, coat off, sleeves rolled, hands braced on the table like a man laying out war.

"Alright," he said. "We're gonna need to stage this right. Blood, body placement, everything. If we're fishing out Royce, it needs to look like we gutted his son ourselves."

Victor lit a cigarette, took one slow drag, then nodded toward the door.

"Hold up."

Lucien raised a brow.

Victor exhaled smoke.

"I got a guy."

Lucien waited.

"Name's Pyotr," Victor continued. "He's tied to my Russians. Ex-FSB, used to stage political kills for optics, made oligarchs look like they got whacked by rivals. Does fake deaths better than the real ones."

Lucien didn't blink.

"He's on U.S. soil?"

"Never left," Victor said. "Lives like a ghost. Keeps quiet, stays mobile. I'm sure his van's still full of props and enough makeup to fake a goddamn war crime. I knew someone in Kiev who used him once. Needed it to look like a rival boss got poisoned and tossed off a balcony. Pyotr staged the whole thing, latex double, press photos, fake autopsy paperwork, had three governments chasing the wrong corpse for a month."

Lucien leaned back slightly.

"Get him here."

Victor smirked.

"He'll fire up the van the second I say the word. I make it worth his time."

His phone was already at his ear.

Across the room, Lena's phone buzzed.

She glanced down.

Blocked number. No contact. No preview.

Just a single message:

You made it further than I ever could

Her stomach dropped fast.

The room around her blurred, the voices, the tension, all muted by that single line on the screen like it had no right to exist.

Lucien caught the shift in her expression.

"What is it?" he asked.

She showed him the screen.

Lucien stared.

Something behind his eyes changed.

She'd seen that look before.

He didn't say a word.

Just slowly lowered the phone, eyes narrowing, mind already shifting.

The past was moving again.

And the past was always at its most dangerous when it stopped staying buried.

Lena's voice came low, almost to herself.

"I haven't gotten one of these texts since Miami."

Lucien didn't look at her. Just stood there, focused.

"If they meant to hit you," he said, "they would've done it by now."

Lena gave a short, bitter laugh.

"I guess gunning me down with a car wasn't dangerous enough."

Lucien glanced at her then, eyes steady.

"I'm serious," she said.

He stepped closer, lowered his voice.

"We'll figure it out. Right now we finish this."

She nodded, lips tight.

Victor spoke up from across the room.

"My guy's two hours out. He's been laying low in Pennsylvania, small town off I-80."

Lucien didn't hesitate.

"Good. Let's get him prepped."

Chapter Forty-Four

THE STRIKE BEFORE THE STORM

Ninety-seven minutes after the call, the floodlights outside the shell property caught the low silhouette of a matte-gray panel van easing past the condemned bodega. No plates. No running lights. Just the soft crunch of broken glass under tires and the faint smell of diesel seeping through the walls.

Inside, Lucien didn't move from the shadows. Victor slid the bolt and cracked the steel door open three inches. Cold air knifed in.

Pyotr stepped through the rear entrance like he'd always been there.

No knock. No warning.

Lucien's gun was up before the door even clicked shut.

Victor raised a hand, fast. "Easy. That's my guy."

Lucien didn't lower the weapon right away. Just stared. "You're early."

Pyotr was mid-fifties. Lean. Pale eyes that didn't blink too often. He wore a navy jacket with no markings, gloves already on, and carried a canvas duffel that looked like it had been dragged through six countries and four body dumps.

Only then did Lucien holster the gun.

"Pyotr," Victor said, as if that explained everything.

Lucien didn't extend a hand. Didn't offer a greeting.

"Can you make it real?"

Pyotr dropped the duffel with a heavy thud, unzipped it, and started pulling out gear: sealed blood packs, medical-grade silicone prosthetics, synthetic skin sheets, coagulated gore.

He looked up once. "Depends how real you need it."

Lucien crossed his arms. "Dead enough for a grieving father."

Which meant it had to look less like murder and more like punishment.

Pyotr gave a slow nod, then turned to Logan, still in the chair, silent and resigned. "We'll need his facial dimensions, bone structure, swelling patterns, neck bruising, blood flow simulation. Might need to crack a rib to make the photos sell."

Logan jerked upright, panicked. "Wait, what?"

Victor didn't even glance at him.

"Shut the fuck up. You're lucky that's not all we crack."

He glanced down at Logan's waist.

"Or worse, cut something off."

Logan muttered under his breath, "Sick fuck."

Pyotr knelt beside him, opened a smaller case, and began measuring his face with a digital scanner.

Victor stepped beside Lucien. "He's everything I said he was."

Lucien's voice came low. "We get the photos out within the hour. I'll ride point with Ghost."

Victor nodded once, then turned his eyes back on Logan.

Now he looked like a man watching his own funeral.

Pyotr moved with precision, laying out wraps, mixing blood packs, adjusting the lights for the camera like he was dressing a movie set instead of staging a fake execution.

Logan sat duct-taped to the folding chair, shirt ripped, a painted slash across his throat, bruises placed in the exact places they would be if Victor had taken it further.

Pyotr didn't talk much, just gave short instructions while applying layers of gore and grime like a butcher with patience.

After twenty minutes, Logan finally groaned. "Is this really necessary?"

Pyotr didn't look up. "Yes."

Logan rolled his eyes, voice hoarse. "Pretty sure my dad's not gonna zoom in to admire the details."

Pyotr glanced at him once, expression flat. "If he doesn't believe it, he doesn't bite."

Victor stepped forward, flicking ash toward the bucket of discarded rags. "You want off his leash or not?"

Logan muttered under his breath. "Feels more like I'm getting put down."

Pyotr adjusted the chair angle by two inches and nodded once.

An hour of work clung to the room, fake blood mixed with sweat and cigarette smoke.

Pyotr didn't look up. "We're close. Just need the blood to dry like it set in real time."

Lucien stood off to the side, arms crossed, eyes tracking every movement without a word.

Victor turned toward him. "Ten minutes. Then we shoot the photo and move."

Lucien gave a small nod, slow, distant.

Across the room, Lena hadn't moved since the message.

But her eyes were sharp now. Like something in her had shifted again.

Like the war wasn't just around them anymore.

It had gotten inside.

Pyotr circled Logan one last time, then stepped back and nodded toward Lucien. "It's ready."

Lucien stepped forward, slow and steady.

Logan sat motionless, hood pulled low, duct tape stretched across his mouth. Blood slicked his chest and neck, some still wet, some dried.

Lucien crouched and drew the burner from his coat.

Before he could lift it, Pyotr stepped in, already moving. "Give me."

He circled the body like a stagehand prepping a shot, finding the right light, the right angle.

No hesitation.

No apologies.

Click.

One photo.

All angle tricks.

All theater.

The kind of lie built for men who trusted their fear more than their eyes.

Lucien stared at the image.

Then sent it.

Ghost received it in under five seconds.

Two minutes later, a reply lit the screen:

393

Got it. Image is live on five dark channels. Code thread labeled: Judas Confirmed. Tagging it to bounty chatter and encrypted drop groups. Anyone watching for Royce will bite on it.

Lucien locked the phone.

Victor looked over. "That it?"

Lucien nodded once. "Now we wait."

A different kind of silence followed.

The kind that came before impact.

Then, Ghost again.

Movement

Lucien's eyes narrowed as he typed:

What kind?

A few seconds passed.

Then the phone buzzed again:

Ping hit a private tower outside Providence. Encrypted, but it matches Royce's routing pattern, same digital routing we tagged before Kearny. He's seen the image.

Lucien stayed still.

He looked at Victor.

Then Logan, still breathing beneath the hood, slumped like something already halfway to dead.

Then Lena.

She hadn't said a word.

But he didn't need her to.

She was already locked in.

Lucien stared at the photo on the burner's screen.

Logan's staged body. Hooded. Bloodied. Lifeless.

It looked real.

Like something you don't survive.

A cartel kill.

A warning.

The kind of violence that makes cops look away and fathers cross oceans.

But it wasn't enough.

Not for Royce.

He wouldn't move off a picture alone. He'd want something physical. Traceable.

A location.

A witness.

Something real enough to touch.

Lucien's eyes narrowed.

They needed to place the body.

And they needed Royce's own channels to carry it back.

Lucien didn't look away from the burner.

He texted Ghost back.

We need a dump site. Cold. Isolated. Enough cover to watch the watchers.

A few seconds passed.

Got one. Burned-out dry dock on the Hudson. Last used in '22. Cameras down. No traffic at these hours. You'll have visibility from a few angles. Sending pin now.

The map link appeared.

Lucien opened it, scanned the coordinates, then looked at Victor.

"We set the body. Let Royce's men come sniff."

"We make one send the message. Then we clean up."

Victor gave a sharp nod.

"You wanted a way out?" Lucien said, looking at Logan.

"You're the reason he comes down."

He turned to the crew.

"Load him."

"We're not setting bait. We're ringing the bell."

The truck rolled through the intersection of 12th and 29th, headlights cut, the air thick with tension. The dry dock rose ahead in stillness, half-collapsed cranes leaning over rusted beams and rotted scaffolding. Hudson water lapped against the stone edge, black and quiet.

A blacked-out van trailed them, carrying two of Lucien's men he'd called in before they rolled out, eyes sharp, orders sharper.

Lucien sat in the front seat of the Rezvani, burner in hand, eyes locked on the GPS pin Ghost had sent. The coordinates were good. The sightlines were better.

Behind him, Logan was slumped in the back, hooded, taped, soaked in fake blood and tension.

Victor checked the side mirror. "Cameras are down. No movement."

Lucien's voice came low. "They'll come. They have to."

The Rezvani slowed to a stop. Behind it, the van doors opened.

Lucien stepped out first, coat collar up against the wind, boots grinding against the gravel.

The city skyline burned behind them.

Money. Glass. Heaven.

But here?

It felt like the edge of the world.

The kind of place where a body could become a message and a message could start a war.

Victor moved alongside him as Lucien's two men climbed out of the trailing van, silent, efficient. Logan didn't speak, didn't even move. He knew not to. He let them drag him from the truck like dead weight, his body slack, blood drying in streaks down his shirt.

They carried him near the rusted hull of a dry-docked vessel. Enough shadow to make it believable. Enough light to make it work.

They laid him out like a cartel trophy, hood still on, head back, blood crusted like it had dried hours ago.

Victor crouched, adjusted the angle of Logan's chin, then stood back.

"Looks real," one of the men muttered.

Lucien didn't respond.

He pulled the burner from his coat, snapped a fresh photo of the setup, and sent it to Ghost.

Body placed. We're in position

The reply came fast.

Intercept window open. One unknown encrypted ping just hit a relay within the city. Could be Royce's people. Stay sharp

Lucien slid the phone back in his coat and scanned the dock.

Three sniper nests, two getaway routes, one goal.

"Positions."

Victor moved left. One man covered high. Another stayed low with eyes on the water.

Lucien just watched the dark.

Watched for the ones watching them.

He knew they were already close.

Twenty slow minutes bled by.

The dock held still. Quiet. Waiting.

Then headlights.

A dark sedan rolled in slow from the south entrance, no rush, no hesitation. The engine cut. Doors opened.

Two men stepped out.

Flashlights clicked on.

They scanned the lot in wide, methodical arcs, cutting across the shadows, the hull, the gravel-strewn ground.

One pointed toward the makeshift kill zone near the rusted vessel.

"There," he muttered.

They moved in.

Approached the body.

Logan lay still, hood pulled low, duct tape stretched across his mouth, face pale under streaks of dried blood. One arm twisted unnaturally behind his back.

Dead.

At least to them.

One of the men crouched low. The other kept watch, hand resting on his weapon.

They didn't see Lucien.

Didn't hear him move.

But they felt him the second he spoke.

"Turn around."

The words landed like a hammer wrapped in silk.

The closer man froze.

The second man jolted. He spun toward the voice, pistol rising.

Crack.

A sniper round split the air.

The man's head snapped back in a mist of red.

He dropped.

The first man reached for his sidearm on instinct.

"Ah-ah-ah." Lucien stepped closer. Calm. Ice. "I wouldn't do that if I were you."

The man froze, eyes wide, chest heaving.

Lucien nodded toward the body. "Logan. Get up."

For a moment, the world held its breath.

Then Logan stirred.

Groaned.

Sat up.

The scout blinked, confusion washing over his face like reality had slipped.

Lucien stepped fully into the light, coat catching wind, eyes fixed on the man like a predator already bored with the chase. "You're going to deliver a message."

The man didn't speak.

Lucien kept going.

"You're gonna say we made an example out of him."

The man didn't run.

Didn't move.

Just stood there, chest rising and falling, one body down at his feet, another risen from the dead.

Lucien's voice dropped, cold. "Phone. Now."

The scout hesitated.

Victor raised his pistol a hair.

That was enough.

The man pulled his phone out, slow, careful.

Lucien nodded toward it. "Send it out. Right now. Photo, coordinates. Confirmed."

The man's thumb hovered over the screen.

Lucien kept going. "Then put out that the body wasn't moved. Wasn't touched. Cartel-style disrespect. Say you barely made it out. That they let you walk to deliver the message."

The scout's hands trembled slightly. But he typed.

Lucien watched the confirmation tick through.

A photo. The body. Coordinates. One word: Confirmed.

Then another line:

"Left where it dropped. No cleanup. They let me walk."

Lucien watched the message send.

Watched the noose draw tighter around Royce's neck.

Not enough to kill him yet. Enough to make him come closer.

"One more thing," Lucien said.

The man looked up, hopeful, maybe. Like he thought that earned him a pass.

Lucien raised the pistol and put one clean round through his skull.

The body crumpled.

Victor stared.

"No loose ends," Lucien said.

Victor moved forward, crouched, and retrieved the scout's phone. Slid it into his pocket without a word.

Lucien didn't have to ask.

Then he turned toward Lena. "Now we wait."

Near the edge of the dock, the burner buzzed.

Lucien answered.

Ghost's voice came low and clipped. "We got movement. Remember that Gulfstream G550 I tracked landing at the Linden airstrip? It just filed a false log out of São Vicente. Takeoff confirmed. En route. Seven-hour window."

Lucien's eyes narrowed. "Royce?"

"It's him. Flight plan's fake, like the others. But he's airborne."

Lucien shifted, staring into the dark skyline. "Any idea where he's headed?"

Ghost paused.

"Not yet. I'm running satellite patterns. If he's coming back stateside, odds are it's private, Jersey again. Linden's still top of the list. But I'd expect he's covering his tracks better this time. No crew manifests. No customs flags. Nothing official."

Lucien's jaw tightened. "Then we get ready for him."

Ghost didn't miss a beat. "I'll have a confirmed landing site soon. You loop your fed yet?"

"Not yet," Lucien said. "I'm calling him now."

"Copy."

The line went dead.

The cold crept deeper as the first trace of sun began to bleed into the sky, not gold, not warm. Just light.

The kind that didn't forgive anything.

Lucien stood near the edge of the dock, arms around Lena, her face buried in his chest, wind biting against them both.

The night had been long. Dark. Hell in pieces.

He kissed her forehead, then her lips, slow and soft, like it might be the last clean thing left in him to give.

"I promise," he said quietly. "This is all gonna be over soon."

Lena didn't speak. Just nodded against him, breath shaky in the cold.

Lucien touched her jaw gently, then nodded toward the Rezvani.

"Get in the truck," he said. "I'll be right there."

She hesitated.

Then walked away.

Lucien watched her go, letting the moment settle.

Now he stood alone.

The cold pressed in. The dock behind him looked like a graveyard the wind kept refusing to bury.

He stayed there a moment longer, breath rising like smoke in the pale light, then pulled the burner from his coat and dialed.

No hesitation.

Three rings.

Then Hall's voice came through, clipped and alert.

"Cole."

Lucien didn't waste time.

"Royce took the bait."

There was no satisfaction in saying it. Only the weight of what came next.

Hall's voice sharpened.

"Say that again. What bait?"

Lucien stared out at the water.

"We found a leak on my end. Logan."

"Logan?"

"He's Royce's son."

A breath on the other end.

"You sure?"

"Confirmed. He confessed. He's been feeding Royce our location data since the start. Every time we shifted position, we were being tracked. Every route was compromised before we touched it."

"Where is he now?"

"Alive. For now. We staged his death."

"You did what?"

"You heard me. Hooded him. Taped him up. Made it look cartel-grade. Sent the image through encrypted bounty channels."

Hall's voice tightened.

"You think that was enough to pull Royce in?"

"It was never about the photo. We planted the body. Royce's men came to confirm. One's no longer breathing. The other made sure the message reached the top."

Lucien checked the screen again.

"My guy's tracking a Gulfstream out of São Vicente. Royce is in the air."

A moment passed.

"You're telling me he's coming back?"

Lucien's voice turned to steel.

"He's coming back to confirm the kill himself."

"You want your case? You want someone to point the public finger at for the bodies in Miami? You want the Newark seizure tied to something bigger than a ghost story? This is it."

Hall's tone shifted, colder now. All business.

"I'll need the SSD. If it's as good as you said."

"It is. Everything. Accounts. Blackmail. Trafficking."

Hall exhaled hard.

"Where's it going down?"

"Not sure yet, but if he's coming in quiet, it'll be Linden. Private airstrip just outside Newark. My guy's clocked his jet there numerous times in the past few months. Three minutes from the port, five by chopper to the city.

It's clean. Too clean."

Then Hall spoke, slower now.

"You realize what this means, Cole?"

Lucien's eyes didn't move from the skyline.

"What?"

"You're making yourself the bait now."

"We already drew him out. Now we make him walk into his own cage."

Another breath from Hall.

"Alright. Send me what's on that SSD. I'll get the warrants prepped. I'll stage an intercept within six hours. Just give me the landing site."

Lucien ended the call. Didn't say goodbye.

He slid the burner back into his coat and turned toward the truck.

The sun crept higher, not bright, just there, casting a washed-out light over the water and the dead.

The war had bled through the night. It stayed in every step.

Lucien climbed into the driver's seat.

Lena was already there, silent, staring straight ahead. She didn't ask what Hall said. Her hand found his on the gearshift, and that was enough.

Victor was in the backseat, pistol still resting on his lap, eyes never off Logan, who sat slumped, wrists still zip-tied, face streaked with fake blood and grime.

Logan looked up, jaw tight. "You're really giving all that to the feds?"

Lucien didn't turn around. "I'm gonna burn your father to the fucking ground."

He hit the ignition.

Victor looked out the window with a tired smirk. "Hope Hall brought gasoline."

They peeled off the dock.

The black van split off into the side streets.

Lena glanced at him. "Where to?"

Lucien didn't look away from the road. "Penthouse."

No one spoke.

No music.

No chatter.

Just breath.

And intent.

The real hunt had just begun.

Chapter Forty-Five
RADIOACTIVE

They rolled into the underground entrance off a side street without slowing. The hydraulic gate was already rising, as if it had been waiting.

Lucien tapped the dash.

The lift swallowed the armored truck whole. The doors sealed. The street vanished.

Lena exhaled slow. Victor stayed quiet, watching Logan.

The platform carried them into Lucien's private tier. No shared access. No building cameras. Just steel, glass, and money no one questioned.

Lucien stepped out first. Same walk. Same silence. Everything else had changed.

They moved through the secured side corridor toward the elevator that ran straight to the penthouse. Victor dragged Logan in last by the back of the neck.

The ride up was silent, thirty-three floors of ghosts stacked beneath them. Every floor below felt like another version of the man Lucien had already buried to get here.

When the doors opened, Lena followed him into the penthouse, the glass walls still holding the memory of what this place used to be.

Not the skyline. Not the marble floors.

The night it held.

The way he touched her like she wasn't breakable.

The way she gave in like nothing else existed.

One of the last nights anything felt alive.

Morning stretched across the skyline, pale against the glass. But the penthouse no longer felt like home.

It felt like a war room.

Lucien crossed to the counter and dropped the SSD like a loaded weapon.

"Let's finish this."

He pulled the burner from his coat and thumbed out a short briefing: the deal, the SSD, Hall's window, everything Ghost needed.

Need eyes on the transfer. Hall wants the drive. Want it done clean

The reply came fast.

Where are you?

Lucien responded: **Penthouse**

Perfect. Use the laptop in your office. I built the secure tunnel into the network stack. It only activates when that device is hardwired in. You plug in, I pull the files. Simple

Hall had given them one endpoint, one key, one window. No second chances.

Lucien turned toward the study tucked behind the kitchen, a clean glass-wrapped workspace left almost untouched.

He pulled the laptop from the desk drawer and hardwired it into the port beneath the desk.

Ghost had buried the tunnel years ago. Hidden. Waiting.

The screen blinked awake, cool blue light spilling across the glass desk. Lucien slid the SSD into place.

The system registered it instantly, directories unfolding like a confession in code. Then the cursor began moving on its own.

Ghost was already inside.

Lines of script raced down the screen. A secure transfer panel opened. Network bars spiked.

Victor stood in the doorway behind him. Lena watched from the glass arch. Logan remained zip-tied outside, barely conscious.

SECURE TUNNEL ACTIVE

FIREWALL NEUTRALIZED

TRANSFER CLEAN

INITIATING SYNC TO FED NODE

They were in.

The weight of it settled across Lucien's shoulders, not like armor. Like inevitability. No turning back. No more silence. Whatever was left to burn would burn now.

The transfer bar crawled across the screen, not slow, but not fast enough to ignore.

1%

3%

8%

Victor watched the code race across the screen.

"They'll never see it coming."

Lucien gave a slight nod. "That's the point."

Morning stretched across the city, too clean for the truth coming with it.

Lena stepped closer. "What exactly is on that drive?"

Lucien didn't turn from the screen. "Everything. Flight logs. Bribe trails. Shadow ledgers. Blackmail clips. Surveillance nodes. Accounts in multiple countries tied to shell corps he thought were untouchable. Ghost unzipped it all."

Victor whistled under his breath.

"Enough to hang him a hundred times."

Lucien's expression hardened.

"No jury. No judge. No retrial. Once Hall's team sees this, Royce doesn't walk away. If the plan holds."

Outside the office, Logan coughed.

Lena glanced back. "You think he knows what's about to happen?"

Lucien didn't look. "He knows."

The screen blinked again.

TRANSFER 63%

NODE LOCK ENGAGED

ENCRYPTION PULSE FIRED

Ghost's commands ripped down the terminal.

TRIGGER BACKEND RECORD CLEANSE

WIPE LOCAL DEVICE LOGS

PING STAGING SERVER: HALL_READY

The burner buzzed.

3 minutes to complete. Breathe if you remember how

Lucien didn't smile, but his fists loosened.

He turned to Victor. "When this finishes, I want eyes on every approach to the Linden strip. Every road. Every hangar door. We don't move. We watch."

Victor nodded. "And when he lands?"

Lucien's voice didn't change. "Hall makes the grab. We confirm the fall."

The transfer crept closer to the edge.

87%... 91%...

The penthouse, once alive, felt like it was waiting.

TRANSFER 100%

SECURE SYNC COMPLETE

NODE CONFIRMED: HALL_01

The screen pulsed once.

Then vanished, wiped clean. Ghost had already buried the trail.

Lucien closed the laptop and stepped back like he'd just sealed a coffin.

The burner buzzed again.

Done. Hall has it. Full decrypt loading on his end now. You're officially radioactive

Lucien didn't reply. His mind was already moving past it. Outside, the city kept moving, unaware something in its underworld was beginning to shift.

Victor shifted in the doorway. "We move?"

Lucien didn't turn. "Not yet. We wait on Ghost. He's still watching the sky."

Victor gave a small nod, resting his shoulder against the doorframe.

Across the room, Lena stood at the windows, eyes fixed on the stillness outside.

Lucien walked toward the front of the penthouse, past the empty stretch of marble and the silent wall of glass.

Logan lifted his head slightly from where he was tied. His eyes were dull, wrists bruised from the ties, fake blood still dried along his collar.

"He's not gonna come."

Lucien walked past him without a glance. "He already is."

Victor moved closer to Lucien. "What's next?"

Lucien's voice stayed calm, low. "Ghost pings us when Royce hits U.S. airspace. Once we've got the window, we loop in Hall."

Victor nodded slowly. "Then we shut the cage."

Lucien finally turned from the window. His eyes were colder now. Fixed. "If he veers, we make him wish he hadn't."

Time passed. Just enough for the weight to settle.

Lucien sat on the edge of a leather ottoman, Lena perched on his lap, arms around his neck, her head resting against his shoulder. The room was dim, still, holding its breath with them.

Victor crossed the room, stretching with a grunt. "I'm fucking starving. What about him?" He nodded toward Logan, still zip-tied and quiet. "Should we feed this piece of shit or just let him chew on his guilt?"

Before Lucien could answer, the burner buzzed in his coat.

He reached for it, thumbed open the screen.

Bird's over the Atlantic. Inbound East Coast. Two hours from touchdown

Lucien stood.

He kissed Lena's temple, then stepped away and hit Hall's contact.

One ring.

"Cole."

Lucien didn't waste time. "You going through the drive?"

"You're goddamn right I am. This isn't a case file. It's a career killshot. Every shred of it. This is everything we need to bury this piece of shit for the rest of his life."

Lucien's tone stayed calm. Cold. "Good to hear because he's two hours from touchdown."

Then Hall's voice dropped, shifting into command. "Perfect. I'm having warrants signed as we speak. My team's already inbound, we'll be in local proximity before he touches down. Airstrip's gonna be boxed in. We'll have eyes on every hangar and enough bodies to lock it tight."

Lucien said nothing at first.

He let the silence sit.

Then:

"After that, we finish it."

Lucien ended the call and lowered the burner, eyes fixed on the skyline. The city looked quiet. But nothing about it felt still.

Behind him, Victor stretched, cracking his neck with a grunt. "Either I eat or someone dies. Flip a coin."

Lucien didn't look back. "Doesn't matter. Both are coming."

Lena rose from the ottoman and stepped beside him. "Do we wait here?"

"No. We move."

He looked to Victor. "Get Logan on his feet."

Victor grabbed Logan by the collar and hauled him upright.

Lucien looked at Logan. "You're getting cleaned up."

Then he stepped out of the room. Quiet. Controlled.

Logan blinked, voice raw. "What?"

Lucien stepped back in a few seconds later and tossed a folded bundle of clothes onto the floor, black tee, dark jeans, boots.

"You're not walking out of here looking like a corpse."

Victor sliced the zip ties with a flick of his blade, not gentle. Logan winced as circulation returned to his wrists.

He moved slowly. Sore. Tense.

Lucien met his eyes. "You fuck this up, one wrong word, one wrong look, I'll drop you in the street and step over the body."

Logan swallowed hard. "I get it."

Victor stepped in.

"No. You don't. But you will."

He held Logan's stare a second longer, then turned away, flexing his hands once.

"I'm hitting the shower. Blood's not even mine, and it's starting to itch."

He vanished down the hall, his footsteps fading into the quiet.

Lucien didn't sit. He stayed standing, eyes on the far wall like he could see through it.

Lena leaned against the edge of the counter. "You trust him to keep quiet?"

Lucien didn't answer right away.

"No. But I trust fear to do its job."

She studied him for a moment. "I've seen that look before. But not like this."

Lucien turned to her, his gaze sharp but quieter.

"Because this time it ends."

Silence settled, heavier than reassurance.

Then Lena whispered, almost to herself. "When it's done, what's left of us?"

Lucien's answer was simple. "Whatever survives."

Ten minutes later, footsteps approached.

Logan returned, a towel slung over his shoulder, a clean shirt pulled halfway down his chest.

"We rolling out, or is this the part where everyone stares at the floor and thinks deep thoughts?"

Lucien studied him for a moment, now dressed and standing near the wall like a man still trying to figure out where he belonged.

Then Lucien looked to Victor.

"Both."

They rolled out just past nine a.m.

The Rezvani moved through the Upper West Side matte black and silent, windows dark, the engine barely audible beneath the hush.

Inside, the tension sat thick.

The streets felt wrong. Not loud. Not quiet. Just off.

Like the city was waiting for something to break.

Lucien drove with one hand on the wheel, the other resting near the dash, his gaze sharp behind the tinted glass.

Lena sat beside him, arms crossed tight, watching the mirror. Victor was in the back with Logan, quiet as the street.

They hadn't slept, but this wasn't exhaustion. It was something heavier, meaner, like the night had left ash behind and they were driving through what remained.

Lena shifted slightly, her eyes catching movement behind them.

A black sedan sat a few cars back. Tinted windows. No front plate.

Lucien noticed. "What is it?"

She didn't answer right away. Just kept watching.

"I don't know," she said finally. "Maybe nothing. Maybe not."

He took the next left without hesitation.

They ended up in a corner diner off 10th Avenue, one of those old chrome ghosts from the sixties, washed in neon and burnt coffee. Booth in the back. Lights low.

No cameras. No questions. Just eggs, coffee, and anonymity.

Victor ordered everything. Lena barely touched her tea. Lucien stayed quiet, phone on the table, burner on vibrate.

His notebook was there again. Black leather. Quiet as a grave.

She'd seen him writing in it the night before. Same calm intensity. Same silence.

The pen rested beside it now, the entry half-finished.

Logan sat across from Lucien, hood up, hands tucked in his sleeves, watching everything and nothing at once.

Minutes passed before Victor spotted the black sedan across the street. Same tinted windows. Same missing front plate. Same dead idle.

"That car was behind us earlier," Lena said.

Victor stood. "I'll check."

He stepped outside.

The sedan pulled away before he reached the curb.

Victor came back colder than he'd left.

"Didn't hesitate. Peeled off the second I stepped out."

Lena tensed.

Lucien tapped the edge of the table once. "Everyone relax."

Victor slid back into the booth.

"No one's relaxing. Something's wrong."

Lucien's voice was calm. "It's the adrenaline. Lack of sleep. We made it out of hell and now the world feels too quiet. But you're not wrong."

Outside, morning stretched across the buildings, bright without warmth, more warning than day.

The burner buzzed once. Lucien unlocked it.

Bird's on approach. Thirty minutes from touchdown

The countdown had moved from the burner to the sky.

Lucien stood, slid the phone into his coat pocket, and looked at them all: Victor, Lena, even Logan, sitting upright now like he could feel the air thickening around him.

"Let's move."

They left the diner without speaking. Outside, the quiet no longer felt empty. It felt watched.

The street was wrong for that hour. No horns. No chatter. Just tension waiting to snap.

They loaded in. Victor shoved Logan into the back, rougher than necessary. The locks thumped closed, and they were moving.

Rubber on pavement. The soft click of Lucien opening the burner mid-drive.

Bird's thirty out. En route to Linden. We're in motion

The reply came seconds later.

Everything's prepped. Perimeter staged. Teams in place. Do not interfere. If we need you, you'll know. Until then, vanish

Lucien dropped the burner into the console tray.

He muttered under his breath, almost to himself. "Never listened to a fucking fed."

Then he punched south, cutting downtown, sliding onto Canal, weaving through morning foot traffic like demons in the seams of the city.

Up ahead, the Holland Tunnel swallowed them in steel, flickering light, and no way back. No one spoke. Victor stared ahead. Lena held herself still. Even Logan sat upright now, alert and wired, like prey finally aware of the predator driving him forward.

They burst into daylight, Jersey opening wide ahead of them, grime and skyline, gray and rising.

Lucien's voice came low. "Twenty minutes out."

No one answered. They weren't just driving anymore. They were closing the distance.

The GPS stayed silent. Lucien knew the way.

They cut through the Jersey highways, past fuel depots, storage yards, and the rusted skeletons of old shipping lines. The closer they got, the quieter everything became.

Victor checked the chamber on his pistol and slid it back into his coat like a ritual.

The urban sprawl of Jersey City gave way to industrial flats, gray and gutted, the kind of landscape that never really came alive.

The burner vibrated. Ghost.

Lucien opened it with one hand, thumb steady.

Touchdown confirmed. Linden airstrip. Hangar Six. Royce is on the ground. Multiple fed units in position. Hall's crew. Unmarked SUVs. Wide perimeter. It's real

Lucien said nothing. He passed the phone to Victor.

Victor read the message and let out a slow breath, like the tension had finally taken shape.

Lucien's voice dropped.

"Time to watch this break."

He dropped the hammer.

The Rezvani surged forward, tires biting pavement. They tore through the last stretch, steel and vengeance moving as one.

This wasn't arrival.

It was judgment.

The kind that didn't need a courtroom.

And Lucien wasn't here to whisper it.

He was here to see it drop.

They rolled up slow along the service road skirting Linden Airstrip, running dark and riding the edge of legal visibility. In the distance, movement. Trucks. Agents. Guns etched in silhouette. Hangar Six sat in the daylight like the final staging ground, steel and silence wrapped in federal precision.

Lucien brought them to a crawl, eyes locked on the jet staged outside Hangar Six, sleek, still warm from landing, stairs already down.

Victor leaned forward. "That him?"

Lucien didn't answer.

Up ahead, federal SWAT fanned out from the lead SUVs, rifles trained on the jet, moving like a black tide across the tarmac. Two agents broke formation and climbed the stairs, weapons drawn, while the rest held the perimeter.

No movement. No return fire. Just silence.

The agents disappeared inside.

Lena shifted beside him. Logan didn't move, fixed on the hangar like a child waiting to meet a nightmare dressed in his father's skin.

The agents reappeared alone.

One shook his head, already reaching for his radio.

Lucien's burner lit up.

Hall.

He answered on speakerphone with a calm he didn't feel. "Talk."

Hall's voice came through tight with frustration. "He's not here."

Lucien didn't blink. "Empty?"

"Ghost ship. Jet landed itself on a pre-programmed navigation loop. No Royce. No pilot. No fucking pulse."

Static crackled faintly through the line.

"No cockpit footage. Manifest's a joke. The whole thing was wired to fly blind. It was built to stall us."

Lucien kept his eyes on the hangar. "Any chance he was on and bailed?"

"Not a goddamn one. Whoever set this up made sure no one could track it."

The line went quiet.

Then Hall spoke again, lower now.

"You're not tracking him anymore. He's tracking you."

Lucien's hand tightened into a fist.

Hall's voice sharpened.

"Consider the deal broken. You're not off the hook, Cole. Matter of fact, you're federal bait. Until this piece of shit sticks his head out, you've got eyes all over you."

His voice dropped colder.

"Do yourself a favor. Don't go rogue. Don't play hero. Stay visible. Stay alive."

Lucien ended the call.

Royce had turned the whole operation into theater. Every second Lucien spent watching the stage was a second Royce spent moving unseen.

Victor slammed the seat with his palm. "Motherfucker!"

Lucien didn't even look up. He was already opening the burner, dialing Ghost.

The line clicked once.

Ghost's voice came through.

"Give me the update."

Lucien stared through the windshield. "Royce was never on the plane. Jet flew itself in on some kind of auto-nav assist. No manifest. No cockpit footage. Hall says it was built to stall us."

Ghost answered immediately. "Definitely built to waste your clock. Either remote-guided or paid hands, but that wasn't transport. That was misdirection."

Lucien said nothing for a moment.

"Yeah," Ghost added. "That tracks."

Lucien's voice dropped. "You got any eyes on air traffic out of São Vicente? Anything out of the ordinary?"

Ghost exhaled lightly. "As a matter of fact, yeah. About twelve minutes after the Gulfstream lifted off, a second bird took flight. Smaller jet. Different tail registry. No clearance flags. Didn't show on FAA radar until final approach, but I caught a relay ping and followed the shadow path. It mirrored the Gulfstream, then peeled off just before New York airspace."

Lucien straightened slightly. "Where'd it land?"

"Dropped just shy of Manhattan. Teterboro," Ghost said. "Didn't even ping local towers until it was breathing runway. Same setup as Linden. Quiet tarmac. No commercial traffic. No questions."

Lucien's eyes fixed on the fence line. "Send me what you've got."

Ghost was already moving. "On its way."

A second buzz lit the burner. New thread.

Lucien didn't read it. Not while the world was still pretending.

He ended the call and stared forward, every nerve pulled tight beneath the surface, like a wire stretched to the edge of snapping.

Royce wasn't coming. Royce had arrived.

The hunt had flipped.

Not through the front. Through the blind spot, exactly where he preferred to become real.

He hadn't escaped the net. He'd stepped inside it and pulled the door shut himself.

Now it was their turn to disappear.

A low gust rolled over the fence line. Dust kicked. Nothing moved.

Lucien finally looked down at the burner. The message from Ghost sat waiting, simple, unassuming.

IMAGE ATTACHMENT
TAIL NUMBER: N61VJ
ARRIVAL TIME: 08:46 AM, TETERBORO
CARGO: 2 CREW, 1 UNKNOWN MALE. NO CUSTOMS. VE-

HICLE PICKUP CONFIRMED
SOURCE: SATCOM RENDITION // PRIORITY FEED
CLEARANCE: LEVEL 4, EYES ONLY

He turned the screen toward Victor.

Victor studied it. "That's him?"

Lucien nodded once. "Yeah. Royce. Slipped right past us."

Not gone. Not hidden. Just closer than he had any right to be.

Lena leaned forward slightly. "Then what now? Do we go after him?"

Lucien's voice stayed low. Final. "No. We vanish for now. He wants chaos? Let him choke on it."

He started the engine. The Rezvani rolled back from the service road and turned away without rushing.

Victor glanced over. "Where we going?"

Lucien checked the mirror, eyes flicking to Logan in the back seat.

"Somewhere they won't find us. And somewhere he will."

Lena leaned toward him. "Hall told you to stay visible."

Lucien's mouth curved slightly.

"Hall thinks I'm federal bait? He can fucking choke on the hook."

This time, Lucien chose where it ended.

Chapter Forty-Six

BLOOD FOR BLOOD

They slipped back into the city, moving through traffic like something built not to be caught, shifting lanes, slipping past the lights.

Lucien drove with the skyscrapers sliding across the windshield. Victor rode behind him, one hand on his knee, the other close to the gun under his coat. Lena didn't speak. Logan barely breathed.

The war had gone still, and stillness was never mercy.

The burner lit against the console.

Lucien checked the screen, answered with one thumb, and put Ghost on speaker.

"You heading underground yet?"

Lucien kept his eyes on the road.

"I've been watching Royce's moves," Ghost continued. "And something clicked. He doesn't strike to kill. He dismantles. Strips away whatever makes you human. He hit your empire. Tried to tear your circle apart from the inside. Planted his own blood in your crew. And now he thinks his blood is on your hands."

Victor glanced forward. He knew where this was going.

"Which means there's one piece left," Ghost said. "One thread he hasn't cut."

Lucien said nothing.

Ghost didn't need him to.

"Lena."

Every war found the softest place left and called it leverage.

Lena sat up straighter, heart already quickening.

"You're not the bait anymore, Cole. She is."

Lucien's voice cut through the car. "No."

"I leak something," Ghost said. "Not loud. Just whispers in the right places. That you left her with someone. To protect her. To hide her. Royce sees that, and he doesn't just take the bait. He burns the trap trying to prove he still controls the board."

Victor nodded. "We get ahead of it. Set the trap ourselves."

Lucien found him in the rearview mirror. "You want to dangle her like raw meat?"

"She's not meat," Ghost said. "She's the only move that turns this from a chase into checkmate. She's your queen, Lucien. The only piece he can't ignore."

Victor leaned forward. "What if we take her to Corsini?"

Lucien turned slightly. "And what the fuck about that sounds smart to you?"

"Giancarlo respects power. And he respected your father. His kid acted like an asshole, you handled it, and he sent word after. That wasn't a war. It was a lesson."

Victor let that land.

"Royce thinks the Corsinis hate you. So imagine what he does when he finds out you forged a truce and left her with them."

Lucien shook his head. "Absolutely not. I'm not putting her in the hands of men we don't control."

"You don't control Royce either," Victor said. "At least with Corsini, we know the rules."

Lucien looked at Lena. "No one's asked what you want."

She reached for his hand and held it.

"I want to finish this."

His grip tightened.

"I'm not afraid," she said. "Not of Royce. Not of being seen. The only thing I'm afraid of is this never ending. I want you free, Lucien. I want us free."

She leaned closer.

"I'd rather risk my life for the future I believe in than hide while you keep bleeding for it alone."

Lucien didn't speak. He looked at her like she was the only thing anchoring him.

Ghost gave them a second before cutting back in.

"We set it right. Royce comes to burn her. Instead, we bury him."

Lucien shook his head.

"No. Royce doesn't die yet."

The truck went quiet.

"He stays breathing," Lucien said. "Hall needs him walking into cuffs."

He reached for the phone.

"I'll call Corsini. Set a sit-down."

Then he looked at Lena.

"We do this clean. Quick. And once he shows his face..."

He didn't finish.

Everyone understood the rest.

The trap was already in motion.

Lucien pulled beneath the West Side Highway and let the engine idle along the curb. The overcast sky pressed dull light through the windshield.

He dialed.

No greeting came. Just a low breath on the other end of the line, the sound of someone deciding whether the call deserved to exist.

Then:

"Took you long enough, Cole."

Lucien waited a moment before answering.

"You're not wrong, Giancarlo. I don't call unless it matters."

"And this matters?"

"I'm not asking for an alliance. I'm offering a move. One that pays both sides."

A quiet laugh moved through the receiver.

"You always were your father's son. Calculated. Arrogant when it counted."

"And you've always been the kind of man who doesn't move unless the stakes are worth it."

The line went quiet.

"Go on."

Lucien leaned back in the seat. The city went on breathing, unaware two men were redrawing territory.

"I need someone kept out of sight. Someone Alistair Royce would want badly enough to burn half the city to find."

"And you thought of me," Giancarlo said. "Last I remember, you put my son on the floor."

"Your son earned the floor. And you sent my father an apology for the inconvenience."

Giancarlo's tone hardened.

"I sent word to Alexander out of respect. Don't confuse that with forgiveness."

Lucien let that sit.

"So this woman," Giancarlo said. "This is your wife?"

Not small talk.

Stakes being weighed.

Lucien didn't hesitate. "Not yet."

A slow breath passed through the line.

"So you're asking me to protect something valuable."

"If Royce comes through your gates," Lucien said, "it means the trap worked. You become the house that held the queen while the king cleared the board."

Silence stretched.

"What do you offer for me to spit in the hand that kept me out of prison?"

"An end to bad blood. No more fences. No more cold shoulders. When this ends, we stop circling each other."

Another moment passed.

"You have twelve hours," Giancarlo said at last. "Bring her before dusk. She'll be protected as our own."

No house ever made a promise like that for free. It always expected the fire to owe it something later.

"Thank you," Lucien said.

"Don't thank me yet, Cole. Wars have a way of spreading. Make sure this one ends before it burns us all."

The line went dead.

Victor exhaled from the back seat.

"The board's set," he said quietly. "Now we see who bleeds first."

Later that afternoon, they drove in silence, the weight of dusk pressing down, slow and certain. The sun hung low, smearing the city in bronze and warning.

Lucien took the long way, not out of caution, but because he wasn't ready to let her go.

Lena sat beside him, eyes fixed forward, hands folded in her lap like she was holding something fragile. Maybe hope. Maybe grief.

Victor sat in the back with Logan, silent, watching the road like he was searching for something only he could see. No one spoke. Ghost had gone dark hours ago, setting the leak in motion.

The trap had been planted.

Timing was no longer in their control.

Lucien finally broke the silence. "You don't have to say anything."

Lena turned to him, her voice calm but threaded with fire. "That's good. I don't know how to say goodbye to a man who's still breathing."

He glanced at her, not long, but long enough. "It's not goodbye."

"Then say what it is."

His grip tightened on the wheel. "It's the last move standing between war and the life we deserve."

Lucien didn't say love.

His kind only admitted it when it was already being aimed at.

They reached the edge of the Corsini estate right before dusk.

The gates opened without delay, all iron and silence. Men with rifles stood at fixed points. Eyes forward. No nods. No ceremony.

A tall man in a tailored dark overcoat stepped onto the front drive. Black hair, lined face, cold posture.

Salvatore Corsini.

He didn't extend a hand. Didn't smile. Just looked from Lucien to Lena, then back again.

"If anything moves that shouldn't, you'll hear from us before it stops breathing."

Lucien held his gaze. "Royce doesn't die yet. I want him breathing."

Death was too easy.

Cuffs were heavier.

He stepped out of the car, walked around, and opened her door. Lena paused for one breath, then stepped out and looked back only once.

Lucien didn't speak.

He just nodded.

She returned it.

The estate doors closed behind her.

He stood there a moment, watching the last sliver of her disappear behind wrought iron and stone.

Men like him could take cities apart and still never learned how to watch one woman walk out of reach.

Then he turned, slid back behind the wheel, and pulled away, but not far.

Three blocks east, with dusk nearly gone and the streets thinning into shadow, he cut the headlights and killed the engine beside a closed loading bay.

Lucien patched his phone into the dash. The screen lit with a silent feed. Ghost had already tunneled into the estate's exterior surveillance grid.

Clean angles.

No sound.

Every approach covered.

Stone walls. Gates. Guards.

No movement.

No sign of Lena.

Still, she felt him somehow.

"We're not gone," Lucien said under his breath. "Just out of sight."

Victor stepped out, circled the truck, and slid into the passenger seat.

For a moment, neither of them spoke.

Then Victor shut the door. "So now what?"

Lucien kept his eyes on the feed. "Now we wait. And if Royce comes,"

He stopped himself.

"When Royce comes."

The car fell still.

Not empty.

Waiting.

Waiting was just another word for loaded.

Outside, the last light drained from the skyline.

Lucien opened his phone.

One unread message from Lena.

Still breathing. Still bored. It's too quiet in here. No one's tried to kill me yet. Starting to feel left out

His thumb hovered, then typed back.

Don't tempt fate. Quiet means it's working

Two minutes passed.

If you're watching me right now, just know I feel it

Lucien read it twice, and for a second, just a second, the war receded.

I never stopped

The screen dimmed.

No reply came.

From the backseat, a voice cut through the quiet.

"Can I speak?"

Victor didn't even turn. "No. Shut the fuck up."

Logan sat between shadows, hands folded in his lap. The smirk was gone. What was left looked worn out.

"Let him talk," Lucien said.

Logan leaned forward slightly, like the words had been sitting in his throat for too long.

"I never wanted it to end like this. The way you all move, the way you trust each other... that's not something I grew up around. You treat each other like blood. I never had that. Not once."

Lucien said nothing.

"I was born inside a cage. My father didn't ask what I wanted. He told me who I was. And I wore it even when it never fit."

Logan looked down at his hands.

"I don't expect redemption. Or trust. But if he dies, if my father burns, and I'm still breathing when it's over, all I'm asking for is a shot to be something else."

He leaned back.

"That's it."

Lucien looked ahead through the windshield.

No one spoke.

Then he unlocked his phone and tapped Ghost's number.

One ring.

The line opened.

"Talk," Lucien said.

"Your feed matches mine," Ghost said. "Exterior's dead still. No digital chatter. No ripple anywhere."

A pause.

"Too still, Lucien. No pings. No shadows. Feels like something moved, then stopped moving."

Lucien watched the camera feed. "Can you access interior?"

"Locked down. No cameras inside. We're blind past the fence. Keep your eyes up."

Lucien ended the call.

His gaze dropped to the phone again.

Lena still hadn't replied.

One second passed.

Then another.

Something in his gut tightened.

He typed.

Let me know you're okay. Say something

Delivered.

Read.

Typing.

The dots danced at the bottom of the screen.

She was replying.

Still typing.

Then they vanished.

A new message appeared.

Same thread.

Same number.

BLOOD FOR BLOOD

Lucien stared at the screen.

His body didn't move. His face didn't change. But something inside him ruptured, quiet and irreversible.

Victor leaned forward, voice cautious. "Was that her?"

Lucien didn't look up. "She was typing."

Victor's breath caught. "Then who the fuck hit send?"

Lucien's fingers closed slowly around the phone. "That wasn't her."

The silence in the truck shifted.

Not waiting anymore.

Deciding.

Victor's voice dropped. "It came from her number."

Lucien didn't blink. "Corsini fucking sold her."

Ghost's name cut across the dash screen.

Immediate.

Urgent.

Lucien answered. "They got her."

One breath came through the line.

"Motherfucker."

Ghost came back lower now, furious but focused.

"I was calling because the exterior feed felt off. I ran a timestamp cross-check. What you're seeing, the stone wall, the gate, the guards, it's the same movement every one hundred eighty seconds."

Lucien watched the looping feed. "You're telling me,"

"Yes. They looped the footage. Someone rerouted the estate surveillance on a three-minute delay. Just enough to look real, but dead underneath."

Lucien stared ahead. "They walked in under cover of stillness."

"And dragged her out the same way."

Silence hung on the line.

Then Ghost's voice changed.

Quieter.

"I've known you a long time, kid. I know your silence."

Another breath.

"It's scorched earth. We're gonna get her back."

The anger sharpened into purpose.

"I'm digging through the log headers now. If they didn't scrub it clean, I'll find the patch point. Someone rerouted the feed manually, which means they either spoofed it from inside or tunneled in remote."

Lucien didn't answer.

His fist stayed clenched around the phone.

"If it was internal," Ghost said, "they didn't just look away. They handed her over. And they knew you had someone like me patched in. That loop wasn't silence. It was a blindfold."

Lucien finally spoke.

"Then Corsini didn't sell her."

The line stayed quiet.

"He delivered her."

Ghost exhaled through his teeth. "I'll keep digging. There's always residue. Metadata. Packet trails. Something. Nobody walks into a fortress without leaving a trail behind."

Lucien ended the call.

No goodbye.

Just the low hum of the dashboard as the feed kept looping.

Stone wall.

Iron gates.

A world pretending to stand still.

But Lucien saw it now.

The stillness wasn't peace.

It was a lie, a mask over a stage already emptied.

Dusk was gone.

In the absence of light, something else began to assemble.

Victor rolled his neck, the tension finally breaking loose. "So what now? We gear up? Put together a crew? Drive straight through Corsini's gate and flatten every motherfucker breathing?"

Lucien kept his eyes forward.

"She's not there."

Victor frowned. "You're sure?"

"That estate was a curtain. She's already gone. He used her."

Victor leaned back slowly. "Corsini still bleeds for this."

"And they will," Lucien said. "Just not tonight."

Victor nodded once. "Tonight's about her."

The message still burned on the screen.

BLOOD FOR BLOOD

Victor spoke again, slower now.

"As fucked up as this sounds, her phone might be a line. A thread straight to Royce. What if he's waiting for us to answer?"

Lucien didn't reply.

His eyes stayed on the phone.

Victor's words echoed back through memory.

Her phone was a thread.

Then it hit.

That day.

Broad daylight. Her scream cutting through the speaker.

He'd shouted, "Turn on your location. Tell me exactly where you are."

A gasp.

Silence.

A van door slamming shut.

She was gone.

He remembered finding her phone facedown on the asphalt beneath a parked car.

But it hadn't been her phone that led him to her.

It had been Michael's.

And by then, Michael was already dead.

Lucien blinked.

The present slammed back into place.

He grabbed his phone and opened Find My.

There.

A dot.

Moving.

Love survived in details war forgot to kill.

"Bingo."

Lucien turned the screen toward Victor.

Victor leaned closer. "How the fuck'd you do that?"

"She's lived this before," Lucien said. "She left location on."

Victor let out a slow breath. "So whoever grabbed her's been broadcasting her the whole time."

Lucien nodded once.

"Or they left it on because they want us following."

He locked the phone into the dash.

His voice dropped.

"Then they just chose how they die."

The engine surged.

And they moved.

CHAPTER FORTY-SEVEN

THE SIGNAL THAT LIED

The city fell away behind them.

They drove like slowing down meant losing her forever. The Rezvani ripped up Ninth Avenue, threading between yellow lights and early-night traffic. Lucien's hands locked on the wheel, tension running from his grip through his shoulders and into his spine.

The phone sat synced to the dash. A single dot crawled across the screen. Lena.

Ghost came through the speakers. "Signal's alive. Upper Manhattan. Just cleared 112th. She's not slowing."

Victor said nothing. He rode shotgun, shoulders squared, pistol resting across his thigh like it had always belonged there.

In the backseat, Logan stared through the windshield like a man waiting to see which arrived first, God or the grave.

Silence filled the truck. No music. No conversation. Just the quiet men carried when the next hour might decide everything.

"Westchester," Ghost said. "She's flying. Highway speeds. Whatever she's in, it's built to move."

Lucien didn't take his eyes off the road.

They hit the Tappan Zee at just under ninety. Steel trembled beneath the tires as the Rezvani tore across the Hudson, the river below reduced to black motion and distance.

"She's past Rockland," Ghost said. "Just crossed into Bergen County. Signal's strong. You're closing, but you're still behind."

"How far?" Victor asked.

"Not seconds. Minutes."

Lucien pressed harder on the accelerator.

The engine roared. Lanes smeared into streaks of light. Exit signs flashed past like the highway was dragging them forward.

A pause.

"Lucien."

"Yeah."

"Signal stopped. Just now. Palisades Interstate Parkway, Exit 2. It's off-grid. No road label. Private. Looks like forest."

The dash washed the interior blue.

The dot wasn't blinking anymore.

It was waiting.

Lucien jerked the wheel.

The Rezvani dove off the exit, headlights cutting into darkness.

They merged onto 9W, winding through Alpine's dense stretch of woods. Trees pressed in on both sides, branches clawing at the night.

Then Lucien spotted it.

A narrow break in the dark.

He turned without hesitation.

Pavement gave way to gravel.

Gravel gave way to dirt.

The road twisted deeper into the trees like it had been carved for something that didn't want to be found.

Then the forest opened.

And there it was.

A cabin. One story. Dead center in the beams. Waiting.

Like it had her inside.

Or wanted him to think it did.

Lucien just stared.

They cut the headlights. Darkness swallowed the clearing. The engine ticked beneath them, hot metal cooling in the silence.

Ghost came back low and clinical, the kind of tone that never carried good news.

"Rerouted a patrol drone from a state grid. It's high above the tree line now. No visuals inside, but thermal's picking up residual heat. Fresh tire tracks, engine warmth near the door. Second set already cooling near the tree line. Someone brought her here, then moved her again. Heat's there, but it's vague."

Lucien kept his eyes locked ahead.

"Anything inside?" Victor asked.

"One faint source," Ghost said. "Static heat signature. Not moving. Could be the phone."

Lucien stared at the cabin. "It's fucking bait."

Victor didn't argue. He pulled his sidearm into view. "Doesn't mean we don't hit it."

Lucien turned slowly, eyes locking on Logan.

"Let's go."

Before he opened the door, Lucien tapped the comm live. Ghost's voice fed into the small earpiece clipped beneath his collar.

Doors opened, and boots hit gravel.

Lucien moved to the rear of the truck and popped the trunk. The hydraulic lift hissed open, revealing the rifle compartment built into the frame. He reached in, pulled a matte-black shotgun, and tossed it to Logan.

Logan caught it midair, eyes flashing confusion. "What?"

Victor stepped in. "Whoa, whoa, what the fuck are we doing?"

Lucien kept his stare fixed on Logan. "Giving him a chance at redemption."

Victor stiffened. "You're putting him on breach?"

"If Royce is watching, I want him to see exactly who kicked his door off the hinges."

Lucien stepped closer to Logan, voice low and direct.

"You go first. Blow the lock. Kick the door. We clear fast."

Logan nodded once, tight.

Lucien turned to Victor. "You've got rear flank. I'm with Logan."

Victor checked his pistol with a dry metallic clack. "Hope you know what you're doing."

"I do."

They moved.

Boots hit dirt. Fast, low, silent.

The cabin sat quiet at the end of the clearing, soaked in pale light, still as the grave.

Logan crept toward the front step, shotgun raised, barrel fixed on the deadbolt.

He looked back over his shoulder.

"Three. Two. One."

The blast ripped through the night.

The lock shattered. Wood split. Logan drove his boot into the door and sent it flying inward.

Lucien and Victor rushed past him with weapons raised, cutting angles through the entry, clearing corners, moving fast but controlled.

The lights inside were already on.

Too bright. Too clean.

Like the room had been staged before they ever touched the door.

A voice drifted from deeper inside, calm and low, almost conversational.

It didn't react to the breach, the blast, or the men sweeping its walls with guns drawn.

It just kept talking.

They moved in formation, Lucien ahead, Victor covering the rear, Logan tight behind them.

The hallway opened into a small kitchen.

Lena's phone sat facedown on the center of the table.

Screen dark.

Waiting.

Lucien stopped.

Beyond the kitchen, through the open archway, a flat-screen TV glowed blue in the living room.

The voice was coming from there.

Lucien's eyes lifted.

Above the screen, a small lens blinked red.

Recording.

Broadcasting.

Royce wasn't just talking.

He was watching.

Static cracked across the screen. Blue light flared, then sharpened into a live feed.

Royce stood in the frame like a ghost dressed in shadow, half-lit beneath a flickering bulb, his eyes bright with surgical calm.

Behind him was Lena.

She was bound to a chair, bruised and bloodied, but still radiant somehow, like a queen dragged from war and chained before an altar.

A wicked déjà vu twisted through Lucien's gut.

He saw another room. Another chair. Another night where he had arrived too late.

But Lena's chin was lifted.

Her fire was still there.

Unbroken.

The man they had chased through blood and betrayal had finally come to meet them, not in person, but on his terms.

Royce leaned closer to the lens, like he could smell blood through the glass. "Glad you could join us, Mr. Cole. I see you brought Mr. Dresnik with you as well."

Neither man spoke.

They just stared, like predators who knew the cage was real, but hadn't decided who was locked inside.

"Funny," Royce said. "I expected your father's son to come roaring through the gates with an army. With fire. With vengeance."

His smirk sharpened.

"But here you are. Just a couple strays, breathing heavy in my shadow. No battalion. No backup. Just your pride bleeding out in real time."

He turned slightly, running a hand through Lena's hair like it was a leash.

"You really thought you were hunting me. But all this time,"

He leaned into the camera.

"I've been hunting you."

Lena sat beneath the light, unmoving. Wrists bound. Hair damp and hanging.

She looked ghost-pale.

Alive by design.

Lucien didn't move. His hand lowered with the pistol, useless against a screen, while his breath began to thicken.

Royce stepped forward, face only half-lit. Calm. Predatory.

"You killed my son."

A slight shrug.

"Not that I mourned him. He served his purpose."

Then he smiled, an expression void of warmth.

"Blood still answers."

Lucien glanced at Logan, silent in the doorway, hidden just beyond the camera's reach, shotgun lowered.

One tear rolled down his cheek.

Lucien turned back to the screen.

Royce's tone shifted.

"And now, I want you to stand there and watch as I take the only thing you were ever capable of truly loving."

The camera zoomed in tighter.

Lena raised her head slowly. Her lip was split. One eye swollen. But her voice came clear.

"I love you, Lucien."

Royce raised the gun behind her.

Point-blank.

Lucien's body moved before thought could catch him. One step. Arm out. A useless reach toward a screen.

"Don't."

Royce smiled.

"Three."

The room vanished around him.

"Two."

Lucien's voice cracked open. "No."

Lena didn't look at Royce. She looked straight through the camera.

"One."

Click.

Empty chamber.

No shot.

Royce smiled like he'd fired anyway.

He stepped back, grinning like a man dissecting pain for pleasure.

"This wouldn't be any fun if I couldn't see the look on your pathetic face in the flesh. You know the one. When everything slips. When kings realize they're not gods."

"Let's make this interesting."

The screen pulsed. Static fuzzed the edges.

Royce didn't move. He just stared through the lens like it was a mirror.

"I left something for you. Think of it as a breadcrumb. Or a fuse."

He tilted his head slightly.

"You've got ten minutes to find it before the next piece of her disappears."

Victor stepped forward. "What the fuck does that mean?"

But Royce was already fading.

The screen dipped to black, then flared white.

A timer appeared.

09:59

09:58

Time didn't count down.

It pressed.

Lucien didn't move. Above the television, the camera kept blinking red, still feeding Royce every breath.

Logan understood first.

Not the timer.

The lens.

He stood half-hidden beyond the kitchen arch, just outside the camera's direct angle, the shotgun low in his hands. His face had gone pale. Whatever tears had been there a moment ago were gone now, burned out by something colder.

Lucien's eyes shifted once, not to the camera, but to Logan.

That was enough.

Logan moved along the wall, slow and silent, keeping his shoulder tight to the blind side of the room. Victor saw it and went still, understanding before anyone spoke.

The timer dropped.

09:19

09:18

Logan raised the shotgun.

The red light blinked.

BOOM.

The camera burst apart in a spray of plastic, sparks, and shattered glass.

The timer kept burning on the television.

Royce's eye was gone.

Ghost's voice snapped through Lucien's earpiece. "You just killed his eyes."

Lucien stared at the sparking hole above the television. "Good."

"No," Ghost said. "Not good. Drone's picking up movement."

Victor turned toward the window. "How many?"

For two seconds, only static answered.

Then Ghost came back sharper. "Tree cover's fucking with thermal. I have heat flickers north side. West line too. Wait,"

Glass punched inward, punctured clean.

A black coin of absence appeared in the kitchen window.

Then the round came.

It snapped past Lucien's temple and blew the cabinets apart behind him, wood cracking open, ceramic bursting, white dust and splinters blasting across the room.

Victor grabbed Logan by the collar and ripped him down.

"Contact!"

The cabin went to war.

The front windows blew inward in glittering sheets. Suppressed fire raked the room in savage lines, chewing through drywall, punching the table apart, kicking splinters off the beams. The timer kept burning on the television, clean white numbers in the chaos, counting down like judgment.

08:41

08:40

Lucien dropped behind the kitchen island as rounds shredded the cabinets over his head. A jar burst beside him, spraying sugar into the air with the glass. It caught the television light for half a second and came down like white ash.

Victor rose into the storm and fired through the ruined window.

Muzzle flash turned his face into something carved from brass and fury.

Outside, shadows broke and scattered across the porch. Low. Fast. Trained. One body dropped behind the rail, but another shape cut along the west side of the cabin, moving beneath the windows.

A burst tore through the hanging light above the sink.

It popped in a shower of sparks.

Half the kitchen fell into violent flicker.

Logan hit the floor hard, breath punched out of him, shotgun clutched to his chest while glass and wood chips rained over his back.

Ghost cut through Lucien's earpiece. "Three on the north approach. Maybe four. One moving to the rear. They moved the second the camera went dark."

"They were always here," Lucien said.

"Yeah," Ghost answered. "And I saw them too late."

Another round cracked through the wall behind Logan.

He flinched, instinct dragging him lower.

Victor shoved him toward the hallway. "You want redemption? Start shooting back."

Logan looked down at the shotgun like it had turned into a verdict.

The front door buckled under another burst. Wood jumped from the frame. Victor fired twice, driving someone off the porch, then dropped as a line of rounds carved over him and tore through the far wall.

Lucien rose just enough to catch movement through the blown-out front window.

A black mask. A rifle. A shoulder turning toward Victor.

Lucien fired.

The man vanished from the frame without a scream, only the heavy sound of his body hitting wood.

"Rear!" Ghost snapped.

The back door kicked open, and a man in black came fast through the mudroom, weapon raised, face covered, eyes dead behind clear lenses.

Logan turned.

Too slow.

Victor was still exposed at the front window. Lucien was pinned behind the island.

For half a second, Logan froze.

The man swung the rifle toward Victor.

Then Logan's face changed.

Not brave. Not clean.

Something meaner.

Survival.

He ripped the shotgun up and fired from the hip.

The blast detonated in the mudroom.

Buckshot tore through the man's chest and throat in a wet red burst, slamming him backward into the wall hard enough to spiderweb the plaster. Blood sheeted across the paneling. His rifle flew from his hands and skidded wild across the tile.

Smoke curled from the barrel in Logan's hands.

He stood there shaking, speckled with blood, still holding the gun like he hadn't decided yet whether he'd fired it or survived it.

Victor's voice came rough. "Again."

Logan pumped the shotgun.

The pump sounded ugly and right.

Lucien moved.

He crossed low through the kitchen as another burst shredded the window above him. Glass cut through the air where his head had been. He reached the dead man in the mudroom, stripped the rifle from his hand, and tossed it toward Victor.

Victor caught it, checked the chamber, and smiled without warmth.

"Now we're talking."

07:32

07:31

The timer kept burning.

Ghost came back sharp. "Two closing front. One west window. Rear looks clear for now."

"For now?" Victor snapped.

"Tree canopy. You want a prayer, call a priest."

A shadow crossed the west glass.

Lucien saw it.

Not the man.

The brief eclipse of moonlight sliding across the wall.

He fired through the wood before the merc reached the window.

The round punched through paneling, flesh, and spine in one clean line.

Outside, something choked.

Then came the sound of a body folding wrong, hitting the siding, smearing blood across the boards before collapsing out of sight.

Victor gave him one quick look.

Lucien was already moving.

"He left something. Find it."

Victor stared at him like he was insane. "We're being shot at."

"We're bleeding time."

They split without discussion.

Victor held the front, firing controlled bursts through broken glass, forcing the men outside to stay low. Every shot had purpose. Every pause was bait. He moved like the room belonged to him now, using the dark between muzzle flashes to turn the cabin into a kill box.

Logan stayed near the hallway, shotgun shaking in his grip, watching the rear door like the dead might get back up.

Another shape appeared beyond the porch.

Victor fired, the glassless window flashing white.

A body dropped out of view.

The cabin breathed smoke, pine, hot metal, and blood.

The timer kept counting.

06:58

06:57

Lucien tore through the kitchen while the walls came apart around him. Drawers hit the floor. Cabinets flew open. Plates shattered beneath his boots. He ripped at the underside of the table with both hands, searching for wires, tape, anything.

Nothing.

Only Lena's phone.

Facedown.

Waiting.

His chest tightened at the sight of it.

Then he saw the chair.

Not the one near the table, but the one pushed slightly back from the wall.

Its legs had scraped fresh lines into the floor.

Lucien crossed to it.

A strip of duct tape clung to the back leg, with dark hair caught in the edge.

Lena's.

His breath stopped.

Beside it, a small smear of blood had dried into the floorboards.

Not enough to kill.

Enough to promise pain.

The whole room narrowed to that strand of hair and the blood beneath it.

She had been here.

Not as a signal. Not as theater.

Real.

Lucien touched the tape with two fingers.

Careful.

Almost gentle.

Then the window nearest the chair blew inward.

A merc came through shoulder-first, rolling over broken glass with a blade in one hand and a compact rifle in the other.

Lucien snatched the chair and drove it into his face before the rifle came up. Wood cracked. The man hit the floor hard. Lucien went down with him, one knee crushing his wrist, pistol jammed under his jaw.

"Where is she?"

The merc breathed hard through the mask.

"Lucien!" Victor shouted from the front room as rounds hammered the opposite wall.

The man tried to twist free.

Lucien drove the barrel higher, angling it up into his skull.

"Where?"

The man's eyes flicked toward the hallway.

Lucien saw it.

He fired.

The shot blew through the top of the man's head and painted the wall behind him.

Lucien rose and moved for the hall.

06:21

06:20

Logan backed away as Lucien passed him.

"What did he look at?"

"The hallway."

"There's nothing back there. I checked."

Lucien didn't slow. "Then check like a man who wants her alive."

Victor's voice carried from the front. "More headlights!"

Ghost cut in. "One vehicle pulling up at the road mouth. Not entering yet. Blocking you in."

The hallway was narrow, cheap wood paneling closing in on both sides.

First bedroom. Empty mattress, bare frame, curtains nailed shut.

Second. A cracked mirror and a folded tarp.

Bathroom. Rust in the sink, mud in the tub.

Nothing.

The timer bled through the walls from the living room.

05:48

05:47

Logan's breathing had gotten louder.

Lucien turned on him. "Look at me."

Logan did.

"This is your father's work. Not his men. His."

Logan swallowed.

Memory crossed his face, ugly and old.

"He never leaves anything where it belongs."

Lucien held his stare.

"Keys. Files. Phones. Evidence. He used to make people tear rooms apart while it sat under something too heavy to question."

A burst of gunfire ripped through the front room.

Victor cursed.

Lucien looked past Logan.

One narrow door remained at the end of the hall.

He crossed to it and shoved it open.

Storage room.

Dust. Damp insulation. Old tools stacked along one wall.

And in the corner, a rusted woodstove sat squat and black, its pipe stopping an inch short of the ceiling like the whole thing had only been staged to look permanent.

Too heavy to question.

Lucien pointed. "Move it."

Logan set the shotgun down and grabbed one side.

Lucien took the other.

They dragged the stove, and it screamed across the floorboards.

Underneath, a fresh square cut scarred the floorboards.

Lucien dropped to one knee and pried it open with his knife.

Inside was a small black steel case.

Red light blinking on one side.

05:09

05:08

Victor appeared in the doorway, rifle in hand, face streaked with smoke and glass dust.

"You better tell me that's it."

Lucien took the case.

From outside, the shooting stopped.

Ghost came back in his ear. "Road mouth's clearing. Vehicle's reversing out."

Victor frowned. "They're retreating?"

Lucien stared at the blinking red light. "They were only here to burn the clock."

He carried the case into the living room.

The timer kept counting.

04:22

04:21

Logan followed, shotgun back in his hands. He looked toward the ruined camera mount, then toward the bodies, then at the case.

For the first time, he didn't look like Royce's son.

He looked like someone standing in the ashes of that name.

Lucien set the case on the table beside Lena's phone.

The room smelled like gunpowder, pine, blood, and burned wiring.

He cracked the latch with slow, steady pressure.

Inside was a burner phone.

The screen lit up, one file already open.

Lucien tapped it.

A map blinked to life, centered on a single dot.

Coordinates.

Then Royce filled the room again, recorded this time. Calm. Cruel.

"Let's see how far love can really run, Mr. Cole. You buried your past behind lock and stone. Now dig it up, or lose what's yours."

Lucien stared at the screen.

The coordinates didn't just point to a place.

They pointed backward.

Victor lowered the rifle. "Where to?"

Lucien didn't answer right away.

The name sat behind his teeth like something rotten.

Then he said it.

"To a past I buried."

The house stood still.

The war didn't.

It had just been given somewhere to go.

Chapter Forty-Eight

THE GRAVE THAT WOKE

Half an hour later, they rolled to a stop, gravel crunching under the tires as the headlights swept across rusted iron gates hanging open like jaws. Beyond them, a cemetery stretched into darkness, the headstones fading beyond the reach of the high beams.

Victor stared out the window. "What the fuck is this place?"

Lucien kept his gaze forward. "StoneHaven."

From the backseat, Logan leaned forward. "Gates are open. Guess that's our invitation."

Victor turned to him. "So we're just rolling into this? No backup? No clue what the fuck we're up against?"

Lucien's voice stayed calm, low. "If we pull up mobbed out, he'll kill Lena for sure."

Victor exhaled through his nose. "So we just walk in blind?"

"I have a plan."

Lucien reached into the console, pulled a sidearm, and turned to Logan. "You wait here. Stay sharp."

He tossed the pistol. Logan caught it, hesitated. "What am I watching for?"

"Anyone that's not us."

Victor opened his door. The cold met them fast.

Together, he and Lucien stepped out, moving through the gate on foot. The cemetery opened around them, rows of headstones half-buried in mist, moonlight leaking through the tangled branches above in thin strips.

Every few feet the wind carried strange noises. Distant birds. Low animal sounds. Something harder to place.

Lucien took out his phone and dialed. The line clicked, then Ghost came through.

"Talk."

"We're here. StoneHaven. It was the location on the burner."

"Where's the kid?"

"In the truck. He's staying back."

A beat of static. "Smart."

Lucien scanned the rows of graves, as if something might rise from them. "There was a case at the cabin. Steel box. Red light. Inside was the burner with one file and a set of coordinates."

"That's how he's moving you."

"Yeah."

Then Lucien added, "Do me a favor. I'm sending you a list of instructions. Follow them. I pushed your transfer earlier, it should clear tonight."

Ghost said, "I'll handle it. Talk to you soon, or see you on the other side."

Lucien looked out across the cemetery. It stretched like a forgotten world. "Talk soon."

Victor adjusted his grip and scanned the shadows between the headstones. "You ever feel like you're seeing shit?" he muttered. "Something moving at the edge of your vision. Like you're being watched."

Lucien kept walking. "Could be paranoia. We don't know what we're walking into. Could be someone out there watching us."

He glanced sideways.

"Or the dead."

Victor stopped cold.

Lucien smirked. "Move."

Victor exhaled sharply. "Not funny."

"How far are we?" he asked after a beat.

Lucien looked through the trees ahead. "Close. Listen. When we reach it, hang back. Stay near the trees."

Victor shook his head. "No way. I've got your back."

"Exactly." Lucien stopped. "If you come with me, nobody's watching ours. I need eyes in the dark. And if this bastard wants my life for hers..."

He shrugged once. "I'll pay it."

Love always sounded simplest right before it asked for blood.

Victor studied him for a moment. "You really love her, don't you?"

Lucien didn't hesitate.

"I do. She's the only heaven I've ever believed in, and I'll drag hell behind me to reach her. No hesitation."

He looked up through the branches. "Crazy thing is, it happened fast. But it never felt random. It felt inevitable. Like I was already hers before we ever met. And she's spent every day since proving it wasn't coincidence."

Victor glanced sideways. "Earlier you said you buried your past out here.

What did you mean?"

Lucien slowed.

"There's a grave behind this bend I swore I'd never stand over again."

Victor frowned. "So why the hell would Royce bring us here?"

Lucien's expression hardened.

"Because he knows my story better than he should."

A breath passed between them.

"And if he dragged us to StoneHaven, he's planning theatrics. Something symbolic. He wants this to hurt before it ends."

Victor shook his head. "Christ."

Lucien kept moving.

"Stay sharp. Whatever he's staging, we're walking straight into it."

They followed the path until it bent, then stopped.

There it was. The same black-marble crypt Lucien hadn't seen since the day he swore he'd never return, framed by two stone pillars, weather-worn and rooted like a wound in the earth.

Around it, the same mausoleums stood where they always had, forsaken monuments to stone and silence. Angel statues loomed between them, chipped and crumbling, their faces hollow, wings broken at the joints. Latin inscriptions faded along the walls like prayers time had stopped answering.

Victor's voice dropped to a whisper. "This is it, isn't it?"

Lucien didn't answer. His eyes stayed locked on the crypt.

Something was wrong.

The crypt doors hung open, just slightly ajar, like someone had slipped inside or left in a hurry.

Lucien's jaw tensed. "They were shut when I left. I locked them myself."

He stepped forward, slow, like something ancient had just stirred beneath the stone.

Victor moved with him.

Lucien held out a hand. "Wait here. Watch the tree line."

Victor narrowed his eyes. "You're sure about this?"

Lucien nodded once. "If this is what he wanted, me alone, then let's give him what he asked for."

He broke into the clearing, footsteps crunching across sacred ground.

Lucien's hand brushed his coat pocket. The burner was already warm.

He faced the crypt and raised his voice, not cracked or broken, just furious.

"Royce! Come out, you fucking coward!"

His echo danced off stone and silence.

"This is what you wanted, right!? This is how you wanted it played out?"

He stepped closer, hands at his sides, every muscle wired and waiting.

"Me in the fucking flesh. By myself. Face to face."

His voice dropped to a growl. "Show yourself."

BOOM.

A floodlight erupted, white and violent, carving Lucien's silhouette into the earth.

BOOM.

Another.

BOOM.

A third, sealing him in a triangle of synthetic light.

And there she was.

Lena, strapped to a metal chair in the grass. Arms pinned behind her, ankles bound. Duct tape over her mouth, streaked with blood.

Tears carved clean lines through the dirt on her cheeks.

Her eyes locked on his, full of panic and hope, and a muffled scream tore behind the tape.

Lucien surged toward her.

"Lena."

"Easy now, Mr. Cole. Let's not be so predictable."

A voice slid out of the dark, not echoed, not elevated. Just there. Close. Too close.

"One more step and she bleeds. Let's not ruin the show before it starts."

A shadow peeled itself from the edge of the light, step by step, calm and deliberate, until the face was no longer a myth, but a man.

Royce.

A smile touched one side of his mouth. Dead eyes. Measured stillness.

"Welcome to the reckoning."

"Fitting place, isn't it? Cemeteries tell the truth. Everyone ends up quiet. Everyone ends up equal. Even kings."

He stepped closer, pacing with the calm of a surgeon.

"You built yourself a throne out of fear and called it an empire. That's why you'll never understand me."

He nodded toward Lena, tied in the grass.

"This isn't revenge. Revenge is for men who still believe in fairness."

His eyes found Lucien again, sharp and unblinking, as he stopped pacing.

"This is education."

He lifted a hand, counting each truth like scripture.

"You can take money from a man. He earns it back.

You can take power. He steals it back."

A small smile ghosted across his face.

"But you take the one person he cannot replace, and you own him forever."

"Legacy isn't what you leave behind."

"It's what you make people do while you're still breathing."

The tripwire at Lena's ankle caught the light.

Then Royce's smile sharpened.

His gaze flicked to the wire at Lena's ankle.

"And tonight, Mr. Cole, I'm going to make you choose."

Lucien froze mid-step.

His fists clenched at his sides, rage flooding him so fast it felt like poison.

Royce paced forward with a predator's grace.

Royce tilted his head, eyes scanning Lucien like he was a specimen on a slab. "You look good. Tighter around the eyes. A little less god in your walk. That's what grief does. Sharpens the edges, dulls the shine."

Lucien didn't speak.

His eyes stayed on Lena.

Still tied. Still gagged. Her body trembling, but her stare never broke from his.

Royce followed the glance.

"Beautiful, isn't she? Funny. I thought I'd have to drag you here in pieces. But all it took was her."

One corner of his mouth lifted.

"You came crawling."

Lucien stepped forward once. "Don't."

Royce raised a single finger.

"She's on a tripwire. You cross the mark, she chokes on steel. Just like that."

"What the fuck do you want?"

Royce took another step.

"I want what I've always wanted. Balance. You tipped the scale, Lucien. Killed my son."

Lucien didn't move. "You used him. Treated him like a pawn. You don't get to grieve that."

Royce stopped walking.

Something colder settled into his face.

"Like I said." A faint smile returned. "Blood is blood."

"You of all people should understand that. Cole blood doesn't wash off."

Lucien shook his head slowly.

"You came after me. After Victor. After Lena. After everything I built."

"You built it on bones!"

Royce's voice rose now.

"You burned empires. Dismantled legacies. And for what? Some idea of clean hands? Love? Don't kid yourself, boy. You're no better than me. You just dress your monsters prettier."

Lucien looked down for half a second.

Then he raised his head.

"You came all this way to die."

Royce smiled.

"Maybe."

His gaze shifted past Lucien. "But not alone."

He motioned behind him.

From the shadows, a second figure stepped forward.

A woman.

Lucien's world cracked.

No. It couldn't be.

She moved like the earth itself hadn't felt her weight in years, her silhouette pulling free of the gloom, heels brushing dead leaves, a long black coat trailing behind her. Then she stepped fully into the light.

Dark hair. Storm-gray eyes. The face he once swore to love until death, lit now by the same brutal floodlight holding Lena in chains. Eyes Lucien knew. Lips he once kissed like promises.

The woman he buried.

Isabelle.

Alive.

Lena let out a muffled scream behind the tape.

Lucien stepped back like the ground had vanished beneath him.

"What's wrong, Cole?" Amusement curled through Royce's voice. "You look like you've seen a ghost."

Royce let the silence stretch, savoring it.

"Then again, family has a way of coming back."

Lucien didn't move.

Couldn't.

The air felt fragile, like one wrong breath would split the moment open.

Royce turned his head slowly and looked down at Lena, still bound to the chair, her chest rising in short, frantic breaths.

Then he smiled, that same thin, poisonous smile.

"Let me introduce you." He looked back at Lucien. "My daughter."

Isabelle stepped beside him.

Her eyes locked on Lucien.

No tears. No warmth. Only something old and fractured behind them.

Not dead. Not the woman he remembered. Something else.

Lucien stared like he was watching his past burn in real time.

"Isabelle..." The word barely made it out. Half breath. Half prayer.

She didn't blink.

Didn't flinch.

Behind her, Royce folded his hands like a preacher before judgment.

"She was mine long before she was yours."

"You just borrowed her."

A thin smile returned.

"A performance. And she played it beautifully."

"I loved you."

A flicker passed through Isabelle's eyes.

Almost something.

Then it vanished.

She tilted her head. Almost apologetic.

"I know."

Lucien's hands curled into fists. "Was any of it real?"

Isabelle's eyes held his. "I didn't fake my death to hurt you. I did it to save you."

Royce stepped forward, his smile coiled tight.

"Lie to him again, sweetheart. Let's make this last."

Lucien took one step.

Royce raised a hand.

No words.

Just the warning.

Another inch and Lena dies.

Isabelle's voice hardened.

"You were never supposed to matter. You were a mark. That's how it started. But something changed."

She looked at him.

"I saw who you were beneath the violence. The man you kept trying to bury."

A quiet breath.

"And I loved him."

Lucien's voice cracked. "Then why didn't you stay?"

She looked at him like the answer carried a weight she could barely hold.

"Because loving you put a bullet on your name."

Her eyes shifted toward Royce.

"And he never misses."

"You were a threat," she continued. "To his control over me. To the life

445

he planned."

Her voice dropped. "When I defected, he didn't see heartbreak. He saw treason. So he gave me a choice."

Her eyes returned to Lucien. "Disappear, or watch you die."

Royce smiled.

Lucien turned toward him, his stare cutting through the light.

"All your power. All your control."

A step closer.

"And still, you couldn't stop one thing."

Royce tilted his head.

Lucien's voice went cold.

"She chose me."

Something shifted in Isabelle's face.

And Royce's smile cracked.

Only slightly.

But Lucien saw it.

And held on.

Isabelle's voice softened, just enough to sound human again.

"There's one thing I never understood."

Her eyes moved to Lena.

"Not how I chose to love you, even when you chose your world over me."

Isabelle hesitated, something tightening behind her eyes.

"But how you chose her."

Lena sat tied to the chair. Bleeding. Defiant.

"You would risk your crown for her. Jeopardize everything you built."

She stepped closer.

"From the shadows I watched you. Not just survive. Transform."

Her voice lowered.

"I don't understand what she is. What she has. What makes her so intoxicating to you."

Lucien's breath ignited.

"It was you. You were the one behind the texts."

He took a step forward. "You stalked her. You rattled her. You dragged chaos to her door."

His voice cracked open. "You caused all of this."

He pointed toward Royce.

"You and that piece of shit standing next to you."

His voice sharpened.

"He murdered innocent people in Miami. At Midnight Club. Just to punish my partner for standing with me."

"He orchestrated the seizures in Newark just to bleed a threat that only existed inside his warped, delusional mind."

Isabelle didn't deny it.

Her voice came smaller now.

"Yes."

"And I'm sorry."

Her eyes held wreckage.

"If I exposed myself too soon, if I appeared at the wrong moment, what would that have done to you?"

She turned slowly.

"But I'm standing here now."

Royce stepped forward. "First of all, I'm not sorry. All's fair in love and war."

Royce lifted a finger, like structuring a sermon.

"And second." He smiled, like the devil making room at the table. "I stand here now with an offer."

Lucien let out a short breath. "An offer?"

"Yes. Isabelle's life, for hers." He gestured toward Lena, tied to the chair, like it was arithmetic.

"One thing you were right about, Lucien. My need for control. It's been a weakness."

The smile sharpened.

"But I'm learning."

He looked between Lena and Isabelle.

"Family, real family, can't be ruled. It has to be shared."

He began to pace. Calm. Intentional.

"I forgive you for Logan. I forgive you for the disobedience. For the insolence. For the story you built for yourself about me."

He stopped.

"Because I see the future."

His eyes lit, feral and unholy.

"I offer you a kingdom greater than the one you're burning in.

Power that makes politicians beg for permission to exist.

And that's just the ground floor of what's coming. The world is rearranging itself, Lucien. You can kneel early or get crushed late."

His voice warmed, almost reverent.

"You think power lives in city halls and courtrooms? That's the surface. The real architects don't sit in government, Lucien. They tilt governments. They don't report the news; they write the mood of entire nations. They lean on markets until currencies kneel. They whisper into the ears of men who believe they run countries and remind them they're temporary."

He stepped closer, as if sharing a secret with destiny itself.

"There are hands above the world, and they're building something new. A structure. A doctrine. A House fit for a new era. And they're watching for the ones who can shape it."

Royce's eyes narrowed, almost disappointed.

"You think Isabelle was random?"

He took another slow step.

"Men like you don't happen by accident, Lucien. Not with your mind. Not with the way people follow you. Fear you. Need you."

His voice lowered.

"You were supposed to become something greater than a king with a bleeding heart."

His gaze flicked toward Lena.

"And then you fell in love."

Royce turned to Lucien, eyes like flame behind glass. "All you have to do is let go. Take back what you lost."

Lucien's grin cracked the tension wide open. "Just like that, huh?"

Royce tilted his head, amused.

Lucien nodded toward Lena. "We remove her from the equation, and suddenly we're all just one big happy fucking family?"

He took a slow step forward. "Life doesn't work like that. Love sure as hell doesn't."

Then he turned to Isabelle, eyes hard. "You expect me to just fall in love with you again? You were a chapter I mourned. She's the whole goddamn book."

Another step brought him fully into the light. "Lena is the life I choose."

Isabelle flinched.

Royce's smile flattened.

Lucien stepped closer to the barrel. "Pull the trigger if you came to. But don't mistake me for a man who can be bargained out of love."

His eyes didn't leave Royce's.

"I'd rather die facing you than live as the man who gave her up."

He drew a deep breath, almost calm. "Without her, everything stops."

Royce's grin twitched into something uglier.

"Then let's test that theory."

He raised his gun.

Pointed it straight at Lena's head.

Lucien's eyes widened.

His hand dove for his pistol.

CRACK.

A single shot split the night.

Royce screamed.

Half his hand was gone.

The pistol clattered to the stone like a bone torn from its owner.

He stumbled back, blood slicking the marble at his feet.

From the shadows, Victor stepped into the light.

Eyes locked. Gun still smoking.

"Told you. I've got your back, partner."

"Dad!" Isabelle screamed, dropping beside Royce.

He clutched his ruined hand. Blood spilled between his fingers as he howled.

She cradled him, shaking.

"Dad, stay with me. Just breathe. Please, just..."

Her eyes snapped to the pistol Royce had dropped.

Trembling fingers reached for it.

Lena screamed through the tape, thrashing in the chair.

Muffled. Desperate.

Lucien's pulse surged. "Isabelle," he warned, taking a half-step forward.

She gripped the pistol.

Turned.

Eyes wild. Heart broken.

"If you can't love me, then no one can love you, Lucien Cole."

She raised the gun, hands shaking.

BANG.

A shot rang out from the dark. Isabelle's chest snapped backward, blood bursting from her sternum. She gasped once.

BANG.

Another slammed through her ribs and dropped her to her knees.

BANG.

A third ripped through her shoulder. Her body tilted.

CRACK.

The final shot went straight through her skull, and she collapsed over Royce's still-screaming body.

A shape separated from the dark, and heads turned as Logan stepped into the light, gun raised, eyes stone, the barrel still burning.

Royce lay sprawled at the crypt's opening, clutching what remained of his hand, blood leaking through his fingers.

He barely noticed as Lucien dropped to his knees beside Lena.

Lucien tore the duct tape from her mouth and worked the knots around her wrists, fast and shaking. Then his fingers found the collar at her throat, a taut filament running from it like a noose to a trigger behind the chair.

He snapped the filament with his teeth, tore the collar open, and ripped it away. Lena's breath came back in ragged pulls as the metal threat fell slack.

She collapsed into him, clinging like he was the last thing in the world still real.

"It's okay. I've got you. I'm right here."

Logan stepped forward.

Gun raised.

Face unreadable.

Royce blinked up, dazed. "Logan…"

His voice cracked. Gnarled. "You, my own son."

Logan stopped above him. "I was never your son."

His voice cut like steel. "You didn't raise a man. You built a weapon."

Royce's lip curled. "You betrayed me, your blood. Your father!"

Lucien stepped in.

Pistol drawn. Expression cold as ice.

"We staged his death. You really thought that cartel photo wasn't fake? You watched it. You believed it. That was the point."

He loomed over Royce now, like judgment incarnate.

"We could've killed him when we found out who he was. But we didn't. We gave him a choice."

"And he chose us."

Logan stepped closer. Looked Royce in the eye.

"You said blood still answers. But blood doesn't make family."

A low thrum built in the air, distant and rising, until it became the unmistakable chop of helicopter blades tearing through the night. Royce's eyes flicked skyward as headlights flared from both sides, sweeping across the cemetery hills.

Dozens of black SUVs and tactical vans barreled in, tires screeching, gravel kicking skyward, red and blue lights strobing across angel statues and broken tombs.

Lucien pulled the burner from his jacket and raised it high.

The chopper crested the treeline.

Its spotlight hit them like divine judgment.

The loudspeakers boomed:

"FBI! DROP YOUR WEAPONS! HANDS WHERE WE CAN SEE THEM!"

In the distance, Agent Hall emerged from his vehicle.

Tactical vest. Rifle slung. Agents flanking him in tight formation.

SWAT stormed in behind him, fast and focused, rifles leveled.

Royce blinked against the light.

Lucien knelt beside him, just close enough to be final.

"The FBI heard everything, Royce." Lucien held up the burner. "Your confession. Your plans. Every word. Live."

He crouched beside him, voice low and measured. "And your digital empire? You thought it was gone. Thought your secrets died with the servers. But we pulled them. Everything. Before the burn."

He leaned in closer.

"Extracted it to an SSD. Transferred it. Then turned the rest to ash."

Lucien rose, standing over him now.

"Your empire wasn't buried, Royce. We gift-wrapped it for the fucking feds."

Royce stared up at him.

Lucien's voice dropped to a whisper.

"Your story ends here."

Royce opened his mouth,

Lucien cut him off.

"You watched your daughter die. You watched your legacy rot. And worst of all," Lucien nodded to Logan, "you watched your own blood bury you."

Logan stepped forward.

Spit, hard, into Royce's face.

Royce flinched, blinking blood and spit from his eyes.

"DO NOT FIRE!" Agent Hall's voice tore through the chaos like a blade.

SWAT surged forward.

Boots thundered. Lights flared. Orders flew.

Royce didn't move. His empire was gone, his daughter was dead, and his last card had just walked away.

Agent Hall appeared beside them, helmet tucked under one arm, vest still dusted in stone and night. His eyes swept the carnage, the blood, the broken crypt, and the body slumped in the dirt like discarded history.

"Christ." He looked from Royce to Isabelle. "You always throw this kind of party, Cole?"

Lucien didn't smile.

He just stood there, chest rising slow.

"I told you we'd bring him in."

Hall nodded once. Solemn.

"You did more than that. You buried the son of a bitch."

He looked toward the perimeter, where agents swarmed with forensic bags and spotlights.

Hall shook his head, almost in disbelief.

"We've got enough here to bury him in every courtroom from D.C. to The Hague. Wiretaps, video evidence, GPS triangulation, hell, that SSD alone reads like a blueprint for organized hell."

He glanced toward the chaos behind them.

"You know what's crazy? Royce didn't just run drugs and rackets. He was an arms broker back in the Cold War days. Fed conflict zones from the Balkans to the Congo. Moved weapons by the container load, sometimes with state-level blinders on. We've been chasing shadows of his shell corps for decades."

He looked back at Lucien, eyes sharp.

"What you just handed us, it's not just the end of a criminal empire. It's a reckoning. And a few people in Geneva, Langley, and The Hague are going to lose sleep tonight."

Lucien's eyes flicked toward Royce, who was being strapped into a gurney.

He didn't fight it.

"He tried to rewrite the world."

"But the world doesn't forget."

Hall looked at him. Searched his face. "You alright?"

Lucien didn't answer right away. He glanced back toward Lena where Victor held her close, his jacket around her shoulders, murmuring something human.

"I will be. But not tonight."

Hall turned, started to walk, then paused. "You should know, this doesn't erase your past. It doesn't buy you sainthood."

Lucien's gaze didn't move. "I'm not looking for redemption."

Hall raised a brow. "Then what are you looking for?"

"Peace."

Then Hall muttered, "Let's get the devil behind bars," and turned toward the agents. "And maybe, just maybe, we can put this nightmare to fucking bed."

A few minutes later, they stood beside the open ambulance.

Lena sat inside, a medic gently checking her bruises and cuts.

Lucien glanced sideways at Logan, a ghost of a grin tugging at his mouth. "Thought I told you to wait in the truck."

Logan looked sheepish, then matched the expression. "Something felt off. Had to have your back, boss."

Lucien raised a brow. "Boss, huh? You think you're back in?"

Victor stepped in, shaking his head, half laughing. "C'mon, Lucien. Kid just murdered his own psycho sister to save your ass."

Lucien turned to Logan again, expression sharpening.

"Let me get this straight. The woman I buried and once thought I loved was your sister, and your father is the man who tried to kill me and torch everything I've ever built."

Logan swallowed. "Half-sister."

Victor blinked. "What?"

Logan shrugged. "I said half-sister. I hated that crazy bitch."

"Stop." Lucien raised a hand. Then extended it. "You're good."

Logan hesitated, then shook it.

Lucien gripped firm. "Go grab the truck. I'm not walking back through this goddamn cemetery."

Logan nodded and turned.

"Oh, Logan."

He paused.

Lucien's grin returned, cold, casual, unreadable.

"You get one last life with us. Don't spend it wrong." Lucien's grip tightened just enough to hurt. "You ever betray me again, I'll slit your fucking throat."

The grin didn't fade.

Chapter Forty-Nine

THE FUTURE

A few days later.

For the first time in a long time, the world was still.

No shadows at the door. No coded messages. No ghosts on burner lines. Just silence, and something dangerously close to peace.

Peace always looked strangest on people who had learned love through violence.

Morning light spilled into Lucien's estate, warm and golden, sliding through the tall kitchen windows where he stood barefoot, shirtless, pouring dark roast into two black mugs.

Outside, the horizon didn't feel dangerous anymore. Just wide, open, and theirs.

Lena padded in, hair tousled, wrapped in one of his old T-shirts, oversized and slipping down one shoulder. She looked like trouble from a dream.

"Smells like caffeine and whatever the hell you're scheming," she said, voice still lazy with sleep.

Lucien smirked without turning. "Morning to you, too."

She wrapped her arms around him from behind, resting her cheek against his bare back. "I was having the best dream."

"Oh yeah?" Lucien asked.

"You were making me coffee. Naked."

He turned, eyes tracing the sleepy glow in hers.

"Close enough."

Without warning, he scooped her up by the waist and sat her on the counter.

She laughed, half breath, half disbelief. "I'm not even awake yet."

"That's fine," he muttered, lips brushing her jaw. "You don't need to be."

His mouth found the curve of her neck. Her eyes fluttered shut.

"I still think about it," she whispered.

He paused. "About what?"

"You. The way you looked at me in that cemetery. Like you'd already made peace with dying as long as it meant not betraying me."

Lucien didn't answer right away.

"There was no choice to make, Lena. You were the only thing in that moment that made me real. Without you, I was just bones in expensive suits."

Her throat tightened. She touched his face. "And now?"

"Now I'm breathing," he said. "For us. For whatever comes next."

Then he pulled back slightly, smirking again, same old devil in his smile. "Get dressed. I've got a few surprises for you today."

"Oh, really?"

He lifted her off the counter and set her back on the floor.

"Shower. Wear something you like being kissed in... or fucked out of."

An hour later, Lucien led her down the same hallway from that first morning, her hand tucked into his. The air felt quieter now, like the ghosts in the house had finally gone still.

They stepped outside into the crisp morning and crossed the stone walkway beneath a pale sky. He guided her toward the glass-paneled garage at the edge of the estate.

At the keypad, Lucien punched in the code. The door hissed open, and the garage came alive in steel and silence.

And there it was.

A blacked-out Porsche 911 Turbo S sat under the LED lights.

Lena stopped. "You didn't."

Lucien leaned against the doorframe, watching her take it in. "Figured you'd need a ride to get to your next surprise every day."

She walked toward the car slowly, fingertips brushing the hood. "Black?"

Lucien shrugged. "Fast. Quiet. Hard to argue with."

She smirked. "Black like your heart."

Lucien lifted a brow. "Careful."

She circled the car. "At least it's not pink."

"Pink's a tactical liability."

She laughed. "Relax. No one's ever seeing you riding passenger in something pink."

"Good. I have a reputation to maintain."

Lucien stepped beside her, arms crossed. "And before you ask, no, Logan doesn't get to drive it. Kid needs to finish therapy before we put him behind any more wheels."

Lena laughed, genuine and unguarded. Then she reached up and brushed her hand down his cheek like she was still trying to believe he was real.

"I don't know what to say, Lucien."

His arm slipped around her waist. "I don't want you to say anything. And I never want you to feel like you have to ask me for anything."

He reached into his jacket and pulled out a black credit card, sleek and metallic, her name etched in silver beside a small custom logo. Then he slid it into her hand.

"It matches the car," he said, that dangerous grin back in place.

She stared at it, stunned. "Lucien, I can't."

Her voice cracked.

"I'm with you because of you. Lose the money, lose the empire. It doesn't change where I stand."

"I know," he said softly. "That's why my empire is our empire now."

She smiled, then looked down again and saw something beneath her name.

Subtle. Elegant.

"Cole Enterprises," she read aloud, almost whispering it.

Lucien nodded once. "Real estate. Energy. Imports. Fashion. Licensing. I've got hands in every corner of the city, and strings that reach farther than the map suggests. Time to start pulling them for something cleaner."

He looked down at her, his hand closing gently around hers, the card still resting in her palm.

"This life? It's been all blood and fire. But that's not what I want for us. Not long term. I'm not just building a future anymore, Lena. I'm rewriting the past. Turning everything I built in the dark into something that can survive the light."

Lena stared at the card again, then back up at him.

"I love that," she said quietly.

"You really mean it."

He nodded. "You went through hell. I thought you deserved a piece of heaven."

Lucien smiled. "Speaking of heaven, that brings me to your final surprise."

He stepped back and slipped his hand into hers. "Let's head into the city."

There's one more thing I want to show you."

He pulled out a slim key fob and pressed it without looking.

A Lamborghini near the back wall blinked awake, low and matte-black.

All him.

Lucien opened her door. Lena slid inside, still smiling. He circled the car and climbed behind the wheel.

For a moment, he didn't start the engine.

Something shifted behind his eyes, and Lena knew that look.

"What is it?" she asked softly.

Lucien rested one hand on the wheel, the other settling on her knee.

"Everything I told you back there, the future, the empire, all of it, it's real."

His hand tightened slightly.

"But there's one last thing I have to take care of tonight."

Lena already knew.

Still, she asked.

"What thing?"

Lucien's eyes went dark.

"The Corsinis."

Lena didn't argue. She didn't question it. She just nodded once.

Then Lucien started the engine.

As they pulled out of the driveway, he glanced in the mirror.

The estate stood silent in the dawn light.

He'd learned better than to trust the quiet.

Lena sat sideways in the passenger seat, legs folded beneath her, watching Lucien guide the car down the open stretch of highway with practiced ease.

She smiled faintly. "Tell me this isn't just a drive to get bagels."

Lucien glanced over, a hint of a smirk tugging at his mouth. "Only if the bagels cost eight million dollars."

She laughed under her breath and looked ahead.

In the distance, the first edges of Manhattan rose through the morning haze.

"So... you gonna tell me where we're going?" Lena asked.

He let the question hang for a moment.

"You'll see."

The skyline sharpened as they drew closer, and the city swallowed them whole.

Streets packed tight with horns, engines, voices. New York moving at the only speed it knew.

Lucien navigated the chaos with calm control, cutting through traffic like he belonged to its rhythm.

They turned onto Fifth Avenue.

The car slowed.

Then stopped.

Lena lifted her eyes, and her breath caught.

There it was again.

The building.

Tall. Brutal. Beautiful.

Old brick fused with polished steel, sunlight spilling down the façade and catching on the brass letters above the entrance.

HEAVEN ON FIFTH

Her whisper barely escaped.

"You opened the club?"

Lucien stepped out without answering, circled around, and opened her door.

"Not exactly."

She stepped onto the sidewalk, sunlight washing over her. In the glass doors, she caught her reflection for the first time in what felt like forever.

Lucien stepped forward and swiped a black keycard.

A soft beep.

A click.

"No more six-digit codes," he said, pushing the door open. "After you."

Inside, the bones of the building remained. Three expansive floors. A sweeping mezzanine. Rooftop glass.

But polished black marble now stretched beneath her feet, warm amber lighting spilling across the industrial finishes. Steel beams still cut through the space, exposed like old scars left on purpose.

Lena looked around slowly.

"It's the same," she said softly. "But completely different."

Lucien nodded. "I kept the scars. I didn't want to erase what we lived through here."

He stepped closer.

"But I built this for what comes next."

She tilted her head. "And this is?"

"Yours."

Her eyes moved to him.

"A fashion house," he said. "A brand. A legacy. Whatever you want it to be."

He gestured around them.

"I saw what this place could become. I knew it had to belong to you."

Lena exhaled softly.

"Lucien..."

His smile faded into something quieter.

"You kept me alive when everything else I touched burned." He looked around the room. "This is how I learn to build something without destroying it."

A moment passed.

"Call it whatever you want," he said. "Just make it yours."

"You're serious?"

"Dead serious."

A slow smile crossed his face.

"Who better for a king to build a part of his world around than his queen?"

Lena looked at him.

"Just us?"

Lucien stepped closer and took her hand.

"Always," he said.

He kissed her knuckles. Then his grip tightened slightly.

"You think I fought through hell for half of you?" he murmured. "I'm not interested in half."

Lena moved without thinking, her spine pressing gently against the cutting table as sketchbooks slid to the floor like possibilities finally loosed.

Her fingers grazed his jaw.

"You already have it," she whispered. "All of me."

It was truth, raw and irrevocable.

She was home.

Lucien tilted her chin up, fingers rough from war and redemption. The kiss he gave her wasn't gentle, but it wasn't rushed either. It was reverent.

They didn't move at first. Just felt.

Not lust.

Not adrenaline.

Ache.

Her hands fisted in his jacket, dragging him down to her. Their chests met. She moaned into him, soft and trembling, like her soul had waited longer than her body.

No ghosts.

No blood.

Just breath.

Heat.

Lucien's hands slid to her hips, lifting her onto the table. He looked at her, really looked.

No masks.

No walls.

"Lucien," she whispered. "I love you."

"I know," he replied. "I feel it in every scar. Every breath we still get to take."

He kissed her again, deeper this time, his hands trailing from her face to her throat, then lower, slow and unhurried.

At the hem of her dress, he paused.

Then lifted it.

Inch by devastating inch.

"Say it again," he whispered. "Say you love me."

"I love you," she breathed.

Then again.

Not for him.

For herself.

His throat tightened.

"Then let me worship it."

He dropped to his knees.

One slow drag.

Deep.

Possessive.

Lena cried out, fingers fisting in his hair. He didn't need guidance. He already knew her. She came fast, shaking, gasping his name like it was the only word she trusted anymore.

Lucien rose, eyes dark, expression hard.

She reached for him, stroked him slow, watching his restraint flicker.

"You want me gentle?" he asked.

"No," she whispered. "I want you honest."

He pushed into her in one deep motion, and the sound he made had nothing to do with pleasure.

It was relief.

Her legs locked. Her nails dragged down his back, desperate and clawing.

He grunted, then fucked her like every unspoken word lived in his hips.

They moved together again and again, her voice breaking on his name. He bit her neck, whispered against her skin, made her say his name like it meant something.

She came again.

He didn't stop.

When he finally did, he folded over her, breath rough, body shaking.

Skin. Breath. Warmth.

No words.

No need.

They didn't speak as they redressed.

The silence between them wasn't empty. It was full, heavy with breath and the sense of something new beginning.

Lucien's hand brushed Lena's waist as he reached behind her and zipped up her dress. His palm lingered at the small of her back a second too long.

She didn't move.

She just smiled softly.

She turned off the lights while he locked the door behind them.

Morning sun broke through the windows, washing over blank canvases, scattered fabric, waiting mannequins, and the disheveled cutting table.

Outside, the city roared again, alive and indifferent.

Lucien opened the car door for her. She slid in, still breathless. When he got behind the wheel, his hand settled on her thigh, and she covered it with her own.

They didn't look at each other.

Touch said enough.

The engine purred, and they slipped into motion.

As he merged into traffic, he said, "One more stop. I need to clear the safe at Enigma before Brinks gets there. Normally, a manager handles it, but Midtown's short-staffed."

Lena nodded and leaned back, letting the city rise around them again.

They pulled to a stop in front of Enigma's entrance. No valet, no line, no bass thumping through the walls. Just morning sun glinting off the sleek black doors and the name etched across the steel that crowned them.

Lena stared out the window, eyebrows raised slightly.

"Wow," she murmured. "So weird seeing this place in the daytime."

Lucien killed the engine, smirking faintly. "Doesn't look so intimidating without the red lights and a three-hour wait, huh?"

She smiled but didn't answer right away.

As she stepped out of the car, her eyes drifted to the spot beside where the velvet rope would've been, the same place she'd stood with Jessica and Christina.

All wide eyes and heels too high, laughing at the idea they'd get in.

They hadn't expected anything more than a picture from the sidewalk.

Until Lucien had stepped out.

No warning. No name drop. Just a quiet word to the doorman, and suddenly they were inside.

Her gaze lingered on that patch of sidewalk.

Then something caught the light.

A glint.

Small.

Gold.

She frowned and crouched.

There, half-caught in a crack between the concrete slabs, was a gold chain.

Her mother's gold chain.

It was tarnished and twisted, bent slightly at the clasp, but it was hers. The same delicate links that had once warmed her skin. The same necklace that man had ripped from her throat and pocketed like nothing.

She froze.

"How?" she whispered.

Lucien turned, watching her.

"What is it?"

She didn't answer right away.

It shouldn't have survived. Not the rain. Not the crowds. Not the months.

Yet here it was.

Untouched.

Waiting.

She bent down and picked it up.

The metal was cold.

She rubbed her thumb across the broken clasp, then looked up at Enigma's dark glass, her reflection caught in the same place everything had begun.

Lucien's voice broke the silence behind her.

"What is that?"

She glanced down at the chain in her hand.

"This was my mother's necklace," she said softly. "The man that night, the one you stopped, he ripped it off my neck. In the moment, I didn't even think about getting it back until it was too late."

Lucien's expression shifted, something almost imperceptible tightening in his eyes.

He caught the word was, then mother.

For a heartbeat, his walls wavered.

He looked at the chain again.

"Guess the city decided to return it," he said quietly. "Let's just hope it doesn't want something back."

Lena smiled faintly, curling the chain into her palm.

"Maybe it's a sign. Things are finally looking up for us."

Lucien brushed a thumb over her shoulder, his gaze drifting up the block.

Then he opened the door for her.

Inside, Enigma felt hollow without the music, shadows cast wide across the marble floor, barstools neatly arranged like soldiers on break. The scent of last night still clung faintly to the air: sweat, smoke, champagne, and something that always smelled of risk.

Lucien led the way down the main corridor. Lena trailed behind, eyes scanning the quiet grandeur of it all. Without the lights and pulse of bodies, Enigma felt like the bones of a myth.

He keyed open a side door, revealing the low-lit corridor leading to the private offices.

"I always forget how quiet this place really is during these hours," Lucien said, trailing his finger along the cool wall as they walked.

"It almost feels like we're not supposed to be here," Lena said, her voice hushed, like the walls were still listening.

Lucien didn't look back. "It's loud when it needs to be. But silence tells you more."

He reached the end of the hallway and opened another door, this one lined with reinforced steel, a keypad glowing faintly at its side. His fingers flew over the numbers without hesitation.

It beeped once.

Then opened.

The vault room was quiet, lined with polished black shelving, a small desk, and two floor safes.

Lena leaned against the doorframe, arms crossed, watching him. "You ever think about walking away from all this too?"

Lucien paused at the safe and glanced over his shoulder. "What, clubs? Or power?"

"Both."

He crouched to open the lower safe, entering another code. "I think about building something with you. Not just keeping the empire. Making it clean. Strong. Real. Everything before you was noise."

The safe clicked open.

Lucien pulled out a large black case.

Stacks of cash. A few sealed envelopes.

He set it on the desk beside him, then opened another drawer, slower this time.

Lena pushed off the doorframe and stepped inside, her eyes moving over the safes, the sealed envelopes, the clean desk.

"This feels permanent," she said softly.

Lucien looked up. "What does?"

"This place. What it holds." Her voice quieted. "Like no matter how far you get from the past, something keeps it breathing."

He paused, then gave that familiar half-smile, the one that never quite touched his eyes.

"It's not about the weight," he said. "It's about what you carry anyway, and what you protect because of it."

Lucien pulled the final stack from the safe and set it beside the rest. The black case brimmed with crisp bands of hundreds, neatly bundled and aligned.

He ran the stacks through the compact bill counter, watching the numbers climb.

10,000. 20,000. 50,000.

By the time the last bundle cleared, he scribbled the final figure on a slip of paper.

$348,200

ENIGMA, FINAL DROP

He tucked the slip beneath the last envelope and closed the lid.

A sharp electronic buzz cut through the stillness.

Lucien's head lifted.

The security feed above the vault door flickered to life, showing the back hallway and the Brinks guard already waiting outside. Dark tactical uniform. Armored vest. Gloved hands clasped in front. Still as stone. Professional.

Lucien gave a slight nod, not to anyone in particular, and stood.

He moved through the vault door, down the quiet corridor, and keyed open the back entrance.

The steel door clicked and hissed, swinging outward.

The Brinks guard stood waiting, broad-framed and clean-cut, uniformed in standard navy and gray. No helmet. Just a ballistic vest, gloves, and the neutral expression of someone trained not to ask questions.

Lucien gave him a nod. "Right this way."

The guard stepped inside without a word, and Lucien led him back down the hall.

They entered the vault together.

The vault hadn't changed, but the air felt tighter inside. Lena stood off to the side, arms loosely crossed, watching it all unfold with quiet detachment.

The guard gave her a glance, then focused on the case.

Lucien gestured toward it. "Counted. Verified. You'll find the receipt in the side slip."

The guard opened the canvas deposit bag. Lucien transferred the stacks, sealed envelopes, and form, then zipped it shut.

The guard fastened the lock and nodded. "You're all set."

Lucien stepped back, hands by his sides. "Appreciate it."

Without another word, the man turned and exited the vault, his footsteps fading back toward the corridor.

Lucien exhaled slowly, eyes still on the vault door.

"Let's go."

He logged the clean transfer, shut the vault, and keyed the locks.

They walked back through the echoing heart of Enigma.

Lucien glanced at her. "You hungry?"

Lena looked over, eyes wide with mock betrayal. "I thought you were never gonna ask."

He smirked. "Perfect. We'll keep it local. Gotta stay in the city anyway. This afternoon, you and I are meeting a few people. Big names. They're ready to help build this fashion empire of yours."

"Ours," she said, bumping her shoulder into him.

He smiled again, softer this time.

"Ours."

They stepped out into the light.

The street was alive, unaware of the ending waiting in its next breath.

Chapter Fifty

HAPPY EVER AFTER?

Lena watched him lock Enigma's doors with that quiet, confident smirk and thought maybe, finally, the fight was over.

Lucien turned toward the street, shoulders loose, breathing easy, like a man who finally believed the day belonged to him.

Then.

POP. POP.

Lucien jerked, his body folding before he collapsed onto the pavement.

"Been waiting for you, motherfucker," a man said, like he'd rehearsed it forever.

For half a heartbeat, Lena froze, her mind trying to rewrite reality. But the blood pooling beneath Lucien didn't lie.

"Lucien!"

She dropped to her knees on the concrete, cradling his head as blood poured through her fingers, hot and relentless.

Chaos erupted. Screams pierced the air; a baby wailed; tires screeched. Yet Lena heard nothing but Lucien gasping, struggling for breath.

"Somebody call 911!" she screamed, her voice cracking in half as she fumbled for her phone, slick fingers barely able to unlock the screen. "Please, somebody fucking help!"

Across the sidewalk, the shooter stood frozen.

Just that man. The one from the maintenance hallway. The one who tried to force himself on her. The one Lucien asked, *which hand*, before he broke it.

Now that man stood motionless, staring blankly at the gun, as if it had acted without his consent.

Then he bolted, disappearing into the chaos he'd unleashed.

But Lena didn't watch him go. Her world had narrowed to Lucien, his eyes flickering, mouth opening wordlessly, but only blood answered.

"Stay with me. Please, baby, stay with me." Her voice cracked, breaking down into sobs as she pressed her hands harder against the wounds. "I need you! Don't you fucking leave me, Lucien!"

His eyes fluttered. Lips parted, trying to say something, but only blood came out.

And still, she held him like she could anchor his soul with nothing but her arms and the sound of his name.

People were gathering now. Phones out. Recording.

"Call 911!" someone shouted.

Another voice: "Holy shit, he's bleeding out!"

Lena looked up and saw the glowing screens pointed at them.

"Why the fuck are you filming this?" she screamed. "Help him!"

Then sirens, far off but getting closer. Red lights washed over the street as the ambulance screeched to a stop at the curb and the doors burst open.

"Gunshot victim!" one of the medics shouted, already dropping to his knees beside Lucien. "What happened?"

"Chest wound," someone yelled from the crowd.

The medic cut Lucien's shirt open with a quick slice. "Jesus. Alright. We've got him."

"What's his name?" the second medic asked, already pulling gloves tight.

Lena choked on the words. "Lu... Lucien. Lucien Cole."

"Stay with me," Lena begged, her hands still pressed against the wound.

"Ma'am, I need space," the medic said, firm but not unkind.

"I'm not leaving him!"

"Then keep pressure right there," the medic beside her snapped, already waving his partner toward the rig. "On three."

They rolled Lucien onto the board.

"Lift!"

The stretcher snapped into place and they rushed him toward the ambulance, Lena stumbling after them, blood smeared across her hands and dress.

"Ma'am, are you coming?" the second medic asked.

"Yes!" she choked.

"Then get in. Now."

The back of the ambulance smelled like antiseptic and blood.

The doors slammed shut. The engine roared to life, cutting through the chaos behind them. Lena sat pressed against the wall, one hand gripping the stretcher rail, the other still clinging to Lucien's, his blood still warm on her skin.

"Gunshot wound to the chest, entry high left," the paramedic shouted over the siren. "Possible lung puncture, pulse is thready!"

He pressed his stethoscope to Lucien's chest, listening hard.

"Breath sounds weak on the left," he muttered. "Shit... lung's collapsing."

Lucien's eyes were barely open, fluttering like he was somewhere between this world and the next. His lips moved, but no sound came out.

Lena leaned forward, her voice raw. "I'm here. I'm right here."

The paramedic didn't look at her. He couldn't.

His focus was the wounds, the vitals, the oxygen mask he pressed over Lucien's mouth.

"BP dropping," the second medic barked. "We're losing him, start another line!"

"Lucien," she whispered, her hand trembling as she ran it through his hair. "You hear me? You stay with me. Don't you fucking go. Not after everything. Not now."

The monitor beeped louder, faster. Then slower. The rhythm erratic, cruel.

"Pulse is fading," one medic said.

"Stay with me, Lucien," the other snapped, pressing harder against the wound. "Don't you do that shit on my rig."

"Pupils sluggish," one of them muttered. "Come on, come on, stay with us, boss."

But to Lena, none of it sounded real. The world felt underwater. Time folded in on itself. Every beat of her heart was a scream she couldn't get out.

She wanted to sob.

She wanted to shatter.

But she couldn't.

Not until he opened his eyes again.

Lucien gasped beneath the mask, blood bubbling at the corners of his lips.

The mask fogged with each shallow breath.

Then the fog stopped.

For a second.

His body jolted once as they hit a bump, and Lena swore the light was leaving him.

"No, no, Lucien, look at me. Look at me!"

Her voice cracked, shattering somewhere between prayer and command. "You said we were building something. Remember? You and me. You don't get to leave me now."

The paramedics exchanged a look.

The driver shouted from the front, "Two minutes out!"

"Hold pressure!" one medic snapped.

"Trauma bay ready?" the other called toward the cab.

"Already called it in," the driver yelled back.

Lena pressed harder against the bandage, feeling the heat of his blood seep through the gauze as tears slipped down her cheeks.

"Please," she whispered. "Please don't go where I can't follow."

Lucien blinked. Once. Barely.

But it was enough to destroy her.

The ambulance jerked to a stop.

Doors flung open.

"Let's move!"

They pulled the stretcher from the back like it was burning. Lena jumped down after it, feet hitting the pavement with a stumble.

Hospital doors slammed open ahead of them.

"Gunshot wounds to the chest, male, late thirties, critical," one of the medics shouted.

A trauma team was already waiting, gloves on, pads ready, faces set. The gurney wheeled faster. Lena tried to follow but someone held her back.

"Ma'am"

"I'm coming with him."

"You can't. You have to let them work."

"Don't tell me no!" she snapped, trying to break free, voice wrecked. "He needs me, he needs me!"

But the double doors had already swung shut.

She stood there frozen for half a second. Then her body gave out, and she dropped to her knees in the corridor. Just collapse.

A nurse knelt beside her, voice low. "Hey. You're okay. He's in the best hands."

But Lena wasn't listening. She stared at the doors like her soul had gone through them already.

Someone helped her to her feet, guided her into the waiting room.

She didn't fight. Didn't speak. Just moved like a ghost, still covered in Lucien's dried blood.

A nurse approached quietly, stepping into her path like you'd approach a wounded animal. "What's your name, sweetheart?" the woman asked, voice gentle, almost maternal.

Lena blinked. Swallowed. Tried to answer. "Le, Le, Lena," she stammered. "Lena Hart."

The nurse gave a small nod, hand brushing her arm with careful warmth. "Okay, Lena. We'll have the doctor come out the moment they know anything. I promise."

Lena nodded once, but didn't really hear her.

The nurse guided her into a metal-framed chair beneath the sterile hospital lights.

Lena sank into it.

She didn't cry. Not yet.

Because if she did, she'd have to admit he might not come back.

Lena sat still, but her hands began to shake.

She opened Lucien's phone with blood-slicked fingers and scrolled until she found Victor.

She didn't hesitate.

The line rang once. Twice.

Then his voice came through. "Yo."

"Victor." Her voice cracked apart on the first syllable. "Victor, it's, it's Lucien... he, he was shot... he's..."

She couldn't get the rest out. Her breath was breaking too fast. The sobs hit her chest like fists.

Victor went silent on the other end.

For a second Lena heard nothing but his breathing.

Then his voice came back, flat and cold. "Where are you?"

"Mount Sinai. He's inside. I don't know if he's..." Her voice pitched up again, throat closing around every word.

"I'm on it," Victor said. She heard wind in the receiver, a car door slamming. "Stay with him, Lena. I'm on my way."

"He didn't even see it coming, he, he smiled and then, God, he was just, he was gone."

Victor didn't say anything more.

Then she pulled up the next name.

Dad.

Her hand hovered over the call button like it weighed fifty pounds before she forced herself to press it.

Then, "Lucien," came the deep voice on the other end. "What is it this time, son?"

She opened her mouth. Nothing came out.

"Hello?" he repeated. "Lucien?"

"Mr. Cole," Lena choked, the words tumbling out like broken glass. "It's Lena. He's been shot. Lucien's been shot. He's in surgery. I... I don't know if he's..."

Silence. Heavy.

Then Alexander's voice, colder than winter steel: "Where are you?"

"M-Mount Sinai," she choked out. "They won't let me in. He collapsed right there on the street. There was so much blood, so much."

In the background, Lena heard a woman's voice break.

"Alexander, what happened? What did she say?"

Evelyn.

Alexander didn't interrupt. He didn't speak. He just breathed, measured and restrained, like someone holding back a scream from somewhere too old and too deep to show.

"I'll be up there tonight," he finally said.

And then, gently: "He's strong, Lena. You know that. If there's breath in him, he'll fight."

The call ended before she could reply.

Lena's eyes paced the hospital corridor, scanning every face, every white coat that passed, desperate for someone, anyone, to walk toward her with answers. With hope. With news she wasn't ready for but couldn't bear not knowing.

But no one did.

Just nurses moving, double doors swinging, and the relentless quiet of not knowing.

Before she could breathe, the phone lit up again.

Victoria.

Lena hesitated for a second, then answered.

"Hello?" Her voice was barely a whisper now, paper thin.

"Lena?" Victoria's voice came through shaky and small, nothing like the confident girl she usually was. "What happened? I just got a call from Dad. He said... he said Lucien..."

Lena couldn't say it again. Her throat burned from trying.

"He's in surgery," she forced out. "Mount Sinai. He collapsed outside the club. There was blood everywhere, Victoria. I couldn't stop it."

Victoria's breath hitched. "Oh my God."

"I'm still in Miami," she said softly. "I wasn't supposed to leave for a few more days, but I'm coming up with Dad. I'm not staying here. I can't."

"I didn't know what to do," Lena whispered. "One second we were walking to the car. He asked if I wanted breakfast. He was smiling, Victoria. He was smiling."

Her voice broke again.

"I know. He only ever really smiled when he was with you. The rest of the time, it was that look, like nothing could touch him. Like he was untouchable. But he's not. He never was."

Lena pressed her forehead to her knees, the world spinning around her. "I'm so scared."

"I am too," she said, voice breaking. "But listen to me. He's my brother,

Lena. He's our fire. He doesn't go down like this."

Another pause, softer this time.

"Hold the line until we get there."

The call ended.

But Lena didn't move.

Then footsteps, not rushed or panicked. Just deliberate.

Her head snapped up as the double doors creaked open and a man in scrubs stepped into the waiting area. His eyes scanned the room until they found her, the girl with dried blood across her arms, her collarbone, her throat.

"Lena Hart?"

She stood too fast. Her balance wavered.

"I'm Dr. Navarre," he said, voice even but low. "I'm the trauma surgeon overseeing Lucien."

She couldn't speak. Just nodded, her grip on the phone tightening like it was the only thing keeping her upright.

"He was hit twice," the doctor began. "One bullet entered through the upper left chest, punctured a lung, fractured the clavicle. The second struck lower, near the ribs. It narrowly missed his heart but tore through a portion of the intercostal artery."

Lena's breath caught, eyes wide.

"We performed an emergency thoracotomy and stopped the internal bleeding. He's on a ventilator. We've stabilized his vitals, but..." Dr. Navarre's voice softened. "He's holding on by a thread right now. The next twelve to twenty-four hours are critical."

She blinked, as if her body refused to understand that any of this was real. "But... he's alive?"

"Yes. But barely. He's sedated. We'll be monitoring for infection, respiratory distress, and cardiac fluctuations throughout the night."

Lena's knees buckled slightly as she sat back down.

"Can I see him?"

The doctor nodded slowly. "One person for a few minutes. He won't wake up, but hearing is often the last thing to go. If there's anything you want to say to him."

He let the sentence hang in the air.

"I need to see him," she whispered.

A nurse stepped in to guide her, but Lena didn't move right away. She stared past them, then finally rose, unsteady, eyes locked forward.

Toward the man who had taken bullets for the empire he was trying to leave behind. Toward the man who smiled before the bullets took him down.

Toward Lucien.

Still fighting, but fading.

And she wasn't going to let him do it alone.

The air carried that unmistakable hospital scent, antiseptic and sterile.

Bright white lights reflected off polished floors and glass walls.

Machines hummed beside the bed, soft electronic beeps marking the heartbeat that hadn't given up.

Lucien lay motionless. Tubes in his nose, another down his throat. His chest rose in shallow waves, the ventilator pushing each breath like a borrowed promise.

His skin looked wrong. Pale where it used to burn gold. Dry at the lips. Eyes closed, lashes unmoving.

The doctor stood near the foot of the bed, voice low.

"Like I said, he's stable and on the ventilator. You can sit with him if you'd like." He gave a short sigh. "He might hear you."

Then he stepped out, leaving her alone with what was left of the man she loved.

Lena didn't move for a moment.

Then she moved forward, each step heavier than the last.

She eased into the chair beside him, the vinyl squeaking under her weight.

Lucien didn't move.

Only the machines answered. The ventilator hissed softly, the monitor tracing a fragile line of life across the screen.

Lena reached out, her hand hovering over his like she was afraid to touch him wrong.

Then gently, she laced her fingers through his.

His hand was warm.

She swallowed hard.

"Hey," she whispered. "It's me. I'm here."

Her thumb brushed over his knuckles, still faintly streaked with dried blood.

She tried to smile. "You were gonna take me to breakfast."

It cracked halfway through.

"You asked me like it was nothing. Like we hadn't just been through everything."

She leaned closer, resting her forehead against the edge of the bed.

"You smiled at me," she breathed. "Right before."

Her shoulders began to shake.

"I don't know what to do if you don't wake up."

She shook her head. "I know you're strong. I know that. But you don't have to fight alone."

Her voice dropped to a whisper. "Just come back."

His hand went slack beneath her fingertips.

"I need you to fight, Lucien. Not for the empire. Not for everything we survived."

She tightened her grip on his hand.

"Just for us."

A long pause.

Then softly:

"For the mornings we haven't had yet. For the places we never went. For the life you said we could build."

She pressed her lips to his hand.

"If you can hear me," she whispered, her voice breaking, "I love you. I love you so fucking much it hurts."

Still, he didn't move.

But the line on the monitor held steady.

For now.

Lena sat beside him, holding his hand like it mattered, like maybe some part of him could still feel her.

The machine breathed for him.

And in that quiet, she understood something she hadn't seen before.

Lucien wasn't the man who set the world on fire.

He was the one who kept a flame alive in the dark.

Maybe that was why the dark kept reaching for him.

She squeezed his hand.

"You're okay," she whispered.

His fingers twitched in hers.

Just once.

No strength. No intention.

But it was enough to make her breath catch.

And then.

A long, piercing beep.

Lena froze.

The warmth beneath her fingertips vanished.

Lucien's hand went limp.

The monitor flatlined.

"No, no, no, no," she gasped, her voice raw, panicked. "Lucien!"

The door burst open. A flood of nurses and doctors rushed in, voices sharp, urgent.

"Miss, you have to step out."

Lena didn't hear them at first. Couldn't. Her hands were frozen over her mouth, her eyes locked on Lucien's still body as someone grabbed the paddles, someone shouted orders, someone pressed into his chest with forceful compressions.

"Miss, please."

A hand touched her arm. Then another. She was ushered backward, until the door shut behind her with a gut-wrenching click.

She stood there, just beyond the glass, her breath fogging the window as she stared through it, helpless, shaking, her world collapsing on the other side.

All she could do was pray the next jolt would bring him back.

"Charging, clear!"

His body jolted violently.

"Again, clear!"

She flinched. His body jumped, then settled. The monitor stayed flat.

"Please," she whispered, her voice barely there. "Please."

Moments later, Dr. Navarre stepped out, scrubs streaked and dark in places they should not have been. He pulled his mask down, eyes fixed somewhere past her shoulder for a beat.

Lena stood frozen in the corridor, throat locked, chest refusing air.

He didn't want to say it, but he had to.

"I'm sorry," he said, voice gentle and final. "There's nothing more we can do. His body couldn't handle the trauma."

The words hit her like impact.

She shook her head. Slow at first. Then faster.

A nurse touched her arm. Lena barely felt it.

"Would you like a few moments alone?"

Her lips parted. Nothing came. She gave the smallest nod, and her feet carried her back before her mind caught up.

The ventilator was unplugged. The tube was gone.

The leads were still on his chest.

Beside him, the monitor showed a flat green line. No alarm. No mercy.

The team filed out one by one, quiet now, eyes down, hands busy with small, careful tasks that meant goodbye. Then the door clicked shut and the world shrank to one bed, one body, one impossible stillness.

Silence.

Lena lowered herself into the chair beside him, slow, like if she moved too fast she would shatter. He looked so still. So unlike himself. Tears ran hot down her cheeks as she reached out, hesitated for one second, then slid her fingers through his.

He was still warm.

That warmth broke something in her.

A sob rose hard in her throat, raw and animal, and she swallowed it down, blinking fast, because if she let it out she would never stop. She couldn't do this. She wasn't ready to let him go.

Her gaze drifted to the small tray beside the bed, the few things they'd taken from him laid out in a neat pile like he was only temporarily gone. That was when she saw it, the small black notebook. Slightly creased. Leather-bound. Quiet.

Something in her stilled, like his voice, low and steady, had been waiting for her inside the silence.

Her fingers reached for it before she could stop them.

She opened it carefully, pages worn at the edges, and saw her name at the top of the first page.

Lena,

I wrote this for you during the nights I didn't think we'd make it.

The kind of nights where I needed to leave you something, in case death reached me before I reached you.

Something real.

Something to hold onto if the world ever stops making sense.

If you're reading this,

it means I didn't make it back to you.

I've seen too much of life's cruelty to believe in coincidence. Somewhere beneath the ash and noise, I still believe there's a hand shaping all this, something greater than the mess we've become.

When I look at what we didn't create, the sky before dawn, the silence between heartbeats, the way your eyes found me when nothing in this world should have allowed it, I know there's a design too perfect for chance.

And yet, I still question.

Why give a man something like this...

knowing it's the one thing he can't survive losing?

Why let me find you...

when I already know how this could end?

I've watched good people break under the weight of evil and still call it faith.

I've watched men kill in God's name and call it purpose.

And now I look at you, and I don't understand how something this real was ever placed in a world like that.

And still, even with all of it, I can't deny there's something more.

I've felt it.

Not in churches. Not in words.

In you.

In the way you looked at me like I wasn't already too far gone.
In the way something in me didn't feel broken when I was with you.
If anything in this world is true...
it's that.
And maybe I was one of the lucky ones.
Because in a world so often clouded by loss, I found you.
Something that stayed.
Something that didn't break when everything else burned.
I have done terrible things in this life.
But loving you was never one of them.
Everything else I touched, I ruined.
You were the only thing I didn't destroy.
If suffering taught me what love costs,
then loving you made the cost worth bearing.
What we had doesn't break.
It doesn't end just because I do.
So if you're reading this,
I need you to understand something.
I'm not gone.
I just won't be where you can reach me.
Every scar you carry, I loved you through it.
Every heartbeat after me still belongs to you.
You don't get to lose me completely.
Because what we built, it was real.
If death reached me first, let it choke on this truth: I was yours.
Maybe that was always the miracle.
Not that a man like me found love,
but that love still found a man like me.
We weren't chance.
We were collision.
And if I have loved, truly loved, then I know:
I have lived.
And I have won.

As Lena reached the final line, something in her shattered. Tears streamed unchecked, blotting the words, the only thing in the room that still sounded like him. She pressed the book tight to her chest, as if force alone could keep him there.

Beep.

Her breath caught.

Beep.

The book slipped from her fingers and hit the floor, pages splaying open.

Beep.

The monitor found him again.

Lena's head snapped up.

Lucien's eyes flickered, distant at first, then sharper, burning back to life when they found hers.

Behind her, footsteps broke into motion in the hall.

She moved toward him like the world had turned fragile under her feet.

"Lucien?"

His mouth parted. Nothing came at first. Then, rough and torn from somewhere far away, he whispered, "Lena."

The door opened behind her.

A nurse stopped cold. "Doctor!"

Whatever was holding Lena together gave out. Her hand flew to his face.

Warm.

Alive.

Her whole body started shaking.

"Oh my God," she whispered. "Oh my God. No, no, no, don't do that to me. Don't ever do that to me again."

The corner of his mouth moved, barely, but it was him.

Her forehead fell against his. Her tears ran over both of them.

"You came back," she whispered.

His breathing hitched. His eyes never left hers.

"I came back to you," he rasped.

Footsteps pounded closer.

"Ma'am, step back," someone said.

But Lucien's fingers tightened around hers.

Weak.

Barely there.

Enough.

"Wait," Lena begged, not looking away from him. "Please, just wait."

His gaze moved over her face like a man trying to hold on to the only mercy he'd ever been given.

Then, with what little strength he had left, he lifted his hand.

His fingers brushed her cheek.

"Will you marry me?"

She laughed through the tears, shaking her head.

"Yes." Then louder, breaking apart with it. "Yes. Of course yes."

Something in his face softened.

Not the king. Not the monster. Just Lucien.

For one suspended second, it felt like the world had made room for them.

Then the monitors screamed.

His body jerked once.

The line went flat again.

"No," Lena breathed.

Medical staff rushed past her this time, hands pulling her back as they flooded the bed.

Her yes still hung in the air.

The book lay open on the floor, ink bleeding where her tears had fallen.

THANK YOU FOR BLEEDING WITH ME
You just watched a king fall.
You felt his last heartbeat under your palm.
You read the words he wrote in case the bullets found him first.
You heard the question he asked while dying.
You answered with blood on your hands.
The world will say Lucien Cole died that night.
Let them.
A body can break.
A pulse can fail.
A man can vanish behind a hospital door.
But legends don't go quietly.
And kings don't stay gone just because the world decides they should.
This wasn't a love story.
It was the first chapter in the making of a myth.
Book 2 begins where your breath stopped.
Beyond the ICU door.
Where machines are still screaming.
Where the empire is holding its breath.
Where wolves are already pacing the dark.
Where a queen is learning what it means to burn the world down just to keep
her king breathing.
The war isn't coming.
It's already here.
If you want to go deeper...
If you want the original soundtrack built for this world...
If you want the artifacts pulled straight out of the universe...
The Lucien Archives are open.
Anthonyblodgett.com
Enter at your own risk.
See you on the other side.

About the Author

Born and raised in Staten Island, New York, Anthony Blodgett spent years shaping emotion through music before turning to fiction. Writing became more than an outlet, it became survival, a way to turn feeling into fire. His work is driven by grief, longing, love, and the unseen forces that linger at the edges of ordinary life. He writes for the haunted, the heartbroken, and anyone who has ever felt too much. His goal is not to comfort, but to confront, to shake something loose inside you and leave it burning long after the final page.

www.ingramcontent.com/pod-product-compliance
Lightning Source LLC
Chambersburg PA
CBHW020647110726
47901CB00001B/76